D0310888

GHOSTMAN

GHOSTMAN

ROGER HOBBS

Doubleday

LONDON • TORONTO • SYDNEY • AUCKLAND • JOHANNESBURG

TRANSWORLD PUBLISHERS
61–63 Uxbridge Road, London W5 5SA
A Random House Group Company
www.transworldbooks.co.uk

First published in Great Britain
in 2013 by Doubleday
an imprint of Transworld Publishers

Copyright © Roger Hobbs 2013

Roger Hobbs has asserted his right under the Copyright, Designs
and Patents Act 1988 to be identified as the author of this work.

A CIP catalogue record for this book
is available from the British Library.

ISBN 9780857521613 (cased)
9780857521620 (tpb)

Addresses for Random House Group Ltd companies outside the UK
can be found at: www.randomhouse.co.uk
The Random House Group Ltd Reg. No. 954009

The Random House Group Limited supports The Forest Stewardship
Council® (FSC®), the leading international forest-certification organisation.
Our books carrying the FSC label are printed on FSC®-certified paper.
FSC is the only forest-certification scheme supported by the leading
environmental organisations, including Greenpeace. Our
paper procurement policy can be found at
www.randomhouse.co.uk/environment

Typeset in Janson Text
Printed and bound in Great Britain by
Clays Ltd, Bungay, Suffolk

2 4 6 8 10 9 7 5 3 1

GHOSTMAN

ATLANTIC CITY, NEW JERSEY

Hector Moreno and Jerome Ribbons sat in the car on the ground level of the Atlantic Regency Hotel Casino parking garage, sucking up crystal meth with a rolled-up five spot, a lighter and a crinkled length of tin foil. They had thirty minutes.

There are three good ways to rob a casino. The first is in the front door. It worked back in the eighties, if not so much anymore. Just like a bank, a couple of guys would walk in with masks and guns and put some iron to the pretty little thing behind the bars. She'd start crying and begging for her life while the manager would hand over the stacks from the drawer. The bad guys would walk back out the front door and drive away, because common sense said that a gunfight would cost the casino more than whatever you'd got from the cages. But times change. The cashiers are trained for it now. Security's more aggressive. As soon as the silent alarm goes, and it always does, guys with guns are coming out of the woodwork. They still wait for you to leave, though as soon as you step back out the door there are forty guys waiting with AR-15s and shotguns to take you down. No two-minute lag like before.

The second is to go for the chips. Take the elevator down from the suites, walk up to the high-roller roulette table, take out your gun and put a bullet right through the double zeros. Everybody runs at the sound of the shot, especially the croupier. Rich people aren't brave, and employees even less so. Once they've scattered, get a bag and scoop up all the chips. Put two more bullets into the ceiling to let them know you're serious, then run out like the devil was chasing you. Sounds dumb, but it works. You're not messing with the cages, so the response time won't be so fast. Security won't be waiting outside like they would be in the first scenario. You might actually make it to the parking lot and, from there, the highway. You've still got the problem of what to do with the chips. If you take enough of them, say a million or more, the casino will swap out all the chips on the floor for new ones with a different design, and you'll end up holding a bag full of worthless clay. Worse, technology is making this gambit obsolete. Some casinos are now adding microchips for counting purposes and they'll be able to track the ones you took. You'll be wanted from Vegas to Monaco in six hours, and the chips will be just as worthless. And if somehow neither of these two things happen, the best you can hope for is to try to sell them on the black market. But if you do that, you'll have to sell them for half face value or less, because nobody wants to eat that rap unless they can double their money. Long and short of it is, chips don't get you anywhere.

Finally, the third way to rob a casino is to steal the money while it's in transit. Take down one of the armored cars. Casinos move a lot of cash. More than banks, even. You see, most don't keep big pallets of hundreds locked up on the premises like they do in the movies. There are smaller cash cages all over the place, not massive vaults with hundreds of millions piled up. And instead of keeping all those stacks of money around, they do what every institution of that size does. When they've got too much cash, they send it to the bank in an armored truck. When they don't have enough, they do the same thing in reverse. Two or three deliveries a day, all told.

Taking down an armored truck isn't really feasible, though. The modern ones are like tanks full of money. Hitting the bank where the money's coming from isn't an option either, because banks have even better security than casinos. The key is to make your move right in the middle of the transaction, while the guys are loading the money on or off the truck. They even make it easy for you. Most casinos don't have a special armored-car depot; too impractical. Instead, the truck parks next to one of the rear or side entrances, a different one every time. The guards open up the back and then walk the money right through the glass doors. This is the golden minute of professional heisting. For sixty seconds, a couple of times a day, more money than a couple of guys could get from half a dozen banks changes hands out there in the open right in front of everybody. All a professional heisting team has to do is get past two or three guys with crew cuts and guns and then drive away before the cops show up. Easy as that. Of course, you need to know when the deliveries are going to happen, and how much money is involved, and which entrance the trucks are going to use, but these details aren't impossible to get. Information's the easy part. Getting away, that's the hard part. If you can snatch the money and disappear in two minutes, you'll end up rich.

Jerome Ribbons looked down at his gold Rolex. It was half past five in the morning.

The first delivery was half an hour away.

It takes months of planning to take down a casino. Luckily for them, Ribbons had done this sort of thing before. Ribbons was a two-time felon out of north Philadelphia. Not an attractive résumé item, even for the kind of guy who sets up jobs like this, but it meant he had motive not to get caught. He had skin the color of charcoal and blue tattoos he'd got in Rockview Pen that peeked out from his clothing at odd angles. He'd done five years for his part in strong-arming a Citibank in Northern Liberties back in the nineties, but had never seen time for the four or five bank jobs he'd helped pull since he got out. He was a big man.

At least six foot four with more than enough weight to match. Folds of fat poured out over his belt, and his face was as round and smooth as a child's. He could press four hundred on a good day, and six hundred after a couple of lines of coke. He was good at this, whatever his rap sheet said.

Hector Moreno was more the soldier type. Five and a half feet, a quarter of Ribbons's weight, hair as short as desert grass, and bones that showed through his coffee-colored skin. He was a good marksman from his days in the service, and he didn't blink except when he twitched. His sheet showed a dishonorable discharge but no time served. He got back home and spent a year cutting chops in Boston and another browbeating protection money out of dope dealers in Vegas. This was his first big job, so he was nervous about it. He had a whole pharmacy in the Dodge with him, just to get his nut up. Pills and poppers and powders and smokes. He wanted to burn away his jitters with a fistful of speed. There were never enough drugs for him. They'd gone through the whole plan over and over to get ready, but Moreno needed more than that. He finished a big bone of crystal meth with a slurp. His eyes watered up. A friend of his had cooked the crank up in a trailer west of the Schuylkill. It was low-quality Strawberry Quick, but he didn't care. He wanted to fix and focus, not get blown out of his mind on crank and paint thinner before the main event.

Ribbons looked at his watch again. Twenty-four minutes.

Neither man spoke. They didn't have to.

Moreno took a pack of cigarettes out of his pocket and lit one, then passed the foil over to Ribbons. He let out two puffs in quick succession.

Ribbons numbed his mouth down with a pull off a pint of bourbon first. Basing meth is a hot and bitter experience. He took his time chasing the drop across the foil between his callused fingers. This wasn't the first time he'd been down this road. The meth felt good, though not nearly as good as the rush he'd get with his mask on and his gun up. He liked to be right in the thick of it.

Moreno watched him, smoked his cigarette and stole a few pulls off the bottle of cough syrup. His heart skipped. A lot of people in the old neighborhood would have paid top dollar for this premium kind of high, but none of them ever did cough syrup anymore. Only him. Makes you see things like you do when you've got fever so high you're on the edge of death. You see God waiting for you at the end of the tunnel. Nobody ever told him about the endless hard breathing, the heartbeat or the things he'd hallucinate once the DXM hit his bloodstream like an eight ball of ketamine. He listened to the radio and waited.

Moreno flicked his cigarette out the window and said, "Got your house picked out yet?"

"Yeah. Blue Victorian. Beautiful place down by the water. Virginia."

"What did the lady say?"

"That it's a buyer's market. Our deal won't be a problem."

They sat quietly for a while, listening to the morning traffic report on the radio. Nothing much to talk about anyway, nothing they hadn't said a thousand times over cups of coffee and blueprints and glowing computer screens. There was nothing more to do but listen to the traffic reports.

They had planned this job way in advance, though maybe it's wrong to say that they'd planned it at all. The man with the idea was three thousand miles west sitting by his phone in Seattle and waiting to make a call. He was the jugmarker. Most robberies are lone-wolf operations that never get off the ground. A couple of crackheads try to knock down a bank and end locked up for the duration. A job with a jugmarker isn't one of those. It is the kind of job you hear about once on the evening news and it never comes up again. The kind that goes off right and stays right. This was a job with strict plans, timing and endgame—a jugmarker's heist from beginning to end. The man with the plan knew everything and called all the shots. Ribbons and Moreno didn't like to say his name. Nobody did.

Bad luck.

Moreno and Ribbons weren't dumb, though. They knew the patterns of the security cameras. They knew the armored truck inside and out. They knew the drivers' names, the casino managers' names, their habits, their records, their phone numbers, their girlfriends. They knew things they wouldn't even need, because that was part of the process. There were a million things that could go wrong. The idea was to control the chaos, not step right into it. Now it was all down to the traffic reports.

After twenty minutes, Ribbons's phone rang. A sharp, crisp chirp, repeated twice over. A specific ringtone for a specific number. He didn't have to answer it. Both men knew what it meant. They exchanged glances. Ribbons sent the call to voice mail, put the drugs back in the glove box, and looked at his watch a third and final time. Two minutes to six in the morning.

The two-minute countdown had started.

Ribbons took a high-fiber cotton balaclava out of the glove box. He put the ski mask on and fitted it until the fabric was snug around his face. Moreno followed slowly with his own. Ribbons connected the wires under the dash and powered up the engine. On the floorboards was a KDH tactical-assault vest with level-four ballistic plates designed to stop rifle rounds from insurgent assault weapons fifty feet away. Ribbons had to wear one. He was the point man. His stomach hung out beneath. Under a blanket in the backseat was a Remington Model 700 hunting rifle loaded with five rounds, fitted with a red-dot sight and modified with an eight-and-a-half-inch AWC Thundertrap silencer— Moreno's weapon. Next to it was a fully automatic Kalashnikov, Type 56, with three mags of 120-grain, full-metal-jacket, boat-tail hunting rounds, thirty in each. Ribbons took the AK and loaded a mag into the receiver, pulled back the cocking lever, turned to Moreno and asked—

"Are you as ready for this as I am?"

"I'm ready," he said.

Again they were silent. The parking-garage lights flickered, then turned off—no need for lights after sunrise. Their Dodge Spirit was covered in rot-brown rust stains. Right in front of them, visible across the street, was the casino's side entrance where the truck would be. The rain streaks on the windshield looked like a kaleidoscope to Ribbons's eyes.

Ninety seconds before the truck was supposed to arrive, Moreno got out of the car and took his position facing the street, behind a road-block. The salt air had eaten the concrete down to the steel rebars. He looked up at the security cameras. They were shifted away. Perfect timing. Casino security's tight enough to have cameras in the parking lot, just not quite tight enough. Moreno had mapped out the camera blind spots and tested them weeks ago. Nobody really cares what goes on in the parking lot at six in the morning. Moreno steadied the forearm of his rifle on the concrete block. He flipped the lens cap off his sight, pulled back the lever and locked in the first round.

Then Ribbons got out. He hustled while the cameras were still shifted away and hid behind the next pillar, in another blind spot. He started breathing deeply and quickly to loosen himself up so he'd be ready to run. The Kalashnikov seemed tiny in his massive hands. He held it close to his chest. He was beginning to feel sick. That old familiar feeling crept into his stomach, like it always did. Nerves. Not as bad as Moreno's nerves, he thought, but still there, every time.

Sixty seconds.

Ribbons counted down the seconds in his head. The timing was very important. They were under strict orders not to move until the exact moment. The sweat made the inside of his gloves slick. It is harder to shoot precisely in latex gloves, but he was also under orders to keep them on until the end of the day. He was as still as the Buddha behind his pillar, even though it was a little too small for him. He didn't even have enough space to pull back his jacket and look at his watch. Instead he concentrated on breathing, in and out, in and out. Seconds ticked away in his head. Water fell in drops off the concrete overhead.

At exactly six a.m., the Atlantic Armored truck slid through the green light at the corner and turned down the street. Both the driver and the guard wore brown uniforms. The truck was ten feet tall and weighed close to three tons. It was white, with the Atlantic Armored logo painted on both sides. It turned in the casino's loading zone and came to a slow, rolling stop under the Regency sign. Ribbons could barely hear a thing over the sound of his own hurried breath.

Armored cars are never easy. They're intimidating machines. It's not just the obvious things, like the three inches of bullet-resistant NIJ-tested armor, or the tires reinforced with forty-five layers of DuPont Kevlar, or the windows made of a transparent sort of polycarbonate capable of stopping a whole clip of ten-millimeter armor-piercing rounds. No, all that's obvious. The more dangerous things about an armored car involve the stuff on the inside. The guards, for example, are trained guys with guns. The inside of the truck's got cameras that record everything that happens in there. There are sixteen gun ports, so the guys on the inside can shoot the guys on the outside. And to top it all off, there are magnetic plates in the strongboxes. If the loot is ever taken off the plate, a timer starts going. If the timer ever runs out, little ink packs in the money explode and ruin the prize. But to a jugmarker and a team with a plan, all those worrisome features fall by the wayside. There is always a weakness. In this case, there were two. The first is obvious: nothing stays inside an armored car forever. Wait for the guys to get out, and all the armor and cameras and magnetic plates mean nothing. The second requires a little more thought, however. The second requires much more cruelty.

Kill the guards, and the cash can be yours.

There were two of them, both in the front cab. One driver and one money handler, with a couple of years of experience between them, or so the research said. One had a family, the other didn't. Once the truck had come to a stop, they'd got out. As soon as they closed the doors, a guy in a cheap black suit came out through the casino entrance to meet them. He was balding and had a name badge over his lapel. He was the casino vault manager. Middle forties, cleanest record a guy could have. Not even a parking ticket. He took a key out of his pocket and handed it to the money handler. Of course, even with his clean record, he was never allowed in the truck itself. Not once in ten years. The uniforms would handle it out here, and he would handle it back in the cage. He waited on the sidewalk and rubbed his hands together.

Thirty seconds.

The driver took another key off his belt and handed it to the handler, who cracked the lock on the back of the truck and climbed in. Back there was a magnetic-plated strongbox built into the side wall of the vehicle and covered with a further layer of bulletproof ceramic armor. His key fit into one of the two locks, and the vault manager's key fit into the other. Nobody had ever robbed an Atlantic Armored truck before. Their service was top of the line, courtesy of paranoid bankers and hotel service accounts worth countless times more than a whole fleet of armored trucks. Security was a big deal in this town. The item in question was a twelve-kilo block of vacuum-packed hundred-dollar bills, in the new style with the shiny metal security stripes right down the middle. The block was subdivided into hundred-bill stacks called *straps*, because of the mustard-colored paper strap banding each pile together for easy counting. Each strap was worth ten thousand U.S. dollars. There were 122 straps in the twelve-kilo block, or $1,220,000, compressed to the size of a large suitcase. The handler slid the money off the magnetic plate. There was a blue Kevlar bag in a drawer opposite. He fitted the stacked cash in the bag, then fitted the bag onto a small carrying trolley hooked into the wall. He put on a pair of sunglasses from his pocket and pushed the trolley off onto the pavement. It was large and awkward, so he had to maneuver it.

Ten seconds.

As soon as the handler got out of the truck, the driver drew a Glock 19 from his holster and held it low beside his hip, which was standard procedure for a delivery like this. He looked bored. This was his first delivery of the day and there would be ten more like it, back and forth to various casinos at different times throughout his shift. He adjusted his grip on the gun and kept his finger off the trigger. The handler locked the truck and gave the casino's key back to the vault manager, who attached it to his belt. The driver scanned the parking garage, then turned back, took two steps toward the casino doors and gestured for the other two to follow with the money.

Time's up. Ribbons gave the signal.

Moreno's rifle bucked gently in his arms. The shot wasn't silent but muffled, like a nail gun firing up close. The bullet hit the driver's head just below the hairline and behind the ear. It went right through his head and exited through the nose. Blood and brain matter painted the sidewalk. Moreno didn't wait to see the body fall. At this distance, he knew where the bullets would go. He worked the bolt and the cartridge flew out. It took him a fraction of a second to switch targets, as if he'd been doing this his entire life. The vault manager was closest, so he was next. The bullet hit him in the sternum and tore through his heart. The third target was already on the move.

The money handler threw himself toward the armored truck. He stumbled on the sidewalk, then hit the pavement and grabbed for the Glock in his holster. Moreno led him through the sight. He took a bead and squeezed the trigger. The bullet missed by a foot. The guard scrambled for cover. Moreno gave Ribbons a hand motion. No chance he'd get the shot from this angle.

Ribbons emerged from his blind spot and raised the Kalashnikov to his shoulder. He pissed bullets, unsuppressed, full-automatic. The gunshots broke the morning silence like a jackhammer in the middle of the night. The glass casino doors shattered as one long, thirty-round burst of ammunition poured from the barrel of his gun. It was the law of large numbers for hitting the third guy. Most of the bullets missed, but one didn't. A bullet caught the handler in the spine, below the heart. He twisted on the pavement from the hit. Inside the casino, people started screaming.

Ribbons hopped over the concrete barrier between the parking garage and the street and jogged toward the armored truck. He dropped his clip, whipped out another and charged it. There was no traffic in either direction. Too early for that. He held the rifle out one-handed, in case somebody else was waiting to come out from the casino and snatch the money first. He stooped down, never taking his eyes off the doors, and used his free hand to try to unhitch the bag, which was fastened to the trolley with big easy nylon buckles. Ribbons hadn't considered, however, how hard it would be to get them undone with one hand, in a latex glove, on a quarter gram of meth, in the July heat. His hand was shaking.

Moreno watched the street through his sight. *Come on, come on, come on.*

Then the alarm went.

It was a loud klaxon with flashers from inside the lobby, meant for fires and earthquakes. Ribbons flinched, then sprayed a burst through the doors to discourage anybody from coming out. The rifle's kickback forced his arm up and sent bullets through some windows in the casino's hotel tower and took out the *R* in the neon Regency sign. His brass shell casings poured out and tinkled on the sidewalk. He shouted. The recoil nearly broke his hand. When he regained control of the Kalashnikov, he kicked the bag to the pavement in frustration. Screw it. He pointed the gun at the last nylon buckle and blew it free.

The money handler gurgled from where he lay on his back a few feet away. His eyes followed Ribbons. Blood frothed up from his mouth and pooled around his face like a halo. Ribbons picked the bag up by the broken strap and slung it over his shoulder. When he passed the dying guard, he looked down at him, lowered the rifle and put a burst of bullets through his head.

Police sirens were audible in the distance, drawn to the gunfire. Eight blocks away, by the sound of it. Thirty-second response time starting now. Ribbons ran as quickly as he could back to the parking garage. He was shaking, even despite the handful of barbiturates he'd swallowed. His eyes were as wild as some savage warrior's. There was still no traffic. The run was easy.

Moreno gave him the open palm. *Run faster, you fat fuck.*

When they were within earshot, Ribbons shouted, "Heat coming in from the north. Open the damn car, let's go!"

They were less than twenty feet apart. Now the cameras didn't matter. Security couldn't identify them in that sort of headgear. They sprinted back to their getaway car. Ribbons hopped over the concrete barrier and Moreno threw the passenger door open for him. Moreno would drive. The whole job had taken less than half a minute. Twenty-six seconds according to Ribbons's Rolex. It was as easy as that: walk up, take the money and run. Moreno had an idiotic smile plastered on his face. He thought everything would go perfect. But no heist ever goes perfectly. There is always a problem.

Like the man sitting in the car on the other side of the parking garage, watching them through the scope of his rifle.

To Ribbons, what happened next was all a blur. One second he was getting into their car, and the next he heard the gunshot and saw Moreno hit. There was a spray of pink mist. Chunks of brain matter and fractured skull hit Ribbons straight on, like shrapnel from a grenade. Ribbons didn't have time to think. He raised his Kalashnikov and sprayed lead blindly in the direction of the sound. There were flashes of light from one of the cars behind him, but Ribbons was out of bullets before he could target it. He got out of the Dodge, dropped the clip, took out another and charged it. He hadn't even shouldered the rifle when a bullet punched a hole through the windshield. Ribbons took a bead on the flashes and returned fire. The next round came right at him. He scrambled around the car toward the driver's seat, letting out shots in quick bursts. A bullet struck him in the shoulder. It hit a ceramic plate. It was a powerful blow that spun and staggered him, but he barely felt it. He recovered and kept shooting. Another shot hit him in the chest above the belly. The hit felt like a sharp, immediate sting. Ribbons shouted. He was out of bullets.

He swore and dropped the empty rifle. He pulled a Colt 1911 from the small of his back and fired the gun one-handed, arm out-stretched, no target in sight. The stupid mask had slid over one eye. He fired in quick double taps to give himself cover fire. A rifle round hit the pillar behind him and sent up a storm of powdered concrete and plaster. With his free hand he pulled Moreno's body out of the driver's seat. There was brain matter blown out all over the dash. Another round hit the trunk of the Dodge. Ribbons could hear it bouncing around against the chassis. The car was still running. Ribbons put it into Reverse. He didn't even bother to close the door, which hung open until Rib-bons was halfway through the two-point turn and momentum slammed it into place. He leaned over the seat and fired through the rear window. Then the mirror, a foot from his head, exploded. *Drive, you idiot.*

Ribbons burned rubber. The Dodge peeled out so quickly it slammed into the row of cars behind it and sent up a shower of sparks. Half blind from the mask and the blood, Ribbons shifted into Drive and barreled down the slope toward the garage entrance. There was no attendant in the booth this early, which was good because Ribbons couldn't see where he was going. The beat-up Dodge crashed through the ticket machine, swiped the booth and fishtailed onto Pacific Avenue. The car careened through a red light and lost control down the wrong side of the road toward Park Place, where Ribbons ducked behind the steering wheel and floored the accelerator. The rims of his tires sent up sparks along the pavement. He could hear cops circling in the distance, going Code 3 with full sirens. Only blocks away now, close enough to be a problem. When he pulled the mask off, drops of sweat showered the dashboard. He glanced behind him. Nothing in the rear window yet. He weaved down the wide Atlantic City boulevards, still flooring it. Moreno, the wheelman, had planned the escape route down to the second. That plan had all gone to hell in ten seconds flat.

Ribbons spun the wheel and screeched through a parking lot and down an alleyway.

In less than ten minutes, the make and model of his car would be out to every cruiser and state trooper for fifty miles. He had to stash the car, the money and himself before the police caught up with him. But first he needed to put *distance*. It wasn't until he'd turned onto Martin Luther King Boulevard that he felt the blood soaking through the clothing under his bulletproof vest. He touched the wound in his chest. It had gone through. Though the vest had slowed and deformed the bullet, it had still gone through twenty-seven layers of Kevlar into his flesh. It didn't hurt, exactly. He had Moreno's crank and a syringe of heroin to thank for that. But it was bleeding fast. He'd have to wash and wrap it if he wanted to stay alive. Proper treatment would wait until later. It would have to.

The phone rang again. That special ringtone. The caller had little tolerance for lateness, less for incompetence and none for failure. The man's reputation relied on that sort of totalizing kind of fear that could cow federal agents and keep murderers and rapists as obedient as schoolchildren. His plans were precise, and he expected them to be followed precisely. Failure was never even discussed. Nobody Ribbons had ever met had failed him before. Nobody still around to talk about it, anyway.

Ribbons looked over at the phone, where it was lodged under the front seat, then reached over and killed the call with his thumb.

Ribbons tried to concentrate on the escape route, but all he could think about was his little blue house on the water. Through the drug haze, he could practically smell the old Victorian and feel the chipped paint on his fingertips. His first house. He kept the image of it in his mind, like a security blanket around the pain of the bullet lodged in his chest. He could make it. He had to. He had to.

Two minutes after six in the goddamn morning.

Two minutes after six in the goddamn morning, and the police were already out in full force, sweeping the streets for him. Two minutes after six in the goddamn morning, and word of the heist was already out to the highway patrol and the FBI. Four people were dead. More than a million dollars stolen. Over a hundred bullet casings on the pavement. This would be one for the headlines.

It was two minutes after six in the goddamn morning, and the police had already woken their detectives.

It took another two hours for someone to wake me.

1

SEATTLE, WASHINGTON

The shrill, high-pitched chirp of an incoming e-mail was like a bell ringing in my head. I woke with a start and immediately put a hand on my gun. I took gasping breaths as my eyes adjusted to the light coming off my security screens. I looked over to the windowsill where I'd set my watch. The sky was still as black as ink.

I took the gun out from under my pillow and put it on my nightstand. Breathe.

When I regained my composure I scanned the monitors. There was no one in the hallway or the elevator. Nobody in the stairs or the lobby. The only person awake was the night watchman, who looked too engrossed in a book to notice anything. My building was an old ten-story, and I was on the eighth floor. It was a seasonal sort of place, so there were year-round occupants in only about half the rooms and none of them ever got up early. Everyone was still asleep, or away for the summer.

My computer chirped again.

I've been an armed robber for close to twenty years. Paranoia comes with the territory, as well as the stack of fake passports and hundred-dollar bills under the bottom drawer of my dresser. I started in this business in my teens. I did a few banks because I thought I'd like the thrill of it. I wasn't the luckiest and I'm probably not the smartest, but I've never been caught, questioned or fingerprinted. I'm very good at what I do. I've survived because I'm extremely careful. I live alone, I sleep alone, I eat alone. I trust no one.

There are maybe thirty people on earth who know I exist, and I am not sure if all of them believe I'm still alive. I am a very private person out of necessity. I don't have a phone number and I don't get letters. I don't have a bank account and I don't have debts. I pay for everything in cash, if possible, and when I can't, I use a series of black Visa corporate credit cards, each attached to a different offshore corporation. Sending me an e-mail is the only way to contact me, though it doesn't guarantee I'll respond. I change the address whenever I move to a different city. When I start getting messages from people I don't know, or if the messages stop bearing important information, I microwave the hard drive, pack my things into a duffel and start all over.

My computer chirped again.

I ran my fingers over my face and picked up the laptop from the desk next to my bed. There was one new message in my in-box. All of my e-mails get redirected through several anonymous forwarding services before they reach me. The data goes through servers in Iceland, Norway, Sweden and Thailand before it gets chopped up and sent to accounts all over the world. Anybody tracing the IP wouldn't know which was the real one. This e-mail had arrived at my first offshore address in Reykjavik some two minutes ago, where the server had encrypted it with my private-key 128-bit cipher. From there it had been forwarded to another address registered under a different name. Then another address, then another. Oslo, Stockholm, Bangkok, Caracas, São Paulo. It was daisy-chained down the line ten times with a copy in each in-box. Cape Town, London, New York, L.A., Tokyo. Now it was undetectable, untraceable, private and anonymous. The information had circled the world almost twice before it got to me. It was in all these in-boxes, but my cipher key could unlock only one. I entered my pass code and waited for the message to decrypt. I could hear the hard drive doing a spin-up and the CPU beginning to work. Five in the morning.

Outside the sky was empty, except for a few lights on in the sky-scrapers, which looked like foggy constellations. I've never liked July. Where I'm from the whole summer is intolerably hot. The security monitors had browned out for a few seconds the night before, and I had to spend two hours checking them. I opened a window and put my fan next to it. I could smell the shipping yard outside—old cargo, garbage and salt water. Across the train tracks the bay stretched out like a giant oil slick. That early in the morning, only a half dozen or so headlights cut through the darkness. The fishing boats cast rigger beams over the nets, and the early ferries were setting off from the harbor. The fog rolled in from Bainbridge Island and through the city, where the rain stopped and the cargo express cast a shadow from the track going east. I took my watch off the windowsill and put it on. I wear a Patek Philippe. It doesn't look like much, but it will tell the correct time until long after everyone I've ever known is dead and buried, the trains stop running and the bay erodes into the ocean.

My encryption program made a noise. Done.

I clicked on the message.

The sender's address had been obscured by all the redirects, but I knew instantly who it was from. Of the possibly thirty people who know how to contact me, only two knew the name in the subject line, and only one I knew for sure was alive.

Jack Delton.

My name isn't really Jack. My name isn't John, George, Robert, Michael or Steven, either. It isn't any of the names that appear on my driver's licenses, and it isn't on my passports or credit cards. My real name isn't anywhere, except maybe on a college diploma and a couple of school records in my safety-deposit box. Jack Delton was just an alias, and it was long since retired. I'd used it for a job five years ago and never again since. The words blinked on the screen with a little yellow tag next to them to show that the message was urgent.

I clicked it.

The e-mail was short. It read: *Please call immediately.*

Then there was a phone number with a local area code.

I stared at it for a moment. Normally, when I got a message like this, I wouldn't even consider dialing the number. The area code was the same as mine. I thought about this for a second and came up with two conclusions. Either the sender had been extraordinarily lucky or he knew where I was. Considering the sender, it was probably the latter. There were a few ways he could've done it, sure, but none of them would've been easy or cheap. Just the possibility that I'd been found should have been enough to send me running. I have a policy never to call numbers I don't know. Phones are dangerous. It is hard to track an encrypted e-mail through a series of anonymous servers. Tracking someone by their cell phone is easy, however. Even regular police can trace a phone, and regular police don't deal with guys like me. Guys like me get the full treatment. FBI, Interpol, Secret Service. They have rooms full of officers for that sort of thing.

I looked at the blinking name long and hard. *Jack.*

If the e-mail were from anyone else, I would've deleted it by now. If the e-mail were from anyone else, I'd be closing the account and deleting all my messages. If the e-mail were from anyone else, I'd be frying the computers, packing my duffel and buying a ticket for the next flight to Russia. I'd be gone in twenty minutes.

But it wasn't from anyone else.

Only two people in the world knew that name.

I stood up and went to the dresser by my window. I pushed aside a pile of money and a yellow legal pad full of notes. When I'm not on a job, I translate the classics. I pulled a white shirt out of the drawer, a gray two-piece suit from the closet and a leather shoulder holster from my dresser. I fished a little chrome revolver from the box on top: a Detective Special with the trigger guard and hammer spur filed off. I filled it with a handful of .38 hollow points. When I was dressed and ready, I took out an old prepaid international phone, powered it up and punched in the numbers.

The phone didn't even ring. It just went right to connection.

"It's me," I said.

"You're a hard man to find, Jack."

"What do you want?"

"I want you to come to my clubhouse," Marcus said. "Before you ask, you still owe me."

2

Even from across the street, the Five Star Diner smelled of cigarettes and aftershave. It was wedged like a garbage can between a restaurateur's alleyway and a porn shop in the drinking half of Belltown, a block from the Space Needle and just shy of South Lake. A pack of motorcycles were parked under the streetlight. The inside was lit by the faint glow of neon and a jukebox full of shiny compact disks. The front door was propped open. Even at this hour the heat hadn't let up.

The cab driver made a rolling stop out front. Compared to the places where I used to work, like Vegas or São Paulo, there are very few bad neighborhoods in Seattle, which is practically spotless by comparison. This neighborhood was an exception. The alley looked like a homeless shelter, full of blankets and bottles and stinking of skunk beer and motor oil. I paid the fare through the cash-sized gap in the plastic shield, and the driver didn't wait around. He drove off as soon as I had my feet on the pavement and both hands off the door.

I walked down the alley and went in through the kitchen. The Five Star was a public place, I figured. It's harder to do anything really awful to someone in a place where anybody with eyes or ears could be a witness. Marcus was trying to tell me that he didn't want to kill me. If he'd wanted to kill me, he wouldn't have bothered to send me a message. He would've found me himself, put a pillow over my head and then a bullet through it, like he did back in the day. Meeting here was like standing on the sidewalk in front of a police station. There was a twisted sort of logic to it. It gave me one reason to take comfort.

Marcus had never killed anyone in his own restaurant before.

Still, he did have plenty of reasons to take me out. A job we'd worked on together had fallen apart, and his reputation had gone down with it. He went from international mastermind to scumbag drug lord overnight. He used to have his pick of the best operators in the world. Now he had to hire scum off the street for protection. After that job I thought he'd never want to see me again. I thought that he'd as soon shoot me as send me an e-mail. But somehow I knew this day was coming. I owed him.

The guard in the back was expecting me. He was a big guy in a denim cut who took a good look at my new face before letting me through. He nodded like he recognized me, but I was sure he didn't. I've changed so many times that even I forget what I look like. The most recent incarnation had brown hair the color of caramel and hazelnut eyes, with white skin from too many days inside. Not all of it's plastic surgery. Contact lenses, weight loss and hair dye can change a man better than fifty grand of knife work, but that isn't the half of it. If you learn to change your voice and how you walk, you can become whomever you want in ten seconds flat. The only thing you can't change is the smell, I've learned. You can mask it with whiskey and perfume and expensive creams, but the way you smell is the way you smell. My mentor taught me that. I will always smell of black pepper and coriander.

I went in past the line cook, who was taking a break with a nonfilter cigarette on the upturned flat of a soup-base can. I nudged behind the flat top through the kitchen where the Mexican fry cook was working. He glanced at me, then quickly looked away. The kitchen smelled of bacon, chorizo, fried eggs and salted butter. I crossed through the servers' doors into the back of the place. Marcus was waiting for me in the eighth booth under a neon Bud Light sign. He sat in front of an untouched plate of ham and eggs, with a cup of coffee at his elbow.

He didn't speak until I was close.

"Jack," he said.

"I thought I'd never see you again."

Marcus Hayes was tall and stringy, like the president of some computer company. He was as thin as a stalk and looked uncomfortable in his own skin. The most successful criminals don't look the part. He wore a dark blue oxford shirt and coke-bottle trifocals. His eyes went bad after serving a six-pack on a work camp on the Snake River in Oregon. His irises were dull blue and faded around the pupils. He was only ten years older than me, but he looked much older than that. The palms of his hands had gone leathery. His appearance didn't fool me.

He was the most brutal man I'd ever met.

I slid into the booth across from him and peered under the table. No heat. I've never been shot at from under a table before, but it would be easy enough, especially for a man like him. A P220 or some other small pistol with a silencer might do the trick. Subsonic bullet. One to the gut, one to the heart. He'd have one of the cooks chop off my hands and head, wrap me up in garbage bags and dump the rest of me in the bay. It would be like I never even existed.

Marcus stretched his fingers in mild annoyance. "Don't insult me," he said. "I didn't bring you in to kill you, Jack."

"I just thought I was burned in your book. I thought you never wanted to work with me again."

"Then clearly you were wrong."

"I got that much."

Marcus didn't say anything. He didn't have to. I looked him right in the eye. He held out his palm, open on the table, and shook his head like he was disappointed.

"The bullets," he said.

I said, "I didn't know your intentions."

Marcus said, "The bullets, please."

I responded slowly. I took the revolver out of my shoulder holster with two fingers, to let him know I didn't plan on using it. I released the cylinder and pushed out all the bullets. I put the handful of hollow points on the table next to his plate. They clattered on the wood like silverware. They rolled around for a moment before coming to a stop halfway between me and him.

I holstered the gun.

"What's this about?" I said.

"Did you know Hector Moreno?"

I nodded slowly. Noncommittally.

"He's dead," Marcus said.

I didn't react much. It wasn't really news. I knew Moreno was heading for an early grave the first time I met him. I was in a bar in Dubai a couple of years ago. I was drinking an orange juice for the ride home. It was a classy place, full of guys in suits. Moreno came up from behind me all dressed up in a new pinstripe Armani. He smoked no-bull cigarettes, two puffs at a time. When he spoke, he mixed in words from a language I couldn't understand. Arabic, or maybe Persian. He fired up a love rose behind the shed in the parking lot when we were done talking. I could smell the freebase cocaine in his clothing and I could see his heart beating through his ribs. He was as much a soldier as I was Santa Claus.

"What does this have to do with me?" I said to Marcus.

"How well did you know him?"

"Well enough."

"How well?"

"As well as I know you, Marcus, and I know you brought me here to listen, not to talk about some crackhead I met on a job."

"All the same, Jack," Marcus said. "Moreno ate a bullet this morning and he deserves our respect. He was one of us to the end."

"The day I give a murderer like Moreno respect I'll eat a bullet myself."

We were silent for a second as I studied Marcus's face. His eyes looked strained. There were brown rings in his coffee cup. There was no steam off the coffee. No little creamer cups, no empty sugar packets. Just crusty brown rings, and a black sludge that started about halfway down. The cup had been poured at least three hours ago. Nobody orders coffee at three in the morning.

"What's this about?" I asked.

Marcus reached into his pocket and produced a wad of twenty-dollar bills the size of a paperback book, wrapped up with rubber bands. He set it on the table. "This morning," he said, "my heist with Moreno went bad. Bodies everywhere, loot missing, feds circling sort of bad."

"What do you want from me?"

"I want you to do what you do best," he said. "I want you to make it disappear."

3

Five thousand dollars doesn't look like five thousand dollars. It never does, even after you've counted it twice, as I'm sure Marcus had. Five grand always just looks like a stack of green paper two and a half inches wide, six inches long and eight inches high. It could be two grand, or it could be twenty. At a certain point, the brain can't count it all fast. It just looks like a lot.

Marcus slid the stack toward me, through the bullets.

I looked at it. "With all due respect, Marcus, I don't get out of bed for less than two hundred grand."

"This isn't an offer, Jack. These are cash expenses. You're going to do this for me because you still owe me. You've owed me for five years."

I couldn't argue. I'm not even sure I wanted to.

Marcus told me all about it. He started thirty minutes before the heist and walked me through it like he was narrating a boxing match blow by blow. There was something broken about the way he talked, as if he'd learned to speak by reading telegraphs or talking to one of those automated phone machines. It was all a series of facts to him, spoken in short bursts, with no time to breathe in the middle. He said, "I sup-pose you haven't heard anything about this, considering it's still early here, but it's all over the news out east. Four people were killed, including Moreno. The target was a big brick of bank money on its way to a casino. Easy as you can imagine. A thirty-second job. I thought even idiots like him and his partner couldn't screw it up. They had to avoid a few cameras, put the scare on a couple armored-car guys, grab the money and drive off. Once they bounced the heat, they were supposed to head north to a self-storage facility, call me and wait it out. It was supposed to be the easiest deal in the world."

"But Moreno ate a bullet." I said.

"And I never got the call."

"Why were you even using Moreno? I can't imagine his partner was that much better."

"They were disposable."

I chewed it over. "What was the take?"

"A million and change in hundred-dollar bills. Exactly how much depended on the casino numbers. First weekend in July, first delivery of the day, it was probably looking more like a million two, million three. Enough to cover the morning cash rush from last night."

"How do you know Moreno got shot?"

Marcus nodded to the television playing in the corner. "One of the robbers got shot. Guy had white skin. Moreno's partner was black. You ever see a security photo on TV before of one of your own guys?"

"Yeah."

"I've seen two."

"When did the job go down?"

Marcus looked at his watch. Like me, he was wearing a Patek Philippe.

He said, "Almost four hours ago, now."

I put my hand on the money. "You want my advice? Wait. Four hours is no time at all. Four hours after my last heist I barely had time to catch my breath, let alone call anybody. I was up to my neck in Vegas heat. I didn't know who was dead, I didn't know who got caught, I didn't know who had the checks. I didn't know anything. The only thing on my mind was getting to the safe house and laying low until hell and the district attorney froze over. And if you think those TV reporters know what happened, they don't. Moreno could be out of surgery and in county jail by eleven. Nobody will know anything solid until noon at the earliest, and you won't be able to move on any of it until the dust settles, probably tomorrow. I know you're worried that this black guy—"

"Ribbons. Jerome Ribbons."

"I know you're worried that Ribbons is vanishing on you, but you've got to wait and see about it. If you go in too hard he might think you're after him for screwing up the heist, and then he'll never show."

"This isn't one of those things that can wait," Marcus said. "The item Ribbons and Moreno stole is extremely dangerous. I'm on a forty-eight-hour clock here."

"The money's dangerous?"

"Yes, the money. The cash money. The goddamn unmarked, shrink-wrapped, sequential, genuine Federal Reserve notes. Shipped specially from D.C. to the Philadelphia Federal Reserve branch for distribution to the casinos in south Jersey. The *notes*, Jack."

"What's the problem with them?"

Marcus nodded at the stack of twenties in my hands.

"They've still got the federal payload," he said.

4

Federal payload.

Two words nobody wants to hear.

Especially not me, and I've never even dealt with a federal payload before. It's like the perverse punch line at the end of the absurd story that's bank security. It has to do with how the Federal Reserve transports cash. Once the Bureau of Engraving and Printing in Washington finishes a print run, they put the freshly printed notes through a machine that lumps the money into thousand-bill wads, each subdivided into hundred-bill straps. At the end of the process, they vacuum-pack the money in cellophane to make it easier to transport. They print a half a billion dollars every day. They spend millions just on plastic wrap, because sometimes a print load can weigh as much as five hundred metric tons. The vacuum packing can bring the volume of each wad down by a quarter, which means more efficient transport. Once the money is wrapped, it's put into trucks. The trucks drive to the Treasury, where the money is scanned by a computer and serial numbers are monetized. Then the trucks drive the money to one of the eleven banks on the backbone of the Federal Reserve. The Federal Reserve banks scan the money a second time, then put it on different trucks and distribute it to smaller banks all over the world. The receiving banks scan the money a third time, then tear open the cellophane and spread out the currency to the masses. But it isn't all inflation. The Fed exchanges older notes with newer ones, so the amount of money in circulation is almost the same, give or take a few percentage points a year. The older bills are collected by the smaller banks, shipped to the bigger banks, driven back to the Treasury, shredded and burned. One big cycle.

To guys like me, a sixty-ton pallet of fresh hundred-dollar bills sounds too good to be true. That's because, as far as I'm concerned, it *is* too good to be true. Nobody's ever tried to rob a Fed truck, not to mention pulled it off, because nobody's that stupid. It can't be done. The reason is that the government doesn't give two shits what happens to the cash while they're moving it. They protect it like all get out with armed personnel and blind-decoy trucks and everything, but the moment they think the bad guys might actually pull one off, they'll torch the whole load. Long story short: the Federal Reserve only pays the government around ten cents for every bill they print, which essentially covers the cost of ink and paper. If the money gets burned, it doesn't really count against the bottom line. All the bank loses is paper. They just order more from the printer and a few smaller banks have to make do with older bills for a while. Meanwhile, if the money gets stolen and the guys get away with it, every single dollar lost in that shipment is inflation. Sure, a couple billion dollars isn't all that much compared to the total GDP, but even the smallest bit of inflation harms the credibility of the whole U.S. monetary system. Word of the heist would get out from Boston to Bangladesh in ten hours. Once there's word that there's a hole in the system, every crew in the country would try to take down the Federal Reserve. One slipup, and Uncle Sam would have a whole other thing coming.

So that's where the federal payload comes in.

The federal payload is essentially an ink bomb placed in all the money that comes out of Washington. Every couple hundred bills, there's a very thin, almost undetectable, explosive device. This device has three parts. There is a packet of indelible ink, a battery that doubles as an explosive charge and a GPS locator that acts as a trigger. While the Feds are trucking the money around the country to and from the banks on the backbone of the system, they keep these big cellophane-covered wads on an electromagnetic plate. The plate's a wireless battery charger, like those things they have now for cell phones. As soon as the cash is removed from the plate, the batteries on the explosive devices hidden in the bills start to drain. If the batteries run out, the cash blows up. If the cellophane gets cut open prematurely, the cash blows up. If the GPS locator hooks up with the wrong satellite, the cash blows up.

Department stores often put tags on their expensive clothing, right? If some dumb kid tries to sneak a Vera Wang out the front door of Nordstrom, a signal gets sent to the little radio frequency identification marker on the dress. You know, those circular little plastic things. The klaxons go off on the door, because the RFID bars can sense when a dress that hasn't been bought yet is moving. If that doesn't bust the kid, then there's a packet of indelible ink attached to the bottom of the dress that'll blow up a couple of feet out the door. When it does, the clothing is ruined and the kid gets caught. The department stores do this because if a piece of clothing gets ruined this way, they can claim a loss of full retail price, plus legal fees and punitive damages from the shoplifter. Also, the prospect of exploding clothing is a strong deterrent. It's the same principle with the federal payload. If the money gets stolen, it's on a timer. Unless a qualified vault manager scans it with a very particular receiving code within a certain amount of time, usually just a few days, the money goes bye-bye. Federal payload is the kiss of death.

Regular banks use the same sort of technology, just without the GPS. If you walk into a bank and ask for all the money, as I have a few dozen times, sometimes there'll be ink packs hidden in that loot too. They're usually set to go off after about two minutes, so once you walk outside, the cash explodes and the police know to look for the guy covered in indelible ink. Those kinds of ink packs can be beaten by segregating the money into different thick plastic bags, so if one ink pack goes off, it doesn't ruin the whole load. But Fed packs are different. The

Fed packs are all bound together. Imagine if the truck broke down, or the electromagnetic plate stopped working. Think about all the time that Fed money spends in the depot, sitting on a big pallet roller while someone finishes the paperwork. Think about how long it must take for a couple of strong guys to load a hundred million dollars off one truck and into another. The system is slow. The Fed timer's set for forty-eight hours, partly because of inefficiencies in the system, and partly because forty-eight hours is the maximum time frame that law enforcement has to reasonably catch the criminals and recover the money using the GPS.

I swallowed. "What the hell was Fed money doing at a casino?" I said.

"Going into circulation," Marcus said. "The average casino moves more cash in a week than half a dozen banks. Hardly anybody brings cash anymore. Customers buy chips with plastic and expect to cash out winnings in bills. All of the bank vaults in Atlantic City combined couldn't cover a hotel casino like the Regency on a busy weekend like this, so the casino got itself classified as a bank. It can draw down directly from the Federal Reserve, because none of the private banks can come close to filling their cash needs. There are a hundred ATMs and thirty gold-rated teller windows in the Regency. That's like ten banks. It's been like that for two years."

"How were you going to deal with the tracking device? GPS jammer?"

"Lead-lined bag. Easiest trick in the book."

"How the hell were you planning on getting around the payload?"

"That isn't your concern."

"Like hell it isn't."

"The money was for a drug deal," Marcus said.

"That doesn't explain anything."

"The money is on a forty-eight-hour clock that started at six Eastern. I was supposed to get rid of it before six Eastern on Monday. It's almost ten in the morning there now. That means I've got less than forty-four hours left to deal with this thing, or else I'm a dead man."

"How were you going to do it?"

Marcus stared at me like I was the slow guy at the table.

People like him do deals every day. Nothing goes wrong. Of course Marcus was going to do deals with his cut. It isn't just good money, it's smart. It's the fastest, easiest, most profitable way of passing off stolen goods. Of course Marcus was going to do it.

I said, "Answer my question."

"You're not understanding me, Jack." Marcus's words came slowly. "We were going to use the cash for a *drug deal*."

Silence.

My hands slid off the table.

"It was never your intention to disarm the money. You were going to pawn it off on some poor bastard who didn't know what he was getting," I said.

A drug buy is exactly as simple as it sounds. One person brings the drugs. The other brings the cash. They trade. It's rarely more complicated than that. I did my first drug deal when I was fourteen. I put a nickel on the park bench, my dealer put a nickel sack in my lap and walked away. If I could do it then, anyone could do it now. Child's play.

Marcus's buy was no different. It was just bigger. With a million in cash, Marcus and his two jokers could buy a whole car full of product at cartel prices. A million in pure acid could fit in a small water bottle. A million in heroin would fill the trunk of a sedan. Coke would take the backseat too. Pot would need a truck. The seller wouldn't even question the shrink-wrapped money. He'd take it and go.

Boom.

Thirty hours later, there'd be one less drug dealer in town. Once the casino blew the cash, Marcus's supplier would find himself with ten thousand or more useless hundred-dollar bills and a direct homing beacon to the federal government. Dealers on Marcus's level can handle losing a million or more if things go south, but very few dealers can survive a swarm of Secret Service agents coming in for the kill by helicopter. Marcus didn't rob a casino because he wanted the money. He robbed it because he wanted a weapon. Marcus wasn't stealing from a casino. No.

He was stealing from a cartel.

I said, "You're kidding me."

Marcus moved forward an inch. "For you it's just a cleanup job. It doesn't matter what trouble I'm in. I'm not paying you for the heist. I'm not paying you to tangle with the casinos. I want to pay you to make sure, make damn sure, that Ribbons calls in, doesn't get caught and delivers the money where it needs to go before the two-day clock runs out. You're my insurance policy, Jack."

"You're completely insane."

"Do you know how many people smoke crystal meth in the Pacific Northwest?" Marcus said. "Everybody. Demand is huge. Pure rock goes for sixty to ninety a gram. Half as much as cocaine, but at fifty times the volume. And that's assuming the meth is just average quality. That's twice as expensive as it is on the border. That's fifty times what it costs to cook up. Think of the profits. On this one deal alone, with one major competitor eating prison or worse because of the bad money, we could stand to make eight-figure profits. Start a half dozen labs. Be on every street corner from here to San Francisco. I could turn the hundred thousand dollars I paid Moreno into a seventy-five-million-dollar industry in six months. So when I said it was a big payday, it was *the* big payday. It all comes down to what's sitting in front of you. Mounds and mounds of it."

I took a long look at the cash.

"It's all the same to me," I said, "whether you're buying straight meth or trying to cook it yourself. I don't do drug deals. You know my rules. I only work for cash or art, nothing else. No exceptions."

"What makes you think you have a choice?"

"Because you're going to let me walk out of here alive," I said. "And I still owe you."

Marcus chewed his lip and gave me a withering look. "I have a jet waiting to take you to Atlantic City. When you get there, I know a few people who'll help you pick up what you'll need. If you won't deal for me, I want you to find the money and call me. I'll figure out what to do from there. I just need this mess cleaned up before it comes across the contiguous forty-eight and shuts me down. I'm not serving time because Moreno got plugged, and I don't care what happens to you afterward. Go ahead, disappear. You clean this up, we're even, got it?"

Marcus gave me a look, then another at the money sitting in front of me. He reached forward and flicked one of the bullets with his finger. It rolled toward me, then off the table.

I pursed my lips.

"I don't like your new face," Marcus said. "Too innocent."

I put the bullet back on the table.

"Why are you a dead man if the cash blows?"

Marcus didn't say a word for a moment. He didn't have to. I could hear sounds from the kitchen. Coffee was percolating behind the counter. Marcus's words were as dry as a stone, as if they'd sucked all the moisture from the air.

He said, "I made the deal with the Wolf."

5

PACIFIC CITY, OREGON

Let me get one thing straight. I despise Marcus with all of my being. But he was right. I owed him.

It happened almost five years ago, on something we called the Asian Exchange Job. Marcus had invited seven of us out to a resort hotel in Oregon to pitch us a heist. It was a huge job for huge money, so he wanted a handpicked crew. I'd been in the game since I was fourteen years old, more or less, but I'd never been handpicked like that before. It was the first time, in fact the only time, I ever broke my rigorous system of anonymity. Marcus got a message to me, through one of my e-mail accounts, which included a latitude and longitude deep in the woods, and I went without knowing a thing about the job. I had no idea what was in store for me. The only reason I agreed to it was that the message also said my mentor would be there. Angela. When my limo pulled up to the hotel, she was waiting, leaning against an ivy-covered brick column and smoking a cigarette. I hadn't seen her in six months. I smiled at her through the glass.

The resort was small and surrounded by forest, but it looked very expensive and Marcus had booked every room in this old brick building that looked like it might once have been a school. The rooms had real keys, not those magnetic swipe cards, and the bathrooms were down the hall. It was like stepping back in time. When I got out of the limo, I couldn't tell if Angela was happy or angry to see me. She took me by the arm and smiled cleverly, like she always did, as she walked me through the lobby. There was no reading her. She was the kind of woman who could talk her way out of anything, even her own emotions. She was an actress and a con artist and at least ten years older than me. She liked to call me *kid*.

We went right to her suite without saying a word. When the door closed, she ran her fingers through my new hair and told me that even with all the changes, she could still remember my face. We had made love once, when I was still fresh meat on the bank circuit and she was money-crazy from a strip-bond job worth five hundred grand. It had been her mistake, she said. We sat at opposite sides of the room now and talked for a while. It was difficult to get used to her new voice, but she smelled just the same. Cigarettes and passion fruit.

The evening came, and Marcus sent word through the porter for all of us to gather around the fire pit outside. He introduced himself with one name only. *Marcus.* I stood next to Angela and listened to him do his cryptic spiel. Angela chain-smoked like it was nothing and whispered in my ear about all the different specialist bank robbers around us, pointing each out with the ember of her cigarette as she went around the circle.

A well-dressed, handsome blond kid named Alton Hill was the wheelman, which means he'd drive the getaway car. If it had wheels and an engine, he could drive it. He sounded like he was from California somewhere. There was a sort of crispness to his voice that didn't fit his pressed and professional appearance. The leather on his driving gloves was worn through, and he was only half-listening to Marcus speak.

The guy next to him, Joe Landis, was a boxman. Boxmen don't open safes, they literally crack them. The safes rarely survive. Joe was a short little guy with big eyes and a small mouth. He was from some part of

Texas, but I wouldn't have been able to tell if Angela hadn't told me. A boxman is half computer programmer, half demolition expert. There are still a few guys who can crack a combo with nothing but their ears and fingertips, but they are a dying breed. These days safecracking's done with a computer, a fiber-optic cable, a high-powered drill and home-made nitroglycerine called "soup." Amateur boxmen have a tendency to go deaf before they get it right. Joe stood off by himself and avoided eye contact.

Nearby was a grifter from mainland China named Hsiu Mei. She had more master's degrees than space on her wall to hang them, Angela told me, and she certainly had the rumpled appearance of an academic. She was beautiful, however. Her skin was the color of brown eggshells, and her black hair was so soft it looked like a strong wind might blow it away. She spoke half a dozen languages and was scribbling in a note-book. She was our controller and linguist.

After that, there were a pair of buttonmen named Vincent and Mancini. Brothers, Angela said. They didn't seem tough, but buttonmen rarely do. They hurt people for a living. These two were small Italian guys who cultivated that greasy Mediterranean look, wore the most hideous matching green ties I'd ever seen and radiated tough-guy body language. They stood next to each other in front of the fire with their legs wide open and their arms crossed across their chests. Vincent spoke, Mancini listened.

And then there was us.

There isn't a proper name for what we do, but we used to call ourselves *ghostmen*. Angela and I were in the business of disappearing. I've helped maybe a hundred bank robbers escape over the years. Not all of it is disguises and fake passports and driver's licenses and stolen birth certificates, either. Most of it is confidence. A ghostman has to be confident in the way he acts, talks and behaves. You could be on the FBI's top-ten list with your picture up in every post office from Bangor to South Beach, but if you know how to act like somebody else and you have the chops to prove it, you could live on Park Avenue and nobody would ever notice. People see what you tell them to see.

Angela and I were professional impostors.

She got her start as an actress in Los Angeles. She was very good at it, like you'd expect, but that didn't translate into success on the screen. Her acting was pathological. She was pure Method. She didn't act, she changed who she was. Casting directors hated her for it. A man might pull off spending his whole life in character, but not a beautiful young woman. She was a different person for every person she met. She'd get cast as a trophy wife and show up as a little girl. Her first measure of success was as a corporate spy. She bluffed her way into an executive-assistant position for a major aeronautics company. Got paid a hundred grand to steal a blueprint for a military jet and deliver it to the next company over. I don't think she did anything else but steal after that. She made enough money to eventually begin creating her own personal roles. She'd wake up each morning and choose who she wanted to be that day. When she found me, she was posing as an FBI agent so she could rob a cartel of counterfeiters. She tricked me into helping her, and I was hooked.

From that day on, I was her apprentice.

These days, I'm the best in the business. I can hit a bank and disappear in two days, and nobody would ever know I was even there. I could talk my way into Congress, if I wanted to. But as good a liar and a thief as I am, I could never hold a candle to Angela. She taught me everything I knew. I watched her flick her cigarette butt and stomp it into the soft, moist earth. I drank a bourbon and listened to the sound of her voice in my ear.

When the meeting was over, Angela took me by the arm and led me off into the forest behind the last cabin. We walked and we walked and we walked until my pupils were like dinner plates. It was as dark as the inside of an eyelid back there. The only light was from the moon behind the clouds. After maybe half a mile, she stopped and turned and stared right at me like she had something to say. She didn't speak for a long time, but when she did, she spoke in her real voice. She spoke in the voice that she only ever used with me.

"What are you doing here?" She looked up and shook her head. "What did he do to get you here?"

"Nothing. He gave me a location, that's all."

"I thought I taught you never to go on a job without all the information up front. I thought I taught you never to trust a stranger, especially if that stranger's planning a job. I thought I taught you to be careful."

"You did teach me that."

"Then what the hell are you doing here?"

I didn't answer. I thought it was obvious. I stared into her eyes for a while. She was a brunette then, with pixie-short hair and lipstick the color of blood oranges. She wore a four-thousand-dollar dress and diamond earrings no woman had worn in two hundred years, because she had stolen them from a museum. To say she was beautiful would be to miss the point. She was anything you wanted her to be. I stood there for a while until she sighed and took me by the arm again. When we got back to the hotel, her dress and my suit were covered in mud. She walked me to my room and said good night in the hallway. I listened to her footsteps down the stairs. That was how the Asian Exchange Job started.

We went to work in the morning.

Back then, Marcus was the man to work for. He wasn't a cartel kingpin yet. He was a full-time jugmarker. He wrote heists the way Mozart wrote music. They were big and beautiful and made money like you wouldn't believe. Five years ago, everybody wanted a shot at one of his jobs, because everything he touched turned to gold. There was a dark side, even then, sure. I'd heard rumors about what happened to anybody who failed him. But those were just rumors. I saw firsthand what happened to the men who succeeded. They flew away rich. Very rich.

Two days later, Angela and I were on a chartered jet with the others, flying from Los Angeles to Kuala Lumpur, Malaysia. Though it was

Marcus's charter, he didn't come with us. He was going to run the whole thing from Seattle by satellite phone. He was like Caesar when he was in the back of his restaurant, but none of us complained. He was going to make us rich.

I was the one who screwed it up.

6

The flight to Atlantic City took five hours.

The jet was a Cessna Citation Sovereign, a midsized two-engine the size of a semitruck, with a range of about three thousand miles. It was fueled and waiting when I arrived at the gate, and there was no security check. The man at the airport entrance took one look at Marcus's limo and waved us through. We pulled up next to the plane on the tarmac and I walked directly up the stairs. I shook the pilots' hands, but we didn't bother with introductions. Time was of the essence here. We were wheels up in five minutes. We had twenty-five hundred miles to fly.

I carried a black nylon bag over my shoulder. Marcus had given me enough time to pick up a few things from my apartment. In the bag was my Colt .38 revolver with the bobbed hammer, which Marcus had given back. A toothbrush. Shaving kit. Makeup. Hair dye. Leather gloves. A few passports, driver's licenses, state ID cards and two prepaid burner phones. The five grand from Marcus, and three black Visa corporate cards with a different alias on each one. At the bottom was a faded copy of Ovid's *Metamorphoses*, translated by Charles Martin. I always travel light.

I was excited to get on the plane. It had been a long time since I'd had a job like this. I'm very picky. When I'm not working, time seems to pass by in a haze. The days blend together, then the weeks, like a tape recorder set on Fast Forward. I sit in my apartment, at the desk facing the window, and watch the sun come up. I read the Greek and Latin classics again and translate them on yellow legal pads, some in German or French as well. Some days I don't do anything else but sit there and read. My translations go on for hundreds of pages. Aeschylus, Caesar, Juvenal, Livy. Reading their words helps me think. When I'm not on the job, I don't have any words of my own.

This was what I'd been waiting for—a job that, for once, wasn't going to be *boring*.

The Cessna was beautiful on the inside. I'd never flown in that model before, but it was like most of the other private jets I'd seen. It had a nose like a hunting bird and two big engines under the tail. The takeoff was like an amusement-park ride, but once we got up five and a half miles, the flying was easy and the engine noise minimal. There were eight seats, plus two for the pilots, and the sticker price was just south of twenty million. For that amount of money, every seat was like first class. There was a full-sized bar in the back of the cabin, a flat-screen TV overhead tuned to a twenty-four-hour news channel, a satellite phone next to the coffee machine and a wireless connection to the Internet. When the copilot came back and said it was okay to walk around, I made a pot of coffee. I still felt uncomfortable. You can barely stand upright in one of these things.

I brought the coffee flask with me back to my seat, poured myself a cup and drank it. I poured myself another and opened up my book. Something was making me nervous, but I couldn't quite figure out what.

After about twenty minutes, a story with the graphic *Shoot-out at the Regency* came on the television and I turned up the sound. The names of the victims were being withheld, but an old picture of Moreno in olive-drab fatigues flashed on the screen followed by a couple of shock shots of the hotel-casino tower and a line of bullet holes in the cement. A news crew was set up on the Boardwalk. I could make out where the heist had gone down by the crowd of onlookers in the background. A female reporter said four people were dead at the scene, one of them a perpetrator, and then added that police suspected two more were on the run, which caught me off guard. I'd suspected there was a third shooter as soon as Marcus told me what happened, but this confirmed it. The heisters had detailed knowledge of the casino's security system, the reporter said, and the investigation was well under way.

Then Jerome Ribbons's mug shot came up.

I nearly spilled my coffee. The picture was a few years old, but it was definitely him. *Wanted for questioning*. Ribbons's name was in all-capital letters at the bottom of the screen next to the number for the tip line, and the reporter did two whole sentences about it. They'd figured out his identity in less than four hours. Shit.

I pushed Pause and stared at the picture for a second. Blinked. Ribbons was maybe four years younger than he was supposed to be. He was scowling at the camera and holding up a booking number. He was a thick man, positively fat, with a boyish face and facial hair the thickness of a Brillo pad. He was hunched forward like a brown bear and his jaw hung open. His eyes were bloodshot and he looked exhausted. The shot had been taken by the Philadelphia Police Department, so he was still in street clothes. The tattoos on his one visible wrist and on his neck told a story. I could make out a stylized stag on his wrist. He'd been to prison and done five years, judging by the number of horns. He was gang affiliated, or used to be, according to the tattoo of a pistol under his chin. His nose had been broken and never quite fixed, and his knuckles were covered in scars.

I recognized him from somewhere. I couldn't remember where.

Unless Ribbons had really messed up at the crime scene, they must've found his name when they ran Moreno's fingerprints. Ribbons was probably on Moreno's known-associates list. It wouldn't have taken long to match the file photo of Ribbons against the surveillance video of the heist. He's pretty unmistakable, considering his size and his history. There aren't a whole lot of six-foot-four cons with stag tats. That would be enough evidence to get his booking photo to the media. By mid-afternoon, everyone in the world would be on the lookout for Jerome Ribbons.

I looked at my watch. Three more hours to wheels down. This was going to make my job very challenging.

I pressed Play again and poured myself another cup of coffee. The report was almost over, and there wasn't anything new when it came on again forty minutes later. I sat and thought about all the things that could've happened since six Eastern that morning. The investigation would've gotten huge fast, because any crime involving the Federal Reserve is a jurisdictional nightmare. The police would have detectives, sure, because people had been killed. The sheriff would have deputies running around, too, because there were fugitives on the run. The FBI would have field agents, because bank robbery is a federal crime. The Secret Service might be in on it, because they're the ones authorized to investigate crimes against currency. The Treasury has its own enforcement agents and, hell, even the Federal Reserve banks have their own security branch. There were probably two dozen guys in cheap suits in Atlantic City by now.

And Ribbons was still at large.

I wondered why he hadn't called Marcus.

When you don't show up or call in after a heist goes down, you're *vanishing*. Vanishing and ghosting are very different things. A whole crew ghosts after a job, so none of them get caught. One guy vanishes, so he personally doesn't get caught. Vanishing is one of the cardinal sins of professional bank robbery. No matter what happens, no matter how messed up things get, you don't vanish, and you *really* don't vanish with the loot. If the plan says meet at the warehouse, you meet at the warehouse. If the plan says check into a motel, you check into a motel. If you vanish on your crew, the whole getaway falls apart, which is the first step to everybody getting caught. In most instances, if you get a bad feeling before the job goes down, there's plenty of time to say you're done, give up and go home. If it looks like things are going bad, you tell your crew you're not feeling it and walk away. The minute the job starts, however, you're all in. Professionals take this very seriously. It's a matter of pride for some people. Some people would rather die than vanish. In fact, many have.

So maybe Ribbons was dead.

Or maybe Marcus's reputation had finally backfired.

Marcus was known for being horrible to the people who didn't come through. Truly barbaric. The rep helped him keep things in line, sure, but I could see why it might make a guy like Ribbons run. I'd heard a story about an electronics man who'd forgotten to disable a bank alarm. Four of Marcus's favorite men got locked up for five years each. Marcus went to the guy's house and made him eat a whole jar of powdered nutmeg. Scooped it into his mouth with a spoon. That doesn't sound so bad until you realize nutmeg's got *myristicin* in it. A teaspoon's okay, but not a whole jar. A few hours after the incident, the guy started dry heaving. Then he developed a headache and body pain like the hangover after a bar fight. An hour after that his heart started racing and his hands were shaking uncontrollably. It took nearly seven hours of that before the hallucinations started. Tripping hard and running a fever of 106, he took off all his clothes and scratched his face until it was covered in blood. A nutmeg trip can last for three days. Some people find it pleasant. Most think it's hell on earth. In some versions of the story, Marcus leaves the guy with a gun with one bullet so he can shoot himself. In other versions, the guy bites off his own tongue and drowns in the blood.

If Ribbons thought that was in store for him, no wonder he hadn't called.

1

I turned off the television and sat in silence for a few moments, closing my eyes and thinking about Ribbons. He'd gotten himself into a world of trouble. When I opened my eyes, I started to transform myself into someone else.

Transforming has always been the easiest thing in the world for me. I unbuckled my safety belt and retrieved my bag from the overhead compartment. In the side pocket was a trio of faded passports, and stuffed under the covers were matching driver's licenses. I had three men with a range of ages. Each one had a different look, career and lifestyle. None of them looked like me, but that wasn't a problem. I wasn't going to Atlantic City anymore. One of these three men was.

Jack Morton was the oldest of the three, and one of my favorite identities. I'd modeled him after a favorite college professor and never gotten into trouble with him before. He had a good, strong, noble personality. When I was pretending to be him, my voice would get deeper and my movements would get slower and more thoughtful. He was kind, strong-spoken and quick-witted. His voice was like melted wax. I laid his passport on my tray table and put the other two away. He was my man.

Although the birthday on the passport put him in his middle fifties,

Jack Morton was barely two years old. I'd created him piece by piece over the course of six months between a couple of jobs. I'd already planted all of his official documents in the record books. I had copies of his birth certificate and his college diploma tucked away somewhere. He'd gone to the University of Connecticut, Stamford, and done moderately well studying ancient languages. Now he worked as an insurance investigator. I liked him because, unlike some of my other names and identities, he didn't have a single file in his criminal record. He was a good man who didn't mind playing rough from time to time. I stared at his picture until my muscles slowly relaxed into the shape of his face. I could feel my expressions changing to fit his appearance. My resting heart rate slowed down, and my hands seized up with the tension of sudden middle age. It's hard to age twenty years in twenty seconds.

I took a long breath, let it out slowly, and became fifty-six years old.

Since Morton's palette was brown, I had to change mine to match. I carefully took out my sharp brown contact lenses and replaced them with foggier, duller, blue ones from my pack. My kit had a small vanity mirror for the makeup. I accented the curves of my face with a pencil and furrowed my brow to emphasize the lines. I smudged the pencil marks with my thumb until they blended in seamlessly with the curvature of my face. I applied very small amounts of dark foundation to my neck, cheeks and forehead. Within two minutes, it looked like I had the wrinkles and deep laugh lines of a man twenty years older.

"My name is Jack Morton," I said in his voice, just to practice.

The hair was next. There are hundreds of products that can change a man's hair color, but I've come to rely on a select few. Speed and simplicity are important. I didn't have the time or space to wash my hair and let the dye sit for an hour. Instead I got my scalp wet in the sink and carefully combed in streaks of instant dye, turning my light blond hair a darker, dirtier, older brown. Once the dye set, I added streaks of salt-and-pepper gray, then swept my hair back and tousled it until it looked careless. I made the eyebrows match with a few touches of a pencil.

"My name is Jack Morton," I said to myself again. "I'm an insurance investigator with Harper and Locke. I was born in Lexington, Massachusetts."

I had a few pairs of glasses in the bag. I tried a few different styles. Wire frames were too trendy. Circular specs were a little too old-fashioned. Thick-framed black glasses weren't right, either. I settled for a pair of rectangular bifocals that slid down my nose slightly. I glanced in the mirror. I looked practically professorial. I tied a small amount of dental floss around my left ring finger and pulled it until it was tight enough to cut off circulation. According to Morton's life history, which I'd written, he'd been divorced for a little over a year. When I pulled the floss off, it left the mark of a married man.

To complete the costume, I'd have to change watches. No insurance investigator would wear such an incredibly expensive Patek Philippe, and, if I was smart, I wouldn't risk someone recognizing it. However, this was the only watch I had with me, and I was quite attached to it. I pushed it back on my wrist to hide it under my shirt cuff.

The combination of all of my efforts rendered me completely unremarkable. I looked like thousands of other middle-aged white American men. I was middle age, middle weight, middle height and middle income. The only thing that set me apart was the expensive suit and watch, but those could be explained away. *At my age, I should care about how I look. It's just part of the job.*

We arrived at Atlantic City International close to four in the afternoon local time. I set my watch forward three hours as the tires bounced once on the runway. It was even hotter here. A blistering ninety degrees, and it wasn't likely to cool down anytime soon. Even the baggage handlers on the runway wore their shirts tied around their heads. With the humidity the way it was, the city felt like it was burning. The pilot gave me his phone number and told me to call when the cargo was ready. I patted him on the back and went down the stairs. The tarmac stuck to the soles of my shoes.

First I needed to rent a car. Then I needed a place to stay and something to eat. But all that could wait until I found the facilitator.

I took out my international phone and pounded in Ribbons's cell number. I knew he wasn't making calls, but that didn't mean he wasn't taking any. He had a cellular code from Virginia, which was a little unusual but not completely unheard-of. People have cell numbers from all over the place. The phone rang. By the time the answering machine picked up, I was already halfway to the rental-car desk. An electronic voice. You've reached this number. Please leave a message after the beep.

I waited for the beep. "Call home immediately," I said. "Father isn't angry, he just wants to hear from you."

I killed the call and glanced down at the screen. Ribbons's number was already logged on the phone's record, permanently written onto the data chip. I took the battery out and crushed the small data card. I threw the phone away in a trash can. I had another international phone in my jacket, but it was the last one.

The federal agent was waiting for me at the bottom of the escalator.

8

I don't run from federal agents. I run from cops, sure, because I might have a chance of getting away. But running from a federal agent is like trying to hide in a labyrinth. You might be able to prolong the chase for a while, but in the end the minotaur's going to catch you. Feds don't mess around. They always get the people they're looking for, so you'd better make sure they're not looking for you in the first place.

The only solution is to play along. I didn't speed up or slow down. I just leaned against the escalator's railing and let it bring me slowly toward her.

I knew who was waiting for me. She had the right wrinkles in her suit and worn-out edges on the soles of her sensible leather flats. Her skin was the color of coffee creamer and she was slender, but not thin. She had curves in the right places and a stern sort of intelligence to her. I imagined that she was a swimmer. Her curly brown hair was bundled back. Shoulder length, no nonsense.

She stepped in front of me and flipped open a leather badge booklet. Inside was a small gold shield with an eagle and the words *Federal Bureau of Investigation.*

She said, "Are you the passenger from the Citation Sovereign?"

"Yeah," I said.

"Can I have a word?"

"What is this about?"

"Do you know a man named Marcus Hayes?"

I didn't answer. Not right away. I would have walked away right then, if she weren't so goddamn pretty. "I'm sorry," I said. "You must have the wrong person. I don't know anyone by that name."

"You just stepped off his jet, so I'm betting you do."

"I want to see your badge again."

"Show me your identification and we've got a deal."

I considered it for a second. It is for moments like this that people carry fake driver's licenses. Travel agents rarely give them a second look, and regular police don't have enough training to tell the high-quality fake ones from the real ones, because every state has different security features. But Jack Morton was clean. If I played the odds, showing her his driver's license would be almost as safe as refusing to show her anything at all. It was within my rights just to walk away, but that would make me look suspicious.

I took the card out of my wallet. She looked at it, then up at me. We matched perfectly. For all she knew, the photograph could have been taken today. If she could tell it was a fake, she didn't let on.

She put the license back in my hand, then slid her shield booklet off her belt and gave it to me. It was a thin leather wallet with the gold insignia and a card in a viewing flap. *Rebecca Lynn Blacker.* Five foot six, pale eyes, tan skin, just north of thirty years old. I took out the card and rubbed it between my fingers. It felt real.

I looked up.

"All right," I said.

She took the badge back. "Mr. Morton, you're in from Seattle, right?"

"Yes."

"You hear about the armored car that got robbed this morning?"

"I saw it on the news on the flight."

"I didn't. I got a phone call. I'm on vacation, you see. I was taking my two weeks down in Cape May. This morning I'm waking up, just about to take a run on the beach, when I get a call from the special-agent-in-charge of the Trenton field office, then another one from the Atlantic City Police. I get in my car and spend three hours getting back to Atlantic City. Traffic like you wouldn't even believe, understand? No coffee, no time for a shower. I just drive and hope the PD sorts it out before I get there, but I pull up at the scene and the police have nothing. Two guys at large and no leads on finding them. So I start making calls. And you know what I find out? That just hours after all hell broke loose here, the Seattle field office snapped some photos of a meeting between an unknown man and a notorious heist-maker. An hour after that, the heist-maker got a Cessna Sovereign fueled and sent it packing across the country right here. This isn't a large airport, Jack. This town doesn't get that sort of itinerary every day."

"An unknown man?"

"One six-foot Caucasian male, mid-thirties, with light hair and brown eyes."

"Then you know it wasn't me," I said.

"I asked you a question about Marcus Hayes."

"It sounds like he loves to gamble."

She shook her head. She had a sort of half smile on. She said, "What are you doing here, Mr. Morton?"

"I'm on vacation."

"You're here to clean things up for Marcus."

"I'm not here for anyone," I said.

"Listen, I get it," she said. "A guy like that says jump, you jump. I read his file. Extortion, murder, drugs, bank jobs in half a dozen countries. If someone like that told me to do something, I might start thinking that I didn't have a choice. Like it's this or prison. But you know what? I've found I do my best work when I'm doing my own damn thing. And I'll tell you, this weekend I'm here by myself. If I were you, I'd try to stay out of this. I'm very good at what I do."

She handed me a business card that had a couple of names on it before hers, but hers was right there at the bottom. "In case you want out," she said, "give me a call."

9

The man Marcus promised me was leaning against the wall under the arrivals gate holding up a piece of paper with *Jack* on it. A young black guy with slick hair and a very expensive suit. I might have mistaken him for just another limo driver if it weren't for his gold-framed eyeglasses and the almost-nervous look on his face. He barely saw me coming until I was right on top of him.

"I'm the man you're waiting for," I said.

We shook hands and he fell in step with me without my having to ask. His voice was soft as silk. "Nice to meet you, sir," he said.

"Who are you?"

"I'm here to help with whatever you require."

"Okay."

"Have you ever used our service before?"

"No."

"Whatever you need, we provide. Your privacy is of the utmost importance to us. Nothing you ask us to do will ever be traced to you. All evidence of our relationship will be destroyed once you pay the balance of your bill. We do not keep records of our clients, nor do we ask any questions of you."

"You running point for me?"

"Yes, sir. Your employer called this afternoon and told me you would prefer it if I didn't ask your name."

"Good. Do I get to know yours?"

"Alexander Lakes."

"That's not your real name, is it?"

"No, sir, it isn't. What should I call you?"

"Sir is fine."

"Yes, sir."

"Ulysses is also good."

"That's a fake name if I ever heard one."

"I have a soft spot for the character."

"There's a character?"

"Homer. Also James Joyce. Don't you read?"

"Newspapers."

I walked with him through the doors and out to where the rental-car agencies kept their desks. I knew Alexander was there to pick me up if I wanted, but I needed my own wheels. I rang the bell for service. When the lady came out with the papers, I gestured to Alexander. He looked at me, then showed her his driver's license and he filled out his information on the contract. He was left-handed, and his script looked like he was performing a surgery. He had perfect cursive handwriting. He paid for three days' rental with a gold credit card. In his wallet I could make out two faded photographs of his children tucked into the flap.

As we walked away from the desk and into the parking lot, he said, "We've taken the liberty of booking you a room at the Chelsea. We know the staff there. Your name, whatever it is, won't go on the register, and there will be no record of your stay. All charges will be forwarded to us. The name they've got is Alexander Lakes."

"When do you get paid?"

"Call me when you are ready to leave, and we can arrange a meeting. If that isn't possible, I can arrange a cold drop or a wire transfer directly with your employer."

"Do you take Visa?"

"Cash or wire transfer only."

"Good."

We stood there for a moment until one of the parking-lot attendants pulled up in a blue Honda Civic, a couple of years old, with one of those bolt-on GPS devices above the dashboard. A kid got out and handed me the keys.

Alexander said, "I could've paid for any car on the lot, sir."

"This one is fine."

It used to bother me to drive an economy car, but it doesn't anymore. More expensive cars get noticed, and that's counterproductive. When you rent a car for a job, you want something invisible. Angela taught me that. There is hardly anything more invisible then a Honda Civic. They do their best to advertise them as unique and youthful, but they're not. They're cheap and identical. There are dozens of model years on the road and nobody can tell them apart. I've grown to like that. The Civic didn't have any bells or whistles or odd shapes or fancy colors. It was just a cheap little import, plain and simple.

I looked back at Alexander. "You drive here?"

"Yes, sir."

"Then drive back. I need some supplies as soon as possible. I need prepaid cell phones, a locksmith set, a knife, a change of clothes and a slimjim. Do you know what that last one is, other than a piece of jerky?"

"A strip of plastic used to break into cars, right?"

"Most people prefer to say 'keyless entry.'"

"Give me an hour. I'll have your items waiting at the hotel."

"Do you have a phone on you?"

"Yes, sir."

"Give it to me."

I waited for him to fish a black smartphone out of his pants pocket. It was one of those new ones with the touch screens that feel like they have buttons, but they don't. I took a look at it, flipped through the last couple of calls he'd made and didn't see any numbers I thought looked suspicious. I put the phone in my pocket.

Lakes stared at me for a beat.

"Did you just steal my phone?" he said.

"It lets me know you trust me."

"And?"

"And I need a phone with a local number."

"You should have my business line, then."

He thrust a card in my face with his name and number on it. *Executive Concierge Services.* I memorized the number and gave it back to him.

"No thanks," I said.

I got in the car and shut the door. Alexander Lakes looked at me for a moment before walking back toward the terminal. I saw him pull out around the corner in a black Mercedes. It was a new model with tinted windows and it looked like a shined-up paperweight. I followed him on the highway heading downtown from the airport until I turned off into the salt marsh. I thought as I drove. He was the perfect lip man. He spoke his employer's words almost better than he did. Almost certainly better. Time was ticking away.

Thirty-seven hours to go.

10

I followed the old two-lane highway to Route 30 through the salt marshes, next to where the Absecon Bay twisted through the flatland like a junkie's vein. Driving toward Atlantic City felt the same as driving into Las Vegas. The highway to both places was empty and lined with the faded billboards and casino promotions I remembered from my childhood. The marshland by the highway reminded me of the desert. Flat and hot and empty. There was hardly any vegetation taller than scrub brush for miles. The casino towers shimmered on the horizon like a mirage. The Honda handled nice and easy.

I zoomed past a billboard that read *The Atlantic Regency: A World Away*.

As I got closer to the city, I could taste the salt in the air. I cranked up the AC to full blast and followed the instructions from the machine on my dash. Back in the Five Star, Marcus had mentioned a self-storage unit north of the city. *Call me and wait it out.* If there really was a unit, it would be my first stop. I owed Ribbons that much. Not everyone who doesn't make a phone call after a heist is vanishing. Some have reasonable explanations for why they went incommunicado, and not all of them are liars. Phones run out of juice. Numbers get lost. People get caught in places with no reception. It sounds unlikely after so many months of planning, sure, but these things happen. If Ribbons had simply broken his phone during the firefight or ditched it in a moment of panic, it was still feasible he could've made it to the storage facility. He could be there right now, just hoping and praying that Marcus would send someone like me, and not a guy with a jar of nutmeg and a pair of pliers. I owed it to him to assume his innocence. At least, for the moment.

I saw the storage sign from almost a half a mile out, growing like a dot on the horizon. The storage center was in a precarious zone between the outskirts of the city and the uninhabitable salt marshes separating the city from the rest of the mainland. The place looked like it had been around for all of a week. The units were old steel freight containers just dumped there in the marsh, surrounded by a fifteen-foot razor-wire fence. There was a plain stucco prefab manager's office in the dirt parking lot. The sign was on wheels. I parked the car and stepped out. It was like walking into a steam vent. The smell of the stagnant water and rusting containers hit me like a blow to the head. I hadn't even got across the lot before my shirt was soaked through with sweat.

Units like these are a one-stop solution to a lot of heisting problems. Sure, the management takes notice if you start sleeping there, but for a quick and private place, a storage unit's hard to beat. A hundred bucks can buy you a hundred square feet for a month. As long as you keep paying the rent, you can keep anything you want in there. Most companies make you flash a driver's license and sign a piece of paper saying you won't use the joint for anything illegal, but there isn't much they can actually do to stop you. If you just need a place to lie low for a few hours, self-storage beats a motel every time. I looked through the fence at the rows of rusted shipping containers. I knew just by looking the place over once that Ribbons wouldn't be there. Having your face on the news changes everything. Suddenly you think about the bored-looking kid who watched you sign the paperwork a couple of months back and start wondering if he could pick you out of a lineup. This place would seem too confining for him. By now, paranoia would be making the decisions.

But Ribbons did have a unit in there.

It was worth checking out.

I ignored the manager's office and walked directly up to the gate. There was an electric box over the handle with a standard numerical punch-code lock. You'd press four numbers and the magnetic bolt would come undone and let you open the gate, even if the manager wasn't around. I tried 1111 and 4444 in case the manufacturer's codes still worked. Neither of them did. I looked up at the fence. I didn't enjoy the prospect of climbing up and slicing through the coils of nickel-chromium razor wire. I stared at it for a moment, then back down at the number box.

I took out the car key. I worked the rental-car insignia off the loop and tossed it. Without the loop, it looked just like a regular key. If I kept my hand around the electronic part, it could pass for the key to anything. I went back to the car and took the rental agreement out of the glove box. I worked the staple out with my fingernail, slipped it in my pocket and put the papers back where I'd found them. I got out again and went straight to the manager's office.

If you're going to convince someone to let you into a secure area, you have to look legit. If you're trying to access a numbered account at a certain Swiss bank, for example, you've got to come in carrying a one-ounce rectangle of pure gold, because certain Swiss banks use gold bricks as part of the passkey to their numbered accounts. It doesn't matter if the gold in your hand is just a piece of lead with spray paint and a holographic sticker on it, so long as it looks right. If I was going to convince someone to open that gate for me, I had to look like I had a key to one of the containers. He wouldn't see me use it, or even really see I had it, but he had to think it was there. Sometimes a single detail is all the disguise you need.

The kid at the counter was maybe eighteen years old with skin the color of pumpkin pie and a dirty uniform. He was sitting in an office chair behind the counter, watching television. He saw me but he didn't get up.

"The gate isn't working," I told him.

The kid didn't look at me. "You put the numbers in right?"

"Yeah," I said, putting a little anger into it.

"Which gate are you using?"

"The front one."

"Try it again. I just used that gate this morning."

"I'm telling you, I was just out there and the gate isn't working."

The kid sighed and looked up at me. He didn't recognize me in the slightest, of course, but I don't think that ever crossed his mind. He just beckoned for me to follow him, like he was tired of having to do this every goddamn day. We walked out the door and went straight to the front gate, where I made a frustrated gesture with my key toward the punch box. Then, like he was dealing with an idiot child, the kid punched in the numbers one at a time, saying them aloud in case my brain was too simple to catch it all. The gate made a buzzing sound and unlocked. I gave him a shocked look, like maybe I thought he'd tricked me, then acted embarrassed. I focused on the emotion and felt my cheeks go red.

"You remember your access key?" he said.

I held up the car key, covering everything but the teeth.

The kid nodded. "Write the code down next time, okay? Don't forget."

When he was out of sight and I was through the gate, I put the key away and walked down the row of units until I found the container painted with a big sloppy *21*. Moreno's container. The lucky twenty-one. The door was padlocked with a key-operated Medeco two-cylinder that was probably supplied by the facility. The doors were bound by a length of chain.

No Ribbons. Considering the lock was still in place, he might never have shown up in the first place, or even intended to. For all I knew, Ribbons and Moreno had been planning to blow off Marcus's rendezvous point from the start.

I took out the staple and straightened it out with my fingers until there was a series of very small bumps at the tip. I took off my tie clip to use as a torsion wrench. I leaned in close so I could get a good look at the padlock. It was harder to pick in the heat, especially without the proper tools, but in a couple of minutes I got the job done. I raked the tumblers with the edge of the staple like a bump key and twisted the tie clip gently until the lever popped. I removed the bolt and tossed the padlock away, then pulled the chain so I could free the doors and pull down the lever that kept them together.

There was something off about this container. From the look of the lock, nobody had been around for quite some time. At least a week. Whatever I'd find inside would be dated at best or irrelevant at worst. Still, it was worth a shot. Ribbons had to be somewhere, and any little thing could help.

Opening the container doors was like scraping a knife across a chalkboard. I pulled from the center with both arms. The unit let out a blast of hot air like a hair dryer. It took a few seconds for my eyes to adjust to the darkness and the stench of rust and old stains.

It was empty.

Mostly.

An intermodal shipping container varies in size depending on the originally intended cargo. They're measured in something called TEUs, or twenty-foot equivalent units, one of which could hold about thirteen hundred cubic feet of material. The common ones you see in the shipping yard are two TEUs, or about twenty-seven-hundred cubic feet. Forty feet long, eight and a half feet tall and eight feet wide. They were designed by the military during World War II to move huge quantities of goods easily between ships, trains and trucks. They're universal now. This one was almost completely empty. No backup car. No makeshift hideout. No ditched equipment. No plans tacked to the walls, no sleeping bags, no maps with lines drawn all over them. I checked twice for any sign that any of that stuff had ever been there, and I couldn't see any.

In the twenty-seven-hundred cubic feet of storage space, there was only a small backpack, more like a rucksack, that sat against the left wall.

I looked around. Left, right. Nothing. Nobody.

I entertained the thought for a moment that the rucksack might contain something dangerous, like Moreno's used needle sharps or some sort of trap he and Ribbons had set up just in case. I also considered for a second the odds that it could be the money, but I'm not that lucky. Or that stupid.

I untied the backpack.

No needle sharps. Not a trap, either.

Something else entirely.

11

A gun.

Not just a gun. At the top of the bag was a goddamn Uzi the size of a pistol, with crude iron foresights and a cut-down folding stock. The action didn't smell like gunpowder and the barrel was still shiny, inside and out. It hadn't been fired in a while, if ever. It was fully assembled and still in the manufacturer's plastic carrying case. There were three spare mags and a box of cheap ammunition underneath. Under that was a strap of twenty-dollar bills, a small Ziploc bag full of pills, a cell phone, a couple brochures and a lighter. Those were the only supplies. I rooted around at the bottom and in the side pockets for anything else, but that was it.

This was a getaway pack.

A getaway pack is a criminal's first precaution. I have more than a few myself hidden around the world. Just in case everything goes completely to hell, the getaway pack is there as a backup. You secure yourself a hiding place and stock it with the bare essentials. That way, when the shit hits the fan you don't have to scramble for anything. The best ones are minimal. The closest one I had was on the roof of a building on the west side of Manhattan, hanging from a wire on the inside of an old chimney that had been bricked up for decades. It had ten thousand dollars, a few credit cards, a clean passport and a Beretta. The pack here contained a fifth of the money and twice the firepower, plus some drug I couldn't identify. Nobody ever packs a change of clothes.

I laid the machine gun out on the floor. It was an old model Micro-Uzi, probably left over from before one of the assault-weapons bans. The ammunition was some Russian import. Nine-millimeter parabellum. I put the box of it on top of the gun. The cash at the bottom of the sack was faded and crisp from the heat. I flipped through the strap. The bills all were dated a few years ago. I took one out and felt the paper. Ones that look that old are more likely to be counterfeit. No watermark. No color printing. No security strip. That's why the Treasury changes the design so often. The counterfeiters try to keep up, but it takes them a few years. By that time, the style has changed again. For these bills, the difference would be in the watermarked cotton paper. Real money is printed on a unique blend of cotton and polyester fabric from a particular factory in western Massachusetts. The fabric gives money its distinctive soft, slightly starchy feeling, because it isn't technically paper. Fakes don't feel the same. I rubbed the bill a few times and compared it to one from my wallet. I'm no expert, but it felt like cash to me, no matter how suspicious it looked.

I pulled one out, picked up the lighter and fired one up. The edge caught and turned black, burning away in black circles that gave off an orange flame. Real money burns with an orange flame, because that's just how it burns. Counterfeits are printed on regular paper, which burns bright red. I shook the bill out and placed the rest of the stack next to the ammunition. Real money.

I took the brochures out next. The top one was a color brochure from a large, nationwide real estate brokerage; it had been folded up so many times that just opening it caused it to fall apart. The other one held a few pictures of old Victorian-style houses, but nothing specific. Inside was a cash receipt from an off-brand gas station down in Ventnor for thirty dollars' worth of regular unleaded, but the date was worn off. I looked at both again for a second, then put them back in the bag. Nothing useful.

I opened the bag of pills and sniffed at the mouth of the bag a few times. They were a pressed white powder, which means they were made in a factory but doesn't tell you much. A lot of drugs come out of factories, even illegal ones. There are whole industrial complexes in South America that press fake Oxycontin. These pills weren't Oxy, though. They smelled slightly clinical, like a polished hospital floor. I thought that they could have been some form of speed, like methamphetamine, but they were equally likely to be aspirin. For all I knew, one of these guys got really severe migraines.

Finally I took out the cell phone. It had a design that hadn't been popular in a few years. I pressed the green button, and I guess it had been charged because the screen flashed on right away and went into start-up. When the logo went away and the home screen popped up, I spent a minute trying to find any stored contacts. The list was completely empty. Then I looked for the list of recent activity. There had been a series of missed calls from a blocked number starting just this morning, but not a single voice mail. The one outgoing call was over a week old. New York area code.

I put all the gear back in the rucksack, took out the phone Alexander had given me, powered it up and dialed Marcus's number.

It picked up within one ring. "The Five Star Diner."

"I need to talk to him."

"Excuse me?"

"Tell him to pick up the phone or I'm going to the casino."

"One minute."

I closed the door to the storage unit behind me. Unless someone came to pick up the rucksack, it would remain there until the lease wore out. Probably another three months. I wondered what might happen then. Police discover weapons caches all the time, but rarely by accident. There would be yellow police tape encircling the unit and guys in black uniforms scratching their heads. I considered taking the cash, but it wasn't worth it. That getaway pack belonged to someone. Moreno or Ribbons, maybe. Marcus, even, considering he was the one who had probably paid for that stuff in the first place. There was still a chance that Ribbons might actually show up, though that possibility was growing smaller and smaller by the moment. If he did, I'd prefer it if he found the phone.

Marcus came on the phone a second later. He said, "What is it?"

"I arrived in Atlantic City all right, but Ribbons never made it to the storage unit. Nobody's been to this place in days. The lock was covered in dust."

"He's vanishing. He probably didn't go to the rendezvous because he knew that would be the first place I'd look."

"Yeah, I get that," I said. "But something's strange. There's only one getaway pack."

"Yeah?"

"Two guys. They weren't going to share a getaway pack. Nobody does that."

"So where's the other one?"

"I was going to ask you," I said.

"How should I know?" Marcus said. "Nobody tells *anyone* what's in their getaway packs, least of all their jugmarker. You know that better than anyone."

"Then I'm going at this thing backwards. You told me how the getaway was supposed to end, but not how it was supposed to begin. If things had gone as planned, you said, this storage unit was where they were going to hide out until everything quieted down. You've got to tell me what happened before that. Ribbons would've ditched his gun and his clothes, right? And what about the getaway car? Certainly Ribbons must have ditched that too. He had to. Probably within a few blocks, even. The news gave out a description of the car, but they haven't said that anyone's *found* it yet."

"They were supposed to ditch the car and burn it, yeah. It should've been a charred hunk of metal by now."

"So then what? Were they on their own to steal another one off the street, with maybe a whole fleet of black-and-whites chasing them? You've got to tell me more about the getaway."

"That's the only part of the job I didn't plan personally. I left Moreno in charge. He was the wheelman."

"Whatever you know, I should know."

"It was a two-car deal. Moreno was supposed to swap the first car for another car they'd already stolen and stashed somewhere. They were going to burn the first, then drive the second out to the storage unit where you're standing right now. I left it up to them to work out the details."

"Did he tell you where they were going to ditch the switch car?"

"They had some big empty building next to a derelict airfield about ten blocks from the casino. The idea was that inside an abandoned building, the switch car could burn for hours before the police would find it."

"Okay," I said. "I can work with that."

I hung up and removed the battery with my free hand. I crushed the body of the phone under my foot and kicked it away. I went out through the gate, got back in my car, started the engine and drove. The afternoon humidity was beginning to let up, and the light glinted off the marsh and caught in the windshields of oncoming cars. By the time I was back on the highway, I was already trying to put together my search strategy. I was already lost in thought. I wanted to go through Ribbons's getaway, move by move. If I could re-create his escape, there was still a chance I could find him alive.

I checked my watch.

Thirty-six hours to go.

12

The Atlantic Regency Hotel Casino was the first thing I recognized on the skyline. It seemed to loom over me on the highway like some giant glass obelisk, impossible for anyone to miss. It was twenty stories and a radio tower higher than the next tallest hotel, which made it one of the biggest resort casinos in the country. A triumph of modern engineering, I thought. The tower was shaped like a white knight on a chessboard. The whole billion-dollar complex had been nothing but a block of waterfront tourist traps just two years ago, and now there it was. They'd worked on it day and night to put it up so fast. The sign was visible from miles away.

I've always been less comfortable with people than with architecture. People can be boring. A well-designed building knows how to keep its secrets. Think the walls of Troy. No human army could break through, but a simple trick, like a horse full of hidden soldiers, could render all that security meaningless.

When I got close, I could feel the ocean on my skin. I drove around behind the Boardwalk near the casino's back and side entrances and circled around looking for a parking space. It wasn't long before I passed the spot where the job went down. The whole area was cordoned off by police tape, and every block for miles around it was packed with cars. The news crews looked like they'd set up camp for good. Vans from every affiliate within a hundred miles were parked with camp chairs set up next to them like they were tailgating. There were cameramen in sunglasses sipping sodas in the shade and a sea of other people. The rush I'd seen earlier on the news had died down a bit because of the afternoon heat, but there was still a throng of rubberneckers standing near the taped-off area. A uniformed police officer was telling them to move along. The *R* in Regency had been blown out over the entrance and there was a spider-bite line of bullet holes leading up to it. The holes would probably be gone by morning, as soon as the police gave the casino the go-ahead. But for now, the place still looked like a battle-ground even though all the bodies were gone.

I found a parking space a couple of blocks away and proceeded back on foot. If I could just see the place where Ribbons and Moreno had been working, I knew that I could put together their getaway in my mind. I could go through the same steps and maybe even see what they'd seen. Think what they'd thought. I walked past the TV reporters and ducked under the yellow police tape. The cop looked at me, but I reached into my breast pocket and took out my wallet. I flashed it at him like I couldn't give a damn. It didn't look anything like a badge, but the better part of my job is confidence. If you behave like you belong some-where, people find a way to believe it.

He waved me through without a second glance.

The casino doors under the Regency sign were locked now and cov-ered in clear plastic sheets. Everything felt strangely empty. At the time of the crime the whole area would have been relatively quiet, but not like this. All the cars had been removed from the parking lot and the bloody spots had been washed away with a pressure hose. The place was like a ghost town. The garage was one of those open-air concrete places where you could drive up ten stories and park on the roof if you wanted. The ticket booth had been smashed out and there was a whole different layer of caution tape around it. I could see the whole job go down, starting with the muzzle flashes of Ribbons's assault rifle. It played out nothing like the simple plan Marcus had described. This was a battle, not a heist.

Moreno had stayed behind with the hunting rifle. I glanced up at the place where he'd hidden. Six in the morning meant minimal traffic, if any. Ribbons was there for pure assault. Moreno had tried to kill all the guards silently, but couldn't. There were holes in the pavement from all the bullets. One of the guards must still have been alive when Ribbons started firing. There was no other reason to let off so many shots. I could see the spot where Ribbons had killed the very last guy. Point-blank, full-auto. The blood was all cleaned up but the bullets had blown away part of the blacktop in a tight little grouping. This was an execution.

I climbed over the concrete barrier into the parking garage. I could tell immediately where they'd parked the getaway car. There were bullet holes in the pillars all around, and marks on the pavement from the burned rubber. The broken glass and auto parts were all gone, but the tire marks and bullet holes were still there. I stood where the getaway car must've been and examined one of the holes in the pillar. It was at least .30 caliber. Someone had been waiting for Ribbons and Moreno. Someone had been sitting at the other end of the parking garage and watching them through the scope of a pretty serious rifle. The bullet had gone at least two inches into the concrete.

The sniper.

Marcus hadn't mentioned a sniper, but the news on the plane had called him "the third man." He had fired thirty yards from one end of the lot to the other. With a rifle like that, it would have been like shooting fish in a barrel. I could understand how he'd been able to kill Moreno with one shot. At that distance, a trained sniper could have killed them both blindfolded. All the extra shots suggested that my shooter was something of an amateur. He'd compensated for his lack of skill with a large number of bullets.

What I couldn't understand was the timing.

The third man had fired on Ribbons and Moreno only after they

were done. A normal person would've tried to stop the robbery in prog-
ress instead of waiting until it was almost over. Hell, even a criminal
with a grudge would've tried to stop the heist before then, since nothing's more dangerous to a criminal's life and livelihood than a high body
count. I considered for a moment that maybe the third shooter needed
a few moments to get his rifle ready. Maybe he didn't have a good shot
until the shit had hit the fan. Maybe he didn't exactly know what was
going to happen. Maybe the rifle was unloaded or in the trunk when
Moreno fired the first shot. But none of those explanations felt right.

The shooter must have known what was going to happen. What
were the odds that he'd just been in the right place at the right time with
the right weapon? The sniper must've known about Marcus's plan in
advance. How the hell could something like *that* happen? Marcus's plans
had only ever got out once before, and that time it was my fault.

Yes, this was certainly premeditated. Efficient. Maybe even personal.
Someone knew the heist was going down ahead of time, set up shop with
an angle already in mind and waited to take the first shot until exactly the
right moment. What was the goal? I didn't know, but I could guess. The
third shooter wanted the money Moreno and Ribbons had just taken. It
was a double heist. Ribbons and Moreno did all the dirty work, and the
third shooter would drive away with all the payoff.

I wondered if he'd bothered to give chase. Probably not. Too risky.
Once Ribbons made it out of the parking garage, the third shooter lost
his window of opportunity. Chasing him down on the roads wasn't part
of the plan. If it took too long, or ended the wrong way, both of them
could get caught. The cops may have been a couple of blocks away, sure,
but after a firefight like this, every squad car for miles would be going
Code 3. Giving chase would also require the third shooter to abandon
his own getaway route. Even the best drivers in the world wouldn't take
that risk.

I looked up at the surveillance cameras. They were several genera-
tions out of date. I'd seen pictures from cameras of that era. The license
plates would have looked like a Rorschach blot. When I checked on the

plane, there was nothing on the news about the cops catching the guy. Maybe his getaway car was still missing too. If that was so, he must have planned his getaway just as well as Ribbons and Moreno had. Maybe even better. After all, the sniper didn't have his face all over the news.

I closed my eyes and put myself inside his head. I became him for a moment and lived through his senses. I felt the rush and the weight of the rifle against my shoulder. I imagined trying to hold my racing breath as I centered the crosshairs on the back of Moreno's head. I imagined counting my heartbeats and correcting for the ocean wind. I imagined waiting for exactly the right moment, for Ribbons to cross the concrete barrier back into the parking garage. I imagined squeezing the trigger, feeling the force of the recoil absorbing into my shoulder and seeing the puff of pink mist as Moreno's body crumpled on the steering wheel. I imagined what I must've been thinking at that exact moment.

There was only one thing on my mind.

Kill.

I stood there a moment longer, then opened my eyes and blinked. When I came out of it, I headed toward the Boardwalk, slipping quickly under the yellow tape, past the cop, into the pedestrian traffic. A man in torn denim shorts blew past me on a rickshaw. For ten bucks, he was a slow, expensive taxi. Not for me. I weaved through the crowd, blending into the sea of bright summer colors. I became invisible. I caught my first sight of the ocean. It churned like a giant black oil slick up against the sand dunes.

When I got back to my rental, I switched on the GPS. It found my current location. I took a long look at the map and moved it around using the arrow buttons. The area looked like a getaway nightmare. One side of the Regency faced the ocean, two others faced more casinos and the fourth emptied to a major arterial road that in turn went to a patrolled highway with a toll booth every few miles.

I memorized the map as I scrolled. I'm no wheelman. I can drive well, if it really comes down to it, but actually planning a getaway route was never among my talents. There was a whole lot of information that the wheelman planning the heist would've known but I didn't have time to figure out. I kept thinking about the clue Marcus had given me. A derelict airport. I'd flown into Atlantic City International, nearly twenty miles away through the salt marshes. There were a few unused airstrips out there, sure, but they were about a hundred times farther away than any reasonable wheelman could accept, especially in the first getaway car. If this was a two-car getaway, I was looking for something within ten blocks, like Marcus said. I scrolled for a few more seconds, putting all my attention into the map.

I read somewhere that there's no such thing as eidetic memory. Nobody remembers everything perfectly, and the people who claim to are liars. I believe it, but even normal people can remember more than they think. Greek poets used to memorize epic poems hundreds of pages long, and they weren't anything special. They did it much like I memorize maps. They did it the same way Angela taught me to memorize things. Slowly, and with a lot of practice.

I saw all the possible routes expand out in my mind, spreading like the branches of a tree.

I found something that looked promising about ten blocks away. It was a route that ran parallel to the beach for a few blocks before turning off into one of the city's poorer neighborhoods. The ending spot looked like a large empty blank spot on the map. There was a listing there for a baseball field, but nothing else. I stared at it, taking my time, and finally could make out where the control tower used to be, and the runways, and the parking lot. It *had* been an airfield once. Now it was just a dead zone of abandoned buildings, not ten blocks from downtown.

I traced the route. Went over all the directions in my head. It was less than a five-minute drive. Three minutes, if there wasn't any traffic. Two, if you were driving like the devil was on your tail. Maybe the third shooter did give chase, and caught up even before Ribbons got there.

And I'd be in for a very bloody surprise.

13

KUALA LUMPUR, MALAYSIA

Our plane landed at five in the evening and the city was cooking. I remember the night clearly. It was winter down there and the sun was hanging on the edge of the horizon, dipping over the ocean and casting the whole city in light the color of blood. We'd followed the sun for most of the thirty-hour flight. I'd watched it through the airplane window over the wing.

Marcus had given us all new passports. Mine was from the United States and had the name *Jack Delton* in it. It didn't look like a fake, either. Even the special laminate felt real when I rubbed it. It would serve as my primary form of identification while I was in the country. Of course I'd also brought a second passport just in case, but that was for emergencies only.

We were all ushered through Immigration with no fanfare. Outside, a white limo was waiting for us. Marcus had arranged everything in advance, which was good. I didn't speak a single word of Malay and didn't have a dime of local currency. I was relying on him completely.

I had no idea how much trouble that would get me.

Malaysia was like no place I'd ever seen before. As we rode to the hotel, I leaned against the limousine door and watched the streets go by. The city was full of wealth and culture, but all of that wealth and culture was scattered around in a way that seemed haphazard to me. The financial district had skyscrapers the size of mountains next to great open spaces with nothing in them at all but dust and crab bushes. The parks had fountains lit up like Las Vegas, but the edges of the city were as poor as the slums of São Paulo. The Petronas Towers dominated the view constantly. They were lit up with spotlights that reflected off the clouds. It was their symbol, I guess. Their Empire State Building and their Golden Gate Bridge and their Hollywood sign all rolled up into one. Everywhere I looked, there they were, glowing in the distance.

By the time we got to the hotel, I was exhausted. It was a nine-hour time difference from L.A. and I hadn't slept a wink on the whole thirty-hour flight. Our suite at the Mandarin Oriental was the size of a small house. I walked in the door and took off my shoes in almost the same motion. There was a basket of fruit on the counter with a personalized welcome card on top, but all I could think about was coffee. I went directly to the small kitchen to look for a drip machine while the rest of the group went into the dining area and started pouring drinks from the bar. I looked out the floor-to-ceiling windows at the glowing super-skyscraper across from us. It was past dark by then and the lights were coming up like distant fireworks.

I'd located the machine and just put the coffee grounds into the basket when I heard Angela walk up behind me. I froze at the sound of her heels on the carpet. They reminded me of when we'd first met.

When Angela took me under her wing, I was twenty-three years old. I wasn't a very careful person. In fact, I wasn't very much of a person at all. I was just a kid from Las Vegas who didn't want to deal with society anymore. I didn't have any particular personality or talent. I'd spent a couple of years at St. John's College in Annapolis, Maryland, but I never made any friends. Outside of my course work, I didn't have any ambitions. No drive. When I met her, I was dreaming up bank robberies on park benches and sleeping in the back of my car. I made a lot of amateur mistakes. Angela trained all that out of me. She taught me how to be careful, how to cut off my last ties with the normal world and how to live like a ghost. One night, she heated up a frying pan on the stove until it glowed orange, then told me to put my belt strap in my mouth and bite down on the leather. With her help, I pressed my fingertips against the searing metal one by one, over and over, until the scar tissue formed and the wrinkles never grew back.

"You're making coffee at this hour?" she said.

"I can't sleep." I said.

"Two sugars for me, then."

She sat down on the couch opposite the kitchenette. I could feel her looking at me, even with my head turned. I poured excess water out of the flask. I filled the machine with water and pressed the button. The machine boiled and dripped. She sat there in silence as I watched the coffee brew until the light went off. I opened two sugar packets for her and then poured hot coffee into two ceramic cups. I stirred hers gently with the handle of the spoon.

"You've been quiet," she said.

"I've never been to this city before."

"No," she said. "It's more than that."

I handed her the cup and sat next to her in a chair in front of the desk by the window. I watched her swirl the coffee and look into it like she was reading tea leaves.

"How much do you know about Marcus?" she said.

"I know his jobs are huge. I know everybody comes away from them rich."

"But do you know anything about him? Anything at all?"

"I don't," I said. "But I barely know anything about you, and I've known you for almost eight years now. Do you know something I don't?"

"I know he's very intelligent," she said.

I nodded. "He seems to have everything figured out. I like that. He looks like he knows what he's doing."

"But you don't *know* if he knows what he's doing."

"You're right, I don't."

She pursed her lips and put her coffee down on the study desk next to us. She crossed her legs and bit her lip as she considered something in her head. She took her time before she said it, like she wasn't completely sure what to say, or how to say it.

"I told him about you," she said after a moment.

I didn't say anything.

"He said he wanted options, so I gave him your blind e-mail. I thought you wouldn't come. I thought you wouldn't even consider it. The way you pick jobs isn't normal. I've seen you pass up jobs that another man would've waited his whole career for. I thought he'd send you a message and you wouldn't even *respond*. You'd be off in the Mediterranean somewhere, reading one of your books, waiting for something more interesting to come along. Sketching old Roman wall paintings or something."

"I'm here," I said.

"You are," she said. "And I'm not sure how I feel about that."

I looked down at my coffee and didn't say anything. Angela dug her feet into the carpet like she was thinking something over that was too big to put into words. We were quiet for a moment. She was lost somewhere in her thoughts.

Then she said, "I want you to draw me a dollar bill."

"What?"

"I mean right now, draw me the best American one-dollar bill you can."

"Is this a hypothetical thing, or do you actually want me to do it?"

"No. I really want you to do it. You probably see a dollar bill dozens of times every day. You've probably spent more time looking at the dollar bill than you've spent looking at your own toes. It doesn't have to be perfect. I just want you to draw me one."

"What for?"

"Consider it part of your education."

"I'm really no good at forgery."

"I didn't ask you to *copy* a dollar bill, I asked you to draw me one."

"What's the difference?"

"This is about the dollar bill in your head," she said. "Not the one right in front of you. Think of it as an exercise in perception. I want to see what you remember, not what you see. I can look at a map and memorize it in an instant. That isn't just something I was born with. I taught myself to do that. I studied mazes until I could copy them after just a glance. It sounds easy, but it isn't. I want to see you do the same thing, starting with the front of a dollar bill. Look, I even have a pen in the proper color."

She opened her purse and took out a green fine-point, felt-tip pen. She put it on the desk next to the pad of hotel stationery. I stared at her. She stared right back at me.

"Okay," I said.

I picked up the pen and started with a rectangle, roughly two and a half times longer than it was wide. At first I thought it would be easy. Who doesn't know what a dollar bill looks like? But as I tried to put it all together in my head, it started falling apart. There were a lot of details. I could remember the general layout. I put the number one in all four corners. I remembered that the top left number was surrounded by a floral design, so I circled it. I remembered that the number at the top right was surrounded by a shieldlike thing, so I added something like that. I put an oval in the center and drew Washington's portrait pretty simply, then put the words *The United States of America* above it. Under the portrait I wrote *One Dollar*. I turned the piece of paper around and showed it to her.

"No," she said. "Try it again."

I took another look to evaluate what I'd done wrong, then ripped off a new page.

I started with the same rectangle, because I knew I'd got that more or less right. I put the numerals in all four corners and put a circle around the top left and a box around the top right. I put the oval with the portrait in the right place, and *The United States of America* and *One Dollar* too. This time I remembered that up at the very top of the bill were the words *Federal Reserve Note*, so I put those in, and I remembered that there were official seals on either side so I drew circles to the left and right of the portrait. I put a row of random numbers under the word *America*, and the words *This note is legal tender for all debts, public and private* under the word *United*. I drew a little squiggly line under each seal where the signatures were supposed to be.

She stopped me before I could finish. "No, that's not it, either."

I crumpled up the sheet and started a third one.

I drew the rectangle. I put the numbers in all four corners.

She stopped me right there.

"Nope," she said.

I tossed the pad of paper away across the desk.

"What do you want from me?" I said.

"I want to teach you something."

"What do you think this could possibly teach me?"

"I want to teach you to think about what you assume you already know."

I glowered at her for a second. Chewed my lip.

Angela took a dollar bill from her pocketbook and put it on the table in front of me, faceup. Brand new. It couldn't have been newer or fresher or crisper if it had just been pressed and cut yesterday.

I stared at it.

It was black and white. Only the serial numbers and the treasury seal were green. My eyes were stuck there, lost in the blackness and whiteness of the bill.

"Memory is a funny thing," she said. "We remember American money as green, even though the fronts of the bills aren't. But that's not the lesson here."

I couldn't take my eyes off that bill.

She said, "This lesson is about trust."

Then she picked up the green pen, stood up and walked away. Her coffee cooled on the desk and sat there until morning, when I finally got up the nerve to pour it out. The dollar bill stayed longer. I still have it somewhere. I keep it as a reminder of something. I'm not sure what.

The next day we went to work.

14

ATLANTIC CITY

I followed the short, twisty route through the heart of the city, reconstructing Ribbons's getaway in my head. I could see him driving in front of me, pushing the limits of the shot-up getaway car until the chassis shook and smoke curled out from the hood. He was wrestling with the wheel. His rims sent up showers of sparks. Coolant and oil were leaking. But Ribbons kept driving. He had to. It was that or go back to prison.

Leaving the casino district was like dropping off the edge of the earth. Back there by the Boardwalk, the city was bustling with commerce. Five blocks farther down, the surroundings felt like a third-world country. In just a three-minute drive, I went from hundred-million-dollar penthouses to blighted slums. This non-neighborhood resembled a crack addict's mouth; row houses stood out like crooked, rotten teeth with huge gaps between them.

I passed a broken fence the city had put up around the abandoned airstrip to keep people out. The place didn't look like much—or anything at all, really. I might have driven past, had I not been searching for it. The Civic's engine was the only sound. Nearby I could see a whole baseball stadium with plywood over its windows and doors. I drove past another rusted fence that separated the landing strips from what had been the airport parking lot. In another era, there would have been security checks and floodlights and closed-circuit cameras every fifty feet. Now, the only floodlights would come in at night from across the thin saltwater inlet at the end of the runway, where the casinos cast long shadows over the bits of pipe and the blocks of concrete where the control tower had stood. Brown grass pushed itself up between the cracks.

The engine ticked as it cooled. I got out and bit the air.

It was a smaller place than you might've guessed. Part of it had been repurposed, part of it hadn't. A couple of places almost looked like a public park, and a couple of others were pure urban blight. Piles of trash. Industrial remnants. Burned-out cars and waterlogged furniture. There were acres of empty buildings and spray-painted concrete blocks that had been torn loose by salvage crews but never hauled away. I saw a few gaps in the fence where a person could drive in, but I didn't. I ducked through one of them and went in by foot. Nature had started to reclaim the land. What used to be roads for baggage trucks and flash pits for runway lights were now dirt paths and concrete sinkholes. The landing strip had become a field again, and the paint had cracked long ago. I guessed that there were periodic patrols, but I saw no signs of recent activity. The No Trespassing signs were worn and painted over with indecipherable street tags. It was like an unclaimed junkyard. I walked through it until I got close to the center, where there was a cluster of abandoned buildings. Two empty red dumpsters and a soccer goal post, left inexplicably on their sides in the dirt, sat sentry over the far runway.

The first building, which I supposed had once been a hangar, was locked from the outside with a chain that had withstood many hoodlums. It was held together by a combination lock with four tumblers, connecting two brown-tinted links. The lock and the chain had rusted together.

The second hangar looked much the same. There was a pile of garbage in between, and I could smell rotting waste and animal feces.

I started off toward the third hangar.

But then I heard it.

It was a sharp chirp, somewhere between the sound of metal hitting metal and the chime of a bell. It was faint enough that I barely caught it over the breeze.

For a soft moment I waited, listening, but heard only my heartbeat. Then the wind picked up and the stench of the garbage hit me even harder. I looked around, in case there was someone there. I moved slowly, very slowly, toward where I thought the sound had come from. I turned the corner, back toward hangar two. This one had double barn-style doors designed to slide open from the center. In the airport's heyday, this building would have protected a half dozen private planes from the elements. Now it smelled like any other rusted warehouse. I looked closer at the chain holding the door segments together.

It had been snapped in two places.

The doors were cracked just a few inches. The inside of the hangar was pitch-black. Two sets of tread marks led into it. I stepped carefully around them. Car prints. Fresh. At that moment, my breath stopped.

Blood.

Caked on the hangar's right door handle was a small red splotch in the shape of a thumbprint. The blood was smeared unevenly over the handle, hanging in thick clots where it had dried and was beginning to flake off.

I slid the hangar doors open.

15

Inside was the getaway car.

It was a '92 white Dodge Spirit—or at least it had been white, before it was crashed a few times and shot up with a rifle. There were spider-vein cracks in the windshield, where bullets had passed through the glass and left perfect small circles. The rust stains on the body were so deep that the paint had started to peel, and all four tires were as flat as strips of paper wrapped around the hubs.

The old hangar felt like a cavern. Back when the airport still ran flights, a hangar this size could have housed four prop planes front to back, or a single five-window Cessna half the size of Marcus's Sovereign. Now the steel floor was thick with grime and broken glass, and the thin insulation on the walls was rotting from the inside out. Stagnant water had pooled under the empty skylights. When the field had closed its gates, the city must have salvaged anything of value. Even the Plexiglas. This would've been the perfect place for Ribbons to ditch this old get-away car and stash their next one. It was dirty and easily overlooked, but no more than a five-minute drive from the Regency. And I'd done it in traffic.

Before I did anything I slid on my pair of leather gloves. I may not have fingerprints, but a guy's hands have more identifying characteristics than you might think. My skin still produces oils that my fingerpads leave behind in a unique scarred, splotchy pattern. Only an expert would recognize them, but it's still possible. Also there's DNA that a smart guy could isolate. I didn't exactly expect to get caught due to something like that, but I wasn't about to take any risks I didn't absolutely have to.

I walked carefully around the marks in the dust, where the treads of two cars had dragged mud in from the field. I guessed that one set of tracks was from Ribbons driving the Dodge in, and the other set from taking the second car out. I peered in through the partly shattered windshield. There were bullet holes everywhere. Big ones, from the rifle. There were deep bloodstains in the driver's-side upholstery, straight down to the foot well. The blood had bonded with the fibers and scabbed there like a permanent dye. Most of it was still liquid, but very thick and dark from coagulation. You'd be amazed by how fast the stuff sinks in and clots. It is hard to remove. It must be washed out with cold water and bleach. I had to do it after a job, once. I leaned over the driver's-side window. Bone and brain matter were scattered through the interior as well. It was so thick in places that it hardly looked real.

Drops of blood tell a story—and they aren't hard to read, if you know what to look for. Moreno must have been in the car when he was shot. The drops on the windshield were fine, less than a millimeter wide, and beginning to skeletonize, which suggested his head had been close to the wheel and the direction of impact came from behind. I traced the angles of the spatter to the area of convergence. The bullet had entered his skull from the back of his head and passed through his midbrain and exited through the forehead. There was high-impact spatter, but nothing suggesting a secondary bleed. The shot had killed him instantly. High-caliber. Well-aimed.

I took a look at Ribbons's blood. Even in this mess, I could tell which blood was which. Ribbons's blood had a different character to it. The drops were bigger. Ribbons's blood-spatter droplets were seven millimeters wide and grouped tightly. They made a stain all the way down the left side of the driver's seat, from about shoulder height down. That wasn't spatter from a gunshot. No way. It was secondary bleeding, which must have taken place after the initial bullet impact. Big drops like that indicated passive spatter, which told me that Ribbons had dumped Moreno's body, but only climbed into the driver's seat after taking a bullet himself. I looked around but couldn't find the high-impact spatter from Ribbons's initial wound, so he must've been shot outside the car.

I put myself in his position for a minute. I closed my eyes and felt his panic and pain wash over me like a tremendous wave. He was running on pure instinct. The getaway plan was the only thing he knew. It was the only thing he trusted.

I blinked and took a closer look at the car. There were tool marks between the window and the weather strip, where one of them had jimmied the lock. The car had been stolen because they knew they'd have to ditch it immediately. Beside the bloodstains, in the cup holder was an empty pint of bottom-shelf bourbon.

I had to put my sleeve over my nose. The car smelled terrible.

The smell was like an air conditioner, but foul. There was something both sulfuric and chemical about it, like gasoline mixed with nail-polish remover. Blood and brain matter don't smell like that. I pointed the light from my cell phone through the windows of the car. Between the front seats was a small leather case. Moreno had held such a case under his arm when we met in Dubai. I never asked, because I knew that inside there would be a bent spoon, a lighter, a length of foil and a glass pipe. It was a case for smoking cocaine and crystal meth. Moreno, I'd heard, preferred to let it vaporize so he could suck it up through a rolled-up bill. When he wasn't smoking or drinking, he'd scratch the sore on his face. When I knew him, he scratched and scratched and scratched.

But the smell wasn't that.

Freebasing smells astringent and slightly metallic. I'd been around enough thugs and addicts to know firsthand, though I'd always refused to join them when they offered. This didn't smell anything like that. It was much worse.

I circled around toward the other side of the car. The stench seemed to get worse by the trunk. Blood was spattered over the left hubcap, with tiny loose bloody chunks of skull lodged in the trim of the wheel well. Jesus. For a moment I could visualize Ribbons panicking, tossing Moreno's body out onto the pavement and shifting into Reverse. The car had rolled over his head and crushed it. The trunk was locked. It took a minute to find the release. Inside was a black duffel bag with empty boxes of discount imported rifle ammunition. The boxes were cut down, as if with a letter opener. Only one unfired round was left and I examined it—7.62×39mm steel-core bullet, almost certainly for Ribbons's AK-47. He might have left it behind during the frenzy, or dropped it while he was loading his magazines. I put the bullet in my pocket, then opened the spare-tire compartment, in case the smell was coming from there. No. I opened a side door to the backseat.

Under the seat was a soft leather briefcase with more ammunition inside. I ran a single gloved finger over the passenger window, and felt the stress cracks. My glove came off marked with dirt and blood residue. The two bullets had cut through the upholstery. They were somewhere deep under the seats, unless they'd gone right through.

I ducked out of the back and closed the door, took a few steps forward and pulled on the passenger's-side door. It was unlocked. I checked the glove box, where I found a plastic bag containing better than half a dozen orange pill bottles. Hemostabil, ibuprofen, dextromethorphan, diazepam, phenobarbital. I recognized a few. Ibuprofen was the major ingredient in several popular over-the-counter painkillers. Dextromethorphan was a cough suppressant. Diazepam and phenobarbital were sedatives, probably to calm their nerves and take the edge off the crystal meth. All of them together looked like the combat cocktail I'd heard rebel soldiers used to take in South America. Behind the drugs was an aerosol canister labeled QuikClot. I recognized the brand, having seen a bit about it on the news a few years ago during the Second Gulf War. Soldiers would spray it on and their wounds would clot over and stop bleeding for a while. It saved a few hundred lives, so they brought it stateside for hemophiliacs. Now anybody could get some, if they knew where to look. Band-Aid of the future. Comes sprayed out of a can.

I could imagine Ribbons parking the car and scrambling to field-dress his wound. But gunshot wounds are tough. They bleed deep. If he was smart, he would have jammed in something soft to plug it up, like a scrap of fabric or even a piece of a hamburger bun, and then tied it off with a strip of his shirt or some plastic wrap. With the QuikClot and some basic first aid, Ribbons could have kept himself conscious for hours after his gunshot wound.

I opened up the leather case between the seats and wasn't surprised by what I found. There was a bent spoon that smelled like vinegar and a couple of fresh needle sharps. There was a thirteenth of methamphetamine with a pink color to it. I dabbed my finger in the methamphetamine and tasted it. It was adulterated with some sort of strawberry flavoring. They were both probably high out of their minds when the heist went down.

I caught sight of a Colt 1911 pistol on the floor of the backseat. I climbed partway into the passenger seat and looked at the smashed-out rear window. Ribbons must have fired the Colt at something behind him, turning in his seat and shooting right through it. Who had been behind him? Were the cops chasing him, or the third shooter, or was all of this just from the ten seconds or so before he could get the engine started?

I could barely think over the hideous smell. The beep I'd heard happened again, and this time it was very close by.

I took out my cell phone and entered Ribbons's number digit by digit. When I pressed the call button, a second later a loud chirp somewhere between a bell and a metal scratch came from the driver's-side door. It echoed against the voluminous hangar walls.

I found the phone, an old clamshell, lodged under the bloodstained seat cushion. Twenty missed calls from a blocked number. The last answered incoming call was five a.m. There was a rejected call at two minutes to six, and then another one two minutes after six. There were several dozen text messages too. All of them *Your father needs you,* all from blocked numbers. The contact list was empty.

The last incoming call was from me.

I got out of the car again and went back around to the trunk. The smell was both disgusting and distracting. I dropped to one knee and shined the light from my cell phone below the undercarriage. I covered my mouth and nose with my sleeve. When I looked under the trunk, my eyes went blurry. Then I saw the source of the smell.

My god.

16

Under the car was a silver-brown five-gallon fuel canister. The valve was broken, and the liquid had slowly seeped out into a large puddle. The side of the canister was marked with a yellow hazard symbol. I instantly knew what it was. Naphtha, also known as Coleman fuel. Made of petroleum and charcoal tar. Very flammable. Extremely. It was slowly evaporating under the Dodge.

Worse, it had been there for more than twelve hours.

When I was just starting out, I did my early bank jobs with whomever I could. I met a wheelman who was a fastidious and clean guy. Always kept his hair just so with that grease that they used to sell in the little round cans. He was the kind of guy who liked the word *slick*. Slick car, slick look, slick moves. He drove a silver Shelby GT500 that was so well preserved that it looked like he'd driven it through a time machine. It had an engine as shined up as a wedding ring and a coat of paint as fresh as an army recruit. He loved that car. After a bank job in Baltimore, where I'd helped him by pretending to be a wealthy customer, we were running from the cops with six hundred grand in bearer bonds, and somehow they'd figured out where we were going to swap our throwaway car for the GT. Once we were in the 500, the wheelman didn't hesitate. He parked the first place he thought was safe and walked down the street to the grocer while I stole us a third getaway car from a hotel parking lot. He picked up five gallons of naphtha on a prepaid credit card without the girl behind the counter popping her gum at him. He dumped the whole canister through the driver's-side window, tossed a match in and let the only thing he'd ever loved burn away behind him. That Shelby was his life. The fuel burned that car down to the chassis. Down to the engine block. His classic car was a cinder by the time the cops arrived. His brand-new tape deck. His vintage fender. His custom leather seats—all toast. We both walked away from that heist with enough money to buy a fleet of those GT500s, but his new one wasn't quite the same, he told me. The Coleman fuel had also burned away its soul.

I took three steps back, remembering what my wheelman had called it.

Torch gas.

I backed quickly away from the toxic fumes. When I was out, I took a long, deep breath. I'd seen what this shit could do. Shotgun casings into plastic puddles. Handgun brass into charred pools of metal. Body parts would burn until even the bones were ash.

I considered turning right around and finishing what Ribbons had started. One little spark would torch away every shred of evidence. Blow it up like the Fourth of July. The drugs would vaporize. The bullets would melt like solder on the chassis. The whole hangar would go up.

But that was the thing.

There was evidence here that I wasn't picking up on. To an expert, this car could tell a story. So far it had told me about Ribbons's state of mind, his health and his getaway plans. But there was more. What about the tread marks leading out? What sort of car did they belong to? And besides, the minute I tossed the match at this wreck, the police would be en route, and I still had business here.

Why hadn't Ribbons torched the car in the first place? He got as far along in the process as dumping out the torch gas; why hadn't he finished the deal? Everything was ready to blow, so it wouldn't have taken much. All he had to do was light a match. Matches can be hard to strike when you're wearing gloves, and maybe going through septic shock from a bullet wound, not to mention shaking from a quarter gram of crystal meth, but it couldn't have been that hard. Maybe he had tried to set the thing on fire, I thought. Matches aren't as reliable as people think. Eight times out of ten, a lit one will go out before it hits the ground. And sometimes, even when it stays lit long enough to hit the fuel, nothing happens. I once saw a guy flick a lit cigarette into a bucket of gasoline. It sizzled out, just like he said it would. Fire needs fuel and oxygen. Liquid fuels, especially in containers, often don't have enough oxygen to catch from a single small flame. But that didn't sound right. If Ribbons was cogent enough to get this far, he would have done anything to set this Dodge on fire. The evidence here could convict him. Hell, even if he'd run out of matches, he could have lit the thing up with the muzzle flash from his assault rifle. There must've been something else going on that I was missing.

I took out the phone again and stared at the numbers for a few seconds. Atlantic City. The number came back to me, like muscle memory.

Executive Concierge Services.

The line opened up a second later. "This is Alexander Lakes."

"I need a wheelman."

"I'm sorry?"

"I'm looking for a person who knows cars. Do you guys do services, or only provisions?"

"We've worked with several mechanics in town. Where should I say—"

"I don't need a mechanic. I need a wheelman. Someone who can fix a broken transmission isn't good enough. I'm looking for someone who can take one look at some tracks in the mud and tell me what sort of car they came from. Someone discreet, who doesn't ask questions and who likes getting paid in cash. I need someone who knows cars like I know how to breathe."

Lakes went silent for a second. Thinking.

He said, "We can provide that."

I listened as Lakes walked his phone into a different room. Because of the nature of my work, the collection of names and phone numbers in my head could fit on a single index card. I rely on fences and jugmarkers to know people for me. It's safer, most of the time. I could hear crickets in the distance until Alexander came back on the line.

"There's a man named Spencer Randall who I've worked with before. He's done some emergency driving for our clients in the past. Very professional, very discreet. He's one of the best drivers I've ever met."

"Does he know cars?"

"Better than anyone."

"Is he in the city?"

"He has an automotive shop in Delaware."

"Don't you have anything closer? Delaware's too far."

"Sir, as I mentioned, we do not keep a list of clients. Only assets."

I shook my head. "Randall's really all you've got?"

"I'm sorry, sir. If you give me a few hours—"

"Give me the number."

In the background I could hear the hum of a computer and the sound of a television with the volume down at the other side of the room. I thought I could hear children playing. He recited the number slowly, and I only needed to hear it once. I terminated the call and put in the new number.

The phone rang seven times.

When someone answered, it was clearly in a machinist's shop. The man on the other end cleared his throat. He said, "This is Spencer Randall. Who is this?"

He had a soft voice and he spoke through his nose a little too much.

"My name is Jack," I told him.

"How can I help you, Jack?"

"I need a wheelman."

The line went quiet for a moment. *Wheelman*, an almost exclusively criminal term, dates back to the early days of professional bank robbery, before John Dillinger and the Chicago Outfit. It was coined by a German guy named Herman Lamm, who was the original jugmarker. A former military man, he was the first person to plan his heists as if they were tactical operations. Before him, bank robberies were all messy, bloody, impromptu affairs. He chose the word for the getaway driver after what a naval captain would call the guy who steered his ship, because, at the time, *driver* was still associated with horses and carriages.

"Who gave you this number?" Spencer said.

"A man named Lakes. You know him?"

"Yeah, I know him," he said.

"I hear you're in Delaware," I said.

"Wilmington. I run a shop."

"I'm in Atlantic City. I'll give you a thousand dollars for an hour of your time, but it has to be right now."

"I'll want to hear the circumstances first."

I paused to think about what I should tell him. "I think it would be better if you saw for yourself."

"Then my answer's no. I don't do any job without getting the information up front. I'm not even supposed to be taking this call. Jesus, I don't know you. I don't recognize your voice. For all I know you could be bringing me into some sort of bait-car scheme."

"It's nothing like that."

"Then what is it?"

"I'm just asking you to look at something and tell me what it is. You'll be in no danger."

"I want more than a thousand bucks. How much are you getting on this job?"

"Nothing."

"Bullshit. Nobody works for nothing."

"Then it's a good thing I'm nobody. Now or never, Spencer."

"Make it five thousand. And I don't run from cops. I see flashing lights, I pull over. As far as I want to know, this is all aboveboard."

"Three thousand."

"Done. Where should I meet you?"

I checked my watch.

"The movie theater by the airport," I said. "Pleasantville exit. You can't miss it. One hour."

"I'm three hours away."

"You're a wheelman. I don't want a Sunday driver."

I hung up and dropped the phone. I didn't smell it before, but even in the open air I was beginning to detect the fuel. Naphtha evaporates clean. Some people use it to strip paint. But it takes a while. Especially with a full five-gallon canister. I turned back toward the dumpsters and crushed the phone under my foot. It broke in half in the dust and battery acid sprayed out like ketchup from a packet.

Time to head out again. One hour, three thousand dollars and a phone for a wheelman. Not bad, I thought.

I walked away toward the Civic and glanced at my watch as I ducked through the fence. Nine p.m., thirty-three hours to go.

Then I saw a black Suburban waiting for me.

17

It was parked across the street near the defunct baseball stadium, the front end peeking out behind a dumpster like it was an elephant hiding behind a tree. The windows were tinted and the engine grille looked like snarling teeth with a Chevrolet logo stuck onto them. It hadn't been there before.

It was official.

I was being watched.

I'm not accustomed to that. Pursued, yes. Chased, certainly. But not watched. Nobody's supposed to know who I am. That's the whole point. There isn't supposed to be anything to trace. No phones, no houses, no girlfriends, no mortgages, no connections. Police might chase a ghost-man for a few blocks down the freeway in the thirty seconds or so immediately after a job, or an Interpol agent might pursue one or more of his identities from city to city for a while, but we never pick up tails. That's just not how it works.

So how the hell did these people find me?

When I got in my car, I adjusted the rearview mirror to get a better look. The Suburban was maybe fifty yards back. It didn't have a front license plate and there were traces of mud on the tires. I just sat there and thought for a moment. I didn't know any techniques for losing a tail. I'd seen wheelmen lose the police fifty different ways, and I even remembered a few, but this was another thing entirely. Losing a tail is slow and spontaneous, not fast and choreographed. When you're being chased after a job, you've had time to prepare for it. You know every street in the city and you've driven the route a hundred times. You've gone out and sat at the side of the road in a fold-out chair, timing the intervals between cars with a stopwatch. When you're being tailed, you've got to improvise.

I pulled the Civic away casually, like I hadn't seen them, and turned left back onto the street. I tried to drive normally, but it was harder than I'd thought. I kept looking in the mirror. The Suburban slid out from behind the dumpster and weaved into traffic behind me. It stayed two cars back, which was a pretty smart move. How often do you pay attention to anything that far behind you? I could see only their boat rack in my mirrors.

I crossed the bridge and went through the park back toward the Regency. The farther I got downtown, the heavier the traffic was. It was evening at the beach, which means lots of traffic. People were getting ready to go home or to go out somewhere. There were eight-car backups at every light. The Suburban closed the distance between us and swerved into the turning lane to cut in line. These guys were good, I thought. The driver was worried I might get to the front of the line at one of the intersections, then go through a light that turned red before they got there. If they stayed two cars back in traffic, they couldn't keep up. Up close, if I ran a red, they could step on the gas and run right after me.

I kept driving. I followed the signs toward the Atlantic City Expressway. The route took me all the way across town past the Regency casino. I got to the highway entrance and went up the ramp toward Philadelphia. The SUV held back a bit and blended into traffic, letting the gap widen again. Two cars between us. I got in the left lane. It got in the left lane. I increased speed. It increased speed.

I took out my last phone and punched in Lakes's number.

"Executive Concierge Services," Lakes said.

"It's me. I'm going to need a new car."

"Is there something wrong with the Civic?"

"No," I said. "I just need to switch rides. Something different. The sooner the better."

"Why?"

"I thought you weren't the kind who asked questions."

"Sorry, sir. I can get that for you right away."

"I want a black Chevrolet Suburban. New model. Can you get me one of those?"

"Yes, sir," he said. "Is there a place you'd like to meet?"

"No," I said. "Just deliver it to the parking garage at the Chelsea. And make sure it's black. Has to be black, got it? Put the key with the rest of the stuff you've got me. I'll come and pick it up when I'm ready."

"I'll need to return the Civic, of course."

"You can pick it up behind the movie theater in Pleasantville. I'll park it near where the emergency exits let out. You'll know where to find the key. And when you get rid of it, I never want to see it again. Return it to the rental agency and dump the record. Get the new car from a different place with a different ID. Understand?"

Lakes said, "It would be much easier for me to do this if you'd just tell me what's going on."

"You've got it backward. You're here to make it easy for me, not the other way around."

I shut the phone.

I looked out at my mirrors. The Suburban was taking its time. Following slow. I was working on another plan to lose it. It was something I'd done once before while running from the cops in Las Vegas. It had worked then, but I'd nearly killed myself in the process. It was worth a shot.

I slowed down until I was going an even fifty miles an hour, drifting into the outside lane. The Suburban did the same. We crossed the salt marshes and kept going for a few miles, all the way into Pleasantville and then off into the pine barrens. The exit for the airport was up ahead. I waited until I could see the sign. *Come on, come on, come on.*

The Exit sign peeked out over the horizon.

Then, without signaling, I jacked the wheel hard to the right. My car slashed across all four lanes in one long dangerous swoop. At the same time, I put the hammer to the floor and blew forward until my engine redlined, weaving four lanes back across traffic toward the exit. Cars behind me lay on their horns. Brakes squealed. A green Mazda jackknifed and spun out of control. It hit the safety rail and sent up sparks as it scraped along a few feet. The Suburban wavered out of its lane and then cut loose.

I took the airport exit at full speed.

I spun through the cloverleaf like a pinball. The street at the bottom of the ramp was totally empty, so I gunned it through the overpass and ended up back on the highway going in the opposite direction. I didn't even touch the brake.

I kept glancing in the mirror, and when the Suburban didn't reappear for a solid two minutes, I let out my breath and regulated my speed. I got off two exits later and scrambled through side streets before coming to a stop at a gas station on the outskirts of the city. I parked around the back and waited with my lights off, watching the road as the cars zoomed by. I must have sat there for ten minutes, waiting for the black Suburban to blow past. It didn't.

I turned the ignition and drove to the movie theater.

18

The theater was a big complex, the sort of place that made popcorn by the hundred-pound tub. It had sixteen screens and red trim all around the stucco exterior. It looked less like a theater than a warehouse. It was across a road and a packed parking lot from a shopping mall, less than ten miles across the salt marshes from Atlantic City.

I hadn't seen the tail for half an hour.

By the time I got there, the sun was on its way down. It illuminated the clouds to the west with bright pinks and purples. Even out here in the pine barrens, I could hear the wind coming in from the ocean. In the map of the city in my head, this was the only major commercial movie theater in this part of New Jersey. I drove around the parking lot for a moment, keeping an eye out for any vehicle I might recognize. Once I was satisfied, I parked the Civic around back, by the emergency exits. It was quiet here—just me and a few dumpsters. To my left, the pavement petered off into a no-man's-land of trash and wild pine trees. The ambient light was deep enough to shade my face in blue. I turned off my engine and waited.

Angela had introduced me to my first real wheelman when I was twenty-three. I'd told her about the slick dude with the Shelby, and she told me I would never have to go through something like that again. No real pro would ever use his own car as part of a getaway. A few days later, she took me to meet Salvatore Carbone. He was in his seventies when I met him, but he was built like a pile driver. He was maybe five foot six and well over two hundred pounds, with not an inch of fat on him. His chest was as wide as most doorways, and his arms were the size of canned hams. He looked like he could run right through a wall, if he wanted to, or bench-press a motorcycle. We shook hands in the back of his auto body shop on West Fifty-third. He lit a cigar and brought me out into his shop. Right in the center was a rusted old fastback, and he told me to get in. He sat next to me in the passenger's seat and said I should take us for a spin. When I told him he'd forgotten to give me the keys, he smacked me over the head. He took out a small knife, jammed it into the key socket and twisted until all six tumblers broke and the car rumbled to life. From then on, he taught me everything a real wheelman should know. He taught me how to plan getaway routes. How to pick up getaway cars. How to spot unmarked cars and bluff my way out of a traffic stop. I was never good enough to be a wheelman myself, but that isn't the important part. I learned which skills I needed to look for.

If I was very lucky, Spencer might have them.

I waited there in the darkness, with one eye on my watch and the other on the street. The sun went down and the floodlights flickered on. They cast deep shadows into the pine trees. Ten minutes later a black late-model Camaro pulled into the parking lot. It was a car that hugged the ground like a slug and moved with the silence of a hunting cat. It was so clean that somebody could've eaten dinner off the hubcaps. The windows were as tinted as could be and there wasn't a front license plate. I watched the Camaro cruise around the parking lot once before turning down the strip of pavement in front of me. It flashed its brights.

I switched the engine on, so the driver would see my daytime runners. I looked at my watch. It had taken him sixty-seven minutes to drive seventy-five miles up the Atlantic seaboard. He was late.

Quarter after ten. Thirty-two hours to go.

The Camaro pulled a little closer and stopped no more than fifty feet away from me in the halo of a floodlight. A lanky guy in an expensive black suit got out. He was long and thin, just a little over six-two, with a large nose and black leather driving gloves that didn't cover his knuckles. He was handsome, too, maybe even a little too handsome. When he bared his teeth they were bright white and as shiny as the silver trim of his car. There was an understated power in his shoulders. He looked a little like James Dean.

I got out and walked around the front of my Civic.

He looked me over, like I wasn't exactly what he'd expected. "You're the guy I spoke to on the phone, right?"

"Yeah," I said. "I expected you in an hour."

"I stopped for a burger."

"Did you really?"

"No. I ran into traffic on the bridge. I had to push almost eighty all the way here, you demanding little prick."

He was joking, I think.

"Do you have something for me, or did I just break traffic laws in three states for no reason?"

I took Marcus's wad of cash out of my jacket pocket and counted out three thousand dollars. I took a couple of steps forward and put the money in his hand, like it was a handshake.

He flipped through the bills quickly. When he was satisfied, he put it in his back pocket, looked at my car and made a face.

"Tell me you're kidding," he said.

"It's a rental."

"You don't want me to work on that, do you?"

"You're working on something I found a couple of miles down the road. What you see you can never speak about to anyone, understand? I'm paying for your time and your silence."

"I'm the master of silence. No need to hold my hand through this."

"I'm sure."

Spencer nodded, like he'd heard it all before.

"I want you to say you understand," I said.

"I get it, I get it."

"Okay," I said. "We're taking your car."

"You just going to leave this piece of shit here?"

I went into the Civic and grabbed my overnight bag. I locked the doors, then bent over and slid the key under the front right tire, until the silver bit disappeared into the treads.

"That's the idea," I said.

Spencer nodded. The inside of his car smelled of air freshener and energy drinks. In the foot well was a whole pile of crushed cans. I had to kick them aside to get in. Spencer pulled out of the theater parking lot slowly and methodically, like at any minute he thought he might have to take off. When we got back on the highway, he cut straight to the left lane and lay on it. The acceleration pushed me back into the seat, but I don't get the same thrill as a passenger as I do when I'm driving. My reflection flashed across in the windshield as the city lights whipped by.

"Were you followed?" I said.

"No. Why do you ask?"

I didn't answer.

The drive took the better part of fifteen minutes, and I spoke only to give directions. Pleasantville to Route 30 and down Pacific back to the abandoned airfield. We parked behind the trees on the other side of the fence where we were covered from the street. Spencer got out first. He took a black box of automotive tools from his trunk, scanned the area with a look of disgust, then fell into step with me and said, "Now what?"

"There are two things I want you to do. I want you to tell me what you can about a junk car that was ditched here. Then I want you to take a look at some tracks and tell me what sort of car they came from."

"What sort of junker am I looking at?"

"A ninety-two Dodge Spirit. Lots of torch gas."

"Fun. Anything else I should know?"

"Yeah. The car's full of blood."

We went through the fence and across the runway toward the dilapidated hangars. It was dark now, dark enough that I could barely find my way. Spencer remedied the problem by taking out his BlackBerry and shaking it until the screen came on. He illuminated the ground in front of us with a pale green glow. I got to the hangar doors and slid them open for him. Instantly the smell of the blood and naphtha hit him head-on. There was a strange blend of horror and recognition on his face. Blood and octane.

"Good god," he said.

"Do you see what I mean?"

"This is the car from the Regency shoot-out."

"Just take a look around, tell me what you see."

"Just looking at this thing makes me an accessory after the fact."

"What did you expect?"

"This is some serious shit."

"Don't complain. Besides, you were an accessory the moment you took my money. The only thing you could pick up now is a misdemeanor count for failing to report, which is nothing."

Spencer gave me a look, shook his head, then got ready to go inside. He handed me his BlackBerry, removed his belt, put down his tools, then wrapped a handkerchief firmly around his nose and mouth like he was a spray-paint artist.

"Why all the preparations?"

"Have you ever left the valve of a gas tank open," Spencer said, "just for a little while on a hot day?"

"No."

"Hot weather makes gasoline and a lot of other flammable chemicals evaporate. The fumes mix into the air, and if it's hot enough they can catch on fire. It's called a flash point. If left in a garage on a hot day, even in an open garage, a bucket of gasoline is a real hazard. Anything could set it off. You ever hear of that woman who blew up a gas station because she was talking on her cell phone? That shit isn't true, but I'm not going to be the guy who finds out why."

He finished tying on his mask and started breathing through it. He stopped for a second when he got a closer look at all the bloody carnage in the car. Everybody does that, at least a little bit. A person has a lot of blood inside him, and it doesn't look pretty when it comes out. He moved slowly, like an artist. He was a good wheelman, I could tell already.

He walked slowly around the thin mud tracks and examined the grooves in the treads. He ran his finger over the surface of the passenger's-side window just to get a feel for it. It was like saying hello, even with the fumes gathering all around him. He was building a relationship with the car the way another man would with a horse, or a gun, or a computer. When he was ready, he dropped to his knees and looked under the carriage. He worked quickly but thoroughly. He held his breath when he got close.

Wheelmen think differently from normal people. They think in terms of cars. For them, a car is a unit of currency. Buying a house costs two cars, or six, or ten. Food for a year is the cost of a fix-me-up. A meal's worth a quarter tank of gas. So when Spencer got close to the dirt around the side of the hangar, he took one look under the car and said, "You shoulda just let this thing burn."

I knew exactly what he meant. The Spirit was as busted as a car could get—blood evidence, material evidence and, of course, an easily recorded make, model and license-plate number. I watched as Spencer drew lines in his head and traced the trajectory of the bullets that had smashed through the front windshield and those that had blown out the back. While I had looked at the blood spatter, he looked at the material damage. He tapped the engine block with his knuckles twice. He didn't like the sound.

He turned to me.

"What do you want me to tell you?" he said.

"I want to know where the driver went."

"Not far, not with all this blood."

"I know that."

Spencer pointed to the tracks.

"There are mud tracks off the Dodge coming in, but there are no such tracks for the car going out. That means this was a one-step deal. There's a little trickle of blood, too, from the driver's-side door over to a patch of ground on this side of the building. From here, it looks like the driver left driving a midsize coupe, maybe sedan, moderate load, with slightly balding tires."

I said, "You can tell all that from there?"

"Yeah. I can."

Spencer took two steps toward me and snapped his fingers like he was ordering a beer. He wanted his BlackBerry. On the screen he had a picture of a naked woman lying on the hood of a yellow Ferrari Enzo. He flipped the phone over and snapped a picture of the grooves in the dirt by the hangar entrance. He examined the photo for a long second. He zoomed into it, as much as he could, until I couldn't distinguish the tread marks from the mud around it. In two minutes, using only a photo, his memory and his connection to the Internet, he'd narrowed down the range of tires it could be to three. After five minutes, he had a match within 70 percent certainty. After ten, 90. He was a machine.

Wheelmen think differently from normal people. They see the little things.

"Your guy drove out of here in a Mazda MX-5," Spencer said. "These are dealership tires for sure."

I nodded. An MX-5, the Miata, is a standard choice for a getaway car. They've got decent acceleration and room enough for two, but the Miata has one thing going for it that lesser cars don't. It can turn on a dime. It can spin through a corner at a speed that could send everybody inside up against the window glass before the tires gave a single inch. It could make it through cutoffs and weave through traffic better than cars that cost eighty grand more. Good moves for a getaway. In a getaway speed isn't nearly as valuable as maneuverability.

Spencer stepped away from the tire marks and took off his gloves. "The thing about the Miata, though, is that there are hundreds of thousands of them. New models are coming out all the time, and have been for the last god-knows-how-many years. Thousands of them could be registered in this half of Jersey alone. It's one of the most popular sports cars of all time."

"Is there anything more specific you can give me?"

"There's only so much I can do, man."

"What do you think about the guy driving the Dodge, then? Do you think he was being chased?"

"He certainly fired enough rounds through the rear window, yeah. But there isn't anything that I can say for certain, other than that there's extensive damage from multiple crashes and half a dozen gunshots. When you came here, did you find those hangar doors open or closed?"

"Closed."

"Then he wasn't being chased. He was just getting sloppy."

"Why didn't he torch the thing, then?" I said. "If he could toss the Coleman fuel under the car, how come he didn't light it up?"

"He did," Spencer said. "Take a look."

He beckoned me a few feet into the hangar, got down on his haunches, and I followed suit. Spencer turned up the brightness on his phone and shined it under the Dodge. I took a good look at the naphtha canister. Next to it was a very small string, almost like a thread, submerged in the gas. Spencer held the light on it. Though it was a few feet long it didn't reach either end of the car.

"You see that?" He said. "It's a fuse. Not a dynamite fuse, exactly, but similar. Homemade. Looks like it was made out of toilet paper and the stuff they put in fireworks. See how the end's burned? Your boy lit the thing for sure, but it went out before it could ignite the gas. My guess is that he was trying to buy himself a few extra minutes before the flames went up, just in case someone noticed the smoke."

"Is there anything else you can tell me?"

Spencer shook his head, ground his teeth together and pointed at the car. There wasn't much to say.

"All right," I said. "If you can't tell me any more, give me a ride to the Boardwalk and then you're done."

"That's it?"

"No, one more thing."

"Yeah?"

"Do you have a cigarette?"

He gave me a strange look as he pulled a pack of Parliaments from his shirt pocket and patted one out for me. I put it between my lips and he took out a book of matches and struck one for me.

I took one long drag.

"Thanks," I said. "Can I have the matches too?"

"Sure." He handed me the matchbook and stood there for a second, looking at me with an odd expression. I couldn't quite place it. After a beat he said, "Jack isn't your real name, is it?"

"What's a real name?"

Spencer nodded like he understood. He lingered for a moment longer, trying to find something else to say, then started across the tarmac back toward his car. I watched him walk off until his body faded into the darkness.

Sooner or later, someone would come by and find this Dodge, then this whole scene would be a mess of cops. They'd find the same things I did—the print, the blood, the drugs, the bullet casings. I looked it all over one last time. When the cigarette was about half gone, I opened up the matchbook and slid the lit cigarette into the fold between the paper and the match heads. The cigarette would burn for a few more minutes on its own, then the ember would hit the match heads and the whole thing would catch on fire. I moved very carefully into the hangar and placed the book of matches at the very edge of the seeping pool of naphtha. I was almost a hundred yards away by the time the ember hit the match heads. It echoed out over the waterway as the fireworks started.

I looked at my watch. Eleven p.m.

Thirty-one hours to go.

19

The Chelsea Hotel was downtown on the waterfront. Spencer dropped me off four blocks away and I walked over, keeping an eye out for the black Suburban that had been following me earlier. The taillights of passing cars seemed to blur together. I took shortcuts through other hotels and casinos, just in case. There was no one behind me.

The Chelsea had a vibe straight out of the sixties. The sign on the tower was illuminated from below by purple floodlights, and inside there were bars and pool tables with the same color scheme. The lobby's furniture was shabby-genteel. I liked the feel of it. It was a place my father would have liked, if he were still around.

I scanned the lobby for security cameras, simply on instinct. They were there, but unsophisticated. I could see the bank of monitors tucked away under the marble façade, barely out of view. Their quality was minimal: no database of footage, no twenty-four-hour watch. The cameras were probably there for insurance purposes. I went up to the counter. The man there was an Asian old enough to walk with a cane. I said my name was Alexander Lakes. The old man looked down at the computer screen for a second then back up at me. He handed me a magnetized room card with a number on it for a place on the third floor. He reached down under the desk and pulled out a minibar key. Smiled like it was nothing. I smiled back at him and didn't say a word.

When I got to the room, at the foot of the bed was a large brown paper bag waiting for me with a card on it that read *Executive Concierge Services*. Before I did anything, I closed the blinds on the window. In some cases, it's better to leave them open. That way you can see things coming. Other times, a blackout is better. A person with binoculars can look through a window from anywhere with a comparable height, and people on the outside always have the advantage. They look in, you see out. It's not the same, looking and seeing. The best way to do it is with blackout curtains with thin peek slits down the sides. The peek slits are too thin to see through from the outside, but wide enough to peek out from the inside, like a duck blind. The person on the inside can peer out, and people on the outside can't peer in. Counter-advantage. Not that a hotel room is particularly safe. The inside is a three-hundred-square-foot concrete sarcophagus with only one exit. I was on the lowest customer floor, three stories up. Good place. Angela taught me to never take a room above the tenth floor or below the second. Ten stories is too high for a fire truck and two stories is low enough for a climber.

I turned on the television and tuned it to the news. It was doing international stories. I called room service for a blackened steak with nothing on it and a carafe of coffee. I turned the TV sound off and opened the bag at the foot of the bed. I looked at the card again and flicked it in the trash.

There was a new black Hugo Boss suit, two white shirts and a blue tie. Under the clothes was a lock-picking tool set in a leather case. Below it was the slimjim, a Microtech Halo knife and a large black electronic key with the Chevrolet logo on it. At the bottom was a pile of prepaid cell phones and their chargers. Everything I'd asked for, nothing I hadn't.

I put everything in my overnight bag and sat on the bed while waiting for my food to arrive. I watched the news cycle around to the heist. Ribbons's photograph didn't feature this time, but they flashed the image of Moreno and put up the number for the tip line. This time there was helicopter footage of the casino area and even a snippet of security-camera footage. Black-and-white, grainy as could be. It wasn't much, but I got what I was looking for: an image of Ribbons in a mask firing his gun, and another of the parking-garage sniper. That confirmed my theory. The sniper had been waiting for Ribbons and Moreno. The video showed someone in what looked like a Nissan with tinted glass. I could see the muzzle flashes out the driver's window. I turned up the volume and listened. The third shooter's vehicle had been recovered, the reporter said, four blocks from the scene in a long-term parking lot. It was stolen a few days before and had been wiped clean.

No word on either suspect.

My steak and coffee arrived. I turned the bill upside down and, using my left hand, signed *Alexander Lakes* in that perfect handwriting I remembered from the airport. It's easier to copy a signature upside down. I don't know why.

I ate my steak and drank my coffee while watching the news on a different channel, but there was nothing I hadn't seen before. I put the tray in the hallway, then went back inside and knocked on the door dividing my room from the next one over, 317. I knocked harder. No sound. I dialed the front desk.

When a man answered, I said, "My wife's hearing a strange sound."

"What room are you in?"

"Three sixteen."

"Where is the sound coming from?"

"The one next to us, she says."

"To your left?"

"No, the one on the right, number three-one-seven. She said it was some sort of scratching."

"Is she certain? I can send someone up, if you like."

"Could you just tell me if there's somebody in there? I can go talk to them."

There was a momentary pause. I could hear him working a keyboard.

"I'm sorry, sir, but that room isn't occupied. Are you sure you don't mean three-one-five?"

"That's what she said, but it's no big deal. Thanks anyway."

I hung up. I took my lock-picking set and cracked the lock on the door between the two rooms. Inside 317 it was dark and the king-size bed was made. I brought all my things over from the other room and closed the door. I took one of my cell phones and set an alarm to wake me up in four hours, then opened my overnight bag and took out my gun. I brushed the cylinder to make sure it was loaded and ready. The cylinder spun around and clicked softly as the bolt stop pin locked into each chamber. I laid out the new set of clothes and put the old ones and everything else in my bag.

Some heisters take a lot of precautions before they go to sleep anywhere. I've met guys who take a newspaper and cover the floor around the bed with it, so they'll hear the footsteps of someone sneaking up on them. I've even known guys who only sleep upright in a chair. I have my own rules, but nothing so drastic. My gun goes under the pillow, loaded and locked. My shoes go to the side of the bed with the laces loose, so I can slip into them in an instant. My clothes for the next day go beside me on the floor. My bag remains packed by the door, and the light in the bathroom remains on so it's not totally dark. I don't take off my makeup, and, when I'm on a job at least, I don't take off my watch. I want to be good to go, and a few smudges don't matter much.

If someone came to kill me in my sleep, I wouldn't be able to put up much resistance. If I had to run, however, I could be out the door in ten seconds. Those are my priorities. Of course, someone *did* try to kill me in my sleep once. In Bogotá, I woke up with a man standing over me with a knife. I shot him twice before he could cut my throat. I got very lucky that time, but you can't count on luck. I doubt I'll ever be so lucky again.

I was still a little bit buzzed from the coffee, so I got my copy of *Metamorphoses* from the bag and spent a few minutes reading to clear my head. I don't need a translation for Latin, but I like to read new translations anyway to see how the translator handled it. There is a finesse to translation that reminds me a little of my job. Translators take another man's story and put it into their own words. In a way, I do the same thing. Angela never quite understood this. I'd try to explain it to her, but she was too quick-witted to really get it. For her, taking on a new identity was like taking a breath. For me, it was a work in translation.

I put the book back in the bag and the gun under the pillow.

I climbed under the covers and closed my eyes. I hardly remember falling asleep. Angela used to make fun of me for sleeping so well. My last thoughts were about us together in that Oregon hotel, listening to the sound of the forest and the crackle of the fire pit down below. If I dreamed, I don't remember anything about it.

But I'll never forget the sound that woke me up.

20

KUALA LUMPUR

On the first morning of the Asian Exchange job, Angela walked across the hall from her bedroom in our shared suite, came into my room and woke me up. She picked up the alarm clock on the bedside table and held it next to my ear. It went off and I jumped. She used to criticize me for being such a sound sleeper. When she slept, it was in hour-long bursts punctuated by insomniac pacing and the occasional cigarette. When I slept, it was like passing into a coma.

"Meeting in an hour," she said.

It took me a moment to blink and get my bearings. Angela was wearing a blue pantsuit with a gold name tag that had the insignia of the hotel on it. *Mandarin Oriental, Kuala Lumpur.* It said her name was Mary. I don't know how she got the uniform but she looked convincing in it, even as a white woman in an Asian city. Her makeup was perfect. She had the thick eye shadow of an exhausted hotel worker. Her shoes were worn-out flats. I looked out the window. The sun was already reflecting off the skyscrapers next to us.

I turned off the alarm.

Angela had an energetic beauty about her—she was an actress, and she had trained for it in college. All I had done in college was read and translate Latin and ancient Greek. I'd never even gone to see any plays, because the whole concept of acting was off my radar back then. I didn't crave attention, I craved anonymity. All I wanted was to do my translations and be left alone. Angela changed all that. She showed me how, by being nobody, I could be anyone I wanted. She provided my real education. I copied people's signatures until I could write in anyone's hand. I learned how to transform the muscles in my larynx until I could speak in anyone's voice. I studied the differences in posture and syntax. But most of all, Angela taught me that I didn't need to be perfect, I needed to be convincing. She once handed me a toy police shield and told me to get a piece of evidence from a real crime scene. I got past the yellow tape, picked up a bullet casing with a pair of tweezers and walked away with it in a plastic bag. That was one of her final tests for me. That's how she knew I was ready.

I moved over to the edge of the bed that morning and sat up. She looked at me, arms crossed, said she was putting on a pot of coffee, then left. When I got out of the shower, she handed me a fresh cup, no cream, no sugar, and told me to get my ass in gear.

She never liked waiting for anything.

The video conference with Marcus happened right there in the sitting room of our suite. In the center of the table were twelve small golden keys, two for each of us, except for the wheelman Alton Hill, who wouldn't do anything but drive. We didn't know what the keys were for at that point, but we'd find out soon enough. All we knew then was that we were supposed to take care of them and take them with us everywhere for the duration of the heist. The room also had a large flat-screen TV with a glowing green camera attached by a wire. Back then, Internet video conferencing was less common than it is now. I remember being fascinated at how Marcus's face jerked and paused on the screen. It was the middle of the afternoon where he was, nearly eight thousand miles away, yet it felt like he was there in the room with us.

We gathered around the table as he described the job. In order to get it all done, we were going to have to start right away. No questions, no second-guessing. His voice was matter-of-fact. He spoke slowly, so we wouldn't miss anything.

"In two weeks," he said, "each one of you will be two and a half million dollars richer."

The take was a block of foreign currencies for the exchange market, the value of which changed depending on who you asked and at what time of day. Liquidated, it was something like seventeen or eighteen million dollars. Yen, baht, yuan, ringgit, you name it. Even with traveler's checks and credit cards, huge sums of these foreign paper currencies found their way overseas every month.

A German-based exchange company was the target. It shipped all their displaced Asian currency back here, to the financial equivalent of a weigh station, before distributing it back into the local economies.

The setting was the high-finance Bank of Wales in an office tower on Jalan Ampang. The money was counted and put in the vault there temporarily, then packaged and sent by armored trucks to the airport to be shipped back to the countries of origin. The armored trucks never moved more than about one and a half million U.S. dollars' worth of currency at any one time, and never did deliveries more frequently than once every hour, on the hour. The vault was top of the line. Time sensitive, time delay, triple custody. In order to take the entire load, we would have to be creative. We would have to do what professional armed robbers usually consider suicide. We would have to drill the vault, which meant we would have to take over the bank.

For at least an hour.

Takeover heists are very risky. They're very rare too. Most bank robberies are as simple as you can imagine. A person walks into a bank wearing a hoodie and sunglasses and hands the teller a slip of paper asking for all the money. The teller empties all the cash from the drawers and the robber leaves. There are no guards anymore, so it's as easy as that. The problem is, there isn't a whole lot of money to be gained that way.

There might be ten or fifteen thousand in those drawers, but that's it. In order to get *real* money, you have to do the whole bank takeover-style, with masks and guns and precision timing. The take's bigger by ten or twenty times because you'll get all the money in the vault too. But the risk's much higher. Go in armed, and you have only two minutes to get out. Even if you don't have any money yet, you leave after two minutes because that is the minimum amount of time it takes for someone to trigger a silent alarm and for the police to mount a response. Each second longer, and your chances of going to prison increase tenfold. If you're there for five minutes, the robbery's gone wrong. If you're there for ten minutes, the robbery's botched beyond repair. If you're there for thirty minutes or more, the robbery's the last thing you'll ever do.

And that's what we were planning: in order to drill the vault, we'd have to be inside for at least an hour, maybe more.

There would be multiple issues. The first was damage control. A takeover heist means hostages. Hostages mean guard duty. We needed someone watching them at all times. If someone wasn't, one of them might get brave. If one got brave, somebody could get hurt. If someone got hurt, more people would get brave. Rinse, repeat—people start dying. None of us liked the prospect of killing anybody whose only mistake was being in the wrong place at the wrong time. We'd need a guy, maybe two guys, to act as babysitters.

Location was another problem. The bank was in a skyscraper thirty-five stories up. Once the word of the situation got out, security on ground level would shut down all the elevators, effectively barring our exit. Even if we managed to get all the way up there wearing masks and carrying guns, we had a very good chance of getting stuck.

The third problem was the getaway. Jalan Ampang, one of the city's most important arteries, is nine lanes wide and runs past a quarter mile of skyscrapers, restaurants and hotels. In the middle of the morning it would be packed with traffic and pedestrians, which meant there would also be a lot of cops. There was a freeway just a block to the north of our target, but the nearest on-ramp was four blocks west. Not to mention that if the alarms went, an hour would be enough time for the Royal Malaysian Police to set up a barrier and wait for the military to send in helicopters.

And finally, even if we somehow managed to get out of the bank and away from the cops, then we'd have to get the money out of the country. Seventeen to eighteen million dollars in relatively low-value foreign currency could weigh anywhere between ten and twenty metric tons. I'm talking about bricks of money the size of hay bales that could fill up a fairly large semi. If we loaded it all onto a waiting jet, it would be too heavy for the plane to make it off the runway.

Marcus's voice was dry as stone as he laid out the whole thing, step by step. He presented all the problems, then the solutions, one by one. Angela was wrong about him. Marcus wasn't intelligent. A dog could be intelligent. A kid playing chess could be intelligent. A guy doing his own taxes could be intelligent.

Marcus was *genius*.

Vincent, the loudmouth of the group, said very clearly, so everyone could hear, "How the hell are we going to move that much money?"

"You're not," Marcus said. "It's never going to leave the building."

21

ATLANTIC CITY

I was woken by a sound coming from the room Lakes had bought me.

As soon as I heard it, my eyes shot open and my pulse quickened. I sat up and suddenly froze, focusing all the energy in my body on listening. I held my breath and pulled the gun out from under the pillow. I looked at my watch. It was just a few minutes to 2 a.m.

It was a hard sound that suggested some sort of heavy movement, similar to the scraping sound a big cardboard box makes when you push it around. Modern hotels have thick, insulated walls. Gone are the days of banging against the headboard, trying to get the amorous couple in the next room to quit it. They use solid doors now and make the walls extra thick, with two layers of foam filler between them. All the sounds made in one room get absorbed into the foam, just like in a recording studio. That meant that if I could hear a sound in here, the sound would be five or six times as loud in there.

I moved very quietly off the edge of the bed and slid on a pair of pants. I put the gun in my pocket, just in case, and picked up one of the complimentary water glasses off the dresser. I crept slowly over to the door between me and room 316 and carefully pressed the glass against it as a listening device. The walls might be soundproof, but the interior doors are just wood. There was a tense moment of silence when I heard only the low thud of my heartbeat and the almost-imperceptible tick of my wristwatch. I waited for the sound to happen again, just to prove to myself that I hadn't been dreaming.

It happened again.

Somebody was pushing the furniture around. I could hear a strained groan of exertion and the low, hard grind of the bed frame shifting over the wall-to-wall carpeting. The groan sounded distinctly female. I could hear her swear once as she pushed. She had a deep voice, a beautiful voice, like she'd once been a singer. I heard the rustle of the bedsheets as she pulled them off, and the flop of the mattress as she turned it over. She mumbled to herself as she worked, but her words were garbled and formless.

I'd bet anything it was the FBI agent.

I knew exactly what she was doing.

She was tossing the joint.

Rebecca Blacker was searching every part of the room, from floor to ceiling, so she wouldn't miss any hiding spots. I heard her take the large generic painting off the wall and fling it on the bed. A moment later, she opened the closet and brushed aside all the metal hangers. I waited to hear what she would do next, but nothing happened for another quiet minute. I could hear her talking, but I couldn't make out the words. I wondered if someone else was in room, but then ruled against it. If she were talking to someone, that person would've talked back.

She must have gotten a key card from the hotel manager. The police need a warrant to search a hotel room only if the hotel manager says no. Managers rarely say no. Police raids are bad for business, sure, but not as bad as having a reputation for harboring criminals. Not in a place this nice, anyway.

Careful not to make a sound, I put the glass down and walked over to the hallway door with almost glacial slowness, then put my good left eye up against the peephole. I looked left and right as far as the limits of the fisheye lens would let me.

Feds have a tendency to work in groups—even when only one agent's assigned to a case, sometimes people from local law enforcement work alongside. I half-expected to look out my peephole and see a uniformed cop out there, or a guy in a rumpled sweatsuit with a detective's shield, or another cheap suit with an FBI badge standing guard. But I was in luck.

She was alone.

Across the hall was a room-service cart with upturned metal covers and a couple of dirty plates stacked on top of it. Other than that, though, it looked like we were completely alone. The hall was empty as far as I could see.

I knew what I should have done. If Angela were there, she would've thrown the overnight bag in my hands and told me to get the hell out right away. She would have told me to walk calmly and directly toward the emergency-exit staircase and go immediately to the basement. From there I'd cut through the kitchen, go out into the garage and get in my car. If she were in charge, she would've yelled at me for being so stupid as to trust a concierge service to book my hotel room. She would've rushed into action the very moment she heard the sound.

But Angela wasn't around.

And I was curious.

I slowly put on my new shirt, jacket and tie, which was difficult because I didn't want to turn on any of the lights. I ran my fingers through my hair a couple of times to make sure I didn't look like I'd just climbed out of bed, then grabbed my bag and went out the door.

The hallway was completely empty, and the door to the room Lakes had bought me was closed. I moved up to it and tried to look through the peephole, but those aren't designed to work like that. All I could see was a blurry splotch the color of the hotel curtains.

I ducked back into 317 and pulled a page from the pad of hotel stationery. I wrote *Courtesy of J. Morton* on the paper, along with one of my
new prepaid–cell phone numbers. I went back out into the hallway and
placed the note over the bill on the empty service cart. I put the metal
covers back on the plates, until the cart looked mostly full, then slowly
rolled the cart over to 316. If she opened the door now, she couldn't
miss it.

I walked down the hallway toward the elevators, took the magnetic
key card out of my pocket and snapped it in two. I pushed through the
doors to the stairs and took them two at a time. The woman was in my
head the whole way. She knew my face now, sure, but I also knew hers.
Better yet, I knew her name and her badge number. If I could get to a
computer, I could access everything there was to know about her. Something in me wanted to find out.

I wondered how long it would take her to figure me out in return.
I knew it was only a matter of time before she'd check the surveillance
cameras and see what I'd done. It was how she'd gotten this far that
bothered me. Alexander Lakes told me everything he would do for me
would stay private. Clearly, that wasn't true. Somehow she'd figured
out where I was staying, which meant Lakes had a very serious security
problem.

I took out a phone and pounded in Lakes's number. It rang. Three
times. He finally picked up on the fourth ring.

"Hello?" I could hear the sound of his bedsheets rustling. His voice
was sleepy.

"You gave me a burned room," I said.

"Who is this?"

"Who do you think it is? You gave me a burned room at the Chelsea.
The FBI's there right now tearing the walls down."

"*Ulysses.*"

I got to the bottom of the stairs and found the exit into the basement, which was wired to trigger the fire alarm if opened from the
inside. I sandwiched the phone between my cheek and shoulder, then

took my knife and slipped it between the contacts for the alarm. I gently eased the door open with my hip and kept the knife there until the door was closed again.

"It's the middle of the night, sir," he said. "How are you sure it's a Fed?"

"I met her earlier. She said I interrupted her vacation."

"A woman? What's her name?"

"She's a Fed. It doesn't matter what her name is."

At this time of night, the parking-garage lights were off and would only turn on if triggered by motion sensors. The only permanent light came from the dim floodlight at the base of the stairs. I crossed to the parking garage, took out the key Lakes had left me and started pressing the button that unlocks the doors. As I walked the lights started flicking on all around me. I got about halfway through the garage before I heard the unlocking sound and saw the car's lights flashing. The black Suburban Lakes had promised me was parked near the exit. It was exactly the type of car I'd been looking for. Brand-new, midnight-black, three-quarters of a ton with three hundred horses and chrome hubcaps.

"Sir, I cannot apologize enough. I can get you another room at Caesars, this time as clean as you can imagine."

"No."

"I have contacts at a motel on the edge of town. I know a wonderful Indian guy there. I'm sure he'll do anything you ask in complete confidence."

"I'll get my own rooms from now on."

"Are you sure?"

"Do I sound confused to you?"

"No, sir. Is there anything I can do?"

"Meet me at the diner at Maryland and Arctic in twenty minutes. We need to talk."

I got in the car. Looked left and right. Checked the mirrors. Took a glance at the row of cars behind me to make sure I wouldn't hit any-thing. Put my hand on the gearshift.

But suddenly I froze and hung up on Lakes without saying another word. I adjusted the rearview mirror again.

There was the other black Suburban, parked two cars down and a row back.

22

It was the same vehicle I'd seen before. Tinted windows, low suspension. The front bumper and the hubcaps were solid chrome. I blinked and tried to get a good look. Yes, certainly the same rig that had jumped me near the old airfield. No front plates.

Son of a bitch.

In the dim half light of the parking garage I could make out two people in the cabin. In the shadows they were nothing more than black silhouettes against an even blacker background. Only the pale white glow of the motion sensor lights above them suggested they were even there. They came into focus in parts—light reflecting off somebody's hair, the dark mass of a torso, the shape of an arm. They blended in like they were made of smoke. Whoever they were, they must have been waiting there for hours. They must have found out where I was staying and parked here in the basement, listening to the sound of their engine tick and cool. Watching the exit. They weren't listening to the radio or drinking coffee or bantering back and forth to each other. They were just sitting there in the stillness and waiting for me to show up.

My hand tightened around the wheel. How the hell did they find me? I took precautions with these guys. I'd lost them on the highway. Switched cars. Spent a good portion of the night sniffing pine freshener in the passenger seat of Spencer's Camaro. Even if they'd picked me up again when I went back to the hangar, I'd wandered around for blocks on foot before checking into the Chelsea. I'd dodged through crowded casinos and other hotels. There's no chance they could have shadowed me. My jaw tightened up like I'd been punched.

Who the hell *were* these guys?

They were almost perfectly still for the better part of a minute, like hunters who'd spotted their prey. I stayed frozen in place with my eyes on the mirror. This time it would be a lot harder to lose them, that's for sure. It would be much harder in a parking garage, in the middle of the night, with almost no other cars driving around. If there's nobody else on the road, it takes an act of God to get away clean. Every move you make they can follow. They had me cornered, and they knew it. In such tight quarters they really didn't have to do very much. They could just pull up in front of the exit and that would be that.

I kept still and watched. A drop of water fell from the pipes overhead and made a slow trail down the windshield.

A dozen different scenarios went through my head. I could turn the engine on, put the pedal to the floor and make a run for it. I could go back into the hotel and try to lose them on foot. I could drive out slowly like I hadn't noticed them and then do my best on the road. Every scenario seemed wrong. I glanced down at my watch. I watched the second hand make a slow, jerking trip around the face.

Two a.m. Twenty-eight hours to go.

When I'd walked into the parking garage, the lights had come on. Wherever I walked, a few small floodlights lit up. Motion detectors. If these worked the way I thought they did, they'd turn off after a short period of inactivity. Without them, the parking garage would be nearly pitch-black. Only the glow of the Exit sign would give any illumination. That would give me a couple more seconds of lead time. I could start the engine and put the car into gear before they could respond. Of course, once I moved more than about ten feet, the lights would snap back on and we'd be in half shadows again. But it might be enough.

I slowly reached forward, put my key in the ignition and turned it to the second position. The dashboard lit up for a moment and the computer screen on the console went from black to a pale blue glow. I flipped the switch that controlled the headlights. I turned everything off that could be turned off. The flashers, the daytime runners, the computer screen, everything. I looked back at my watch.

Any second now.

The first light I'd walked past in the far corner of the garage by the staircase started flickering and went out. Another one went out a second later, then two more. Then another two, then three. The whole process would take about twenty seconds, I guessed, because that's how long it had taken me to walk over to the car. I counted it down on my watch.

Ten seconds. The whole garage was returning to nearly pitch black.

Five seconds.

Three.

Two.

The light over the SUV behind me emitted a loud click and flickered out.

One.

Darkness. My breath was slow and deep. I started the engine. The red warning lights on the back of my SUV must have looked like a signal flare going up.

I threw the car in Reverse and lay on the gas. The tires squealed as I did a kamikaze turn in Reverse, shifted back into Drive and slammed it. The motion-activated lights had a slow catch-up. I got nearly twenty feet out before they snapped back on. I sped up the ramp to the ground floor and cut two corners very close. Nobody was in the attendant's booth, which was good because I had no intention of stopping. I went through the exit at thirty miles an hour.

Still, my plan didn't get me the lead I was hoping for. The other guys must have been ready. The warning lights were their starting pistol. Just as I fishtailed onto the street, I heard the other Suburban roar past the booth after me. There was no pretense anymore. They didn't care about staying invisible. They wanted to run me down. Their brakes screeched as they sailed over the curb.

I was maybe fifty feet ahead. *Come on.*

I milked the accelerator for all it would give me. The gearbox shifted up, then up again as I spun through a red light on the corner of Pacific and Chelsea. It was a big dirty turn that threw me through three lanes of light traffic. The other Suburban corrected course and kept after me.

These guys were no cops, that's for sure. They were gunning for me.

I followed the map in my head. Southbound on Pacific would get me westbound onto Providence. There was a parking lot that I could cut through there as a shortcut onto Atlantic. From Atlantic onto Albany. Albany to O'Donnell Park. A few more blocks, then the ramp to the freeway. There were over three hundred streets in the city and I'd memorized all of them.

Each of my senses was in overdrive now. I could hear the sound of the tires on the pavement. I could feel the treads gripping the small bumps in the road. I could smell the exhaust.

I skidded onto Atlantic and switched directions. Initially the light traffic had seemed like a problem, but now that this had become a flat-out chase it was beneficial. We got nearly ten blocks, blowing through every red light along the way.

I spun through a cloverleaf past a billboard for the Atlantic Regency and took the overpass onto the highway. The engine drowned out the horns of the cars I blew past at nearly twice the speed limit, which is insane in southern New Jersey. I swerved through traffic like it was standing still.

Still, the Suburban was gaining on me. They tapped my rear bumper and I felt the sickening tug of my wheels sliding uselessly on the pavement. I wobbled between two lanes for a moment, nearly hitting a car as we blitzed past.

I briefly thought of putting the car into the highest gear and trying to outrun them, but that idea faded just as quickly. The engines were evenly matched, and they were more familiar with the SUV's handling than I was. They could run me down in a matter of minutes.

The Suburban came around until we were neck and neck, then the driver lay on the horn and swerved into my lane, trying to bash me. I ran over the rumble strip and nearly spun out in the emergency lane. The Suburban roared by, then slowed, the driver still blowing the horn. I could see the person in the passenger seat gesturing at me. He waved his hand toward the side of the road. *Pull over.* The next tap nearly launched me into the guardrail.

The next exit wasn't for another five miles, and clearly these assholes weren't interested in following me around. I didn't really have any choice. Either I pulled over or they'd run me over. It was as simple as that.

I put my flashers on, reduced my speed and started to pull over. Their Suburban drifted behind me for maybe half a mile in the emergency lane. It reduced speed until it was twenty yards back. When my car came to a stop, so did theirs.

Silence.

Nothing happened for a moment. I sat there without turning off the engine or moving my foot away from the gas. They turned on their high beams, so I couldn't see what they were doing in my mirrors. I listened to the quiet rush of the cars next to us, and the crickets in the pine forest to my right. It was a waiting game now.

I took my gun out of its holster and placed it under my thigh.

A few moments later, the driver's door opened and a man got out. His boots made such crunching sounds on the gravel between us that he might as well have been wearing spurs. He came into focus after about ten feet. He was a short man with bleached-blond hair and skin the color of porcelain. He walked with a swagger, like he was coming up to tell me the air in my tires was low. I could make out the number 88 tattooed into his neck. Where I come from, eighty-eight was code. Eighty-eight was the numerological equivalent of HH, because *H* is the eighth letter in the alphabet. HH was code itself. It was an abbreviation of a common phrase in prisons all over the country: *Heil Hitler.*

The blond rapped his knuckles on my window and motioned for me to roll down the glass.

"We'd like a word," he said.

I didn't say anything, just kept my hands on the wheel.

He pulled a small gun out of a little holster in his belt. It was a slick draw. In one quick motion he had reached for it, pulled it out and pointed right at me through the window. He had a bead on my head before I had time to even think about reaching for my heat.

"A word, please," he said.

If I wanted to, I could've slammed down the accelerator and shot off like a rocket. I could have run over the blond's big toe before his pea-brain reflexes could manage to squeeze the trigger. A Suburban has a pretty good pickup for a big car, and I was still in gear and my engine was all warmed up. By the time he knew what was happening, his bullets wouldn't hit anything but air and glass. He'd maybe get three shots out at me, all wide, all unlikely to hit, before I'd be halfway off down the highway with enough of a head start to lose the tail. If I wanted to, I could drive off right now. But what would that get me?

I *still* had no idea who these guys were.

I rolled down the window and he gestured that I should get out. I slowly reached forward and took the key out of the ignition and opened the car door. I slid my revolver up my thigh and into my pocket at the same time. A smooth move, I thought. It must have been, because the blond didn't say anything or frisk me or anything. He stayed about a yard back and kept his gun on me. Once I got out, he shut the door and waved the barrel of the gun behind us toward his Suburban. I could smell his breath. Garlic and menthol cigarettes. He marched me back, then opened the back door on the passenger side and nodded for me to get in.

As soon as I did, the man in the front passenger seat turned around and swung a sawed-off shotgun in my face. This guy was twice the size of the blond and had the same neck tattoo. One load of triple-aught buckshot at this range would blow my head clean off.

"You've got the wrong guy," I said.

The blond closed the door and got back in. "No," he said, "we don't."

"I'm just here on vacation. I'm an insurance investigator."

"We know who you are."

"I seriously doubt that."

"You checked out Ribbons's storage unit yesterday afternoon. You're no insurance investigator. You ain't even a cop."

I was silent.

"You're Marcus's man," the blond said.

"I'm not anyone's man."

The blond went silent. I watched as he put the Suburban into gear and pulled out from the side of the highway. He drove carefully and with great precision, so I wouldn't be tempted to try to get the better of them. The gun felt heavy in my pocket.

"Where are you taking me?" I said.

The blond jeered at me like I was stupid.

"You've got an appointment," he said.

23

The drive in the back of the SUV was mercifully short. They took me along the highway out into the salt marsh. I watched my assailants as we drove. The headlights reflected light back into the cabin that mixed with the faint light from the computer screen in the center console, giving everything a strange white glow. The blond had eyes the color of an old rust stain and arms that looked like they were carved from wood. The other man's eyes were bright blue, his hair was red, and he was younger than the blond by maybe ten years. He didn't stop staring at me the whole ride. He didn't even blink. Along his knuckles he had a tattoo that read *Fourteen Words*. Someone had told me what it meant once. It was something to do with white people and their kids, like, *We must secure an existence for white people and a future for white children*. The exact wording differed depending on what prison you grew up in.

The guy with the shotgun took out an old prepaid cell phone. I saw him punching in numbers, but I couldn't make out which ones. He held the phone very close to his face but never took his eyes off me. He didn't speak much, and when he did, he spoke softly so I couldn't hear. Even so, I could tell what he was doing. He was informing his employer that they'd found me. He was asking for orders.

"What do you want with me?" I said.

"Shut up," the blond said.

He then turned off the highway onto an old dirt path that led into the vast empty marsh. We drove along for maybe ten minutes until we were out in the wilderness. The tires sunk into the loose, sandy ground and the SUV bobbled up and down. The going was painfully slow. We were in the middle of nowhere near the mouth of the Absecon Bay. I could still see the Regency tower glowing off in the distance, but the highway sounds and the buzz of civilization were fading. All I could hear now was the wind blowing across the marsh.

We came to a slow stop.

We waited there for a few minutes with the engine running. The darkness surrounding us was unsettling. I listened to the sound of the two men breathing in front of me, closed my eyes and wondered what would happen next.

Were they waiting for orders to kill me?

I banished the thought as soon as it came into my head. If that's what they had in mind, they wouldn't have put me in the backseat. It would involve too much cleanup. No, they would've thrown me in the back of the rig, because that's easy to clean. The blond would have put a knife through my ribs as soon as I stepped out of the car. Then, when I started to fall, he would have caught me and carried me the rest of the way to their Suburban. He'd have thrown my body in the back, and that would be that. By now I'd already be in four pieces, separated down the spine and across the stomach, and wrapped up in garbage bags or something like that. If they wanted me dead, they wouldn't have gone to all this trouble. They wouldn't have taken the risk of leaving me alive. Every minute I kept breathing increased the chances that I might turn things around on them.

Suddenly headlights flashed through the back window. I turned around, shielding my eyes from the high beams, and took a better look. Another black Suburban was rumbling up across the marsh. It took a good five minutes to close the distance, but when it did, it parked across from us on the other side of the trail.

The blond didn't give me a second look. He pressed the button that unlocked my door and said, "Get out."

I pulled the door handle and climbed out. The path between the cars was worn deep with car tracks. In every direction stretched miles of empty marsh with nothing bigger than a shrub between here and the highway. I watched my reflection grow larger in the tinted windows and then opened the rear passenger door of the second vehicle.

The man waiting for me inside had very dark features. Dark hair, dark skin, dark eyes. Eyebrows like caterpillars. He looked like one of those guys you see on the news walking around in a palace in some oil emirate, doing business with the Saudis or buying tanks from the Russians, not dealing crank. His charcoal suit was probably worth twenty grand. But the most striking thing about him were his eyes. Even under the bright glow of the cabin light, he had eyes the color of black ice.

I knew exactly who he was.

I'd heard countless stories about him over the years. In some, he was a barbarian. In others, he was a sophisticate. But one story in particular stuck with me. It was the story I got from Marcus himself, back when we first met in that Oregon hotel five years ago. After he'd made his selections, he leaned over the table where a group of us were sitting and told us all about a man he knew. They'd been childhood friends, Marcus said. Classmates from kindergarten on up. They'd dated the same girls. Ate at the same restaurants. When they were still in school, the man he knew started selling cocaine, and soon subdued the dealer for his corner and shoved him into an abandoned warehouse. Broad daylight, no mask. He'd knocked the guy out with a wrench and then duct-taped a plastic bag over his head. It wasn't a suffocation move, though. The bag had a few holes in it for air. The kid then waited for the man to come to. When he did, he pressed the nozzle of a can of purple spray paint into one of the holes. He sprayed and sprayed and sprayed until he could hear the metal ball rattle around at the bottom of the empty can. The paint went into the bag, and the fumes went into the guy's lungs until he couldn't scream. There's plenty of nasty stuff in paint—butane, propane, industrial solvent, heavy metals. He breathed all of it into his bloodstream. The kid tore the plastic bag off and left. The man survived, somehow, but the solvent in the paint had crossed his blood-brain barrier. When he got out of the hospital, he could only sit and drool and take shallow breaths. He'd gone blind and needed dialysis. To the higher-ups in the cartel, it was a simple and brutal message. If the kid wanted to, he could run an empire with a can of royal-purple spray paint.

And for the next forty years, he did. He was born with the name Harrihar Turner, but nobody ever called him that. He had another name, one that only a few drug dealers dared to say aloud. A name that, once heard, nobody ever forgot.

The Wolf.

24

"I was wondering when we'd meet," the Wolf said as I slid into the back-seat next to him. Even out here in the summer heat, the leather was cold as winter. The air conditioning must have been set to arctic. The Wolf wasn't armed because he didn't need to be. The skinheads with the shotgun were parked right next to us, and there wasn't anywhere to run. His driver probably had a gun too. I looked at the Wolf like I didn't have anything to say.

"You're not exactly what I expected," the Wolf said. "From what I was told, I thought you were a much younger man."

"I don't know what you were expecting," I said. "I am who I am."

The Wolf nodded meaningfully. "Indeed. And you also know who I am, yes?"

"I do," I said. "Your name's Harry Turner."

There was an abrupt silence. He wasn't expecting this answer, either. "Who told you that?" he finally said.

"People," I said.

"Marcus."

"Just people."

"Your people are right, that is one of my names. But I've never been a fan of *Harry*. It is a corruption of my real name, Harrihar. Do you know what *Harrihar* means?"

"No idea."

"It's an Indian name. It is one of the names of Krishna, an avatar of Vishnu, who, according to some sects, is the supreme god of the Hindu religion. Vishnu is the preserver, the all-knowing and all-powerful protector of the universe. *Harry* doesn't quite capture the full meaning, wouldn't you say?"

"I guess," I said.

"But maybe you know me by yet another name. Something a little more memorable."

"They call you the Wolf."

"Good." The Wolf shifted forward in his seat. "Then at least you understand who I am."

"How'd you find me?"

"Come now, I can't tell you that. You might try to stop me. Suffice it to say, however, I can follow you anywhere."

I sniffed.

"You're Marcus's ghostman, are you not? I can tell. I can see it on your hands. The pads of your fingers are as smooth as the skin of your nose."

"I don't work for Marcus," I said.

He smiled. "I'm sure you don't. You're a free agent. You only work for yourself, don't you?"

I didn't say anything.

"Do you watch a lot of news?" the Wolf asked. "In my home there is always a television on. My wife gives me no end of grief about it. In every room I step in, I turn it on, and sometimes I forget to turn it off. It is almost an unconscious habit. I eat my breakfast and I watch the news. I go to work and I watch the news. I talk on the phone and I watch the news. I hardly notice it anymore, but she does. We are talking and I am listening to her, but I am also listening to the news. She gets upset. But I have to watch, understand? You never know what they're going to show next. This hour it might be a story about a girl who went missing somewhere, and I can tune it out of my mind like it was never mentioned in the first place. The next hour, it will be something else. It could be a story that could change the whole course of my day, or maybe even my life.

"You see, I was on the news once. They didn't show my face or say my name, but a local affiliate was doing a story that involved one of my businesses. A little girl had wandered off from her parents and gone missing for a few days. They'd found her, after a while, passed out in an empty lot next to one of my mechanic shops. She didn't look hurt at first, but when they checked her out, they saw something was wrong. Her eyesight had gone blurry. They did blood tests and found she'd been exposed to massive amounts of phosphine gas. It was a mystery because there were no aluminum phosphide pellets—you know, rat poison—anywhere around where they found her. Just the odor of rotting fish. The news people were baffled. What they didn't know was that this mechanic shop had a meth lab in the basement. The fumes had been ventilated out through a pipe into the empty lot the night before. The little girl had been playing there and accidentally breathed in a huge lungful, enough to cause her to pass out. The cooks hadn't noticed what had happened, so they finished the batch. The fumes dissipated, but the little girl was still lying there, not fifteen feet from the ventilation duct. If the news people had found out about the vent, it would have set my operation back almost a quarter million dollars.

"So as soon as I heard about it, I got in my car and drove out to the abandoned lot. From there, I circled through the neighborhood and drove and drove and drove until I found the little girl's brownstone. Then I parked down the street, walked back to the brownstone and climbed in through one of the windows. I went to the parents' room and did them both with a stun gun, so they wouldn't wake up. Then I went to the little girl's room and told her not to scream. She cried and cried, but then she listened to me and didn't make a sound. She was so scared that she could hardly move. She could only take heaving breaths and cry silent tears. I carried her down to the kitchen in my arms and set her down on the counter next to the sink. I poured a glass of milk and gave it to her, and she drank it. The next glass had drain cleaner in it. With milk it has the right texture. She drank half of it before she had to stop. It gave her blisters on her tongue, so I held her little nose and forced the rest of it down her throat. After that, it took another twenty minutes for her to die. Choking and vomiting blood as the drain cleaner dissolved away her insides. She stopped crying after a while. She just sat there and looked at me with those big soft brown eyes, taking shallow breaths. She slumped over in a bit and didn't wake up. Her face covered in blood, her eyes bleeding, her brain dissolving. I left her body right there, next to the open chemical cabinet. After that, the news people didn't say another word about the mechanic shop."

"Why are you telling me this?"

"Because I'm the one who had Moreno killed," the Wolf said. "And if you don't bring me the money from this morning's heist, I'll have you killed too."

25

The car was silent except for the wind off the ocean whipping up against the glass. The lights from the highway cast long shadows through the pine trees to the west. Atlantic City hummed in the distance.

My throat was dry.

The Wolf said, "Atlantic City is mine, Ghostman. I know every ounce of marijuana and every thirteenth of methamphetamine that gets traded here. I knew about Ribbons and Moreno for months. They talked to the same people I talked to. Spent money at my casinos. Had rooms in my apartment complexes. Parked their cars on my street corners. Marcus must have been an idiot to think he could pull a job in my city without me knowing."

"You must've known Marcus was going to pay you with money from a job," I said. "He was a jugmarker for close to twenty years."

"I knew. But I also knew what they were stealing. How do you think Marcus got the tip about the federal payload in the first place? Do you think it just came to him in a dream, or up through the grapevine like stories the tough guys spin in bars? No. He talked to people who talked to people who knew. And believe me, every person who knew also knew me."

"But if you knew about Marcus's deal in advance, why did you let Moreno and Ribbons go through with it? Why shut them down *after* they'd stolen the money?"

The Wolf sighed. "This is the thing about you thieves. You have no tolerance for complexity."

We were silent for a moment.

"Tell me exactly what you want," I said finally.

"I want to offer you a deal," the Wolf said. "A bargain. You are going to take all that money Marcus stole from the casino and put it on Marcus's plane come Monday morning. You are going to let it synch up with the satellite trackers and then explode."

"That will send Marcus to prison for fifty years," I said. "A death sentence for a man his age."

"Now you're beginning to understand. If Marcus could use the money as a weapon, so can I."

I cleared my throat. "You said you were going to offer me a deal."

He gestured out to the salt marsh. "I'm not going to bury you out here."

"That's not much of an offer. If you don't kill me, Marcus will, even if he's in prison. There are people very highly invested in his operation. I might not work for him, but I'm not stupid."

"Yes, he might try to kill you, but you should consider your situation in the short term. Out there, those ocean winds can get very loud. At night they sometimes start howling through the marsh reeds in big gusts. They sound exactly like screams, the locals say. Some people at the edge of the city will swear up and down there's someone out there in the marsh screaming his head off. The effect is so convincing that tourists have been known to call the police. When the police tell them it's just the wind, they don't believe it. They go out in the middle of the night in their dungarees and their beach shirts, looking for the person screaming. But they never find anyone. It really is just the wind, you see. Real screams don't carry that far. They barely carry more than fifty feet out here."

I didn't say anything. The wind gusted against the window and blended in with the sound of the Wolf's air conditioner.

"One way or another," the Wolf said, "you're going to help me. Do what I say and I'll put you on payroll. We'll make a lot of money together. If you choose to disregard what I say, this will be the last conversation you'll ever have. I'll kill you just to send a message. Bury you out here under a sand dune so when the weather changes all that will be left are your teeth and that expensive watch on your wrist."

I looked out the window at the other black Suburban, where the two men were staring off into space. Maybe listening to the wind.

"I don't have the money yet," I said.

The Wolf turned his head a fraction of a degree toward me. "Oh, of course you don't. If you did, you wouldn't still be here. What I don't understand is why Marcus sent a ghostman to find it and not an army of his thugs."

"I can get the money for you, but you have to let me go."

"So you can skip town and disappear on me? No, Ghostman. You're trained to disappear. It's practically all you do. If you're going to work for me, you won't leave my sight for the next thirty hours. We'll go and pick up the stolen money together, in the company of my men. It's the only way you're leaving this marsh in one piece."

"How do I know you won't shoot me in the head the minute I show you where the money is?"

"Because I recognize a good ghostman when I see one," he said. "And I've already had enough bloodshed for one day."

"Somehow I don't believe that."

"Then think of it this way. You do what I ask and at the very least you'll live just that much longer. It could be a few hours, a few days or a few years. But it will be longer. If you don't do what I ask you'll be dead in the next thirty minutes, right after you finish digging your own grave."

"Believe me," I said, "that sounds like a good deal. But I don't have what you're looking for, and there's no hope of finding it with you breathing down my neck."

"I'm not going to revise my offer."

"That's too bad, because I can't take it. If you offer me a twelve-hour window, it's a done deal. Believe me, I hate Marcus as much as you do. But I can't give you something I don't have yet."

"I still don't believe you."

"And you have good reason not to. I'm a world-class liar. But I don't care if you believe me or not. Your whole operation bores me."

"*Bores* you. I'm threatening your life and you're worried about being bored?"

"Aren't you?" I said. I opened the car door, cracking it just a little.

"Do you understand what getting out of this car means, Ghostman?"

I nodded and said, "I'll take my chances with the sand dunes. Get back to me when you come up with something more interesting."

The Wolf didn't say anything as I got out and slammed the door. He glared at me through the window, like I was some sort of puzzle he couldn't figure out. Maybe he thought I was bluffing. Maybe he was bluffing and didn't expect me to call him on it. In any case, he gestured to his driver to start the car. They turned around and drove slowly back toward the highway, leaving me behind with his two skinheads.

I looked at my watch. Quarter after 3 a.m.

Twenty-seven hours to go.

26

I watched his Suburban bob and buck down the trail, mud splashing up every few feet. The flat lands were full of wet sinkholes. The wind off the ocean picked up. The marsh grass was screaming.

I knew better than to run.

You can't run from a shotgun. A 12-gauge, triple-aught, three-and-a-half-inch Magnum launches eight to twelve lead balls at about nine hundred miles an hour. And after a few feet the bullets start to spread out into a small deadly cloud. Each ball's eight and a half millimeters wide and weighs as much as a nickel. Just one could blow a man's brains out. Running wouldn't do a damn thing.

And there wasn't anywhere to hide. There was a pine forest maybe five miles west and a couple of giant energy windmills some ten miles east, but everything in between was as flat as the desert. Plus they had a car. If I did manage to get out of shotgun range, they could just turn on the engine, drive up and run me over. Even on this sort of terrain, I couldn't get away clean.

I watched the Wolf's Suburban disappear into the distance. The air tasted like salt water. I took a breath and let it out slow.

I heard the car door open behind me and saw the blond get out.

He stood there and blinked. His empty expression suggested that he wasn't looking forward to shoveling six feet of wet marshland over my body when he was done killing me. The redhead got out soon after, but looked different. His eyes were wide open and his brow was slick. Sweating. He lifted the shotgun to his cheek and pointed it at me.

"Sorry about this," the blond said.

I didn't say anything. Didn't move.

The blond walked around the back of the SUV and opened the door there with a push of a button. He had all sorts of supplies back there. Duct tape, wire, hacksaw, knives. He came back carrying a shovel. It was a long wooden thing with a rusted head. It must have been five feet long, at least, and caked with dried earth from the last time they'd used it. The blond stopped a few feet in front of me and threw it on the ground between us.

I looked at it and said, "I'm not picking that up."

I didn't even want to touch it. A shovel isn't a very good weapon. It will destroy someone if you hit them with it, sure, but that's the thing. You can't hit someone with it. It's too heavy and awkward. It takes too long to wind up and get it swinging forward. Then if you miss, you're already committed to the swing. It takes even more time and effort to stop the momentum and try again. Anybody could see it coming. Some people might freeze up and take the blow, but not these guys. The blond would pull out his gun and they'd both shoot me before I'd finished my backswing.

I looked at them.

"You made your choice, man," the blond said.

I listened to the screaming wind and took another long look at the casino towers off in the distance.

"Think of it this way," the blond said. "You dig, you get to live a little longer. If it takes you two hours to dig a grave, that's two extra hours. I'm not going to lie to you. You won't get an opportunity to escape. But if you dig, at least you'll have some time to think about things. Make your peace with god or whatever."

"What's your name?" I said.

The blond and the other guy traded glances. The redhead gripped the shotgun tightly, like he was afraid it might slip away from him.

"If I'm going to die," I told them, "I should at least know your names."

The blond was reluctant. After a moment he said, "I'm Aleksei."

"Martin," the other guy said.

"Aleksei. Martin. I've got money."

"You really think you can buy your way out of this?"

"At least out of the digging," I said.

I reached into my pants pocket. Before I touched the money, though, Aleksei put his hand on his belt, where he kept that small gun. It was a Ruger LCP compact. Made out of that light metal stuff they use for airplanes. It was so small he could have kept it in his shirt pocket.

"Slowly," he said.

I took out two grand in fresh bills, all bound together in mustard-colored paper straps. I held it out so they could see it, then I tossed the whole wad in the dirt between us.

"Let me go," I said, "and I can give you ten times that. It's in the satchel in my car. I've got a whole pile of cell phones too. They're yours."

"You won't buy us," Aleksei said.

I held out my left hand. "Just look at my watch."

Aleksei and Martin both took a step forward. I put both my hands up.

Aleksei extended his palm, as if I was supposed to take the watch off and hand it to him. Then he took another step forward, like he thought I was being difficult.

That's where he made his big mistake. Now we were less than three feet apart.

And there was that shovel between us.

I stomped the head of the shovel as hard as I could and the handle pivoted up like a lever. I grabbed it with both hands and threw it like I was lobbing a sledgehammer. The blade connected with the bottom of Aleksei's jaw, which snapped closed and sent part of his tongue flying.

I let go of the shovel, took another step forward and grabbed his right arm, twisting his wrist until it locked against the nerves at the base of his arm. He squealed in pain. In the same motion I took the gun out of my pocket, wrapped my arm around his neck and stuck the muzzle against his temple. It took hardly any work at all. When I was done, he was my human shield.

I turned to Martin and said, "Drop it."

He ogled me for a moment, like he hadn't really seen what just happened. He adjusted his grip on the shotgun. A few seconds passed. Aleksei wriggled against me, blood pouring out of his mouth and down his chin. I stepped to the left and the shotgun followed me.

"You drop it," Martin said.

"Not going to happen."

Martin looked at me, then my revolver, then his friend.

"I'm very good at this," I said. "You don't put the gun down soon, I'll shoot Aleksei here right through the jaw. At this distance, I'll kill him and then kill you before you get that clear shot you're looking for. That's all you're doing, right? Looking for a clear shot?"

Martin's little neo-Nazi brain was working overtime now. I could see it. He was wrapping and rewrapping his pudgy little fingers around the shotgun's rubberized grip. His palms were as moist as the marsh. A line of sweat was forming along the *Fourteen Words* on his knuckles.

Aleksei gargled. Now the blood was going down his throat.

There was another gust of wind.

"Unload," I said. "Right now."

He aimed it away from me and worked the pump. The action opened and a red shell popped out. He worked the slide again and another shell came out. He kept pumping until all six shells were on the ground. He cocked the gun open so I could see the firing chamber was empty, then dropped it to the side of the road. He looked back at me with his hands hanging by his thighs. I could hear him breathing.

"Good," I said, then pointed my pistol at his head and blew his brains out.

The bullet hit Martin in the left cheek, just below the eye. It went through the roof of his mouth and exited through the base of his brain, where all the nerves meet up. Blood and brain matter and shards of bone painted the sand behind him. His body dropped like it was made of lead.

I let Aleksei go. He stumbled forward, trying to regain his balance. Before he could take two steps, however, I hit him in the back of the head with the butt of my revolver and he flopped forward facedown into the mud. The blow must have rattled his brain, because he twitched in the dirt for a few seconds, then stopped and went out like a light.

I took a moment to breathe.

No sane person enjoys killing, but it isn't as bad as people make it out to be. They say killing's the worst feeling a guy can have, that it's like dying a little on the inside. It was never like that for me. I didn't feel much at all, really, just the pressure building in my chest like a bad case of heartburn. Breathing suddenly gets a little harder. Colors a little bit brighter. My problems seemed a little simpler and my thoughts a little faster, due to the adrenaline. All that would pass, if I gave it a few minutes. I just had to think about something else and focus on the task at hand. There was no shame in this.

These men were weapons.

I never considered leaving them alive. Mercy would be a mistake. As long as they were alive and able to hold guns, the Wolf would send them after me. Hell, even if the Wolf wasn't in the picture, these guys would come after me on their own, because I'd got the better of them. Some guys don't know how to walk away and move on once they've lost. The idea of revenge would bounce around in their heads like a subsonic .22-caliber bullet too slow to blow its way out. They'd come after me until I was dead, or they were. As long as they were alive, and had all their limbs, they were weapons.

I patted Aleksei down. I pulled the Ruger from his belt and checked it. I dropped the magazine and pulled the slide back just far enough to see the nine millimeter in the chamber. I tossed the gun in the marsh. His passport was in his breast pocket. *Aleksei Gavlik*. Wallet and cell phone. The keys to the Suburban. I took his keys and scrolled through the contact list on his phone. None of the numbers had any names attached, but there had been more than fifteen calls in the last ten hours to one number with an Atlantic City area code. The Wolf. I memorized the number, then snapped the phone in half and threw that in the marsh too.

I went over to Martin and did the same thing. He had a wallet with a driver's license giving an address down in Ocean City. Besides the shotgun and another set of keys, there was a small folding knife attached to his belt. I tossed it into the marsh too. I picked up the two grand I'd dropped on the ground, dusted it off and put it back in my pocket. I wiped the handle of the shovel down with my shirttail and hurled it as far as I could.

Aleksei groaned and started moving again. His legs struggled uselessly through the mud.

I went over and shot him in the back of the head. I wiped a spot of blood off my tie and walked away.

I hit the cylinder release on my revolver and dropped the bullets and the empty casings into the ditch, then unscrewed the bolt handle and removed the rubberized grip. I cocked the gun back and pried the hammer spring free, then pulled off the hammer and firing pin and threw it as far as I could. The whole gun was in eight little pieces in less than a minute. I'd trail out the rest of the pieces along the side of the highway. It could take a team of men several months to find and put them all together again.

I closed up the back of the Suburban, got in, backed up along the path until there was a place to turn around, then drove out to the highway. As I left, I listened to the quiet hum of the insects.

27

KUALA LUMPUR

Every heist starts the same way. After Marcus told us what to steal and how, we had to go case the joint. That, however, can be almost as risky as the robbery itself. It takes dozens of hours to get ready for a good job. You've got to know every inch of the target bank, from the door to the back of the vault. You have to memorize every teller's name, every security guard's badge number and every hiding place on every floor of the building. Do the glass doors have electronic locks? Does the vault have a time-lock mechanism? When does the bank manager leave for coffee, and how does he or she take it?

You have to know everything.

Therefore, you need to go into the bank and take a good, long look around. Twenty minutes won't do. Two days is more like it. This observation period provides the professional heister with a unique set of problems. You have to have some sort of reason to be there in the first place. Bankers often notice when someone walks in, looks around for an hour and then just leaves without doing any business. And worse, even if you manage to scope the joint out without any of the employees noticing, there are cameras. Sure, they aren't an immediate threat, because nobody gets arrested for walking through the front door and not doing anything, but cameras can become a serious problem later. Once you've robbed the place, investigators can scrub back through old footage to see if someone matching one of the robbers' height and weight ever came through before. Every walk-in over the past six months gets investigated. If they make a match, they can put the picture on the news and they're one step closer to catching you. So if we wanted to have a closer look at the inner workings of our bank, we had to go in as people we weren't.

Enter the ghostmen.

Hsiu Mei was our controller. She'd stay in the van on a wireless link connected to our earpieces. She could translate for us, if necessary, but would really act as our guide. She'd gone over the schematics for the building again and again, drinking pot after pot of hot green tea from a Styrofoam cup.

Angela and I were going inside.

We spent several hours in the morning preparing our disguises, and Angela was absolutely radiant. Her costume was a red Gucci summer dress, a platinum bracelet set with expensive rocks, heels in the latest style and a handbag to match. She didn't look anything like the woman I'd known for years. This Angela was a good twenty years younger and a few million dollars richer. Her contact lenses were an almost phosphorescent green and her hair was long, black and perfectly straight. Her lips were the color of blood, and it looked like she'd stepped out of a magazine. She wasn't Angela anymore. She was Elizabeth Ridgewater, an heiress from New England.

I looked a little different. I wore a plain black suit and a dark tie in a style that had gone out of fashion a couple of seasons ago. My makeup made me look only about ten years older, and my hair was a deep brown that made me look menacing. I worked my face until it was stuck in a nearly permanent scowl. I was William Gold, Ms. Ridgewater's personal bodyguard.

Angela handcuffed a Halliburton briefcase to my wrist. It was a light aluminum number with layers of foam on the inside for added protection. I could hear something small but heavy shifting around when I lifted it.

"Let's go," Angela said.

We got out of the van and walked through the revolving doors into the lobby. She led the way, of course, walking with the confidence and grace of a woman who could afford to buy anything that came into her sight. I kept my head down behind her and slipped on a pair of dark Ray-Bans. People were looking at us, which makes me feel uncomfortable, even when in disguise. I'm more comfortable pretending to be just another nobody.

The target building was called the National Exchange Tower, a thirty-five-story skyscraper with a helipad on top. As we went through the lobby, I made a quick appraisal of the ground floor. None of the doors required any sort of access key or swipe, and there wasn't a metal detector out front like some buildings have these days. The receptionists didn't even speak to us when we went toward the elevators. One looked at us and nodded, but nothing else.

Only the top portion of the building belonged to the bank itself. As I walked by, I took a look at the list of tenants posted next to the elevator doors. The lobby took up the first floor. On Two were offices for the building administrators, supervisors, cleaning staff and security personnel. A law firm had Three and Four, and the next eight held a large fabrication company. There was no thirteenth floor, but Fourteen through Twenty-one belonged to an oil company. Twenty-three and Twenty-four were under renovation, and Twenty-five was some sort of electronics start-up. Only the top floors, Twenty-six through Thirty-five, belonged to the bank.

And only one of those floors housed the vault.

Most of the bank's floors were of no interest. Two were just customer-service call centers, and the other five were offices for account managers. The floor with the vault was at the very top. Floor Thirty-five was the bank's primary foreign-currency depot, and it was the one we'd have to take over. As far as the schematics told us, there wasn't much up there besides a few managers, some safety-deposit boxes and roughly eighteen million in cash.

Once we were alone inside the elevator, I pressed a button on my watch that started a timer. With an accurate blueprint of the building and the time of the trip up, we could calculate the speed of the elevators. With the speed of the elevators, we could estimate call-button times and override-delay times.

Once the lift jerked into motion, Angela gave me a concerned look. "Anxious?" she said.

I shook my head. "I'm having the time of my life."

It took us two minutes to reach the top floor. We watched the numbers change in silence. When the doors finally opened, a bank manager was there to greet us. I shot a look at Angela but she didn't return it. There must be some sort of sensor that alerted the top floor whenever an elevator was heading their way. This man's position and readiness to greet us was too good to be a coincidence.

The top floor resembled a regular bank, except it was thirty-five stories up. The elevators opened onto a reception room that was twenty by thirty and furnished only with a few couches facing the window. Opposite these were teller stations sectioned off with Plexiglas and a few double-locking doors through to the back. I could make out a few cubicles behind the teller stations, and behind them, far in the back, a secure elevator and the massive round door to the vault. The emptiness was part of the aesthetic, I suppose. No frills, all business.

The manager shook hands with Angela and greeted us in Malay. Angela answered in English. "I'd like to inquire about a vault-deposit box."

It didn't take much more than that to get his attention. He smiled and greeted us again in English, then invited us back to his office. Angela looked like the type of woman who didn't like to waste any time, and the manager could clearly see that. He led us through one of the double-locking doors and down a row of offices to his own. Once we were settled in, I held up the aluminum case and Angela unlocked the handcuff on my wrist. I sat back and didn't say a word. The less I spoke, the better it all seemed. It felt like we could have done the whole transaction without saying a single word.

"While I'm here, I need a small vault-deposit box to keep an item of particular value to me," Angela said. "If I can, I'd like to see what sort of security you offer."

"I assure you, you've come to the right place. We offer a range of security boxes with some of the finest antitheft technology in Asia."

"I was told you also offered vault security."

"We do, but our vault-security boxes are reserved for our corporate clients who wish to secure assets worth five million British pounds or more. Our private safety-deposit boxes, which are located in a separate room just across from our vault, will more than satisfy your needs, I can assure you."

"I think in my case you might be willing to make an exception."

Angela unlocked the other part of the handcuff, took the briefcase in her lap and opened it up to show the manager what she was talking about. Inside was a rock about the size of a man's fingertip. It was almost the color of a ruby, but a little too clear for that. It was a red diamond, the rarest color in the world. This diamond had been dug up almost three hundred years ago somewhere in India, and then owned at one point or another by two European kings, three princesses, two sheiks and three billionaires. At auction, it would fetch just over fourteen million dollars. It looked like a frozen drop of blood.

This was the Kazakhstan Crown Diamond.

It wasn't the real Kazakhstan Crown Diamond, of course. That was behind two inches of bullet-resistant glass in Abu Dhabi. This was a fake, but a very good one. It was made of cubic zirconia treated with a slight amount of cerium to give it the same rare red hue as the original. Anybody with a few years of experience and a jeweler's loupe could've seen it wasn't the real thing, but that wasn't going to be a problem. The case was piled with forged documents—insurance, provenance, appraisal. The rock simply had to look valuable, and let me tell you, it did that perfectly.

The manager's eyes went wide for a moment, but he suppressed his reaction right away. It's part of the job, I suppose, to show little appreciation for the valuables he was tasked to protect. The slightest hint of avarice could set off alarms in a potential client. It was important to do everything by the book, with little variation. He took a glancing look at us and sat back in his chair.

"I am willing to pay any premium to keep it safe," Angela said, "provided you can offer me the level of security I'm accustomed to. I've had problems with Malaysian banks in the past."

She was playing a very delicate game. She had to convince the manager to let us look around the vault, without actually buying a box there. We wanted him to turn us down, ultimately, so we wouldn't be as memorable. If he accepted her offer and we backed out at the last minute, he'd remember our visit for sure, and that might come back to haunt us. Angela's voice was equally gentle and pretentious; she simultaneously came off as desperate enough to warrant consideration but arrogant enough to merit rejection.

While Angela and the manager chatted for a few minutes about the vault, I was memorizing the positions of the security cameras. The whole bank was wired up with black security domes situated in the ceiling to provide redundant coverage of every square inch of the bank. There was one above each teller window, another behind it, one over each cubicle and four more facing the vault. The only place not covered were the employee-only bathrooms built into the far wall.

I politely excused myself to visit the facilities so I could sniff around a little better. Once I was out of the office, I whispered, "Cameras."

Hsiu Mei whispered back to me through the transmitter in my ear. "Take a good look at the secure elevator in the back room, next to the vault and the safe-deposit boxes."

The secure elevator she was talking about was next to the vault and entirely different from the one we rode up in. This elevator had heavy doors made of solid steel and a state-of-the-art call system. The person at one end could have a conversation with the person at the other end through closed-circuit television. I gave it a hard glance as I walked by.

"Dual-custody, card-lock," I whispered.

"Jesus," Hsiu said. "And the vault?"

"Triple-custody," I said. "Time-release, time-delay, three-part mixed dial."

Hsiu swore in Chinese. The vault was a total monster. It had security features from several top manufacturers all piled on top of one another. I moved on before I drew any suspicion. By the time I got back to the office, Angela was wrapping things up. We'd gotten most of what we'd wanted. Ideally he would have shown us the vault, but we knew that wasn't going to happen. A floor manager like him might approve, but a vault manager would shoot him down in a second. We wouldn't get close to that vault unless we already had an account, and opening one would be far too risky. Angela thanked the man and cuffed the case back on my wrist, took my arm and led me quietly out the door. She looked disappointed and frustrated.

That part, it turns out, wasn't an act.

Once we were back in the elevator Angela pressed the button to make the doors close, then paced once around the compartment and looked carefully at each of the light fixtures. There were hidden cameras, of course, but no microphones. Most elevators don't have audio security, but she checked anyway. Once she was sure we weren't being recorded, she leaned up against the brass bar on the back wall and whispered in my ear, "This bank's a goddamn deathtrap."

"I love it," I said. "Did you see that vault?"

"The vault's Diebold Class II, with a time-specific triple-custody delay lock, which means three managers have to enter three different codes known only to them simultaneously, and at certain times of the day known only to them, and once they do, the vault doesn't open right away. It starts a timer that opens the safe half an hour later. Yes, I saw the fucking vault."

"I'm going to love getting through that thing," I said.

"No you're not, because we're walking away. If the vault weren't enough of a problem, once we have the money we're only a block from a police station and only a five-minute drive from PGK headquarters. That means helicopters and assault teams. We can expect guys in black masks and body armor dropping from zip lines, just like in the movies. We'll be in cuffs before we ever touch that vault door. Or we'll be dead."

I said, "Did you think stealing over seventeen million bucks was going to be easy?"

"I expected it to be survivable. This isn't."

I shook my head.

"We should walk away from this job," Angela said. "Vanish. Go to Prague. Book a suite in the Boscolo and stay there for a month."

"Where's the fun in that?"

"I'm not doing this because it's fun," Angela said. "I want to get rich and live a normal life."

"Do you know how bored I am being *normal*?" I said. "I live for challenges like this."

"It'll get us killed."

I shook my head and said, "Then that's how it's got to be."

28

ATLANTIC CITY

I drove in silence for a while. I was halfway to Hammonton before I spotted my abandoned Suburban on the side of the road. I was lucky that the state police hadn't spotted it and called for an impound. When I parked behind it, I could hear a single car passing in the other direction. The highway was empty at this time of night.

Angela used to say she had a list of rules for surviving as a ghostman. Among them were only three she never broke and never changed. I used to call them the Big Three, like they were some sacred catechism handed down to us by god himself. The first: Never kill unless you don't have a choice. The second: Don't trust anyone you don't absolutely have to. The third: Never make a deal with cops.

The last one was strictly practical. The police aren't in the business of letting criminals get away. No matter how corrupt a cop might be, he's still sworn an oath to protect and serve the people and laws of his jurisdiction. You could call me a cynic, but an oath is an oath. You can't cut a deal with somebody who has sworn to take you down. Simply put, police are the enemy, and no amount of talk, money or drugs will ever change that. And the cop isn't always the problem.

Sometimes the guys in your crew are.

There's a word for a heister who talks to the police—several, in fact. *Snitch, rat, stool, fink.* In some parts of the world, just giving a so-called peace officer the time of day is enough to earn a trip to the hospital courtesy of your associates. Nobody is more reviled than a guy who spills to the law. A person who vanishes on a job has a chance of earning redemption, if he works hard enough, but a snitch might as well sign the cops' affidavit, go home and kiss a Beretta. A witness-protection agreement isn't worth the paper it's printed on.

Jugmarkers are notorious for taking revenge on people who rat on them. Some don't even kill snitches right away. They kill a guy's whole family first, just to get his attention. They'll send somebody with a box of knives to work over the snitch's mother. Then they'll kill the girlfriend. Then the brothers. The sisters. The children.

Then time's up.

I couldn't stop thinking about Rebecca Blacker. I could see the black eyeliner running along her lower eyelids and her hair spilling over her shoulders in rough tangles. I pictured her badge booklet. The woman in the picture was so much younger. Full of youthful excitement, anxiety, terror. The one I met was cool and calm and jaded. She was a different person now. I wondered how long it would be before she'd try to take me down, or if she was trying to already.

I used the sleeve of my suit to wipe down the wheel of the SUV, the gearbox and the door handle, both inside and out. I remembered to wipe the passenger and rear doors too. I took off the jacket, tie and shirt, which had blood on them, and threw them in the backseat along with the last two pieces of my revolver.

I went back to my SUV and pulled on a new shirt from my satchel and put on my old suit jacket, then went back to Aleksei and Martin's SUV and opened the back hatch just to see if they had anything useful there. In addition to a second shovel, there was a length of green garden hose, two sweatsuits, a torch lighter, a spool of low-gauge wire, wire cutters, pliers, three knives, a box of large black trash bags, a hacksaw, duct tape and a hammer. To a naïve observer, this might have looked like an everyday collection of home supplies. But low-gauge wire is twice as good as rope if you want to tie someone down. Double-ply contractor bags can hold fifty pounds of human flesh without leaking. A garden hose can hurt worse than a baseball bat, if you know how to swing it right. A hacksaw can do lots of things.

This was a torture set.

I took the sweatpants and ripped them down the center and tore one of the halves in half again. I straightened out a length of the wire that was roughly two and a half feet long, then wrapped the cotton fabric around it.

If I wanted to, I could have cleaned up this SUV out here in the pine barrens for the cops to find. Wiped down like this, they'd probably just return it to the owner. Hell, if I'd wanted to make a few bucks, Alexander Lakes could recommend a half a dozen chop shops that would pay good money for it, no questions asked, and have it cut down to parts by morning. But I didn't want to play it safe.

I wanted to send a message.

I went to the side of the SUV and opened the fuel cap, then fed the wire and cloth into the tank until I felt it hit the bottom. There wasn't a whole lot of gas in there, which was a good thing. Less gas means more oxygen. I made sure the end of the rag was good and soaked with fuel before pulling it out again. Once I did, I pushed the other end of the wire down into the tank until it hit bottom, so this way the whole rag was soaked in gasoline, including a little two-inch tuft protruding from the fuel cap. I backed away from the car a little bit and held the torch lighter to the gasoline-soaked fabric and waited for it to blacken and shrivel up. I tossed the lighter through the car window and walked away.

I opened the other Suburban with the wireless key. I got in, started the engine and pulled out back on the highway with my hazards on so anyone in the right lane could see me coming. I checked my watch.

Exactly 4 a.m. It was still too early for the car-rental companies to be open, and I needed to switch vehicles soon if I wanted to stay inconspicuous. The Wolf would have eyes all over the city looking for a black Suburban with these plates. And I had to assume the Fed knew the make and model as well. If she could find the hotel room, she'd certainly be smart enough to figure that out too. How many rental cars could have been parked in the Chelsea garage? Ten? Twenty, at most?

Behind me, the torn fabric burned slowly, like cotton does, until the flames crawled down the fuel pipe. Fumes don't usually ignite by themselves, but liquid gasoline mixed with oxygen does. The rag had to burn all the way down to the fuel in the tank.

I was a hundred yards away when it did. The engine exploded and all three-quarter tons jumped two feet to the left. A second later, the fire ignited the plastic, fabric and leather in the cabin and sent the whole car up. It would burn like that for hours, if they'd let it. The Suburban must've been worth eighty grand with all those options, but it would be scrap metal by the time I got to my exit. The flames illuminated the pine trees like a giant bonfire and sent smoke drifting across the highway. I drove until the dancing lights were just a speck in the distance and the only thing I could smell was the salt coming in off the ocean.

I had to go be a rat.

29

The highway back toward the city was as empty as the Sahara, the Suburban's headlights revealing only pavement and the faded yellow lines down the center of the road. Off to the side were casino billboards. With the SUV going sixty miles an hour, they all seemed to blend together, like they were caught by a time-lapse camera. The wind was coming in hard against the windshield now, carrying bits of trash and sand.

I wasn't four miles into the drive before one of my cell phones rang. It was still in the bag I'd left on the passenger seat. I fished it out and saw that the incoming number was the one Rebecca Blacker had given me on her card. I flipped the phone open and sandwiched it between my cheek and my shoulder so I could talk and drive.

"Took you long enough," I said.

"Jack Morton's a real pain in the ass, you know that?" she said. "I searched that room for two hours before I found your goddamn note."

"I was beginning to think you'd somehow missed it. And don't you ever sleep? I didn't expect you to call until morning."

"I'll sleep when I'm back on vacation."

"Can I ask why you were searching that room?"

"I found the getaway car," she said. "Thought you'd know something about it, also that I might find something linking you to the scene."

"I don't know anything about that."

"Sure you don't," she snarled.

"What happened?"

"The ACPD found it two hours ago. What's left of it, anyway. It was blown to hell in a building out by the old airfield. Somebody covered it with enough fuel to raze the whole goddamn place. All that's left is a bunch of twisted metal and a couple parts made of that heat-tempered material that doesn't melt. It took an hour just to identify the make and model."

"Tough break."

"You know, Jack, I've seen a lot of torched getaway cars before, but I've never seen a car blow itself up a full seventeen hours after the job went down."

"You think somebody got there before you."

"Two people. We found footprints at the scene. Fresh ones. You wouldn't happen to wear size-eleven shoes, would you?"

"I prefer boots. Better ankle support."

"If you're just going to play games with me, I'll put out a warrant."

"No, you won't," I said. "You don't have anything on me."

"Then give me something," Rebecca said. "You're the one who left me this number, and I refuse to believe you did it just to fuck with me. You wanted me to call you. At least tell me why."

"Are you tracing this call?"

"Excuse me?"

"This phone has a built-in global-positioning system," I said. "They all do, these days. The chip in the back sends out a blip every fifteen seconds with its exact location. Coordinates, down to about ten meters. Latitude and longitude. That means you should be able to figure out where I am. Come on, you're a Fed. You should be all over this."

"You want me to know where you are?"

"I want you to know where I've been. Specifically, where this phone has been for the past hour or so. And if you go back long enough, I'm sure you'll see I was nowhere near your burned-up getaway car."

"You could just tell me where you were, you know."

"I was out along the highway. But you'll want the coordinates."

"And what were you doing out along the highway?"

"Just taking a drive."

"At three in the morning."

"I like the night air. Good for the lungs."

"You stumble across anything interesting?"

"Just do it, will you?"

"Are you helping me," Rebecca said, "or just trying to piss me off?"

"Neither. I'm telling you I went for an evening drive and left my phone on."

"You're so full of it."

"You want to know where I was or not?"

"Honestly? I want your shoe size."

"Ten and a half. Wide."

A pause. I could hear her breathing. Her breath had a simple, quick cadence to it, like she hadn't had the time to take a deep breath and let it out in months, maybe years. I could hear her fingers on a computer keyboard.

Then she said, "We should meet."

"Is talking to me on the phone a problem?"

"I'd prefer to talk face-to-face."

"You just said you might put a warrant out on me. I think I prefer a little distance, for the time being."

"I'm not after you. Marcus Hayes can rob Fort Knox for all I care. He's not my case. All I want are the people who turned this city into a bloodbath this morning, so I can go back down to Cape May and salvage what's left of these shitty two weeks. And considering that burning white Dodge, I think you owe me."

"I told you, I don't know anything about that."

"You want me to go out along the highway or not?"

"All right. Clearly we're both awake, so let's meet in the hotel coffee shop in an hour. A place like that never closes."

"Which hotel?"

"You know the one," I said. "You spent half the night there moving furniture around."

"Fruitlessly, I might add. You didn't even take the chocolates off the pillows."

"How'd you find that room, anyway?"

"I told you," Rebecca said. "I'm very good at what I do."

"One hour."

"See you then."

I ended the call, then removed the plastic cover from the back of the phone and pulled out the battery. Under that was the SIM card, which gave the phone a number and made records of all the incoming and outgoing calls. I took it out and snapped it in half between my fingers, then flicked the pieces out the window. I looked at my watch. Quarter after 4 a.m.

Twenty-six hours to go.

30

When I passed May's Landing, I punched Marcus's number into another phone and waited as the screen turned from black to green. The phone rang and Marcus's man picked up before the third ring, like he was sitting there waiting for the call. I glanced at my watch. It was almost 1:30 a.m. in Seattle, so Marcus should've been fast asleep. Instead his man was poised and ready. The reception was low.

"The Five Star Diner," he said.

"Put him on."

"Who is this?"

"Nobody."

Things were quiet as he walked the phone into another room. People like Marcus can afford to have a guy with a flat Midwestern accent screening all the calls. This one's voice was like cough syrup. The diner had three lines that I knew of, and each was always answered the same way. The guy would say the name of the diner, and if you didn't convince him you were important in thirty seconds or less, he'd hang up and you'd never get the boss on the line.

Marcus came on a few seconds later. He sighed and sounded tired, but there was something else in his sigh. He sounded afraid.

"Hello?" he said.

"Marcus, it's me."

"Jack. I've been trying to get in touch with you for hours. What happened?"

"You tell me, Marcus." I said. "You think I don't know you set me up?"

He went quiet. I took the exit that would take me back through the pine barrens.

Marcus had stopped breathing for a beat or two, then let out a breath to say, "I don't know what you're talking about."

"The Wolf knew your plan long before Ribbons and Moreno even got close. Now, you're too smart to underestimate a man like him, so either you're working an angle on this I don't understand or you're much stupider than I thought."

"That's not possible," he said. "There's no way the Wolf knew the plan."

"I talked to him myself. He tried to kill me."

"Jack, he's got to be reaching. He has to be. If the Wolf really knew I planned to rip him off with the federal payload, why did he agree to the deal? Why did he even let Moreno and Ribbons into the city? He would have put bullets in their heads before they even got past the pine barrens."

"He said he was planning on double-crossing you. He was going to leave you holding the money when it blew, so you'd take the fall for it. Now he's asked me to put the wired money on your plane and wait for it to blow up. But you knew he'd try that, didn't you? You were working another angle."

"What the hell did he do?"

"Have you been watching the news? Do you know about the third shooter? The Wolf told me that was his hit."

There was silence over the other end of the phone for a second.

"You met with him," Marcus said.

"Yeah, I did."

"Jesus," Marcus said. "You're working for him."

I sniffed.

"For all I know," Marcus said, "the Wolf's wired into this call right now, coaching you through this conversation word by word. What did he offer you?"

"Your head on a platter. But I didn't take it."

"I should hang up."

"Listen," I said. "There's going to be a double homicide on the news in the morning. Two of the Wolf's men out in the salt marsh got shot through the head. That should be proof enough where my loyalties are. As far as I know, this line is clean. Just you and me. But if you don't start talking, I can't promise our relationship will stay friendly. If you don't tell me everything, I have no reason to keep your best interests in mind, okay? You can't owe a favor to a dead man."

Marcus didn't say anything.

"You *are* a dead man," I said. "You understand that, right? I bet that if the Wolf can't set you up with the trap money and send you to prison, he'll try to kill you outright. He certainly wants to kill you, Marcus. Right now, I'm your best chance of stopping that. So talk."

"I didn't set you up, Jack."

Marcus took a breath and exhaled, his breath coming in big gasping bursts like he was having a panic attack. I listened to him hyperventilate for a while and thought about how much he liked to play games. He wasn't the kind of guy who freaked out when he got caught in a lie. He was a calm, collected liar and a world-class poker player. He'd do this if he really and truly thought he might have something to lose, or else it was just for effect. Even the way he was breathing could be part of the setup.

"Here's my problem," I said. "If the Wolf was behind the third shooter, why did he kill Moreno and try to kill Ribbons right then? Why didn't he wait until Moreno and Ribbons had gotten well away from the casino before robbing them? Waiting as little as twenty minutes would have doubled his chance of success and limited his police exposure. So either he's lying to me or you are."

"I don't know what you want me to say," Marcus said. "I really don't."

I knocked the phone against the side of my head in frustration. Marcus was messing with me and we both knew it. The whole conversation felt like a brick at the bottom of my stomach.

"Okay," I said. "But you're going to tell me before this thing's over."

"Do you have the money, at least?"

"No. Ribbons is still in the wind."

"How the hell can that be?"

"I think he's dead."

"What?"

"He was shot," I said. "I found that white Dodge they used. The parts that weren't totaled from multiple crashes or shot through with bullet holes were covered with blood. I'm no expert on gunshot injuries, but I can't imagine someone losing that amount of blood and living very long. Considering we haven't heard from him, I think he's dead. And even if he's still alive, he can't have much time left. We've got to start watching the hospitals and morgues."

"Ribbons won't go to a hospital."

"He's dying."

"He doesn't care. He's a two-time felon. If he gets caught, he goes away for life. No parole after twenty years, no plea bargain, no reduced sentence with good behavior. Life. Guys like him would rather bleed out on the streets than die in prison." Marcus paused. "What are you thinking?"

"I'm thinking Ribbons is holed up, then. He must've gone someplace to hide, hoping that he could ride it out, and by the time the drugs wore off and he realized how grievous his injuries were, it was too late.

You know, like an old dog crawling under the stairs so it can die alone. But I'm not sure he wouldn't call for an ambulance. I've met a lot of people who told me they'd rather die than go back to prison, and every single one of them was full of shit."

Marcus said nothing.

"I need to know if you can think of any places he might've gone to. Places that were important to him. Where he could lay low for a while. And don't tell me about any motels. A guy bleeding like that can't check in anywhere."

"Maybe he went back to the scatter."

A scatter's where a guy sleeps the night before a job. It's different from the place where the job is planned. You don't shit where you eat. Heisters don't ever work in the scatter. They don't talk, they don't drink, they don't eat, they don't clean their guns. They do nothing but sleep there. A scatter's set up so you can get out in thirty seconds flat if you have to. Heisters don't bullshit in the scatter. They respect it. You're never ever supposed to return there. Then again, you're not supposed to get shot, either.

"You've got the address?" I said.

Marcus gave it to me slowly, like he thought I needed to write it down. I said the name of the place back to him, just to make sure I'd heard it right.

"What do I do about the Wolf?" I said.

"Don't get killed."

"That's not what I mean. You two are at war now. You realize that, don't you? You're going to have to kill him or else he's going to kill you."

"Just make sure you get that cash," Marcus said. "If it blows and the GPS syncs up, there's no way to stop this thing. I'll take care of my business. You just take care of yours."

"Got it."

We were silent for a second.

"Marcus," I said finally, "if I find out you're setting me up in any way, or even thought about setting me up, I am going to find you and kill you. I hope you understand that."

I pressed the end button and threw the phone out the window. It got sucked back by the wind coming over the side of the car and hit the rear passenger window before spinning off to the side of the road and exploding into a dozen pieces.

31

The diner, a free-standing American joint with a neon sign featuring a steaming cup of coffee, was located in an otherwise empty concrete lot across from a boarded-up strip mall. Through the big glass windows you could see everything that was going on inside. A man in a white hat was greasing down the grill and the only waitress was refilling the coffee machine behind the bar. Two customers were sobering up in a booth near the door and a young busboy mopping the floors all around them. He was wearing headphones.

Alexander Lakes was seated in a booth toward the back.

He was trying to play it cool, but he was obviously nervous. His back was as straight as a board and he kept looking around like he was expecting something to jump out at him. There was a matrix of black coffee stains on the table in front of him. Even though he seemed quite alert, he didn't notice me. When the chime went off as I came through the door, he didn't look up. I came up from behind and he jumped when I put my hand on his shoulder.

"You been waiting long?" I said.

"Over two hours," he said. "Where have you been?"

"I got caught up in something."

He glanced quizzically at my shirt. "What happened to your suit?"

"Ruined it."

I slid into the booth opposite him. He put his right hand on his coffee cup and dropped the other into his lap. His eyes were bright.

"What's wrong?" I said.

"I was worried you might try to kill me over that burned room."

"Is that why you're pointing a gun at me under the table?"

Lakes looked like he didn't know what to say. The kid mopping the floors came around to us. The bass rhythm on his headphones sounded like somebody scratching on a linoleum floor. Under the fluorescent lights every small imperfection on his uniform was as clear as day.

Lakes waited for the kid to pass. Once he did, I heard the hammer of his pistol shifting forward and the safety engaging. Lakes discreetly pulled a small automatic up from under the table and put it back under his jacket.

"How did you know?" Lakes said.

"As soon as I sat down, you slid your left hand under the table and started drinking coffee with your right. I saw you write at the airport— you're left-handed. So if you were just sitting there drinking coffee, you'd be holding the cup with your left hand. Most people use their dominant hand to drink, if they're not eating. Instead, your left hand's under the table and there's no bulge under your armpit. You noticed me come in, but tried to look like you hadn't. You also looked nervous, so I assumed you'd have a gun."

"It was just a precaution," Lakes said.

"Are you still on my side?"

"Depends," he said. "Are you still going to pay me?"

"I was planning to," I said. "But the gun's a real surprise."

"I had to, when you consider my position. I've heard things, you know. Marcus Hayes doesn't have a reputation for forgiving or forgetting. I was worried you might make me chase this coffee with a whole jar of nutmeg, and I wasn't about to let that happen."

"That's Marcus's thing," I said. "Not mine."

"How should I know? I don't know you, or your reputation. I don't even know your name."

"Then now you know one thing about me. I don't kill people unless I have a very good reason to. Your slipup at the hotel doesn't make that cut."

"In ten years," he said, "nothing like that has ever happened before."

"What?"

"In ten years, I've never had anybody bust one of my safe houses. We've had an impeccable record."

"What happened this time?"

"My guy at the hotel desk lost his nerve," he said. "Told me the FBI came around with a description of a white guy, six feet, hundred and eighty pounds, mid-fifties. They made it sound like they'd deport him if he didn't roll. He was worried they'd take his kids."

"That description could've fit anybody. He had deniability."

"As I said," Alex continued. "Nerves."

I took out the two thousand dollars and put it on the table next to the box of napkins and the bottle of ketchup. The hundred-dollar bills were still a little dirty from the pine barrens.

Lakes glanced at the money, then back at me. "You're not really as old as you look, are you?"

"How old do you think I am?"

"It's hard to tell. You look younger now then you did before."

I pointed up. "It's the fluorescent lights."

Lakes didn't say anything.

"This is how it's going to be," I told him. "You'll take this money and you'll get me some police records. Then you'll take the Suburban I parked out front and get rid of it. You'll rent me a new car—something low-profile, like before. You'll buy me some new clothes—suit, shirts, shoes, you name it—and you'll get me a small, reliable handgun with clean numbers. Or no numbers at all. Nothing that can get traced back to you, okay? I'll call you in a few hours and by then I want all of these things done. Do you understand?"

"What do you need records for?"

"You don't need to know. Just get me the police reports from the last week or so. Reported robberies, thefts, murders, all that. Any dirty cop or lawyer could get me what I need in thirty seconds. I want to know everything they know."

"Anything in particular?"

"Yes," I said, "but I'm not telling you. I don't trust you."

Lakes nodded slightly and looked at the money again. Ben Franklin's face was staring back at him. No currency printed in the United States features a smiling face. They're all staring out with dead seriousness. Only Franklin seems to stare right out at you, though. His eyes follow you at every angle like the Mona Lisa's.

"This isn't nearly enough," Lakes said.

"The money's for the records, not you. You should be able to get any cop you like for two grand."

"I understand that, but you've got to realize how much I've spent on you already. After this hotel problem, which I'm not going to charge you for, I'm running this operation at a sizable net loss. Four hundred here, six hundred there. Adds up. And to be honest, I'm not sure I believe you're going to pay me at the end. You might just disappear."

"My credit's good," I said. "You'll get paid."

Lakes shook his head. "You don't have any credit. You don't even have a name."

"So if I disappear, just bill Marcus. You might not trust him, either, but you know him. That should be good enough."

Lakes nodded, staring at the stack of money on the table.

"I need your keys," I said.

"I'm not giving you my car. You still haven't given me my phone back."

"I destroyed your phone," I said, holding out my hand, palm up.

"You asked for a car," Lakes said. "I'll get you a car. Give me two hours. Any model you like. Options too. But I'm not giving you my wheels."

"I don't have two hours. I need a new car, right here, right now. Either you let me take your car or I'll go out and steal it."

"No. No way."

"This isn't a choice, Lakes. The keys. Now."

"You won't steal it. You can't."

"Then let's call Marcus about it."

Lakes thought about it for a second, then took a set of keys out of his pocket, laid them on the table, worked one off the ring and slid it over to me. On the base of the key was a winged, stylized B symbol. Bentley.

"You were in a Mercedes earlier," I said.

"One's for business, the other's for pleasure."

"Which is this?"

"Take a fucking guess."

"I'll bring it back in one piece." I started to get up.

Lakes touched my arm. "You know," he said, "they found one of the getaway cars from the heist this morning."

"Where'd you hear that?"

"On the news. It was burning. A Dodge, they think. Took two fire trucks to put it out. They say somebody got to it before the cops did. Not the robbers, somebody else. They found fresh footprints that don't match any from the casino."

"Is that so?"

"If I were you," Lakes said, "I'd lay low for a while. Check into a motel out of town. Get some sleep. Wait for this heat to blow over. I don't know what you're up to, but that's what I'd do."

I took the key to the Suburban out of my pocket and put it on the table next to Lakes's coffee. He shot it a sideways glance and then looked back up at me.

"I'll call you in a few hours," I said. "Get me those records. And get rid of the Suburban. I never want to see it again."

Lakes didn't say a word more. He kept his eyes on me until I was all the way out the door. I checked my watch. Five a.m.

Twenty-five hours to go.

32

GENTING HIGHLANDS, MALAYSIA

So, let me explain how I got into this mess in the first place. Let me tell you about the mistake I made that ended Marcus's career as a jugmarker, put me in his debt for almost five years and nearly got me killed.

We should start with the shotguns.

Our buttonmen, Vincent and Mancini, wouldn't work without them. There was no talking them out of it, either. If they were going to go into a bank, they said, they wanted 12-bore pumps full of double-aught buckshot under their coats. Marcus tried to tell them that in Malaysia it was much easier to find a pair of old Russian assault rifles than it was to get 12-gauge shotguns, but there was no reasoning with them. So we needed a gunrunner.

Liam Harrison was our guy.

He was a fat man of Australian extraction with a shaved head but heavy stubble everywhere else. He had a middling reputation; he'd come through a couple of times before, but he was known on the circuit as more trouble than he was worth. His only recommendations came from friends of friends and hearsay going a couple of years back.

We met out in the Genting Highlands, maybe fifty kilometers out of Kuala Lumpur, a few minutes after dawn. Three of us were handling this part of the job. Hsiu Mei was translating, I was there to check the guns and make the exchange, and Mancini would guard the paper bag with our money in case anything went wrong. Holding a paper bag may not sound like an important job, but believe me, it is. More than one robber has died because somebody wasn't holding the money during a tense deal.

I first caught sight of Harrison when we came around a corner on the mountain road. He slumped against an old white MG Montego behind a clump of trees like he'd been waiting there for hours. He was leaking sweat out of every pore. He had on shorts that came down to his knees, sandals that were caked with mud and an AC/DC T-shirt that hadn't been washed in days. He was holding an open bag of green soy crisps. I could make out the outline of a big handgun tucked into the elastic strap of his waistband.

We pulled up and got out of the car slowly. I left my door open and looked left and right in case Liam had brought anybody with him. We stood a few feet back for a while, careful not to approach too close in case it looked like we were going to try to jump him. Meanwhile, Harrison didn't move an inch.

"You guys lost or something?" he said.

"All the roads look the same around here," Hsiu said.

"You're ten minutes late."

"Clearly you had breakfast plans," Hsiu said. "I hate those little crisps."

"An acquired taste. Do you want to get down to business?"

"Is this a good place?"

"Don't worry about it. The police rarely come out this far on these rural roads. The only people who do are the locals and a handful of tourists taking day trips. There isn't a petrol station or restaurant for ten kilometers. If somebody drives by and sees something, they won't talk. Or if they do, by the time the police arrive we'll be long gone."

"All right," Hsiu said. "How do you want to do this?"

"I'm going to open my trunk and you're going to look inside. Nothing's loaded and the ammunition's hidden. Once you've picked out what you want, we can talk price. Are any of you packing heat right now?"

Hsiu looked at me, and I looked at Mancini. I shook my head. No guns.

"I figured you for bad guys," Harrison said. "Do you mind that I'm carrying?"

"Just no sudden movements," Hsiu said. "And keep it in your pants."

Harrison gave Hsiu a sleazy grin, then went around to the back of his old Montego and put a key in the trunk. He threw the thing open and stood back, so we could get a look.

Harrison's selection wasn't the best I'd ever seen, but it wasn't the worst, either. He had a pile of old plastic pump-action shotguns with white scratches on the gunmetal around the foresight and the magazine-loading port.

"Today's special," Harrison said, "is a pump-action Benelli Super-nova, black tactical pistol grip. It's mostly plastic, but it's got this steel skeleton inside, right? Makes it super-lightweight and durable as hell. You can drop this thing and kick it around and rub sand all over every-thing and it will still fire."

I raised my hand to shut him up, then pulled out a shotgun that weighed about eight pounds and was the length of my outstretched arm, shoulder to fingertips. I opened the action and took a look inside. The gun had a magazine tube for four shots, which was good but not great. Some shotguns can hold up to eight. It was a bulky black thing made of synthetic plastic that felt almost like rubber. I remember thinking how big it felt. It was so big that Harrison had to keep the guns lying sideways in the trunk. Of course, it wouldn't remain this big for long. Mancini was going to take a jewelry saw to the butt and barrel above the forearm grip. By the time we were done, these guns would fit in a briefcase. I listened to the chunk-chunk of the action.

Hsiu looked at me, then at Mancini. He nodded his approval, and so did I. Then she said, "How much?"

"Thirty-five hundred each."

Mancini opened the paper bag of money he'd brought and took out a wad of ringgit notes. He started peeling bills off. Once he had 10,500 counted out, he handed the bills to Hsiu, and Hsiu passed them to Harrison. It was all orchestrated so Harrison would never get within five feet of our bankroll.

"Ammo?" Hsiu said.

"I've got two-and-a-half-inch Magnum double-aught buckshot, high wad, factory-pressed. Box of twenty-five for five hundred."

"We'll want two boxes."

"I want to see you guys lock the guns in your trunk first. After that I'll give you the ammo. Understand?"

Hsiu shot me a look. I nodded, and slipped past Harrison and picked out the three best-looking shotguns from the pile and carried them like a load of lumber back to our car. I laid them sideways in the trunk, then closed it. I felt everyone's eyes on me the whole time.

Something was wrong.

I don't get premonitions, but I can sense danger. Every good ghost-man has that instinct, because a big part of the job is knowing when to get out. I've walked away from jobs before because something felt sideways, and I had the same feeling now. I knew, right then and there, that Harrison was pulling something over on us. I just didn't know what yet, and I didn't have the confidence to tell Hsiu and Mancini to walk away when everything looked like it was going so well. So instead I leaned against the trunk and waited and watched and tried to calm myself down. I flexed my hand into a fist.

Mancini peeled off more money for the ammunition. He passed it off to Hsiu as before. Harrison snatched the cash from her hands and shoved it in his pants pocket without counting it, then opened the passenger door on his Montego and came back with two big brown boxes of shotgun shells. He tossed me one box, then the other. I caught them and put them in the backseat. I opened one up to verify that he'd sold us the right sort of ammunition and then gave him the thumbs-up.

Harrison wagged a finger at me. "You're the ghostman, aren't you?"

"No," I said. "I'm just the bagman."

"You sure? The bagmen I know don't do heists much."

"What makes you think we're planning one?"

"I hear you're the man to talk to about passports."

"You heard wrong," I said.

"Is that so? I'm told you've got some of the best work available. Real holograms and everything. I heard you people carry passports that could fool a real passport agency."

"No," I said. "Not that good."

"Come on," Harrison said. "Let me at least see."

I just wanted to shut him up. I didn't like talking to him any more than I liked working with him. Everything about him disgusted me—his line of work, his appearance, his breath, his bloody accent. I just wanted to go back to the city and get on with it. In short, I wasn't thinking. I'd been distracted by the strange feeling at the bottom of my stomach.

I took the passport with the name Jack Delton on it out of my jacket pocket and handed it to him. He rubbed the laminate with his fingers to check the texture, then flipped through to the page with my picture on it. He scanned it closely, looked up at me to check the photo and then back at the passport.

"Beautiful work," he said. "Is it pronounced *Dalton* or *Delton?*"

"Delton. Jack Delton."

"Where'd you get this?"

"From a jugmarker," I said. "You done?"

Harrison handed the passport back to me, then winked and grinned like we'd just become best friends. "Yeah," he said. "We're done. You want to sell me one of those, give me a call, okay?"

"Yeah, sure."

I kept an eye on Harrison as I got back in the car. Mancini got in next, and Hsiu last. Before she closed the door, Hsiu gave Harrison a little half-baked salute, as if to say, *It was a pleasure doing business with you.* He returned it, then made an L shape with his fingers and thumb and pointed it at us like he was aiming a gun. He dropped his thumb and muttered, "Pow."

I couldn't shake the odd feeling that we'd done something terribly wrong. I couldn't quite put my finger on it. We started the engine. Hsiu let out a long sigh, like she was glad the deal was over. Mancini clenched and unclenched his fists until he could sit still. I took a long breath and held it. I was also glad it was over. Maybe a little too glad.

Because then it hit me.

It was a sinking feeling. Right then I knew exactly what was wrong with this picture. The realization was like a fifty-caliber bullet ripping through my head and blasting out the other side of my skull. I cursed to myself. If I were a smarter man, I would have figured out what was wrong much sooner. Goddamn it. It was so obvious now. I tried to keep calm.

"Hold on a bit," I said, tapping Hsiu on the shoulder. "I'll be right back."

I got out of the car and held up one hand to shield my eyes from the sun. When he saw me coming back, Harrison got out of his car and gave me a look. He shouted from across the way. "Problem?"

"No," I shouted back. "I just want to ask you something."

I walked briskly to close the distance between us. Harrison took a few steps and leaned against the trunk of his Montego, placing the bag of crisps on the hood and giving me a little smile as I came within talking distance.

"What is it?" he said.

"I want you to clarify something for me."

"I don't offer refunds, if that's what you're after."

"Nothing like that."

I kept walking forward until I was uncomfortably close to him. He held his ground. "Hey, man, I thought we were cool."

"Just one question," I said.

"Okay," he said. "What is it?"

"How'd you know I was carrying a passport?"

I didn't wait for him to respond. Before he could even think about it, I lunged forward and pulled the revolver from his belt. We were less than a foot apart at this point, so I could see the look in his eyes as I turned the gun on him. He tried to grab it back, but it was too late. I cocked the hammer, pushed the barrel into the spot where his gut met up with his ribs and squeezed the trigger. He was close enough that I could smell his breath as I shot him.

Bam.

The bullet took him off his feet. His body dropped and rolled away from me, all the way down the small storm gulch at the side of the road. I could smell the gunpowder and the smoke rising up from the barrel of the gun. The birds took off from the nearby trees.

It happened just like that. One second Harrison was leaning against his car, and the next he was face down in the creek with a bullet in his stomach. He twitched a few times, then stopped. I could see the runoff turn red around him.

It didn't take long for my partners to respond. Mancini opened our trunk and grabbed a shotgun in one fluid motion. One hand pried a shell loose from one of the boxes and shoved it into the loading port while the other hand worked the action by the forearm to chamber the round. By the time my hearing returned, he was ten feet behind me with the gun shouldered in a cross-arm stance, and the foresight was trained at my exact center of mass.

Hsiu took longer. She scrambled from the car and came to a stop a few feet behind Mancini. She said, "What the hell was that?"

I let the .44 Magnum hang loose around my finger by the trigger guard, so they knew I hadn't gone berserk. With my other hand I took the soy crisps off the hood of Harrison's car, turned around slowly and raised a finger to my lips.

Don't say another goddamn word.

Then, as they watched, I pulled a wireless microphone from the crisps bag.

I was wondering why he'd never put a crisp in his mouth, and now I knew why. Inside was a recording device the size of a wallet that had been secured to the inside of the bag with scotch tape. It wasn't the most high-tech device in the world, but it was good enough. At such close range, it probably transmitted every word we said. I dropped it to the ground and crushed it underfoot. Hsiu and Mancini looked on with growing unease.

I said, "We just got made by an undercover cop."

33

ATLANTIC CITY

As I drove, I could see the first rays of light peeking over the skyscrapers. The sunrise wasn't like those big majestic ones they show in travel brochures. It was like a dim lighthouse well offshore whose beam kept getting brighter and brighter. The early-morning fog had settled in and covered everything with salty dew.

My skin was beginning to smell like dried blood.

Lakes's Bentley was a new Continental with a black-on-black paint job and a cream leather interior. It was a fast, expensive toy, with a computer screen in the center of the console that controlled everything. Lakes's music came on when I started the engine. Vivaldi's *Four Seasons.* The engine sounded like a house cat purring.

I refreshed my makeup in the parking lot of the Chelsea Hotel. If Lakes had noticed the difference, Blacker would see through it in a second. It doesn't take long to do this though, once you've put on the disguise. All the big changes were still there from the day before. The hair, the eye color, the glasses, the walk, the voice. I only needed to brush up the age lines and color on my face. When I was done, I looked as good as new. It wasn't quite as convincing without the suit, but I did the best I could.

Ten minutes later, I parked on the street across from the hotel and paid for half an hour in quarters. The coffee shop in the Chelsea lounge was just getting ready for the morning rush. Rebecca Blacker was waiting for me by the bar in one of those plush leather chairs, legs crossed, facing the hotel door like she expected me to be late, which, of course, I was. The cigarette in her hand was burned down to the filter. She saw me right away. Put her hand up like she thought I might not see her.

She dropped her cigarette butt in her coffee cup. "I have to say, Jack, I'm surprised you came."

I didn't say anything, just took the chair opposite her.

She said, "No suit this time?"

"It's at the cleaners," I said. "Isn't there a law against smoking inside?"

"There's one against armed robbery, too, but that doesn't stop people from doing it."

She gave me a look and took out another cigarette. If I didn't know she'd been up all night, I would never have guessed it. Her jacket was wrinkled around the elbows and her shirt was open down to the second button, but her eyes were as sharp as ever and her eyeliner was fresh, as if she'd just put it on. The waves in her hair cascaded smoothly down to her shoulders. The man working at the counter started to come over, but she waved him away.

"I went out to the spot you mentioned on the highway," she said. "You have a nasty habit of running into bad people, you know that? That car you burned belongs to Harrihar Turner."

I shrugged. "I don't know what you're talking about."

"I'm getting damn tired of you saying that."

I shook my head. She wasn't going to get an answer out of me.

Blacker sighed. "Do you have any idea who Harrihar Turner is?"

"He's the one they call Wolf, right?"

"Yeah," she said. "*The* Wolf, like it's some title of nobility. The man likes to pretend he runs this city, and he might well. At one time or another we've had him on murder, meth, heroin, child prostitution and a dozen other things, but nothing ever sticks. He parades around town like he's the mayor."

"Scum, by the sound of it."

"Yeah, but scum with deep pockets. I've lost witnesses to that guy."

"The justice system at work."

She snarled.

"You should see if he's connected to that heist you were talking about," I told her. "A guy like that could easily have tried to knock over a casino."

"You have any basis for that claim?"

"Just the amateur opinion of an interested citizen."

"Come on."

"I didn't promise you anything," I said. "If you think I'm going to hand you this thing on a silver platter, wrapped up just for you with a bow on top, you've got another thing coming. I'm just saying what I'd do, if I were you. Give you a reason to keep me around."

"You're trying to give me a reason not to lock you up."

I nodded. "That too."

Blacker leaned back in her chair. "From my position it looks like you're trying to shift the heat. You're giving me this garbage about Harry Turner so I won't go after Marcus Hayes, but you know I will."

I shook my head. "You've got that all wrong. I hope you catch both of them. I hope you catch everyone involved in this heist and put them in jail forever. If this Wolf guy is half as bad as he sounds, a life sentence is better than he deserves."

She sniffed. "Sure."

"You've got to look in the right place, though. You told me before that you didn't care if Marcus Hayes robbed Fort Knox. Now, the Wolf's somebody you *do* care about. If you can get him for this, it'll be a big score for you."

"Where should I be looking, then, Mystery Man?"

"Find the third shooter," I said. "That should give us something to talk about."

We were quiet then for a moment. Blacker stared right at me and blew smoke. She knew she wasn't going to get much more out of me. I was walking a fine line, after all. She knew I was involved, but I wouldn't say anything that might incriminate me. I had to keep my cool. She understood that. If she wanted my help, she had to play the game. She didn't have to be happy about it, though. She was looking at me the way mothers do when they want their children to shut up.

Then she said, "Who are you, really?"

"We've already been through this."

"Sure we have."

"I told you already."

"No, you told me a story," she said. "Which was bullshit, by the way."

"I am what I said I am. I'm just a guy on vacation."

"I don't have to take this from you, you know."

"No, you don't. But I'm here, and you're here, and that has to mean something."

"It does. It means I know what you're trying to do," she said. "And that's not all I know."

"What else might that include?"

"I know you've got a hidden agenda here. One that you're not telling me. Maybe one that you're not even telling Marcus. You know more than you let on. I think a whole lot more."

"I already told you who I am."

She nodded as if she'd had enough of that line to last a lifetime. I was playing her, sure, and she was playing me right back. For the shortest instant I could see the exhaustion in her eyes.

She tossed the cigarette in her coffee cup and it sizzled. "I know you're not Jack Morton, and I can prove it."

34

Her gaze—fixed directly on me—resembled that of a poker player desperately searching for a tell. She wanted to flush me out, to see if I was lying. The coffee machine made a sound and a group of people came out of an elevator carrying bags. The hotel was beginning to come to life. A guy in leather took the table across from ours and opened up a copy of *The Wall Street Journal.* The morning staff were changing the flower arrangements on the front desk.

"You don't know what you're talking about," I said.

"The Seattle office sent over a couple photographs of the man they saw meeting with Marcus H yesterday," Rebecca said. "He looked like you. He looked a lot like you. Maybe a little too old to be your son, but he could've been a nephew or younger brother. So I ran the number on your driver's license to see if you had a relative around that age. I didn't find any. In fact, I didn't find *you*. Washington State never issued a license to a man with your name and photo, and the home address on your license is an empty lot near Tacoma. So it's a fake. I think your whole identity's a fake."

"You must've got the license wrong."

"I remembered it right," she said. "And you've got a fake ID. That's a felony in some states. And worse, you used that fake ID to lie to a federal agent. People get twenty years for that sort of thing."

"Yeah, but not me."

"What makes you think so?"

"Because you still don't have anything on me."

She didn't even blink.

"The way you remember it," I said, "I showed you my license. But that's not how I remember it. I don't recall showing you anything. In fact, I don't think the license you're talking about ever existed. You can search me. You're not going to find it anywhere. You're crazy if you think I'm going down for this."

Rebecca was quiet. She took her pack off the coffee table and patted out another cigarette. I looked in her coffee cup. There must have been a half a dozen butts in there already.

"So I suppose there's no reason for me to ask who you really are," she said.

"If I were to tell you my name, you wouldn't believe me in a million years."

"Try me."

I shook my head. "You wanted to see me face-to-face for a reason, and it wasn't just to tell me about some car that caught on fire."

"I want to offer you a deal," she said.

I leaned forward.

"I'm going to go out on a limb here and say that I think you're after the money. And you know what? So far, you're the closest one to finding it. But if you do, there's nothing you can do with it. Do you know why? That cash is wired with enough explosives to kill anybody who tries to open it. Did Marcus tell you that?"

I didn't say anything.

"The money's useless, Jack. Unless you have the right codes, there's no chance in hell you can take even a single bill without ruining the whole load. So you might be closest to finding the money, but it won't do you any good. If you try to use it, you're fucked. So let's make a deal.

If you find it, call me and tell me where it is. Once I've retrieved it, you can disappear like you were never here. I'll leave you out of the investigation. I'll say I found the money from an anonymous tip. You won't even be mentioned. This way I'll get the evidence I need, and you'll get a chance to walk away with your life and reputation intact."

"I don't have a reputation," I said. "Somebody just told me that."

"At your age, with your skill? I'd bet anything you do."

I shook my head. It was the main paradox of my profession. I was known as the best in the business, but not at all otherwise. I smiled and let her think what she wanted.

"There's one other thing," she said. "Something I've been thinking about nonstop since you flew in yesterday, but every time I try to reason it out, I get nowhere."

"Yeah?"

"Why did you take Marcus's jet into the airport?"

I was silent.

"After a high-profile heist like this one, you must've known there would be hordes of cops watching all the flights. If you'd wanted to get here anonymously, you would have told your pilot to take you to Philadelphia—or, hell, even Newark. Then you could have driven in or taken the train. It would have taken a few extra hours, sure, but nobody would've blinked an eye once you got here. You'd be totally alone and anonymous. Instead, you took a plane right into the middle of everything. Why'd you do that?"

I kept silent.

"I think you *wanted* to be seen. You wanted someone to know you were here. No, not just anybody, you wanted *the FBI* to know you were here. You wanted us to know of your presence. I just can't figure out why. What could you possibly have gained from that?"

"You," I said.

She gave me a puzzled look.

"I gained *you*," I said. "I got you thinking about Marcus. Once that plane landed, you've been thinking about how Marcus is involved. Now you're thinking about the Wolf. You're connecting the dots."

"Why would you want that?"

"Because I already told you," I said. "I'm not here for Marcus."

"Then what are you here for?"

"The same reason everybody comes here," I said. "I love to gamble."

35

I was light-blinded when I walked out of the Chelsea. The sun had come up hot and fast and the fog was burning off. The whole Boardwalk was coming back to life and the tourists were just hitting the beach. I made my way down the boards until I came to a small breakfast place that was already open. It was a hole in the wall with specials scrawled all over the windows and door. I ordered four eggs and coffee and sat outside, watching the people pass by. I drank four cups and tried to think.

Angela and I used to go to cafés on busy streets and watch people all the time. We'd sit there near a crowded intersection and watch them go through the crosswalk. We'd make notes, sometimes, so we could talk later about the ones we'd noticed. We'd come up with lists of things we observed. We'd pay attention to how people moved their hands when they talked. How they walked. How they wore their clothing. The goal was to see them as they really were, when they didn't know they were being watched. "A person in a café's invisible," she used to say. "Everybody sees, but nobody really *looks*."

I was looking for the Wolf's men.

It was only a matter of time before they found me again. The Wolf wasn't stupid. Even an idiot would've figured out what had happened to Aleksei and Martin by now and sent a crew out to get me. I took a look around to make sure there wasn't anyone within earshot. The Boardwalk was full of sounds that would drown out aural surveillance. Pedicabs clacked on wooden boards. Amusement rides wailed with sirens. Storefronts blasted their radios out the front door at maximum volume.

I flipped open a new phone and dialed Alexander Lakes. He answered on the first ring.

"I got you access," he said, in lieu of a greeting.

"Yeah?"

"I have a phone number that will put you in contact with someone in the police department. Dirty as hell, cautious as can be. This guy likes to meet on his own terms. He's just as careful as you."

"Does this contact have a name?"

"No."

"Not even an alias?"

"You sound surprised. Half the people I work with don't use their real names, including you. This one just doesn't use a fake—he uses no name at all. The way he works, he doesn't need an alias. He's too quick and clean for all that."

"How do you know he's a cop, then? How do you know he really has the access to the things he claims to?"

"He's come through before. You've got to trust him."

"I've never been one for trust. How does he get paid?"

"I dead-dropped the money for him half an hour ago. He'll pick it up when he feels ready."

I looked at my watch. I must have taken a longer breakfast than I thought, because it was almost 7 a.m. already. Definitely late enough to call a cop on the day shift. I said, "So how does he want to do this?"

"You're going to call a number. He'll let it go to voice mail. Once he's checked you out, he'll send you a text message. The text message will give you another number to call, which will hook you up to his phone-over-Internet protocol. Very difficult to trace. He'll give you what you want right there, right then. You'll speak only on the phone. Don't ask about meeting him. For this amount of money, he'll give you about five minutes. After five minutes he'll hang up, whether you're done or not."

"He's careful."

"He's a dirty cop. He knows all the ways he can get caught."

Lakes gave me the number. I memorized it and said it back to him as I pulled a twenty out of my wallet and left it on the table. "Is this guy going to be ready to do business?" I said. "This guy is no use to me asleep."

"He's awake. He's always awake. This guy's the hardest-working dirty cop I'd ever seen."

"Let's hope he never goes clean on us."

"I got you a Honda Accord," Lakes said.

"What color?"

"Red."

"Red's hardly low-profile."

"Compared to the custom midnight-black paint and detail on the hundred-thousand-dollar sports coupe you're flying around in now, this is a goddamn invisibility cloak."

"At what point did you stop calling me 'sir'?"

"About the time you stole my car."

I went back to where I parked the Bentley and took out a different cell phone without hanging up on Lakes. I pounded in the number Lakes had given me. It rang as I walked. The voice-mail message wasn't personalized—just a generic prerecorded voice that said I should leave a message at the beep. I ended the call before the recording started. I put the other phone up to my ear and said to Lakes, "I rang your guy. How long am I going to have to wait for his text?"

"It shouldn't be long. He's got to get to a computer."

"Right."

"Meet me at the diner. We'll swap cars again."

"I might be a while," I said. "I've got to go check out an apartment in the projects."

"Don't let anybody steal my car."

I hung up.

Two seconds later, my second phone beeped and I flipped it open. The sender's number was restricted, and the message was eight capital letters with two dashes between them. I pressed the numbers that corresponded to the letters on the T9 pad, putting in zeroes for the dashes. The phone rang twice before it picked up.

"Hello?" The voice was deep, slow, booming and robotic. He was using a voice changer.

"I hear you have access to information," I said.

"This is correct."

"I'm looking into the theft of a Mazda Miata in Atlantic City. Unresolved case, reported missing sometime in the last two weeks."

There was silence for a bit, almost as if the line had gone dead, but it hadn't. This was a product of the voice changer, I think. A voice changer shifts the tone of human-range sounds down by several octaves. Cheap ones also augment background noises, leading to indecipherable, alien-sounding static on the other end. Expensive voice changers, like this one, edit that out entirely and transmit dead silence.

The voice on the other end said, "There are two hits."

"Tell me."

"A green 2009 Miata was reported stolen from Margate eight days ago and a white '92 Miata yesterday from the Borgata downtown."

The second car wasn't right. It was too old to match the tire tracks out at the airfield, and the date was wrong.

"Tell me about the first one," I said.

"Mazda Miata, 2009, hunter green, New Jersey license plate Xray-Zulu-Victor-nine-three-Hotel. Reported missing from a parking space near Jerome Avenue Park eight days ago at eleven hundred hours. Last seen the previous night around midnight."

"Okay," I said. "Can you delete the report?"

"Done. The hard copy is still in the records, however, if they ever go looking. Anything else?"

"Yeah, one more thing."

"Shoot."

"Can you give me the name of the guy who filed that report?"

"Oh, yeah," the voice said. "A guy named Harry Turner."

36

Shit.

Moreno and Ribbons had stolen one of the Wolf's cars and used it for the heist. Why the hell would they do that? It made no sense to me. My mind raced for explanations, but nothing I could come up with worked. Were Moreno and Ribbons trying to throw off the police or something? If they were, it was a downright stupid plan. Did Marcus order them to do it? I don't think so. It wouldn't accomplish anything except pissing the Wolf off even further.

Huh.

I drove around aimlessly for a while to clear my head before starting off in the direction of Ribbons's scatter. I chewed over the new information like it was a piece of gristle. I couldn't make heads or tails of it.

I was lost in thought when I caught sight of a white Mercedes in my rearview mirror. The windows were tinted, but through the hot sunlight I could make out the faint silhouette of a single driver who kept his head abnormally low near the dash, and his hands at eleven and three on the wheel. I couldn't make out his face, but then again I didn't have to. I knew he was one of the Wolf's men.

That happened fast. I didn't expect the Wolf to find me for another two hours. In a way, though, I was glad that his men had caught up with me again. As long as he kept sending people after me, I knew I was doing something right.

I let the man follow me two cars back from one end of the city to the other. I went south. He went south. I turned left. He turned left. I made it easy for him. I drove slowly and signaled all of my turns. Once I reached the edge of the city I continued along the coast, turning down a thin two-lane road that wound through uninhabitable marshland punctuated with thin intercoastal waterways. Even though there were few other cars on the road, the white Mercedes still chose to follow me. After a few minutes we were in the middle of nowhere and the rest of the traffic had disappeared. It was just me and him. We were maybe five hundred feet apart now with nothing but the ocean beside us. I made it easy for him to see me and follow. I didn't want to shake this tail. No.

I wanted to ask a few questions.

Of course this would've been a lot easier if I still had a gun, and even easier if it weren't broad daylight and anybody out for a leisurely drive could see us. There were no other cars on this stretch of road, but at this time of day somebody could drive by at any minute. This was a problem. I had a plan, and that plan had certain requirements. If the plan went wrong, the last thing I wanted was for some good Samaritan to call 911 on me and for this whole deal to end with a police chase. Hell, even if the plan went perfectly, the trick I had in mind was pretty dangerous. I didn't want anybody to get hurt. At least, nobody who didn't have to.

I looked at my watch. Quarter to 8 a.m. Good god. We'd been at this for almost an hour.

I took my foot off the gas and let myself coast gently.

The trick I had in mind was simple. Now that we were the only two cars on the road, if I were to suddenly come to a stop, say, because of an engine failure, the driver in the white Mercedes would have to make a choice. He would either have to keep going and drive past me, which would mean leaving me behind and possibly losing me, or stopping also, which would mean, out here in the middle of nowhere, that we'd have an encounter. One way or another, I was going to have a conversation with the driver of that car.

I let myself drift along for a good minute or so. The road was smooth and flat. Once I was under ten miles per hour, though, I flicked the hazards on and pulled directly into the center of the road. I tapped the brake and came to a full stop. The engine ticked and cooled.

I kept my eyes on the car behind me. The Mercedes faltered as it came around the bend and into full view. That was the moment of truth—the driver was making his choice to speed up or slow down. The Mercedes closed the distance between us and I watched it grow bigger in the mirrors. He definitely wasn't going to stop. He swerved far out into the right lane to give me some room, but instead of slowing down he was speeding up. Once he was even with me, he honked his horn as if to say, *Screw you, buddy*.

Then I stomped on the gas.

A Bentley Continental has 560 metric horsepower, a twin turbo-charged engine and a top speed around two hundred miles an hour. Needless to say, when I hit the gas, the car took off. I jacked the wheel as if I was going to ram him. The driver panicked. He jerked left to avoid getting hit and instead slammed into the left-lane guardrail facing the ocean. His car tottered on two wheels for a second before the metal finally gave out and the Mercedes careened off the edge. It flipped over once and splashed down into the surf.

I pulled to a stop at the side of the road and got out.

37

KUALA LUMPUR

The first few days after I killed Harrison were tough. Killing a cop is one of the worst things that can happen during a heist. Law enforcement has a knack for bringing cop killers to justice. They spare no expense. Homicides have high clearance rates, and homicides involving the police are even better. Those murders get solved. Period. Every criminal with half a brain knows this.

Of course, we didn't know for sure the guy I killed was a proper cop. Harrison was a white guy, which means he was less likely to be undercover for the Malaysian Royal Police, but that didn't mean he wasn't undercover for somebody or other. He could've been an Interpol agent, or paid informant, or even an FBI attaché. If he were any of those, we could be in just as much trouble. As soon as a body with a badge hits the dirt, the only smart thing to do is run and hide for as long as it takes.

So that's exactly what we did.

We ran.

The whole crew went radio silent less than four hours after the shooting. We were each allowed to keep one phone on in case Marcus called, but we couldn't contact anyone else for any reason. There was a protocol we'd all agreed to follow in case something like this happened. We'd lie low in the city for six days. If Marcus contacted us about resuming the job, we'd do it. If Marcus didn't contact us, however, we'd call the job a wash and get out of the country. For those six days, though, we needed to be completely off grid. We'd leave our scatters only for food and water, nothing else. No phone calls, no Internet, no shopping, no conversations. We'd talk to no one, write to no one and leave no trace of our existence. If you forgot to bring a razor into the scatter with you, you weren't going to shave. We gathered in the Mandarin Oriental for the last time the afternoon right after the shooting. Even though it was daytime, it was raining by then and it felt like night. Alton Hill sat on a couch in the corner, filling his getaway backpack up with stacks of fifty-dollar bills. The rest of us stood around the video-conferencing table and discussed what we would do. There were a lot of sympathetic nods as I described the events out in the Highlands. We generally agreed that I had done the right thing, if a little rashly, so we'd keep an open mind about keeping to the plan. In six days we'd either be back to work planning this heist or halfway across the globe on separate jets, never to see one another again.

When the meeting was over, it took me less than thirty seconds to collect my things and get out of the hotel. My gun was under the pillow and my bag was packed by the door. I slung the duffel over my shoulder and walked out without a second glance. Angela took the same elevator with me, and we watched as the floor numbers steadily counted down. I was nervous because we hadn't been able to get in touch with Marcus. I couldn't stop thinking about that story with the jar of nutmeg. Angela touched my hand. We looked at each other. Once the elevator reached the bottom we'd be strangers again, but for a moment we were simply ourselves. She smiled at me and said, "Does this bank job really mean that much to you?"

"It means everything," I said.

"Then I'm with you," she said. "I have your back, no matter what."

We didn't have to say anything after that. The silence was all we needed. When we reached the lobby, the door chimed and opened.

I went to my scatter the long way, by cab down Jalan Ampang all the way downtown to where it merges into Jalan Gereja. My room was in a small place behind a laundry with a hand-painted sign. When I got there I put my bag next to the door and my gun under my pillow, then sat at the edge of the bed and stared at the wall for what felt like an hour. I watched the sunlight drain away along it until the room was dark. I listened to water gather along the ridge of the showerhead until it formed a large drop and fell. My scatter was empty and plain and cheap and poor. It was everything I wanted and nothing I didn't. I closed my eyes and let myself sleep.

A scatter is more than just a hiding place, you see. It's where a guy gets his head right before the robbery. Everybody has a different approach. Some guys are so stressed they get sick beforehand. They'll spend the whole night coughing and puking and swearing to god they'll never pull another job, but when they wake up the next morning, all of a sudden they're as calm as can be. Some guys try to work themselves into a frenzy. They spend the whole night thinking about their abusive dads or their unfaithful ex-wives or some other thing that gets them mad. That way when the job starts, they're so angry they don't care if they have to hurt someone to get what they want. Some guys fill whole notebooks with lists of stuff they're going to buy, so their greed takes over. Some guys meditate. The result's always the same. Everybody finds a way to deal with the fear, so when they show up on the job they're ready to work. The scatter is as much a mental safeguard as it is a physical one.

Over those six days I translated Ovid's *Ars Amatoria* onto a yellow legal pad. When I was done I read my translation over a few times. It was forced and inelegant. I put my lighter to the corner of the notebook and watched as the fire consumed the words, then put the smoldering ashes in the wastebasket. My translations never flowed as well as I wanted them to. As hard as I tried, I could never make the words feel like my own. They lived only in the moment that I translated them, and died as soon as I put them on the page.

I got a text message from Marcus on the sixth day. *Just a setback*, it said. *Be ready to go on Friday.*

I remember feeling relieved. I was embarrassed about what had happened out there in the Genting Highlands, and to hear the heist was still on made me feel better about it. I'd done the right thing, I told myself. And I stand by that. Killing Harrison was the right thing to do.

But that wasn't my mistake.

My mistake was failing to make sure he was dead.

38

ATLANTIC CITY

The wrecked Mercedes wasn't much to look at—just a pile of steaming metal with the roof battered a few feet into the surf. The rear wheels spun lazily in the air at awkward angles. If it weren't for the sharp, acrid smell of motor oil and burned rubber, it would've been hard to tell how long the car had been there. It was already beginning to look like another feature of the beach. The thin strip of sand between the road and the surf was littered with massive rocks and other inhospitable detritus. Coke bottles. Cigarette packs. Plastic bags. The waves crashed up against the wrecked car and sent bits of white froth and sea trash flying.

I put a hand over my eyes to block the glare off the ocean and took in the view, following the thin line of the horizon from the piers of the distant Boardwalk to the foggy shore farther north. Nobody had walked along this beach in a very long time. I could taste the salt from the ocean spray. If I wanted to, I could just drive off. If the driver didn't come to, it might be days before somebody stumbled across this wreck.

But the guy in the Mercedes did come to. And he started screaming.

It wasn't what you'd imagine, though. He didn't have enough air for that. The sound he made was more like a desperate gurgle. Because the car had landed upside down, the man's head was jammed into the surf and every new wave that came through flooded the interior. He was screaming because he couldn't breathe. If I left him like that, he'd drown in a matter of minutes.

I walked slowly down the hill and waded into the water. The driver's door was stuck pretty bad, so I had to use my foot for leverage. I planted one foot firmly in the sand and tugged on the handle. The door came about halfway open before it got stuck in the sand.

The man was barely conscious. He was strapped in upside down and his safety belt kept him from moving his head clear of the water. I reached over him through the door and unfastened the belt. He fell forward over the steering wheel and started flailing like a hooked fish. I grabbed him by the collar and pulled his head out of the water. Blood was running down his face from a cut in his left eye. Some glass had shattered and sliced him up pretty good. I think his ankle was broken, too, because it was wedged unnaturally between the accelerator and the foot well. I got a better grip and dragged him out through the surf onto the beach.

That's when I saw the gun.

He had a 9mm Beretta with a silencer under his jacket. As soon as I let him go, he went for it. He brought his arm up in a wide arc and pulled on the butt protruding from his shoulder holster. He had a grip on it, but couldn't pull the gun out. The six-inch silencer made it just a little too long and awkward to draw while lying on his back.

I hit him with both fists in the solar plexus. His arms turned to jelly as he gasped and doubled over. The gun fell out then, but I kicked it away. He scrambled after it, so I stomped on his broken ankle.

His scream was primal.

I walked around him, picked up the Beretta out of the sand, pointed it near his face and fired off a round. The bullet made a sound like a whip crack and the gun made a low *cha-chunk* as the cocking slide opened the breach and ejected the spent brass.

The man stopped fighting. He fell onto his back again, writhing in pain. He coughed and coughed until salt water and bloody spit bubbled out of his mouth and he could breathe again. He couldn't speak, though. A shard of broken glass must have cut his tongue right down the center. I could see the frothy blood trickle from the corner of his mouth and up from his lips.

The Wolf's man was a big white guy with plain looks. He didn't look like a tough guy. He was wearing a leather jacket, sure, but his pale baby-blue eyes and round face belonged to a man who was soft on the inside. He looked more like a guy on vacation than a member of a vicious drug gang. I grabbed him by the collar but his jacket ripped in half. Under the expensive leather were prison tattoos. Faded blue-and-black markings. He was covered with gang tags he'd picked up for the price of blood in Marienville or Bayside or someplace. On his left shoulder was a black swastika no bigger from side to side than a silver dollar. Next to it was a bleeding heart with four tears bursting out. I gave up trying to move him and let him fall back against the sand.

We were silent for a second. The breeze came in off the ocean with the sound of seagulls. The Wolf's man was crying blood. It soaked through his eyebrow down his cheek to his neck and spread through his shirt. He spat out a tooth and a wad of bloody phlegm.

"You know," I said, "I love moments like this."

He closed his eyes. I got down on my haunches next to him so we could have a talk. I grabbed his cheek and turned his face toward me. He might have been crying, but it was hard to tell. There was too much blood.

"You hear me?" I said. "I love moments like this. It's all over your face. Right now you're looking at me with more intensity than you've probably put into anything in your whole life. You're fully inside this moment, because you're afraid I'm going to kill you. Do you know how rare that is for me? You're not worrying about your credit-card statement or your mortgage or how many cigarettes you have left before you'll have to buy a new pack. No. Right now every fiber of your being is focused on me and this gun."

I tapped the end of the silencer against his chest. The man was breathing like a machine, practically hyperventilating. His one good eye was as wide open as could be and focused on my face like a laser. I don't think he could stop looking at me if he tried.

I glanced at the wrecked car and then out over the ocean. The air smelled like salt water and gasoline. I breathed in through my nose, relishing it. It reminded me of something, but I wasn't sure what. I let my breath out and looked back down at the Wolf's man.

"I only have one question," I said. "I think you know what it is."

"Tracking device," he said, the blood now gushing through his teeth. He started to reach into one of his pockets. When I saw he wasn't going for another weapon, I let him. He pulled out a simple black cell phone that was still powered on. On the screen was a highlighted portion of a map with a blue arrow showing our exact location.

"Where's the signal coming from?"

"You," he said.

"Is it one of my phones?"

"They put a bug on you."

I took the phone from his hands and moved it around. The location of the dot didn't change. It must've been some sort of GPS tracer, which means the signal could have been coming from almost anything. The Wolf might have slipped it into my clothes or one of my cell phones. I'd seen GPS trackers as small as buttons before. The professional-grade trackers don't even need their own power supply. They can run for weeks on a hearing-aid battery and track a location down to a point the size of an oversized armchair. I sighed and pointed the gun back at the man's chest.

"I'm not going to kill you," I said. "Don't get me wrong, though. I don't particularly mind killing guys like you. I've done it before. But you're going to get through this alive. Consider it my way of thanking you. You see, when I flew in yesterday I was afraid this job was going to be too easy. Before I got off the plane, I was worried that I'd find the heist money right away and I wouldn't get to do anything fun in the process. It's a good thing you guys showed up. Without you in particular, I never would've got to enjoy this moment. All the colors are a little brighter. The air tastes a little better. Even the sand feels good. There's no drug out there that feels like this."

I pressed the gun into his sternum with one hand and went through his pockets with the other. He had a black leather wallet in his left pants pocket. His driver's license said his name was John Grimaldi. He was six feet tall and had an address out in Ventnor. He was just a little over thirty years old. The license had been issued a few years before. In the photo, he was almost handsome. I took the license and threw the wallet on his chest.

"Are they listening to me right now?" I said.

"I don't know."

"I hope they are," I said. "Even if they aren't, I hope you are, John. There's a reason I'm telling you this. The Wolf is going to find you, after all. When he does, he'll want to know what I said. I want you to tell him a few things, okay? I want you to make this clear to him: I don't belong to anybody. I'm not Marcus's man, and I won't be his. I'm just here because I've spent the last six months staring at an empty wall in my apartment and waiting for something interesting to come along. This *is* interesting. I live for moments like this. So if the Wolf wants to stop losing his men one by one, he should leave me alone or make me another offer. This time, however, it had better be interesting."

The man's good eye stared up at me in terror. He nodded with desperate eagerness.

"I hope you remember that, John." I said.

Then I took a look at my watch, pressed the end of the gun against his knee and squeezed the trigger. The silencer made a thump that echoed out over the water. His eye fluttered for a second before he passed out from the pain. I picked up his phone, tossed it into the ocean and walked back up the hill to the Bentley, taking the pistol with me.

I looked at my watch. Eight a.m.

I had twenty-two hours to go.

39

I checked into a small motel at the edge of the city. The desk clerk barely looked at me. It was still only morning, long before any reasonable check-in time, when he handed me the key. It would do for a few hours of anonymous privacy.

After a couple of years in this profession, cheap motels are like your second home. You get used to certain things. The Gideon Bible's always in the same place. The bedsheets all have the same quality. The rooms all have a piney, freshly scrubbed smell at first, but that soon fades into its natural, dirtier musk. This one smelled like ammonia. I took a long breath through my nose, closed the blinds and put the chain on the door. It felt like coming home.

Once I was sure I was alone, I took out my cell phones. It's easy to check a cell phone for added GPS trackers. If it's hardware, it's easy to find. There isn't a whole lot of extra space in there. If it's software, it's easy to turn off. Once the battery is out, it all turns off. First I scrolled through the menu interface to make sure that each phone's built-in GPS transmitter was switched off. They all were. Then I cracked the phones open to see if they had been tampered with. One by one I removed the batteries, SIM cards, fractal antennae and digital-memory cards. Nothing looked out of the ordinary, so I put them all together again. Once I was done, I lay back on the bed for a while and thought it over. They obviously weren't tracking me that way. Huh.

I turned the shower on to make some noise. The water came up slowly from the pipes with a low whine. In the other room I turned on the television with the volume all the way up. I didn't really think that their bug would have audio, but I didn't want to run that risk. After what happened with Harrison in the Genting Highlands all those years ago, I've had nightmares about hidden microphones.

I went through my overnight bag and my clothes after that. It wouldn't have taken much sleight-of-hand for one of the Wolf's operators to slip a transmitter on me. I stood in front of the bathroom mirror and carefully combed over my body. I turned each of my pockets out. I emptied my bag and flipped through my copy of *Metamorphoses*. Nothing.

I gave myself a long hard look in the mirror. After two days with little food and no rest, I was actually beginning to feel as old as I looked. Jack Morton had seen a little too much action lately. It was time to change. I wiped the condensation off the mirror. My makeup was running in the heat.

I took off my clothes and stepped into the shower for a good long while. My arm had developed a string of bruises where Aleksei had struggled to free himself during our fight. They were turning black in the center already.

Once I toweled off, I got my makeup kit out and placed the ID card I'd taken off the man in the Mercedes in the corner of the bathroom mirror. I focused on his face for a while and tried to mimic his fearful yet confident expression. He had deep, sunken eyes and an empty, black-and-white pallor. Even though he lived in a beach town, he didn't have the slightest hint of a tan. He looked lost, somehow.

"They put a bug on you," I said in his voice.

I repeated the phrase twice, perfectly. After a few seconds I could feel the age shedding off me. I took a breath and it felt fuller. My shoulders straightened up and my eyes became a little brighter. My joints lost their arthritic tremble and my smile lost its practiced character. I flexed my hands until they felt young again. When I spoke, I had his soft Atlantic City accent. I said, "My name's John Grimaldi."

John's palette was black. That black leather jacket made him look like he was on his way to a club. He was a stylish guy who didn't mind if he had to sweat for it. I used some hair dye and a lot of gel to turn my hair black and slick it down flat. I drew in a widow's peak with a small makeup pencil.

"My name's John Grimaldi," I said. "But you can call me Jack. I'm from Atlantic City, New Jersey. I do a lot of different things, you know?"

As I put my clothes back on, I couldn't stop thinking about this bug he said they'd placed on me. As long it was active, I was in danger. The next men the Wolf sent wouldn't have orders to follow me around at a safe distance. The next men he sent would have orders to kill me. It didn't matter how anonymous the motel was. If they tracked me here, I was dead meat.

I could only think of one more place it could be hidden.

I packed my things into the overnight bag and smoothed the wrinkles out of my clothes. I left the key to the room under the welcome mat and walked over to the Bentley.

It's easy to track a car. Most have built-in GPS devices anyway so the owner can track the vehicle's location remotely if the car's ever stolen. Even if those features are disabled, however, an add-on tracker like LoJack can be very difficult to find. They're small enough to fit almost anywhere and there are hundreds of places you could hide one in a car. Before I got back in the Bentley, I circled around and ran my hand under the bumpers and along the grille. I checked under the seats, in the glove box and in the trunk.

I only found the tracking device when I got on my knees and looked at the undercarriage. It was a two-by-three-inch white box attached to the chassis between the left tire well and the wheel by some sort of heavy-duty adhesive. It had a durable rubberized exterior and a glowing green light. Goddamn.

Alexander Lakes had sold me out. I cursed and shook my head. He must have been tracking all the cars he gave me. That was the only way the Wolf could have got to me so fast. The more I thought about it, the more sense it made. Of course he worked for the Wolf. Everybody in this whole goddamn town did.

I pried the device off with my knife. It was very light. I slipped the knife through the gap in the plastic and pushed until the light on the device went out and the signal died. I looked at my watch. Eleven a.m. I had been at the motel for three hours.

Nineteen hours to go.

40

KUALA LUMPUR

I had no idea how bad that heist would go. I don't recall much of what happened in the days that led up to the job, but I remember feeling both confident and scared. Fear is part of the job, of course. Anybody who isn't scared to walk into a bank with a gun is nuts. But we'd all done this before, so I thought I knew what I was getting myself into. I thought I knew the routine. I thought I knew the bank. I thought I knew the people I was working with. I thought I knew the mistake I'd made, and I thought I knew the risks involved with that.

I had no idea.

At seven on the morning of the heist, the wheelman came to pick me up from a prearranged pickup point not far from my scatter in an old panel van. The detail on the side was in a mix of Malay, English and Arabic with an address for a window-cleaning company down in Subang Jaya. Window-cleaning companies get something of a free pass while driving around urban centers. The guys who run parking lots and do building security tend to cut them more slack than they probably deserve, because nobody wants a job that involves hanging from a wire forty stories up and cleaning shit all day. Alton nodded at me with a cigarette between his lips from the driver's seat as I opened the rear doors and climbed in the back. His black gloves made a stretching sound on the wheel.

This was the plan—the wheelman would pick us all up from different places around the city, we'd do the job and then we'd leave the country right away. It was much riskier now after what had happened in the Highlands, but we were all willing to take that risk. It took an hour to pick everyone up. We met Angela at the loading dock behind the Crown Plaza. We got Vincent and Mancini by a bus stop in the business district, under a billboard advertising a cell phone. Joe Landis and Hsiu Mei were having breakfast in a coffee shop out by the forest.

Everyone was feeling good about the job except Angela. Usually she bubbles with manic energy before a job, but not this time. Now she was cold and distant, staring off through the van windshield as she chewed a stick of nicotine gum. I wanted more than anything else to talk to her, but I knew it wasn't the right time for that. She needed the silence.

Once everybody was in the van, we parked in an empty lot down the street from the Bank of Wales building and started getting into disguise. Vincent, Mancini and I were going in as security guards. We had hats with an armored-car company's logo and dark sunglasses to cover our eyes. We pulled the baggy uniforms on over our clothes so we could rip them off in twenty seconds flat in the elevator and change into a different costume for the bank floor. Mancini fitted himself with a nylon shotgun rig. I watched as he took one of the shotguns out of the bag, loaded four bright red double-aught buck shells into the loading port and then slid the gun into the apparatus. Next to that was a bandolier of small, powerful tear-gas grenades. Once the uniform was on, though, it didn't look like he was carrying anything at all. He took out a box of shotgun shells and poured extras into each of his six pockets.

"How much longer are we going to wait here?" Hsiu said.

"Don't you have a watch?"

"I mean," she said, "just what are we waiting for, exactly?"

Angela squeezed forward and pointed at the satellite phone on the dashboard.

I'm not sure how long we sat there, but it probably felt longer than it really was. We could all smell one another. Grease and gasoline, cigarettes and alcohol, clove and coriander and black pepper. Every little sound was amplified by the tight quarters. Alton took out a cigarette, but Joe Landis immediately put a hand over his lighter.

"Do you have any idea how much nitroglycerine I have in my bag?"

The wheelman made a face and flicked the unlit cigarette out the window. He said, "You mean I can't get a smoke until this whole thing is over?"

"Here," Vincent said. "We've got something for you."

Mancini took a small vial out of his pocket and shook out about a quarter gram of cocaine onto the cardboard box holding the shotgun shells. He shaped the coke into messy lines with the edge of his pinkie finger and sent the first one up his nose. Vincent went next, then Joe and Alton. I sat there and listened to them until the vial was empty.

The satellite phone on the dashboard rang and vibrated. Nobody answered it; we just let it ring. We all knew it was Marcus, letting us know exactly what time it was and exactly how long we had before the point of no return. If there was a problem of any kind, we could've picked up the phone right then and told him. If we were running late, he'd adjust the timetable. When the phone stopped ringing, we knew exactly how long we had.

We had two minutes.

Alton started the engine and pulled out. The bank was less than a quarter mile away. After Angela and I had cased the joint, we'd decided to break in through the secure elevator. Thirty seconds later, our old panel van rolled down the steep incline into the skyscraper's underground parking garage. The guy at the gate waved us through without a second thought. Like I said, window cleaners always get a pass.

We turned into the lowest of the two subbasement parking levels and pulled into a dark slot not fifty yards away from the secure elevator.

We turned off all the lights and inside the van it was very dark. Now we just had to wait for the first armored truck of the day to arrive. My tritium watch hands glowed an eerie blue.

One minute.

I'd done my research. This elevator was something of a specialty item. Since the vault was on the thirty-fifth floor, the bankers had no easy way of getting shipments of money up that far. The dedicated elevator was their solution. Instead of having armored cars park on the street and walk the cash through the lobby and up using the regular elevators that anybody could take, the deliveries would arrive down here and be sent up on this special dedicated two-point elevator. It was more than secure, of course. The shaft was loaded with motion detectors, so nobody could climb up, and it only stopped on this level and Thirty-five, which severely restricted access. The compartment itself had walls made of tempered steel and an emergency satellite phone that would connect automatically to the Royal Malaysian Police if the elevator ever stopped unexpectedly. The lift system had two high-tensile chromium cords, a magnetic safe lock and four emergency manual wall brakes so nobody could break in and get the money. And best of all, to get the thing to go, a bank manager at the top and an armored-car driver at the bottom had to look at each other over closed-circuit television and swipe their ID cards at exactly the same moment. Nobody other than the vault manager and the delivery team would ever see the inside of that lift. I'd seen the schematics. It was one of the most secure elevators in the world.

Today, however, it was our ticket in.

The van was dark and stuffy. Joe tapped his fingernails on the case holding his lock-pick set. He was nervous. We all were.

Thirty seconds.

We heard the armored truck coming. I raised my head and looked out through the dim, eight-inch-square window in the back of the van.

It was an older, cheaper model built on the chassis of a Ford F550 pickup. The windshield was divided into two flat planes of inch-thick bulletproof glass, and the entire body was covered by maybe half an inch of steel armor. There were gun ports in the walls and doors, though not more than usual, and the tires were puncture-proof, sure, but not strong enough to stop a shotgun blast. In the States no self-respecting bank would use such a vehicle, but in Malaysia this was the best they could get. Back then, these deliveries weren't nearly as high-tech as they are today. A lot can change in five years. There were none of those magnetic plates or GPS trackers or streaming color cameras that make modern armored vehicles so impenetrable. The only technology this rig had was a single CB radio in the cockpit, so the truck could go missing for close to thirty minutes without raising any suspicion.

Inside were three men: a driver, a money handler and a guard. The driver would stay in the cockpit and keep the engine running in case they had to make a quick getaway. The money handler would unload the money onto a cart, and the guard would stand outside next to him with a gun drawn to make sure nobody tried anything. We'd all done the research about these guys. The driver was the new guy on the team. He'd been on the job less than six months and had never fired his weapon except on the range. He had his hair cropped tight like a fresh recruit. The money handler, however, was a pro. He'd been doing this for five years, and not much else, apparently. He didn't have a wife or girlfriend and didn't see his family on a regular basis, either. He'd done nothing but deliver money to and from banks and businesses. He had a grim face and small eyes. The guard protecting him was the youngest by several years, though he was more experienced than the driver.

Once the vehicle made a complete stop, the driver put the hand brake on and left the engine idling. The guard opened the passenger door and stepped out and walked around back. He knocked twice on the rear door with his knuckles. The money handler opened the doors from the inside and hoisted a big blue nylon bag of valuables down to him.

Ten seconds.

I could hear the time ticking away on my watch. Angela was breathing hard next to me. She wasn't nervous or anything. She was breathing like that to flood her body with oxygen so she'd be ready to go when the moment came. I kept my eyes glued to the armored truck and the elevator.

The handler passed two more bundles of money down to the guard, who piled them up at his feet. The money handler briefly disappeared from view, then came back pushing a small dolly cart that he rolled haphazardly out of the truck onto the pavement. The driver lit a cigarette, leaned forward to adjust the air conditioning and cracked the door ajar a little, craning his head around to see how things were going. A second later, the money handler hopped down with something I didn't expect—a large black assault rifle with a reflex sight slung by a strap over his back. We hadn't planned for that.

Five seconds.

It was a goddamn G36. Next to a flight wing of police helicopters, that gun was the last thing we wanted to see. It could put out thirty NATO rounds in a little over two seconds. Each bullet could go through our secondhand body armor and out the other side, no sweat. If we didn't do things exactly right, someone was going to die. I stopped breathing.

Time's up.

Angela gave the signal.

Vincent and Mancini jumped out of the back of the van with their shotguns. They charged the armored truck like football players and shouted orders at the guards. Mancini ran toward the money handler and Vincent toward the driver. Before they could register what was happening, our buttonmen were shoving shotguns in their faces.

"Don't move!" Vincent yelled in English, then in broken Malay to make sure he got the point home. He pressed the muzzle of the shotgun to the driver's temple. The man dropped his cigarette and put his hands up right away in surrender.

The other two didn't give up so easily. Mancini had two targets and only one gun, and the money handler had that rifle on his back. When he got close to the truck, he pointed the shotgun at the guard. As a result, the other guy tried to grab the assault rifle off his back. Before he could get a grip, though, Mancini stepped over into melee range and bashed his head in with the butt of his shotgun. The money handler's nose exploded in a torrent of blood and he stumbled backwards. The assault rifle slid under the truck. The other guard threw his hands up in the air.

Hsiu and I jumped out of the van.

Hsiu's job was easy. She had to hold the men hostage. When most people think of hostages, however, they're picturing ropes and handcuffs, but those are crude measures for neutralizing anybody. Do you know how much rope we'd need to tie up thirty people, or even just these three? I don't. Hsiu had an elegant solution: a jet injector. A jet injector is a medical device shaped like a gun, but instead of firing bullets it uses a very powerful blast of pressure to shoot medicine directly through a patient's skin without rupturing it in any way. There's no blood or needle. The medicine goes right through the dermis and instantly into the bloodstream. No switching nozzles, no risk of transmitting HIV/AIDS, no need to clean it between uses. The jet injector just *works*.

Hsiu ran up to where Vincent had the driver pinned and pressed the nozzle of her jet injector under his chin. The gun made a soft pneumatic sound. It took all of two seconds for the tranquilizer to take effect. The driver went as limp as if he'd been shot through the head. One second he was conscious, and the next he was comatose. His body dangled from the door of the armored car.

Hsiu tossed the injector over to Mancini, who pressed it to the forehead of the guy with the busted nose. He dosed him right between the eyes. The guy wobbled for a second and then fell to the floor. Mancini tossed the injector to me as I grabbed the third guard by the collar. I tossed him up against the side of his truck, pulled the gun out of his belt with my free hand and threw it away.

All this happened in the first fifteen seconds.

I pressed the nozzle of the injector against the soft spot of his neck, near the jugular, and said, "I'm not here to hurt you, but I will if I have to. I'm just here for the bank's money, which is insured. No harm will come to you if you do everything I say, got it?"

He stared at me with a blank expression.

"What's the name of the bank manager on duty today?" I asked him.

He started babbling something in Malay that I couldn't understand. His voice had a crisp squeak to it that made him sound like a seal. I slammed his head hard against the back of the truck. He winced and his eyelids fluttered.

"I know you speak English," I said.

"He says he doesn't want to die," Hsiu told me.

"He should act like it, then," I said. "The bank manager's name. Now."

The young man went limp in my hands. He was frozen in fear. I could see it in his eyes when he stared up at me. He didn't look like a man who thought he was going to die. He looked like a man who didn't exactly understand what was happening to him. He gazed at the jet injector in my hand like he was seeing it in a dream.

I moved it from his neck up to the soft spot between his eyebrows. "One more chance," I said.

"His name's Deng Onpang," he muttered.

"What color is the code card today?"

"Red."

"Thank you," I said.

Then I squeezed the trigger—producing another soft pneumatic sound—and fired a load of drugs between his eyes. The young guard stumbled forward and touched the spot on his forehead. He was surprised he wasn't dead. A second later his knees went weak and he crumpled. I caught him in my arms so he wouldn't hit his head and lowered him to the floor. He was comatose by the time he got there.

I pulled the access key cards from his belt and flipped through to the red one. We were not only about the same age but also of similar height and weight. I snatched his company-logo baseball cap and put it on. Given my uniform, I looked a lot like him. The makeup had been easy. Most of it's in the eyes. I'd used eyeliner and tape to mimic the general shape and now adjusted the brim of the cap to cover up the rough parts.

I'd used a tanning spray to match the color of my skin almost perfectly to his. I'd dyed my hair black. Someone would have to be very observant to tell the difference. Now I just had to fool the manager on the other end of that closed-circuit television set.

This was my moment, after all. In order to get the elevator doors to open up, I had to convince Deng Onpang that I was the same guard he'd seen nearly every day for almost three years. I tried to keep the sound of the kid's voice in my head so I wouldn't mess it up over the CCTV. A hat and a costume might make me look like him, but now I needed to sound and act like him. I took a deep breath.

I pressed the call button. The small screen next to the elevator lit up with the face of an older gentleman in an expensive suit. I greeted him with a Malay phrase I'd practiced a thousand times, until I could pronounce it with the perfect accent.

"*Kantung-kantung,*" I said. It means "pouches."

"How much this time?" he said, happily in English.

"I do not know. It is sealed, and my driver has the manifest."

"How is your wife?"

"Things have been better," I said.

I held up the red code card. Deng Onpang did the same, and we swiped at the same time.

Deng said, "The elevator's on its way. See you soon."

"Good," I said. "We'll be ready."

41

ATLANTIC CITY

I was driving to the address Marcus had given me when one of the phones started ringing. I reached over to the passenger's seat and fished it out, then looked at the caller ID. Instead of a number the screen read *FBI* in big blue letters. I flipped the phone open and cradled it between my cheek and my shoulder.

"Yeah?" I said. "You there?"

"Hello? Who is this?" Rebecca Blacker said.

Shit. I forgot I'd switched to John Grimaldi.

"It's me," I said quickly, falling back into Jack Morton's voice.

"You sounded different."

"You know what a good shower can do."

"Better than anyone," she said. "But you're in big trouble, Jack."

She didn't sound menacing or dire, however. She said this with an excited sort of glee, as if she'd just made a particularly savvy chess move. And I could tell by how she said it that *she* was the cause of the trouble she was warning me about. The low growl of her smoking habit wasn't in her voice anymore.

"The good news is you'll get to see me again," she said. "The bad news, well, the Atlantic City Police Department just issued a warrant for your arrest."

"Really? What are they charging me with?"

"You're wanted in connection to a double-homicide last night. Two bodies were found out in the salt marsh this morning with bullet wounds. Both victims took shots to the head, one of them at nearly point-blank range. The car you sent me to last night belonged to one of them, so they linked you to the killings by extension."

I sniffed. "That's all you need to get a warrant these days? I've never even been out in the marshes."

"This is serious, Jack. Did you kill those guys?"

"I don't like killing," I said.

Rebecca sighed and banged the phone against something hard. "It doesn't matter if the warrant won't hold up," she said. "If I want to find you, I'll find you. There will be men looking for you at all the airports and on all the highways. There's going to be a photo of you in every patrol car by the end of the hour. Three hours after that, every police officer for six states will know your face."

"Where the hell did they get a photo of me?"

"Airport security camera."

I cracked a smile. Rebecca Blacker was playing me good. She was the one who filed for the warrant, probably. In the United States, the police have to have a signed affidavit proving probable cause before they can issue an arrest warrant. She was the only person who could've written such an affidavit, or suggested the airport-security photo, or connected me to the murders, or even knew I was in Atlantic City at all. Blacker had put me on the wanted list so I'd have no choice but to play things her way. It was clever, I had to admit. She had something to hold over my head if I didn't cooperate in her investigation.

"You're out of luck, then," I said. "Jack Morton has already skipped town."

"Bullshit."

"Okay, so you've got me," I said. "What do you want?"

"I'm supposed to ask where you are."

"That's not going to happen."

"I'm also supposed to tell you to turn yourself in."

"I like that idea even less. Enough with the act, okay? You got a warrant out on me. Congratulations. Now you've got a bargaining chip. However, if you wanted the ACPD to catch me, you would've triangulated this number instead of punching it into your phone. You're a smart woman. You wouldn't have called me unless you wanted to make a deal. So deal."

"How do you know I haven't already triangulated your phone?"

I looked at the sky through the windshield. "I don't hear or see any helicopters."

"I could've called in a squad car."

"Then I'd know you weren't really trying."

"Okay, here's the deal. I want you to drive out to the field office right now. You need to offer yourself up to the FBI. If you give me all the help I need to resolve the Regency shootings, in return I'll make sure the two bodies in the marsh go down as self-defense. If you don't, I'll give you two counts of first-degree murder."

"You won't ever see me in a jail cell," I said. I didn't mean to sound boastful, but it came out like that and I immediately regretted it. I meant it merely as a matter of fact. I've never been arrested before, and I certainly wasn't going to get caught because of a baseless warrant and a police dragnet. If Rebecca wanted me in handcuffs, she'd have to put them on me herself.

"I hope you know what you're getting yourself into," Rebecca said.

"Police don't scare me."

"I'm not talking about the police. Those murder victims belonged to Harrihar Turner's drug ring. This morning I thought you'd just torched one of his cars. Now his men are dropping like flies. Do you have any idea what that guy's done in the past?"

"I've heard a few stories," I said. "Why would you clear me on self-defense?"

"It isn't the first time those two have been suspected of burying people out in the salt marshes."

"Then I guess I don't have to give you anything after all."

"If you come in, I can protect you."

"I'm flattered," I said, "but I'm fine on my own. I'll call you later and we can meet. But I'm not going to an FBI building, and I'm not turning myself in. I'm still just an interested citizen."

"Not anymore. Now you're a wanted man."

"And I have you to thank for that," I said. "Do you put arrest warrants out on every man you meet?"

"Only the ones I want to catch."

"Okay," I said. "I'll talk to you later."

"If you don't, I'll see you at your trial."

I threw the phone out the window and it flew over the guardrail. Damn, Rebecca Blacker was good. I looked at my watch. Noon.

Eighteen hours to go.

42

The projects are never designed to look like the projects. They're designed to look like anything else—suburbs, developments, apartment houses, you name it. Project housing's a good deal, considering the alternative's a privately owned slum, but a project's still a project. Take a good look and you can smell it. The block of uniform government houses was separated from the rest of the street by a row of short-growth pines and a wood-chip playground. A billboard for fast loans hung low over a row of dumpsters beyond it. Someone had broken all the streetlights. A bad neighborhood just looks like a normal one in the daytime, but the people who live there know what's up. The playground was as empty as a graveyard.

Ribbons's scatter was a cheap hotel next to a pizzeria. There was a sign out front, facing the trash cans, that was hand-lettered by the same guy who did the one for the pizzeria. Hotel Cassandra, color TV, weekly rates. There was no manager's office I could see. The front door had mail slots with handwritten names under them. The graffiti on the stucco walls looked like bad modern art. The ground-floor windows were covered with bars.

Even rich crooks get cheap scatters. The poor can live anonymously better than rich people. Slumlords don't ask for pay stubs, references or two forms of photo identification. All they want is cash for two weeks in advance.

I walked inside.

Ribbons's room was on the first floor up a short flight of stairs and down a dusty hallway under a burned-out light. His number was nailed just above the peephole. There were small cracks in the door near the handle, where somebody with a very long screwdriver and a considerable amount of upper-body strength had used leverage to pry open the dead bolt. The wood around the lock went first, and the force had pushed the dull steel bolt through the frame and out the other side. Everything snaps with enough pressure. I took a step back.

The police don't open doors with three-foot screwdrivers. When they go to serve a search warrant on someone who isn't home, nine times out of ten they go in with a master key they might have picked up from a neighbor or the landlord. When that doesn't work, they use a lock pick. When neither of those work, they occasionally use a fireman's tool or battering ram to get through the door, but those two things are last resorts and leave a very different breakage pattern. No, it wasn't the police who did this. Somebody else had got here before me.

I looked left and right down the hallway. Opening a dead bolt using leverage is very loud. It would have been loud enough to draw attention from occupants of nearby rooms, but even if they heard they probably didn't do anything. I could hear a television playing in the unit across the hall. Nobody calls the police anymore. They never help.

I took out Grimaldi's gun and checked the silencer, then pushed the door open slowly with my left foot. It swung open lazily on the hinge and made a sound like fingernails on a chalkboard. I scanned the area before taking a step inside. I cleared the main room first, then the bathroom and the kitchen. There was no bedroom. The main room had a fold-out cot in front of an old color television. The vertical bars over the windows cast long shadows over the floor. I checked the closet and in the refrigerator.

Nobody home.

I put my gun away and closed the door.

Ribbons had been fastidious. I'd expected his scatter to be a mess of old rolling papers, pizza boxes and empty beer cans, but instead it was as empty and clean as a prison cell. The walls were bare, and his clothes were packed in a small black Samsonite case on the floor. Sheets were clumped up at the bottom of the cot, and the trash was tied up in bags by the door. The whole place reeked of ammonia and Lysol, as if it had just been cleaned.

I started going through his stuff. I pulled the sheets off the cot. I pulled the drawers out of the dresser. I shot through his kitchen. There was a hot plate next to the fridge and a single pan, spoon, fork and knife in the sink. There were two empty cans of chicken noodle soup in the trash. I checked each of the kitchen drawers. They were all empty. I did the bathroom next. Next to the sink was a box full of razor-blade cartridges, but no razor or shaving cream. In the shower was a single bar of soap, still in its wrapper. Under the sink was a bottle of cleaner and a couple of spare rolls of toilet paper. In the mirror, wedged between the glass and the frame, was a picture of an older black woman I assumed was Ribbons's mother, and a real estate agent's business card with some number written on it in blue ink. I took the card and flipped it over. On the back was written, *Blue Victorian, Virginia.*

Drug users know all sorts of places to hide things. Headshops sell stash jars that look and feel like normal household products but contain secret compartments. I've seen shaving cream bottles that really produce shaving cream, but also have a false bottom for stashing cocaine. A motel room's a goldmine. Behind the refrigerator. Under the vegetable crisper. In the toilet tank. Inside a ceiling light. I made an inventory and checked each spot. I worked my way back into the main room and took another look at Ribbons's luggage. I didn't bother trying to guess the combination on the zipper lock. I put the bag on the bed and pulled at the zipper until it tore free.

Inside was a Colt .38 Saturday night–special revolver. It was an old model, matte-black, with a hammer spur filed down to a nub. They call this a "pillowcase gun." The hammer spur has to be filed down like that so it doesn't get caught on some pillow fabric, cock back and blow your brains out. The butt was wrapped twice over in duct tape. There was rust under the finish from years of neglect. The registration numbers were a distant memory. I checked the cylinders—six bullets—and dropped the old brass in the trash. Next to the pistol was a black cylinder as thick as a soda can and twice as long. It was heavy and had four large holes at the ends, three on one side and one on the other. I recognized it immediately.

It was an Uzi suppressor.

There's no such thing as a silencer, in the literal sense. A gun always makes noise, because the expanding gases that drive the bullet break the sound barrier when it leaves the barrel. A suppressor cools and absorbs some of those gases so the shot isn't quite so loud. Even a very good suppressor, though, doesn't make that polite little spit it does in the movies—more like a whip crack or a phonebook falling on a cement floor. The purpose of a suppressor isn't to take somebody down quietly. The purpose of a suppressor is to keep the shooter from going deaf when he uses it.

Under the suppressor were various bits of clothing. One sweatshirt. One pair of sweatpants. One knit cap. One basketball jersey. One pair of faded sneakers. Two pairs of jeans. I closed the bag and took another look around the room. No phone. No computer. No cash. No bag for personals. I checked the pockets of his clothes and all of them were empty.

Ribbons truly respected the scatter.

He hadn't been living here long, though. Even lifetime criminals hang movie posters on the walls and keep spare toothbrushes in a cup next to the sink. Ribbons hadn't even taken his clothes out of his suitcase. He'd left them there beside the bed, still folded, ready to go at a moment's notice.

His place looked pretty much like mine.

I took out the cell phone in my pocket and pounded in a few numbers. I pressed the green button but the call didn't even ring. It just gave me the quick-paced disconnected symbol. I checked to make sure I had the number right. His realtor didn't want to be reached, clearly. I was about to put the phone away when a thought struck me.

It's hard to describe it. One moment I was walking out the door of Ribbons's scatter with nothing, and the next moment there was a slide-show of things I'd seen playing in my head. Little pieces of information popped up and then disappeared so fast I could barely remember them. The map of the city I'd memorized. The pills and money in Ribbons's getaway pack. The bent heroin spoon in the shot-up Dodge. The numbers written on the back of the realtor's card. The Uzi and the silencer left in oddly different places. The Wolf's cryptic story about the little girl. *Virginia*.

I put in Marcus's number.

The phone rang, then the familiar Midwestern voice answered. "You've reached the Five Star."

"I'm looking for Marcus. It's the ghost."

There was a delay while he carried the phone back to him. I could hear every footstep and every clang of the kitchen equipment.

When Marcus finally spoke, his voice was on the edge of collapse. "Jack?" he said.

"Marcus," I said. "I know where the money is."

43

Here's how I explained it to him. Every for-sale house in the United States has a number. Not just a street address, but another number as well. A code, of sorts, called a MLS, for Multiple Listing Service. When a realtor puts a house on the market it gets a six- or seven-digit number which allows any realtor in the country to look it up off a database so, for example, an agent who lives in Philadelphia can look at houses for sale in Atlantic City without having to drive out there.

Ever since the economy went into the toilet, however, there have been hundreds of thousands of houses on the market that nobody wants. Everybody's selling but nobody's buying. This goes for fore-closed houses, especially. They sit there with For Sale signs for a few dozen months, then start to rot. And an abandoned house is the perfect place to hide out after a heist. The people who used to live there are long gone, and there's no chance that someone might come around to look at it after so long. It can be hard to find one out of the blue, but it's a lot easier if you know a dirty real-estate agent or bank-property manager willing to "rent" you the place for a short period of time under the table.

The seven digits on the back of that business card weren't a phone number. They were the number for a house. And Virginia isn't just a state. It's also the name of an avenue in Atlantic City.

"But do you have anything to back up this theory of yours?" Marcus said.

"I'll go check it out now."

"I don't want promises. I want to hear you've got the money, and then I want to hear that you've buried it so deep you'd need an excavator to get it out."

"It won't be long," I said. "This is the sort of place I'd go if I were on the run."

"But Ribbons isn't you. You're good at this."

"There's no need to remind me."

I could imagine Marcus chewing his lip. "Has the Wolf given you any more trouble?"

"Not for a few hours now."

"Let me know if anything happens. I want to be done with the East Coast as soon as possible."

"Got it."

I shut the phone, stripped out the battery and dropped it in a trashcan down the hallway. I carried the rest of the phone a little farther, snapped it in half, then tossed the pieces down a storm drain.

I got back to the car. I cranked the engine and turned on the GPS device in the dash. I wanted to be absolutely sure where I was going. I pressed the buttons and scanned the city from the sky. I looked up and down the length of Virginia Avenue, then took another cell phone out of my pack and powered it up. Once the screen went white, I started dialing the Wolf's number. The phone rang once. Twice. Three times.

"Hello?"

"Hello," I said back, "who is this?"

It wasn't the Wolf. The voice on the other end of the line was thick and gravelly. The connection was poor. I waited for the line to clear up, but it didn't. All I could hear was the rush of the car under me and the rumble of a thick male voice.

"Nobody. Who the fuck are you?" the man said.

"This is the ghostman. I want to talk to the Wolf."

"He doesn't want to talk to you. In fact, when he finds you he's gonna take a hammer to all of your fingers."

"Believe me, he wants to talk to me."

"You're a walking dead man, you know that?"

"Yeah. But I'm a very rich dead man."

There was a pause.

The guy was thinking, breathing heavily. After I moment I heard the sound of the phone rub up against some fabric. A few seconds later there was the sharp sound of the phone changing hands and someone else drawing his breath.

"What do you want?" the Wolf said.

"I want to make a deal."

44

The line went silent for a moment, and I could hear people talking quietly in the background. The connection still wasn't any good and I couldn't make out the words, but it sounded like the Wolf was speaking to one or two other people in the room with his hand wrapped around the phone to mask his conversation.

After a moment, the Wolf came back on and said, "You must have a death wish, Ghostman."

"Can I tell you what I'm suggesting?"

"No, you fuck. You think you can kill two of my men, hospitalize another, total two of my cars and walk away alive? You've made your last mistake, Ghostman. I'll sink you into the salt bog myself."

"Like I just said, I want to make a deal."

"You have ten seconds before I hang up and tell every man I've got to bring me your heart in a Mason jar."

"I've got something you want, though, and I want to offer you a chance to get it. I think you have to make a deal with me, because otherwise you'll face dire consequences. If you work with me, you win. If you don't, you lose."

"What makes you think I'd deal with you after what you've done?"

"Because I know where the money is, and you're a smart man."

"A smart man would as soon put a bullet between your eyes as look at you," the Wolf said. "A smart man would know exactly how dangerous you really are and put you down before you kill anybody else."

"Then let me give you another reason," I said.

"What?"

"You want to destroy Marcus more than you want to punish me, and I'm the best shot you've got to make that happen."

"You make a lot of presumptions, Ghostman."

"But I'm not wrong."

There was a brief moment of silence. For all the tough talk, the Wolf was a rational, intelligent man. The vitriol just gave him more time to think. He knew I was right. I wasn't his biggest problem. If he could make Marcus my enemy, he'd forget about the three bodies and two cars in a New York second.

"Your voice is different," the Wolf said.

"I changed it."

"So what do you want?" he said.

"I want two hundred thousand dollars in cash or bearer bonds."

He snorted. "You're out of your fucking mind."

"That's my offer."

"You think too highly of yourself. I might be willing to offer you your life for Marcus's head on a platter, but nothing else."

"Threatening to kill me won't get you anywhere. I got away from your men out in the salt marsh without even trying. I don't think you could catch me if you put everyone in your whole organization on my case. So if you want Marcus out of the way, you're going to pay me two hundred grand. Otherwise I'll bury the money, let it explode at the bottom of a hole somewhere and walk off like nothing happened. That's my offer."

"I'd rather see you dead."

"Then this is the last you'll ever hear of me," I said. "Send Marcus my regards from prison. I'm pinning the heist on you."

"How do you suppose you'll do that?"

"I can make sure the money gets stashed away in a place that's very important to you. That way, when it blows, the cops will swarm down over your operation like angels on Judgment Day."

"You think you can blackmail me?"

"Yeah," I said. "I think I can."

The Wolf was silent for a moment, which was strange. He didn't just stop talking, he stopped breathing.

"Hello?" I said.

"I'll give you a hundred thousand," the Wolf said.

"Two hundred. That's less than a fifth of what's in the federal payload. Don't make me drive this hard, Harry. I don't have a care in the world. I've already got the money. You shouldn't try to push me around."

"Is that a threat?"

"Depends on your counteroffer."

"I can give you fifty grand tonight, then another hundred on Monday. Any more would be reckless."

"Like hell," I said. "I'm not staying in this shithole until Monday. Two hundred grand tonight, or I walk."

"The banks are closed, Ghostman. I can't get that kind of cash together until they open. My bankroll isn't liquid. I don't keep big piles of cash just sitting around."

"You don't? That makes you the first drug dealer in history who doesn't have a cash problem. You know the Colombians have to build extra houses just to store all that money? You heard my price. Now cut the bullshit."

"One-fifty tonight, but no more. If you want more than that, I'll see you in hell."

I was silent for a moment, then said, "Okay, I can live with that."

The Wolf made a sound somewhere between a sigh and a grunt. "Come to my suite in the Atlantic Regency in a few hours. I'll have your money waiting."

"You have a suite in the Regency? What a coincidence."

"You sound like you don't trust me."

"Your man just said you'd break all my fingers with a hammer. No, of course I don't. I wouldn't trust you for the time of day."

"I own the title to an abandoned strip club on the corner of Kentucky Avenue and North Martin Luther King Boulevard. We can meet there."

"I'm going to choose the place," I said.

"You've negotiated as far as you're going to get today, Ghostman," the Wolf said. "Let's not continue this game, shall we? You'll do the deal on my terms or you won't do the deal at all. If you think I'm intimidated, you're gravely mistaken. You will bring the federal payload to my club, alone, or the next time you see me will be through a cloud of spray paint and a plastic bag. Now, are you in or are you out?"

I was quiet, just to make him wait.

"You've got yourself a bargain," I said.

45

Ribbons's house was a one-story on North Virginia Avenue fifteen
blocks from the Boardwalk. It didn't take me long at all to find it. The
place couldn't have been more than twenty blocks from the Regency
and I knew where to look. The neighborhood was strangely nice. If I'd
just been driving down the street, I never would've imagined Ribbons
ending up here. The pavement was wide and smooth, and the shrub
pines lining the sidewalk rustled in the sea breeze. People with real jobs
lived in this neighborhood. People in neighborhoods like this had health
insurance and retirement accounts and children playing in their yards.
Ribbons had been hiding out in plain sight. He picked a spot where no
one would think to look for a strung-out junkie with one or more bullets
in him.

After driving up and down the street for a while, I spotted the blue
Victorian. I parked across from it and winced at the glare when I got out.
The house itself was hideous. It looked like it had once been a grand
summer home, but hardly any of its former beauty remained. The front
door had plywood nailed over it, as did most of the windows. A large
wooden For Sale sign was stuck in the lawn behind the mailbox, but
it was slowly rotting from salt erosion and covered in graffiti tags, so I

couldn't see the name of the realtor. The house paint had peeled away to almost nothing, and the windows on the second floor were smashed out and were open to the elements. I looked up at it and whistled.

I'm a connoisseur of hiding places and this one was great. First off, domestic residences are wonderful, and not just because they're protected from searches by constitutional law. Ribbons could stay in there for days without much discomfort, and nobody would wonder much if he came and went. Second, it didn't have a paper trail. The only person who could link him to this house definitively was the real-estate agent he'd bribed to get the address. Third, it didn't fit the profile. It was in a neighborhood just a little too nice to attract the kind of police scrutiny that could ruin the whole arrangement, but not so nice that people would notice him living there. The place was *perfect*.

And Ribbons's stolen hunter-green 2009 Mazda Miata was sitting beside it.

The car had been through hell. The front lights were smashed out and there was a dent over the left-side door as long as a small desk. The vehicle was parked halfway behind the bushes in such a way that the license plate was facing away from the street. I could make out little specks of blood and dirt on the driver's-side window. The car was there, but Ribbons wasn't in it, of course. At least he'd made it inside. I'd hate to die in a Japanese car.

I walked up and kicked the front door hard enough to knock the bolt through the frame. The door practically fell off its hinges. Then I gave the plywood a couple kicks and the whole mess caved in on itself.

As I said, the place had once been beautiful. The wallpaper was an expensive floral pattern full of lush leaves and ripe fruits. Along the ceilings ran ornate crown molding, depicting plum vines twisting off in all directions. It was beautifully done, but the walls were dark and stained brown with watermarks and the lights were all broken. In one corner someone had spray-painted *Nothing is stronger than habit*.

The inside of the house was dark and hot and wet and rotten. Thick particles of dust hung in the air, and it took a moment for my eyes to adjust to the darkness. I flipped the nearest light switch, but nothing happened.

There was a trail of black blood dried into the carpet.

Right after I saw the blood, the smell hit me all at once—something like rotting fish, feces and gunpowder. The drops of blood got more frequent toward the center of the house, down a short hallway and past a closet and bathroom. It looked like someone had painted a long black brushstroke on the carpet.

Ribbons.

His Kalashnikov was leaning against the doorframe. The action was blocked with blood and covered with gunpowder residue. There were other things strewn along the blood trail. A latex glove. A Colt 1911 magazine. A 7.62×39mm bullet. A black ski mask.

He was here, all right.

And he was still alive.

46

When I found him, Ribbons looked more like a corpse than a human being. His eyes were glazed over and his breath was shallow. The rise and fall of his chest was the only sign that he was still alive at all. His voice was a hoarse, parched whisper.

"Water," he said.

He was slumped against a wall in the living room in a pool of blood. His Kevlar vest and sweatshirt were soaked. His face was pallid and his feet were swollen. He looked peaceful, except for his eyes. They were leaking a green pus from the sides. The bullet had hit him three or four inches or so above the belly button and punched a hole through his vest. Two other bullets that hadn't gone through were safely lodged in the vest. I could see the dots of crumpled lead sticking out from the ceramic trauma plates. A long streak of blood ran along the wall where he'd fallen against it and slid into his current position. The blood was now so old that it was beginning to turn black.

Most people shot in the chest don't last fifteen minutes. The hydrochloric acid in the stomach usually leaks out into the blood, you see. This causes some sort of shock, which kills fast. The victim goes into a coma and dies minutes later. This bullet, however, hadn't reached the stomach. The vest had slowed it down too much. It had come to a slow stop in Ribbons's fat without ever reaching his intestines. It was still lodged inside his abdomen and slowly cutting farther into him every time he breathed.

Maybe twenty hours ago a surgeon, a very good surgeon, could've saved him. Not now. The color was already gone from his face. The gunk forming in his eyes was a sign of infection. So was the sound in his lungs. Now he was just waiting to die.

"Cop?" he whispered.

"No," I said. "Father sent me."

"Water," he said. "Please."

I didn't respond. Just stood there.

"Water."

I looked back down the hall. I told myself I was looking for the money, but that wasn't it. If the money were in the hallway, I would've noticed it already.

"Please," he said. "Water."

Ribbons's face was marked with dried blood and his hands were caked with it. His lips were as dry as sand. He made eye contact with me and his gaze didn't waver. "Please, man," he said.

"Where did you put the money, Ribbons?"

"Please."

"I need the money first," I said.

Ribbons didn't say anything. His fingers twitched and he pointed farther down the hallway. I turned my head and followed the line of his gesture out of the room, down the hallway, then stood up and went that way, deeper into the silent house. The bedroom still had an old bed frame and dresser, but it felt empty, and all the shadows gave me a sense of unease. Ribbons had never gotten a chance to live here. The place never had a soul.

I waded through the darkness by sense of touch. The light from outside came through the cracks in the plywood like red laser beams. In the distance I could hear cars rushing along the highway.

The money was in the closet.

I knew what it was without having to open the bloodstained blue Kevlar bag. I picked it up and started toward the front door, but stopped before I got there. Ribbons could barely lift his head to look at me standing there in the doorframe. It was like he was weighed down by a thousand bricks and every little movement took a monumental effort to complete. His lips moved, but no words came out. Praying, maybe.

"Water," he said.

"Yeah, okay," I said. "I'll get you water."

I left him alone in that room, but just for a minute. The kitchen was two doors down, next to the dining room, and it had a breakfast nook. I waded through the darkness and turned on the tap and it sputtered for a bit, but then water came out. I opened drawers, but they were all empty. I made a makeshift cup with my hands and let them fill with water. I waded back through the shadows to the living room. Ribbons's fingers twitched when he saw what I was doing.

"Please," he said.

I swore and knelt next to him in the pool of blood and vomit. I held my hands to his lips until the water ran into his mouth and down his chin. He drank like he couldn't get enough. He asked for more. I made another trip and gave it to him. I didn't say anything. Just watched him drink. When he was finished, we were silent for a while. The old house creaked and whispered. I knelt next to him and he tried to keep his eyes on me. It was quiet.

Then Ribbons said, "Shot."

"Yeah," I said. "One got through. You're dying."

He shook his head a little and twitched his fingers again. I followed his gaze over to a black nylon bag in the corner of the room, just out of his reach.

"Shot," he whispered.

I pulled the bag over to us. Inside was a box of nitrate gloves, a lighter and a syringe. He slowly and painfully gestured at the side pocket.

Inside was a sandwich-sized plastic bag with a twist-tie filled with a few crumbles of a brown substance the texture of pancake batter.

"Shot," Ribbons gasped.

I was looking at half a gram of heroin.

"Please," he said. "Shot."

There are few things in the world I hate more than heroin. I hate it more than people who sell children for sex. I hate it more than killing a woman. I hate it more than the feeling I get when I've been alone for so long that I have to stare in the mirror and practice speaking until my words sound human again. There are very few things in this world that trigger that part of me, but there it was. In my hand.

Ribbons was asking me to kill him.

A shot of heroin would be fatal. Ribbons had lost enough blood that his system wouldn't be able to handle it. A normal dose would hit him twice as hard, like drinking a whole bottle of tequila after giving blood. Even the smallest amount of junk could cause an overdose or, if it didn't, at least slow his breathing. In his condition, he might suffocate under his own weight. If I left him alone to bleed out on the floor, he might make it another six or seven hours. If I gave him the shot, he'd be dead in a matter of minutes. Seconds, if I didn't get the dose just right. And I wouldn't get the dose just right. I'd never measured out heroin before in my life.

Ribbons didn't take his dull, bloodshot eyes off me the whole time. He breathed in and out. I could hear the sickening sound of the fluid settling at the bottom of his lungs.

"If I give you this," I said, "it won't kill the pain. You've lost too much blood for that. You'll be dead before I can pull the needle out."

His voice was barely a whisper. "Please, man."

I took out the silenced Beretta and put it to his head.

At this range, a single bullet would put him out of his misery before he would know what was happening. He'd be dead instantly. I pressed the barrel into the soft spot between his eyes until I was sure he understood what I was offering him.

Ribbons shook his head.

"Please," he whispered. "Shot."

I hesitated. I could handle putting a bullet in his head, but not this. I'd shot people before. I knew how it would happen. The trigger would resist, then lock back, the hammer would fall, the muzzle would bark and Ribbons's brains would splatter across the wall. It would be like flipping a switch. He wouldn't even feel it. A fatal overdose was something else entirely, though. I didn't know how long it would take. I didn't know how much to give. I wasn't ready for that. I told myself that I didn't want to fuck it up, but that wasn't the real reason I didn't want to do it. That wasn't the real reason at all.

My mother died of a heroin overdose.

Ribbons whispered something, but it was too faint to hear. The sound pulled me out of my thoughts. The pool of blood around him was spreading. It wasn't noticeable before, but I could see it now. Every few minutes it grew a few fractions of a centimeter wider like water from a pinpoint leak in a drainage pipe. His lips were moving but he didn't make a sound. Maybe he was talking to someone who wasn't there. Maybe he was saying good-bye, if only to himself.

His breath wheezed in and out, in and out.

I picked up the heroin off the floor.

There was a soup spoon in the nylon bag next to the ammunition, and a travel pack of cotton swabs. I put the syringe, the heroin and the swabs on the floor next to Ribbons. I took a small amount of the brown substance and placed it in the bowl of the spoon, then carried it into the kitchen and dribbled a little bit of water over it from the tap. I used the lighter and placed the spoon over the flame. It didn't take long for the water to come to a frothing boil and for the heroin to dissolve. I took the spoon off the heat, tore a little bit of cotton off one of the swabs and put it in the spoon. I sunk the needle into the cotton and carefully pulled the heroin solution into the syringe, using the cotton as a filter. I knocked the air bubbles out of the needle and looked up at Ribbons. His mouth opened and closed like a fish gasping for air.

I took off my belt and crawled forward until I was beside him.

He put his right arm between my legs. The blood on his hands smeared onto my pants and soaked my knees. I rolled up his sleeve and slowly wrapped my belt around his upper arm as a tourniquet. I tapped the inside of his elbow until the veins appeared under his skin. He had tracks up through to his shoulder from where he'd shot up again and again. It took me the better part of a minute to find a usable vein. If I missed I might accidentally shoot into his muscles, and his death would be even slower and more painful because the injection itself would burn until the moment the overdose killed him.

I stuck the syringe into his arm. The needle went in sideways along the length of the vein until it hit the dark brown wrinkle where I could tell he'd shot up before. I pulled the plunger back slightly. A little blood went into the needle and blossomed out into the brown liquid like a flower.

"Please," Ribbons whispered.

I couldn't think of anything to say.

I pressed the plunger down. I could see the surface of his skin begin to flush red. Once the syringe was empty, I pulled it out and laid it on the floor. I took my belt off his arm. It was done.

It's hard to watch a man die. A few seconds after I gave him the shot, Ribbons started to feel it. The pain drained away from his face. His eyes opened wide, like he was waking up, and he let out what sounded like a sigh of relief. For a moment, just a moment, all the pain was gone. His pupils tightened up into pinholes and his head rolled back. He stared at the ceiling with such intensity that it looked like he was seeing god himself up there. The moment passed, though. Ribbons's face went red and his eyelids drooped down again. Beads of sweat formed all over him. After a few minutes, he went limp against the wall. Soon the seizure started. His eyes closed and his head slumped down to his chest. His mouth frothed up bits of spit. I watched his breath get slower and slower until the shaking stopped and he was dead.

I was kneeling in a pool of his blood.

I went back to the doorway and picked up the blue lead-lined Kevlar bag. Inside was a little more than $1,200,000, forty GPS trackers and seventy explosive ink packs. I walked out the door and went to the green Mazda Miata in the driveway.

I looked at my watch. Four p.m.

Fourteen hours to go.

47

KUALA LUMPUR

The secure elevator opened right up. Once we were inside, Hsiu took a can of black spray paint from her bag, shook it and fired a long black stream into the camera dome. It didn't matter if security saw the blackout, because nothing could stop that elevator once the cards had been swiped. Once we were in, we were in.

We wasted no time. Once the camera was done, Vincent, Mancini and I dropped to our knees and started changing into our bank costumes. Each of us had a different disguise. Mancini had a baggy old olive-drab military surplus jacket and a black high-fiber balaclava to cover his face. Vincent wore a bright blue shaggy wig, a hooded sweatshirt and a Ronald Reagan mask. I had a black shirt, a tan jacket and a Guy Fawkes mask. Angela had a plain blue pantsuit and a hockey mask. Joe Landis had a full-face welding mask with just enough room for his glasses and Hsiu had a clear plastic thing that obscured all of her features. When we cased the joint, we'd calculated that it would take the secure elevator one minute and twenty seconds to reach the top floor. We could change into our costumes in half that.

The Halloween shit wasn't just for show. Heisters who wear gaudy costumes are less likely to be remembered than robbers who wear plain, forgettable ones. The masks and jackets give hostages something to look at. If the robber wears something bright and flashy, the hostages won't remember anything else. That way, once the costume is discarded, so is the memory of the man. Without the costume, the robber is just another face in the crowd.

I strapped on a pair of white latex gloves. We all had to wear gloves, even though Angela and I didn't even have fingerprints. We didn't want to leave any shred of biological evidence behind, including formless smudges. The only exception was Joe Landis, our boxman, because he couldn't do his job wearing gloves. It takes some serious finesse to open a bank vault, and we weren't about to handicap him. Instead, he had a gallon jug of ammonia. He'd splash that on everything he touched and it would work just as well. While we were getting our gloves on, he was in the back of the elevator attaching an oxygen tube to a six-foot thermal lance.

Vincent nudged me on the arm and held out the butt of the money handler's G36 assault rifle we'd retrieved from under the armored car, as well as a small belt full of magazines. I gave him a look and hung the gun by the strap around my back. I could tell he was beaming at me through his Reagan mask when he cocked the slide on his sawed-off 12 gauge. Mancini gave me the thumbs-up and grunted with similar enthusiasm. They were more than prepared for this. They were *ready to rock*.

I turned away and chewed my lip, watching the floor numbers ratchet slowly up above the control panel. Twenty-five stories. Twenty-six. There was a faint *bing* every time the number changed. Twenty-seven stories. Twenty-eight. Twenty-nine.

My palms were sweating under my gloves. I always get the shakes right before I go into a bank. I closed my eyes and tried to focus all my anger. We were nearly there.

Bing.

The elevator came to a jerking halt and the doors slid open. A young vault manager was waiting for us. She looked up and then froze in fear, dropping the papers she was holding. I don't remember much else about her, but I'll never forget her scream. It wasn't even particularly memorable. Like most, it started like a high-pitched yelp and ended in hysterical sobbing. The timing was what threw me off. During most robberies, it takes a few seconds before someone lets out a yelp. Sometimes there is even this strange pregnant silence through the whole thing because everyone's too shocked and scared to move. But not this time. As soon as the elevator doors opened up, the woman started screaming.

I grabbed her by the hair and threw her into one of the teller windows.

This was a good thing, actually. Malaysia has several different major languages, and her scream transcended all of them. Everyone in the bank knew instantly what was going on, even if they couldn't understand a word of what I was about to say. I swung the assault rifle around and raked the ceiling with a burst of automatic fire.

"Nobody move!" I yelled. "This is a robbery!"

A lot of things happened at once after that. Vincent jumped over the bulletproof plastic shields onto the counter behind them and pointed his shotgun at the tellers. He told them to move away from their stations and not touch the money. There were silent alarm buttons under the counter, and even if the tellers didn't have the nerve to touch those there were passive alarms triggered to the money in the drawers. If ever the last bill was taken out of a cash drawer, the alarm would go off.

At the same time, Mancini took to the main floor. He moved from the back of the bank to the front, pointing his shotgun at everyone in sight and herding them all into the lobby. Once he got to the emergency-stairway exit door, he opened it up, pulled a tear-gas grenade from his bandolier and tossed it through. Within twenty seconds the gas filled the entire stairwell, down at least two stories. Without ventilation, the stuff would stay there for an hour and it would be nearly impossible for anyone to climb up those stairs without a gas mask. As a further measure, Mancini jammed the door closed and sealed it with a heavy-duty bicycle lock. Nobody in, nobody out.

Hsiu stepped out into the lobby and pressed the call buttons on the other four elevators. Two elevators opened up right away. Once the doors were open, she placed a small strip of duct tape over the laser sensors that kept the doors from closing on someone's hand. As long as the tape remained there, these elevators wouldn't move unless released by a fireman's key. They wouldn't time out, either, which means it would be difficult for building security to take them offline or start an override. She coated the cameras over the elevator buttons with a long blast of spray paint. Over the next two minutes she'd wait for the other two elevators to arrive and take them out of commission the same way.

Angela was already in the back. Deng Onpang, the manager, was in his office behind the glass cubicles. She grabbed him by the collar before he got a chance to stand up and promptly slammed his head against the edge of his desk. He reeled and fell to the ground, stunned. We call this sort of treatment a "head jog." If we think somebody is likely to give us trouble or try to trigger an alarm, we open with a blow to the head. It not only lets the guy know we mean business but also discombobulates him and makes it harder for him to act rationally. A guy with a minor concussion won't do shit. Once he was on the ground, Angela pulled Deng's shirt open and ripped the vault and safe-deposit keys from around his neck. Knowing there was a panic button under his desk, she dragged him out of the office by the collar and threw him onto the lobby floor.

Joe didn't waste any time, either. He went straight to the vault door in the southeast corner, near the heart of the skyscraper. In less than twenty seconds he was on his knees and taking his drill equipment out of his bag. There was another vault manager less than two feet from him, but the man was frozen against the wall in total panic. Mancini motioned for him to back off with the muzzle of his shotgun.

I jumped up on the nearest desk and said, "We're not here for your money. We want only the money in the vault. It's insured, so you won't lose anything. If you obey my instructions, you will be unharmed. Now get down on the goddamn floor."

Hsiu echoed me in Malay, although it wasn't strictly necessary. For many purposes, banking included, English was still the language of record. We knew all the managers had at least a working grasp of it. The translation was just to make sure nothing important got lost in the frantic energy of the moment.

I pointed my gun at the people in the lobby. When you're holding an automatic rifle you don't have to be particularly threatening. The gun does most of the talking. They looked up at me in total fear, put their hands up and slowly lowered themselves to their knees. Once most of them were on the floor, I had only a few stragglers to deal with. I went into the glass enclosures where the bank officials worked and dragged the last three managers out from under their desks. Two were Asian, one British. These guys were front-end managers, so we knew they wouldn't have panic buttons or safe-deposit keys. I threw them on the floor like everyone else. I went back into the offices to check again, in case someone was still hiding there. I pulled the cords to their desk phones out of the wall. Once I gave him the all-clear sign, Vincent stepped down from the counter and marched the tellers and the crying vault manager into the crowd that was starting to huddle together in the corner farthest from the elevators. Mancini examined each one. He didn't have to do much else but stand there and look serious. They were as complacent as sheep.

One by one, I checked each of them for hidden weapons, starting with Deng Onpang. I tapped his pockets, shoulders and ankles with my foot. Once he was clear, I moved quickly onto the next hostage, then the next. Time was of the essence here. The whole process took less than half a minute. All told, we had thirteen hostages: two tellers, six other bank employees, two customers and the three armored truck guys whose bodies we'd have to bring up later. None of them were armed, though most had wallets and cell phones.

"Take out your cell phones and remove the batteries," I said. "Slide the phones over to the opposite corner. Don't try to call anyone or send a message of any kind. We're jamming the wireless, so that won't work and will only make us angry. Do it now."

Hsiu echoed me in Malay to make sure everyone understood.

I kept a careful eye on the hostages as they produced their cell phones. We didn't actually have a cell phone–signal jammer, but to claim we did increased the odds of easy compliance. The process went smoothly, for the most part. One of the managers said something in Malay that Hsiu translated as "I don't have one." I was suspicious so I checked his pockets but I didn't find anything, so I left him alone and told Mancini to shoot him up with tranquilizer. I didn't want to take any chances. I stomped on each of their cell phones.

"All clear," I said.

"All clear," Angela said.

Hsiu and Vincent were behind the teller windows. "All clear."

Joe was striking his thermal lance in front of the vault. "All clear."

Mancini looked over and gave me the thumbs-up. *All clear.*

I smiled. Just like that, the bank was ours. I took a deep breath and looked out the window. The Petronas Towers were shimmering there in the distance. I looked at my watch. We'd been inside for exactly sixty-five seconds. The easy part was over. I took another deep breath and let it out slowly. My pulse was fast and I had to keep it under control.

Then the woman started screaming again.

She was crouched in the center of the group on her hands and knees. The tears rolling down her cheeks mixed with her eyeshadow in thick black globs that dripped off her chin and soaked into her suit. Her arms trembled and her face twisted up into a horrible look of sheer pain. I could see a trickle of blood make its way down past her hairline, following the curves of her face to her chin. I felt sorry for her. I tried not to, but nevertheless some part of me was suddenly burning with guilt. I looked away and tried to block out her screams, but I couldn't. She was breaking my concentration. It felt like she was screaming directly at me, practically calling out my name. I asked Mancini to pass me over the jet injector so I could fire a load of drugs into her neck. Ten seconds later she was fast asleep, but that didn't change anything.

I felt guilty, but even more than that, I felt powerful.

48

ATLANTIC CITY

I wondered how long it would take before someone discovered his corpse. The smell was already atrocious, but people might overlook a smell coming from a house like that. The real-estate agent who sold him the address might find him on a routine visit, but that could take weeks. By that time the soft tissues in his body would have started to putrefy. His face would be unrecognizable.

I thought about Ribbons's last request for a few moments. All he wanted in the world was one last hit. I wanted to find that despicable, but couldn't. I have an addiction too, and it's every bit as self-destructive.

I stopped first at Ribbons's stolen Mazda Miata. When I opened the door, the smell made me gasp. It was like fish blood and rancid meat. I got over it in a moment and took a deep breath. The seat was coated with Ribbons's blood and body matter, but it was all dried up and blackened after two days in the summer sun. I could see the spots where the spray-on clotting agent had worked and the spots where it hadn't. I shut the door and left it there.

I got back in Lakes's Bentley. I wasn't entirely sure the car wasn't bugged, but it was better than the alternative. I got in and I tossed the blue Kevlar bag onto the passenger seat.

I had to stash the money before I did anything else, clearly. Of course I'd threatened to put the money somewhere connected to the Wolf, but I wasn't going to follow through on that. I didn't need to. The Wolf would buy my bluff either way. Now that I had the money, every minute I spent with it I took a risk that it might explode. My mind explored the map of the city while I drove. I took the road down the coast back into the heart of the city, imagining all the different hiding places and weighing the pros and cons in my head.

I was almost at the Boardwalk when the sky began to rumble and grow very dark very quickly. A storm front was coming through. Red thunderclouds were already flashing heat lightning over the ocean. The humidity was beginning to condense into acid rain. A minute later huge drops plopped down on the windshield and it was pouring full-blast. I looked up at the angry sky and flipped on the wipers.

The place I chose was a strip of abandoned beach just south of the city near the Absecon Inlet. It was a place just a little too rocky to serve much of a purpose. It was halfway between a beach and a cliff. There was a sharp turn in the road to direct traffic away from the deadly rocks and surf.

There were several benefits to hiding the money in such a place. This beach was far enough off the beaten path that nobody would simply come along and find the bag hidden among the rocks in the next few hours. Second, the tide was going out. That way there was no chance that the money might accidentally get swept away with the tide, no matter how big the waves got. Third, if the explosives managed to go off, I'd rather have them blow up out here where they wouldn't hurt anyone. I wasn't about to hide explosives somewhere a kid might find them.

As soon as I got out of the car I was soaked down to the bone. I slung the blue nylon bag over my shoulder and I pulled a cell phone out. I put in one of Marcus's numbers to send him a text message.

No luck, it said.

I took the battery and chip out of the phone and tossed the parts behind the sand dunes, off an old strip of two-lane highway past a sign warning people to stay off the beach. The wind hit me straight on, hard and epic, whipping my hair back and forth in one direction, then in another. After about a hundred feet I emerged from the stubby beach brush and faced the surf directly. It wasn't that inky sort of dark—it was the kind of dark where it looked like someone had turned down the lights on the world. The air was as thick as soup. I made my way across the beach by the pale blue light from the city reflected off the ocean water.

I came to the edge of one of the largest sand dunes and stood there for a moment. The sea was more or less empty now. The tide was high and a storm was coming in. What few clouds there had been in the sky that afternoon had all been sucked up into the storm front brewing off the coast. Driftwood and bits of old beach trash, beer cans and spent fireworks lined the tidewater. A soaked blue child's blanket. An empty gallon jug.

Off to my left maybe a hundred feet was a berm of heavy rocks that stretched out maybe another hundred feet into the ocean to break the force of the waves coming into the harbor. At the end the water crashed up against the rocks hard enough to polish them clean.

When I was a child I used to dream about seeing the ocean. When you grow up in Las Vegas, you never learn to associate sand with water. I've been moving around the world since I was twenty years old. I haven't stayed in one place for more than a year since I stopped introducing myself to people with my real name. I've missed the sand. I thought for a moment where I might want to go after this. I couldn't go back to Seattle, that's for sure. I thought about the wide-open desert. If I could find a job out there, I would, if only to remind me of home.

I jammed the blue bag between two rocks. It fell just deep enough between them that it rested a few inches above the frothing water but well out of sight from the casual observer. If it came time for the money to explode, all the stained bills would be carried out to sea and washed clean by the frothing waves. They'd still be destroyed, but the effect would be the same. Before I went any further, I needed to be sure of that. I took out a cell phone and snapped a picture of the money, just so I could have proof. The Wolf would ask for the money in advance. I'd give him a picture instead.

I made my way slowly back to the car. I punched in the number for Information into the cell phone and asked for listings at the local marina. It took me a while to find what I was looking for, but I eventually got through to a company called Atlantic Maritime Adventures. The guy on the other end said, "How can I help you?"

"I'd like to buy a boat," I said.

49

Alexander Lakes was waiting for me at the diner. He looked even worse than he had twelve hours ago—his eyes were bloodshot and his face was wrinkled with stress lines. There was a heavy two-day stubble poking out in patches from his chin and neck, and a coffee stain down the middle of his tie. He hardly moved when he saw me. He raised his hand slowly off the table and waved.

The place was nearly empty. It was getting into the evening now and the whole vibe was different. Rain was thumping against the glass windows. Burgers were frying on the flat top and steam was rising off the coffee machine. The line cook gave me a double-take as I walked by. I couldn't quite figure out what it meant. Maybe I reminded him of someone he'd seen before.

When I got close to the booth, Lakes said, "You look different."

I shrugged and said, "I'm getting that from all sides today."

"No, you look like a whole different person. I barely recognized you."

"I hope you brought what I asked for."

He picked up a white dress shirt from the shopping bag full of clothes next to him. A black Calvin Klein suit, a red tie and a belt.

"And the gun?" I said.

"Thirty-eight revolver, like you were carrying before. I've scratched the rifling on the barrel and removed the serial number, so it's totally clean. It's cheap and it'll make a lot of noise, but it packs a punch."

He set it down on the table for me to see. It wasn't much better than the gun I'd taken off Grimaldi, but it would do in a pinch.

"Okay," I said.

I slid into the booth across from him. Lakes immediately shifted back in his seat as if afraid. There were coffee stains on the table and a hamburger on a plate between us that he'd hardly touched—the meat had started to go brown in the middle and stiff around the edges. He must have been on his twelfth coffee refill. All the empty single-serving creamer cups were next to the ketchup. He must have been here all day.

"How long have you been waiting?" I said.

He looked at his watch. "Nearly all day now. When you said you'd probably take a while, I thought, you know, like an hour or something."

"Do you have a car for me?"

He reached into his pocket and pulled out a fat electronic key on a rental-company chain. He slid it to me across the table. He moved with a strange mixture of exhaustion and terror. His arm shook a little. I looked at the key and put it in my pocket.

"This is the red Accord parked down the block," he said. "It's registered under the name Michael Hitchcock, so if you get pulled over you've got to pretend you know him. Hell, with your new look you could pretend to *be* him. He's a white male with dark hair and thirty-five years old."

"Has there been any news?"

"There's a warrant out for your arrest, but you probably already know that. Your face was all over the TV. They've got some airport-security photo of you circulating. A pretty good close-up of you talking to some FBI chick. They also listed your height and weight and date of birth. I was worried, but I guess I don't have to be. You don't even look like the same person now. What the hell happened?"

"I fixed myself up before driving over. Took a shower."

"Must've been one hell of a shower."

"I can't wait to get into that new suit."

Lakes nodded. "You need it."

Lakes nodded in the direction of the television over the bar. The sound was off and a commercial for the Atlantic Regency was playing, but I got the point. He'd spent hour after hour doing nothing but watching my face flash over and over again on the news and worrying if he might get caught. Now my face was different. A lot of people have a hard time getting used to that.

We sat in silence for a while, and I watched him nervously drink more coffee and finger the center button on his jacket. He was waiting for me to say something, but I wanted to take my time. Lakes had been betraying me to the Wolf. I wanted to make him sweat.

I picked up the revolver, checked to see all six cylinders were loaded and put it back on the table, facing Lakes. Then I took out the tracking device I'd taken off his Bentley.

He froze with his coffee cup halfway between the table and his mouth. It took him a second to recover and put the cup back down. Once he did and looked up at me, he was panicked. He knew what he'd done. He knew what I'd do in response. He'd been giving me bugged cars and selling my location. In my line of work, a betrayal like that usually merits a bullet in the brain. A betrayal like that is *unforgivable*.

Lakes swallowed hard.

"Were these on every car you gave me?" I said.

He didn't say anything. Lakes was like a deer in headlights. I could understand why he didn't want to answer. If he lied and I found out, I'd kill him. If he told the truth, he'd be incriminating himself and I'd kill him. Whatever he said, it would end badly for him.

"So," I said, "if I go outside right now and look under the Accord you got me, will I find one of these?"

Lakes didn't say anything. He nodded.

"You've been giving the Wolf every detail, haven't you?"

Lakes didn't move.

I sighed, then put my right hand on the revolver and with my left covered it with napkins. The diner was quiet, and sitting in the deep, high-backed booth we were almost invisible. I pulled the hammer back and the ratchet made a soft click as the cylinder snapped into place. The chamber was loaded and locked with a 130-grain hollow point.

"I should've known better, actually," I told him. "You're the only fixer in this town, and the Wolf's the only marker. I should've realized you were either working for him or too incompetent to qualify. It was my own damn fault for trusting you."

Lakes looked down at the gun and didn't say a word.

"You can speak, you know," I said. "I'm not about to kill you without hearing your side of it. As a matter of fact, now that I know you're working for the other team, I think we'll have a stronger relationship. I have good reasons for keeping you alive. Of course, I also have good reasons to keep this gun locked and cocked."

Lakes still didn't say anything.

"Have you ever heard the phrase, *'Flectere si nequeo superos, Acheronta movebo'*?"

Lakes shook his head and whispered, "Is that Latin?"

"Yeah, it's Latin."

"I've never heard it before."

"Do you want to know what it means?"

Lakes stared back at the pile of napkins and said, "I'm not sure if I do."

"You do. Believe me, you do."

"Okay. What does it mean?"

"It means a lot of things. I first encountered the phrase when I was a kid, in fact. Back then I used to read everything I could get my hands on. Every time a new book popped up on the rack at the supermarket, I'd buy it, and if I couldn't afford it I'd read as much as I could right there in the checkout line. I lived in the library. I'd get in people's way sometimes, because I always had my head down. But even though I read so much, I never really found a book I liked. I found most books okay—they'd be thrilling, or romantic, or scary, or true, but none of them really seemed to satisfy me somehow. There was always something missing. So I kept on. I did the literary stuff. I read *Gravity's Rainbow* by Thomas Pynchon. *Midnight's Children* by Salman Rushdie. *The Name of the Rose*. They didn't really move me, though. Then one day, somebody gave me a copy of *The Aeneid*. Do you know the story of *The Aeneid*?"

He shook his head.

"How about Troy? *The Iliad* and *The Odyssey*? Trojan horses and sea monsters and all that?"

"Yeah, I know that stuff."

"*The Aeneid* is an epic poem about the founding of Rome. It's sort of a sequel to *The Iliad* and *The Odyssey*. It follows a young man named Aeneas who escapes Troy after it falls to the invading Greek armies. With the remains of his people, he sets sail across the Mediterranean. He has adventures, falls in love, fights bad guys, experiences the supernatural. He did everything I liked to read about when I was a kid, and then some. I felt I *was* Aeneas. Like him, my real parents were out of the picture. Like him, I felt I was destined for something big. Like him, I was bored with an everyday life. And like him, I wasn't a good guy. At least not in the traditional sense. Aeneas had to do bad things to get where he needed to go."

"You read Latin when you were a kid?"

I shrugged. "Some kids collect model planes. I read Latin. It isn't that hard to understand. I loved reading so much, plus I wanted to be Aeneas. But, you see, Aeneas knew his destiny, because a prophet had told him. I had no idea what would happen to me. Most days I felt like I wasn't destined to be anything. I felt like I didn't exist, except when I was reading that book. The only other time I felt more alive was the day I first bashed a man's head in and robbed him in broad daylight."

"Why are you telling me this?"

"I want you to understand why I'm doing this, and I want you to tell the Wolf too. Do you think you can remember that? Wrap your head around it?"

Lakes didn't say anything.

"*'Flectere si nequeo superos, Acheronta movebo,'*" I said. "It's a quote from the book. It's also a personal motto. I remember reading it for the first time and sitting back and thinking, *This is what I've been missing.* That one line summed up everything I'd been feeling up until then. It made all of my anger and confusion and hopelessness go away. It made all my little problems make sense. I've been saying it to myself ever since as a reminder."

Lakes bit the side of his cheek. "You haven't told me what it means."

"It means, *'If you can't reach heaven, raise hell.'*"

50

Lakes placed his palms flat down on the table. He was sweating and when he withdrew them his hands left steamy prints behind on the laminate. When we first met he seemed a cool guy, but everything was different now. A gun pointed at your belly can do that. A bullet of sweat inched over the ridge of his forehead and fell down his cheek.

I nudged the pistol to the left a little, indicating that he should stand up. He slid out of the booth with careful, practiced ease. I kept the gun on him the whole way. If he was going to make a move, he'd try it now. He was standing, I was sitting and the gun was well within his reach. If he was serious about getting away, he'd grab for it. A braver man would have. He didn't. He stood at the end of the booth with a nervous expression.

"Pay for your meal," I said. "Leave a nice tip."

Lakes pulled out a wad of cash. He flipped out a few twenties and laid them next to his plate. His face was turning red. I could only imagine the sort of things going through his mind.

I picked up the bag of clothes he'd brought me with one hand and kept the gun pointed at him with the other. I laid the new suit jacket across my right arm, hiding the gun from sight. Lakes backed up a step to let me get out.

I eased up, careful to avoid giving him an opening. I wagged the gun toward the door. "Walk," I said.

The line cook gave us another suspicious look, but I ignored him. All sorts of things happen at a diner. For all this guy knew, I was just walking my tired friend home for the night. Suspicious looks don't mean squat. I held the door open for Lakes and the bell chimed. He slipped through without any sudden movements.

Once we were outside, he said, "What are you going to do with me?"

I prodded him. "Walk."

We went over to the Bentley in near total silence. There was a pawn shop across the road that still had its lights on. The storm had cut through the heat and the evening wind was cool, but Lakes was sweating through his expensive silk suit anyway.

"He's going to kill us both," he said.

"I've been expecting Marcus to kill me for years."

"No. The Wolf's going to kill us."

"You, maybe. I made a deal. I'm going to trade him the money from the casino heist for a significant cut of the profits."

"He made a *deal*?"

"You didn't think I'd be walking away from this with nothing, did you?"

"I thought you worked for Marcus," Lakes said.

"I don't work for anyone."

Lakes shook his head. "Look, the Wolf just doesn't make deals. He's going to kill you. If you go in empty-handed, he'll torture you until you tell him where the money is. He'll start in on you with a can of bear spray and a lighter."

"I'm not going in empty-handed," I said. "I've got two guns now."

"You'll never pull it off."

"I'm not stupid. I know he'll try to cheat me."

"If you let me go, I can mislead him," Lakes said. "I can make sure you get away."

"Uh-huh," I said.

I popped open the trunk to the Bentley. The inside was coated with a thick layer of heavy-duty trash bags which I'd attached to the interior walls with duct tape. Trash bags and duct tape are criminal staples. Any worthwhile crime involves them. In this case, they'd contain the smell. A body could fester in a trunk lined with trash bags for months before attracting attention.

Lakes froze when he saw what was inside. Part of me expected him to make a run for it. Another part expected him to finally throw a punch or make a move for my gun. That's what I would have done. But fear does strange things to people, I've learned. Even when they're facing certain death, some guys just can't fight back. It's like they're paralyzed. They just can't do it. It was like that for Lakes right then. His breath stopped short and his feet were glued to the concrete.

And I wasn't even really trying to kill Lakes. Hell, I didn't even want to hurt him. I just wanted to put the scare on him. He'd spend a few sweaty hours in the trunk terrified to death before someone would find him. Sure, he'd sold me out to the Wolf, but I never would have got this far without his help. Plus, murder isn't my thing. I don't kill unless I have to. Rule number one.

"Please," Lakes said. "I'll do anything."

"I thought you'd say that," I said. "And there is one more thing I want you to do."

I grabbed Lakes by the neck and gave him a head jog against the bumper. The slam opened up the skin on his forehead. He recoiled from the blow, stunned. Any harder and it would have put him out. I took him by the collar and the belt and tossed him headfirst into the trunk of the Bentley. After a blow like that, he practically helped me do it. He was a big guy, but I made it work. I let his arms flop down around by his head. He rocked back and forth and clutched his face. He was as soft as butter.

I slammed the trunk and looked at my watch. Quarter to 7 p.m.

Eleven hours to go.

51

KUALA LUMPUR

The police helicopter came in from the east and made a low pass overhead, sounding like low churning thunder as it clipped by us. I watched it through the tinted-glass window until it was low against the morning sun. It was a cut-down version of the Eurocopter Twin Squirrel, painted with bright markings for better visibility. Two PGK snipers in black combat gear were seated over the hang bar. They looked back at me through binoculars equipped with night-vision, which seemed surreal in the mid-morning light and heat, but made a twisted sort of sense. If they were to take the bank back by force, they'd cut the lights and gas us first, then go in with night-vision and take us down blind.

The chopper hovered outside the window for a moment before accelerating forward again. It circled the building eight times before it flew off and was immediately replaced by another identical helicopter. I noted the numbers on the tail. The Royal Malaysian Police had only six helicopters in the whole country, and they'd sent out the two newest ones just for us.

The bank itself was eerily quiet. We'd moved the hostages into a back room behind the offices and shot them up with enough tranquilizer to keep them asleep for a few hours. The only sounds were the high hiss of the thermal lance and the endless churning of the helicopter blades. I looked out the window. Thirty-five stories down, the police had established a three-block perimeter with Unimog police trucks and yellow wooden barriers. Beyond that, all of downtown was blocked up with bumper-to-bumper traffic.

We'd been in the bank for forty-seven minutes.

The reason for our presence, of course, was directly behind me through two double-locking, teller-controlled doors and a sheet of bullet-resistant Plexiglas. We had yet to open the two-ton, triple-custody vault. Joe had been trying to spring the damn thing for three-quarters of an hour and only now was getting close. Of course, vaults require serious prowess. Even the best safecrackers in the world try to avoid them. But as fast as Joe worked, we all wished he'd go just a little bit faster. While he drilled, the police force outside grew stronger and stronger, and all we could do was watch.

We'd all been expecting this and taken a lot of precautions. We knew the cops would get involved eventually. Nobody spends nearly an hour robbing a bank without that happening. If we'd been lucky, right now there would have been only a couple of squad cars outside and a few dozen armed officers in the lobby. Instead we had helicopters flying overhead and an army of PGK elite officers setting up a barricade around the building. It was just a game of chance, I guess.

The sound of drilling filled the air. I won't pretend I can crack a safe, but I know how it works. In order to open this kind of vault, three different codes need to be entered into three different dials at a particular time. Each code was three units long, with numbers between zero and eighty. That means the master-vault code consisted of nine numbers between zero and eighty entered in a particular order at a particular time. That's a hundred trillion possible combinations right there. If someone were to try them all by hand, entering one number every five seconds, it would take one hundred billion years to guess the combination. The universe is only a little under fourteen billion years old.

Joe Landis did it in forty-eight minutes.

Joe Landis used a thermal lance, a fiber-optic scope and a black-box listening device. The lance was a six-foot pole attached to a canister of pure oxygen that would burn on one end at eight thousand degrees Celsius. He used that to drill a very small hole through the lock. The fiber-optic cable went through the hole, once it cooled down a little, so he could see the lock's inner workings. The black box allowed him to hear the gears with superhuman precision and detect the slightest click of the drive cam falling into place. With these tools, Joe could look at each dial, see the open notches on each wheel and line them up. After that he worked backward to deduce the combinations. Of course there were ghost notches, phantom clicks and panic codes he had to watch out for, but Joe knew how to work around those. Once he figured out the code, he had to set the vault's internal clock forward so it would open less than half an hour after the code was entered, and he did it with ease. He was the best I'd ever seen.

And then music came to my ears: "Guys, we're in."

That's all Joe had to say to get us to come running. I watched as he entered the codes, his brow covered in sweat but his hands steady. He twisted one dial back and forth and back, then moved on to the next, then the next. As he put in the very last code, there was a click. He gave the lever a spin and the door slowly cracked open.

Jackpot.

The vault room was the size of an office and piled thigh-high with money. Purple ringgit, red yuan, teal baht, blue rupiah, orange riel, green dong, gray kip—a rainbow of currency. Vault rooms themselves, though, are always a little disappointing. Once the shock of seeing all the money wears off, the cash room is just another high-security box.

We wasted no time—we'd calculated it would take five minutes to pack it all up, so it took us four and a half. We had to take precautions. After we opened the cash cages, we checked the money for booby traps. A few bricks of cash were loaded with hidden ink jets that would explode as soon as they got more than thirty feet outside the building. *Bait money*. Before we could pack the real stuff up, we had to take the ink packs out. Unlike the federal payload, however, these ink packs were big, dumb and easy to spot. They required us to flip through and examine all the bills first, which was an inconvenience but not a deterrent. It took us just a minute more.

Then, after we'd removed all the hidden ink packs, we had to break the thin green straps holding the bills together and throw them away. The straps weren't an immediate threat but could cause problems down the line. Each paper strap had the name of the bank on it, which would become evidence that the money was related to the theft later on. As soon as those straps were gone, though, nothing short of getting caught red-handed could tie that money back to this heist.

I could hear the helicopter rumbling over us again. I wondered how long it would take before they sent a squad up the staircase with assault rifles and body armor. Hsiu's hands were shaking as she filled a black garbage bag with hundred-ringgit banknotes.

"Are we going to do anything about that?" she said.

"About what?"

"The helicopter," she said.

"Our first exit plan is shot," I said. "We can't leave through the roof anymore. Somebody get the wheelman on the radio."

Vincent came up behind me, tapped me on the shoulder and handed me our black Motorola two-way radio unit. Of course the cops would be listening in on all the frequencies, but this particular radio was equipped with a 256-bit digital scrambler that made all the encrypted transmissions sound like white noise. The cops could be eavesdropping on our exact frequency and not even know we were there. I pressed the talk button. "Window washer?"

"Here," Alton said.

"Our rooftop diversion is shot, so we've got to go to plan B. Get the armored car. We'll have to drive away dressed as guards. If we do it right, nobody will even know it's us."

"Could get hairy. It's only a matter of time before the cops figure out we used the secure elevator. They could move on the garage any minute and turn this whole place into a shooting gallery."

"We'll have to take that chance," I said. "Have the truck ready to go as soon as the elevator doors open, got it?"

"Hurry up."

"Roger," I said. I tossed the radio back to Vincent.

"What the hell do we do now?" Hsiu said.

"Make a deposit," Angela said.

She produced the two gold keys Marcus had given each of us and held them out. They were keys to the safe-deposit boxes.

Remember how the bank manager had offered Angela a private safe-deposit box outside the vault at a greatly discounted price? Months before we even started planning this heist, Marcus had rented twelve of the bank's largest private safe-deposit boxes through one of his offshore corporations. The boxes were legally rented, with paperwork and every-thing, under various fake identities Marcus controlled. Right now those boxes were empty.

We were here to fill them up.

This is how it would work. Instead of taking the loot with us, we would stuff each of Marcus's safety-deposit boxes to the brim with cash and then walk away. You see, even if a bank gets robbed, the bank can't just open up all of their customers' private safe-deposit boxes and see if anything was taken. Those boxes are private, and the bank has no right to know what's in there. Unless ordered by a court of law, those boxes remain locked no matter what, even after a robbery. If we stuffed the money in there, we could each come back years later under new iden-tities and collect the money completely legitimately. Twenty percent would go to Marcus, of course, but that didn't matter. Just by thinking of this plan he'd made us all filthy rich.

It was genius.

And these safety deposit boxes were big, too. Each box was two feet wide, two feet deep, and three feet long—that's twelve cubic feet. With twelve of those, we're talking 144 cubic feet total. At optimum capability, we're talking more than three million banknotes. Averaged out, that's somewhere in the range of thirty to fifty million dollars' worth of untraceable, nonsequential cash money. I smiled as I pulled the keys from my pocket.

It would all move less than twenty feet.

52

ATLANTIC CITY

The Wolf's men were waiting for me at the abandoned strip club. They weren't being obvious about it, but I knew they were there anyway. I could see the corners of their elbows and the smoke from their cigarettes through the cracks in the plywood over the windows. One of the Wolf's black SUVs was parked two blocks down the boulevard, between a chain-link fence and an empty parking lot. I'd passed it driving up.

The club itself was a long-dead relic of Atlantic City's bad days. The sign had been covered over with graffiti to the point of illegibility, and the plywood nailed over the windows had deteriorated and started to rot. Weeds poked up through the pavement in the parking lot and shriveled ivy had climbed up the stucco walls. This place had been nice once, but that had been years, maybe even decades ago. The neon lights under the awning were broken. The traffic light at the corner of the boulevard was slowly blinking red.

I parked, got out and slammed my car door so they'd hear me coming. Once I got out, I put my hand up so they could see me too. The rain dripped down my palm and collected in the cuff of my new shirt.

It had started up again on the drive over, this time as a low drizzle that wouldn't let up. When I was within earshot, I put my hand in my pocket and gripped the Beretta.

I was halfway across the street when one of the Wolf's goons came out to greet me. I crossed over into the parking lot and stopped maybe ten feet away from him.

He was a sinewy guy in a black hooded sweatshirt with the top down. All the hair on his head had been shaved off, even his eyebrows, and there was a tattoo of two interlocking hammers on his forehead. He gave me a toothless grin and lifted his hoodie to indicate that he had a big Baby Eagle automatic handgun in his waistband.

"Take out your gun," he said. His voice was heavy and slurred. "I'll give you five seconds."

I took out the Beretta, dropped the clip and pulled the slide to knock the live round out of the chamber. I showed him the empty chamber and the magazine so he'd know the gun was harmless, then tossed them both in the dirt between us. I put my hands back in my pocket and shrugged.

"Where's the Wolf?" I said.

"Waiting," the guy said. "Now I need your other gun."

I took my hand out of my pocket. I showed him both empty palms and shrugged.

"You got it," I said.

The man looked at me suspiciously, then took a few steps forward as slowly as if he were under water. He brushed my arms aside and patted my torso down until he found the lump, then reached around my back and pulled out the revolver. He pointed it at me and kept patting me down with his free hand to make sure I wasn't carrying anything else. His breath smelled like menthol, gun oil and crystal meth.

I glared at him and felt the rain dripping down my neck.

The guy took a step back, but kept his eyes on me just in case. He released the cylinder on my revolver and swept the ejector rod. The brass fell out and scattered over the pavement.

"Now you're the only one with a gun," I said.

He smiled at me through his crooked teeth and took the Baby Eagle out from his belt and released the magazine. He pulled the slide and the bullet in the chamber popped out. Then he held the magazine out for me to see and flicked the bullets out of the spring release with his thumb. The bullets fell to the ground one by one.

Click, click, click.

Our bullets rolled around and slipped into the cracks in the pavement. I didn't say anything. I didn't even move. We stared at each other across the pavement like gunfighters in some old Western. The wind picked up and blew rain into my face.

The Wolf stepped out through the front door. His pale suit was perfectly dry, even in this downpour. Water came pouring down around him off the awning.

"Come in," he said. "We'll talk."

The club was like a sieve. Every three feet, water came down in thick sheets from holes in the ceiling as large as pitcher spouts. After so many years of misuse, the water didn't even pool up on the floor anymore. It fell from the ceiling straight into the foundation through large gaps where the floor had caved in. Another one of his men was waiting inside. He was wearing a big thick bomber jacket and standing silently in the corner.

The Wolf pointed to a set of rusty folding chairs. They were the old metal kind that were made of cheap Chinese steel. Between them was an overturned paint can and a length of plywood that served as a table. I followed him inside cautiously.

"Sit," he said.

I pulled back one of the folding chairs and I scanned the new guy up and down for weapons. I didn't see any, but there are plenty of places a guy could stash a knife, or a little Ruger like the one Aleksei had out in the salt marsh.

"Sit," the Wolf said again.

As I sat down the Wolf gave me a strange smile. He pulled up a chair across from me, held out his hand and snapped his fingers. The guy behind him opened his bomber jacket, took out a chrome .357 Magnum revolver and placed it into the Wolf's open palm. The gun was huge— easily as long as a baby's leg and as powerful as a small rifle. It was a Tau- rus Model 65 single action, which means it weighed almost two pounds and could fire six rounds in less than ten seconds, if the shooter was any good.

I looked at it, then at the Wolf. "I thought we were going to make a deal," I said.

The Wolf gave me that strange little smile again. He held the gun up, hit the cylinder release and swept the ejector rod so the bullets fell into his hand. He set the empty gun on the table between us and let the bullets drop beside it. They didn't make the normal soft clinking sound. They made the heavy sound of 200-grain power slugs, each of which was as fat as a quarter and capable of leaving a hole in a man the size of two fists. He nudged one of them with his fingertip, and it rolled off the edge of the table into my hand.

"I want to see the federal payload," he said.

I turned the bullet over. *Magnum* means "big" in Latin. This one was a semi-jacketed brass hollow point as long as my pinkie finger. It was as excessive as the gun designed to fire it. I put the bullet back on the table, setting it on its rim.

"After you show me the money," I said.

"No, you first," the Wolf said. "You don't have to give me all of it, just prove that you have it."

I made a face and flicked the bullet. It fell over and rolled back to the Wolf. He caught it before it fell.

"What sort of proof are you looking for?" I said. "You know I didn't bring it with me. Once I see that you've come in good faith, I'll tell you where the payload is and you can do whatever you want with it. Until then, I'm not doing anything."

"Have you ever played Russian roulette?" the Wolf said.

I didn't say anything.

"I like to gamble," he said. "So do you, from what you've told me.

There are six chambers in this gun, and let's just say this one bullet. I don't know which chamber the bullet's in, so either the gun will fire when I pull the trigger or it won't. It's a game of statistics, you see. The first time I pull the trigger, I have a sixteen percent chance of blowing your head off. If I pull the trigger again, the odds jump. Twenty percent. Then twenty-five percent, then thirty-three percent, then fifty percent. Do you understand? Every time you play, your odds get worse."

The Wolf picked up the revolver, opened the cylinder and slid the bullet into one of the chambers. He spun the cylinder back, cocked the hammer and pointed the gun at my head.

Then he squeezed the trigger.

53

The cylinder turned, the hammer dropped and the gun clicked as the firing pin hit an empty chamber.

The Wolf spun the cylinder and pulled back the cocking hammer, then put the gun down in front of him. I listened to the rainwater dripping on the concrete. Normally, with a big gun like that, you can see where the round's chambered just by looking. But not in a dark room where the only light came through cracks in the plywood over the windows.

"You said you wanted something interesting," the Wolf said. "This is it. Tell me where the money is, and we can drive over and pick it up. After that I'll give you your share, and then we can both go home."

"You and I know you'll kill me right after you get the payload."

"I wouldn't be so sure," he said. "I might kill you right now."

The Wolf pointed the gun at my head again and squeezed the trigger. I could see the chambers shift around, the trigger lock into place and the hammer drop.

Click.

I took out my cell phone and flipped it open. I brought up the photo of the blue bag sitting on the rocks and held the phone out for the Wolf to see. I knew this moment would come, but not that it would come under these circumstances. The Wolf didn't just want proof that I had the money. He wanted to show me that he was willing to risk it on a game of Russian roulette.

"That's it, then?" he said. "That wasn't so hard, was it?"

"Now you know I have the money," I said. "I want to see my cut."

"You're clever, Ghostman, but not very smart. I still have the whole night to work on you. I can make you talk, if I have to."

"You think you can break me in a couple of hours? Good luck. You know, I'm not weak and I'm not dumb."

"I have ways."

I shook my head. "I'm not scared of your gun."

The Wolf held it up. "Oh, this? No, this is just for my own amusement. When the time comes you'll talk, but not because everyone talks. You'll talk because you'd rather play my game than sit here and wait for me to kill you. You'll talk because you don't have any other choice."

He pointed the gun at my face again and pulled the trigger.

Click.

He laid the gun down on the table between us. I stayed silent for a minute and looked at my reflection in the barrel.

"You'll talk," he said, "because after all you want to live more than you want to get paid."

"You've got it backward," I told him.

The Wolf cracked his knuckles and folded his hands on the table.

"You're the one who wants to live," I said, "and I'm the one who wants to get paid. If I were to die right now, I'd be okay with that. You don't know me, but I'm not in this to win. I do this because I can't think of anything more interesting to do with my time. If you were to kill me or torture me, right here, I wouldn't say a word. Then, once you kill me, you'll have a big problem. I've stashed the money, and nobody but me knows where it is. Worse, who knows when and where it might blow? It could be in one of your safe houses or in some dive where your boys work. That way, when it blows the money gets tied back to you. You'll do time for murder and aggravated robbery."

"Fat chance," the Wolf said.

I shrugged. "At the end of the day," I said, "I think you care more about keeping your ass out of prison than you do about breaking me. Even if you don't believe me when I say I've hidden the money someplace detrimental to you, you'll make a deal anyway. It's much cheaper for you to make a deal with me than take another chance with that gun."

The Wolf stared at me in perfect silence. He was a calm and expressionless statue.

I went on. "Marcus was planning on pinning everything on you, Harry. He always has a hidden agenda, and you played right into it. It took me a while to put all the pieces together, but I did. You see, Marcus knew you'd figure the heist out. He even knew you'd be stupid and prideful enough to try to co-opt it as your own. By sending two idiots to rob the federal payload, he *coerced* you into robbing the federal payload yourself. Marcus *wanted* you to kill Moreno and Ribbons. He *wanted* you to take their loot as your own. He *wanted* you to try to use it against him. Hell, he even ordered Moreno and Ribbons to steal one of your cars just to antagonize you, because he knew that once you had the money, he could tell everyone he knew you were planning to cheat the cartel. See, nobody can steal a federal payload and walk away clean, not even Marcus, one of the greatest jugmarkers in the world. You thought you could? You're just a drug dealer. You pretend to be powerful, but the cartel owns you. For a man in your position, reputation's worth far more than a truck full of meth. If Marcus said you were crooked and the news backed him up, the cartel wouldn't touch your money. In fact, I don't think the federal payload even has to be hidden in a place directly connected to you in order to implicate you in the heist. I think that if the money were to blow up anywhere near Atlantic City, the result would be the same— cops swarming all around you and your reputation in ruins. Your name will be on the top of every investigator's list for the next twenty years.

All of your money will be suspect after that. Every drug dealer in the world will know you as the man who stole the federal payload. Your only chance to avoid taking the heat for the casino heist is to find that money and get it as far away from here as possible. That way, when it blows, you can pin the whole thing on somebody else. If you don't, the cartels will tear you to shreds. So guess what? I think that if you can't make a deal with me, your career is over."

The Wolf picked up the .357 Magnum from the table, pointed it at my head and pulled the trigger. The hammer fell and clicked.

I didn't flinch. I didn't even blink.

"I want my hundred and fifty thousand dollars."

The guy in the bomber jacket shifted uncomfortably. His muscles were suddenly as tight as drums.

"If you kill me," I said, "you'll lose countless times that much. Once the cartels get word you stole a federal payload, even as payback, you'll never make another deal. But we can still both win here. Give me what I want and I'll make your money problem disappear before the sun comes up. It's your only chance to get out of this spotless. We trade. A hundred and fifty grand for one point two million."

The Wolf dropped the cylinder on his gun, slid another bullet in, spun the chambers, pulled back the hammer and fired.

Click.

"You're testing your luck," I said. "Every time you pull that trigger, you run a chance of shooting *yourself* in the head. You can't break me and you won't get me to back down. So take the deal."

The Wolf put the gun down on the table. The corner of his mouth twitched just once. It was his tell—a brief glimpse into his thoughts that was over almost as soon as it started.

"All right," the Wolf said. "Here's my offer, and you better listen well, because you won't do better. I might not feel like killing you, but I can kill that cute FBI agent you've been working with instead. Give me the money or she'll be a corpse by morning."

54

"Do what you want with her," I said. "Your deal with me remains the same."

I slowly reached across the table and picked up the .357 by the barrel. It was heavy, like someone had taken a normal gun and tied a brick to it. In response the Wolf's guy pulled a short polymer automatic from his back pocket and pointed it at me. It was a hole puncher, chambered with .22 Long Rifle, with a barrel shorter than a credit card. A gun like that wouldn't be very accurate, but at this range it would be a miracle if he missed.

"Easy, Ghostman," the Wolf said.

"I just want to show you what I care about," I said.

I held the gun out and showed it to him. There were two bullets in it now, not just one, so the odds were different. I spun the cylinder and pressed the barrel to my temple. Pulling the trigger was as smooth and easy as tearing silk. The chambers turned and the hammer dropped.

Click.

I pulled the trigger again. I listened to the sound of the chamber ratchet snap into place, the hammer sear lock and the trigger drop.

Click.

The Wolf's expression changed. He was uncomfortable. Like he didn't know what I was going to do next. Like maybe he thought I'd blow my own brains out just to show him I could. He shifted around in his seat.

I pulled the trigger again.

Click.

I put the gun down and gestured to the goon in the bomber jacket, who also looked nervous. "Before I play again," I said, "could I bum a smoke?"

He nodded at me and smiled. I must have impressed him. He stepped forward, keeping his gun pointed at me, and patted a Marlboro loose from his pack. He took out a Zippo and leaned in to strike it. I put the cigarette between my lips and waited until he was right up close. I took two puffs, then picked up the Magnum, pressed it under his chin and pulled the trigger.

Bang.

The pistol bark was muffled, as if I'd fired it through a pillow. The bullet punched a star-shaped hole in the top of his head and carried his brains out after it. The expanding gases peeled the flesh away from his skull and sent blood and bone fragments flying everywhere.

I kicked the table over and pushed until the Wolf toppled over and was pinned on the floor by the big sheet of plywood. My intention wasn't to hurt him, just to keep him busy until I could take care of his men. I spun around and pointed the gun at the skinhead, who'd suddenly appeared at the door. I squeezed the trigger several times but nothing happened. *Click*. One of the rounds the Wolf put in must have been a dud—or maybe it was too wet to fire.

The skinhead smiled like a demon and charged me. Neither of us had loaded guns, so a second later we were inches apart. The guy slammed the Magnum out of my hand like he was brushing off a fly. I jabbed him hard with my left, but it was like punching a block of concrete. He was quarried out of solid prison and chiseled on the yard equipment by some sculptor who didn't care much for what the finished piece would look like. My first punches were useless. His weren't. He got off a wide and messy body shot that knocked the wind out of my lungs; two inches higher and he would've shattered some ribs. I didn't bother to block, however. I attacked with everything I had. I landed an uppercut and could feel his jaw crack and whatever teeth he had left come loose. It was a blow that could've killed another man, but not this guy. He didn't even seem shaken by it. He smiled as if to say, *What else you got?* Then he wrapped his hands around my neck and threw me against the wall hard enough to crack the plaster and started squeezing. Though I punched him four or five times in the chest, he didn't even flinch. My vision started to get fuzzy as he cut off the oxygen to my brain.

I raised my arm and brought my elbow down like a hammer on the soft part of his inner arm. I nailed him right below the junkie vein, between his track marks, and heard a bone snap. He let go and stumbled away from me in agony.

I followed up with a jab to the nose. The cartilage shattered and the skin on my knuckles opened up and spattered his face with blood. I followed through with a cross like a freight train. The skin on that hand opened up too. He went like he was going to trip me, but I already had too much of an advantage. I landed another elbow on his skull in that spot where all the bone plates meet up. The old head jog. He stumbled away, stunned. I jumped on him and wrapped an arm around his neck. I pressed my other elbow into the back of his head between his spine and his skull and held it there. I had to keep this choke hold for ten seconds. That's as long as it takes. The sleeper hold cuts off blood to the brain, so it works faster than suffocation. It's like pressing the power button on a laptop. After a few seconds, the whole thing goes dead.

The skinhead stumbled around the room, trying to pry my arm off his neck. He slammed me against the wall again but couldn't dislodge me. The blood from my hands dripped down his skull and ran into his fluttering eyes. He couldn't make a sound. He opened his mouth like a fish drowning in air, then his whole body drooped forward and went limp. I let him go and he fell to the floor like a sack full of rocks. He'd wake up in a few hours with the worst headache of his life.

In the meanwhile, the Wolf had unpinned himself and was scrambling for the plastic automatic the dead guy had dropped. I ran over and kicked as hard as I could just as his hand reached the gun. The gun slid across the floor and dropped through a hole in the floorboards. There was a splash as it hit the water in the basement.

The Wolf looked up at me, shaking the hand I'd just kicked, and scrambled a few feet toward the door, but stopped when I stood in front of him. His suit was ruined. I picked him up by the collar and said, "Give me one good reason."

"A hundred and fifty grand," he managed. "In my hotel room. Give me an hour. If that's not enough to satisfy you, I'll see you in hell."

"What room number?"

"Penthouse," he said. "No games this time."

Then I dropped him back on the floor and walked out.

55

KUALA LUMPUR

Everything about the getaway went wrong the moment the elevator doors opened. As soon as we arrived in the second subbasement, I was hit by a giant ocean wave of light and sound. I didn't know exactly what was happening to me, but I knew one thing.

It was a goddamn police trap.

I don't know how it happened. Right before we got in the elevator going down, Alton had given us the all-clear. No police in the garage. Police were barricaded outside the garage, sure, and on the street all around the building, but the second subbasement was completely open and clear. Somehow in the minute and forty seconds since then, the situation had changed.

Now I was on the receiving end of a grenade.

The blast didn't take me off my feet, but it blinded me. I couldn't see or hear anything. I could feel someone grab my shoulder and pull me out of the elevator. I could feel the pavement under my boots. Finally I could make out gunfire. It sounded soft, at first, but soon became roaring. My vision started to come back. There were heavy muzzle flashes from the foot of the garage. A skirmish line of Royal Malaysian police officers was firing at us from behind a barricade of police cars. The muzzle flashes lit up the corner like shooting stars. A tear-gas grenade between us poured out billows of thick yellow smoke.

I pulled up the G36 assault rifle, pressed it against my hip and let loose a stream of bullets at the barricade. I was firing blind. Each shot sounded like the low punch of a bass drum instead of the intense crack of a gun. Hsiu still had me by the shoulder. The armored car was just a few more feet away. We were all running toward it. I hoped like hell that Alton hadn't been hit.

Then I watched Joe Landis go down. A bullet struck him in the head maybe two steps in front of me. His body didn't so much fall as slump over given all the equipment on his back. He was dead before I could do anything, and his pack was still loaded with nitroglycerine.

The Italian brothers came out of the elevator next with their shotguns raised. They pumped the actions so fast the red shotgun shells collided with one another in the air.

The police had made a choke point at the garage opening. They must have rushed down at the last minute in Unimog police trucks. I couldn't see them all, but from this distance I could make out two men in black berets crouched on the bed of the second truck. They let out steady bursts of gunfire from automatic MP5A2 submachine guns. A bullet clipped Angela's pack.

My mag was out. I hit the release and pulled it off, then fumbled another one from under my shirt. Before I could pull the bolt spring, I felt a heavy punch in my chest. I was hit. The bullet knocked the wind out of me and I stumbled back. I couldn't breathe. Another one hit me, then another in quick succession. I was weighed down by the equipment on my back and still shocked from the first hit, so I fell over. I rolled back and forth on the pavement for a few seconds. I inhaled as hard as I could, but nothing happened. My lungs wouldn't let in air. It was like someone was sitting on my chest.

Hsiu and Vincent saved me. They came from behind and grabbed me by the arms and dragged me over to the armored truck. Vincent loaded me in the back while Mancini knelt next to us and licked shots out the back of the truck. He pulled the G36 from my arms, finished reloading and opened fire at the police in quick, controlled carbine bursts. He switched targets like he was blowing up glass bottles on a shooting range. Once I was secured, he tapped the roof twice, shut the doors and the car took off squealing.

I glimpsed Alton through the small window into the cab. He veered left, hard. I was thrown against the right wall. Angela climbed next to me over the bags of supplies. She started to say something, but the words never came out.

The armored car plowed through both of the police trucks, which didn't stand a chance. They crumpled against the armored car's grille and were dragged sideways for ten feet up the ramp until they were launched apart in different directions.

The standard armored truck is equipped with sixteen gun ports that look like little mail-slot windows. You slide them open from the inside by a handle and they're just barely large enough to squeeze a shotgun muzzle through. They work on the principle that it's almost impossible to shoot a target that small from the outside, unless you're standing right next to it.

There were two on the rear doors.

Mancini slid one of them open. He took careful aim down the aperture sights through the little metal hole and emptied round after round into Joe's body. I could feel the vibrations of a car crash behind us, then an explosion. The nitroglycerine in Landis's kit went. That shock wave coursed through the pavement. Muzzle flashes filled the dark space, then the smell of burned gunpowder and vaporized concrete. It was so thick it seemed like smoke. Hot brass poured out of Mancini's action. He reached down and pulled a clip from my vest and charged the G36.

I was in a special universe of pain. I writhed around on the floor of the truck, taking short and fast fish breaths. I could barely see. Everything was dark. I peeled my hat off and clawed at my chest until the shirt came open. Under it was a tactical vest with two titanium trauma plates designed to stop assault-rifle bullets. A trio of 9mm hollow points were stuck inside the left plate. They'd cut through the Kevlar just over my heart. I picked one of them off. It looked like a mushroom.

Angela screamed something in my ear, but I couldn't hear it. The only thing I could hear was a high-pitched ringing, like a fire alarm going off inside my skull. She tapped me on the ears and her gloves came away with red specks. The blood was dripping down from my eardrums and soaking into my shirt collar.

She screamed and screamed at me until I could hear her.

"Did one go through?" she was saying.

"I don't know," I said. "I can't breathe."

"Keep calm!" she shouted into my ear. "You were shot three times and hit by a flashbang. I don't see any other blood, so you should be all right. Maybe broken ribs, that's all."

A flashbang grenade emits a sound ten thousand times louder than a shotgun blast and a sudden flash of light as bright as the sun. It uses magnesium and ammonium nitrate. Makes the target wish he was dead. I felt like I was swimming in static. I can best describe it as a migraine headache that was happening over my entire body.

Angela took a vial of cocaine out of her jacket pocket and poured half of it into her palm, which she then clamped over my mouth and nose. The powder rubbed into my face and smeared into my stubble. I felt the cool numbing sensation of the drug. I breathed in. The pain in my chest subsided and the world snapped into focus. Everything that had been black and white was suddenly in bright Technicolor. Angela pointed at me with her other hand and said, "Are you going to be cool?"

I nodded.

I was better than cool. I felt like a wounded god.

Angela took her hand off my mouth. She grabbed a radio from somewhere and shoved it in my face. It took a moment in my dazed, coked-up state to recognize it as the large black police scanner that Hsiu had been carrying.

"It just said your name," said Angela.

"What?"

"The goddamn police scanner just said your name. They've got helicopters coming in, and the police frequencies are shouting your name around like you're the one running the show."

"I don't understand," I said.

"Goddamn it." Angela shoved the radio in my face again. "How do they know about Jack Delton?"

I didn't know what she was talking about at first. I was dumbstruck and couldn't focus on anything except the ringing sound of Mancini's gunfire. It took me a few pregnant seconds to put all the pieces together. My eyes went wide when I realized what I'd done. I finally knew the magnitude of the mistake I'd made. I finally recognized the mistake, the simple mistake, that would haunt me for the next five years. I couldn't hear anything but Angela's voice.

"How the hell do they know about Jack Delton?"

Right then, I knew.

56

ATLANTIC CITY

I got into the Bentley and drove. As soon as I pulled out onto Kentucky Avenue I grabbed a cell phone from my overnight bag, powered it up and slammed in Rebecca Blacker's digits. The phone rang and rang, but nobody picked up.

The Wolf had finally offered me a straight deal: 150,000 clean dollars for 1.2 million dirty ones. That didn't mean I trusted him, however. I'd done everything short of killing him. I'd killed three of his men and put another two in the hospital. Men like that are replaceable, sure, but it's rare for any gang to suffer that many casualties in such a short period of time. There would be enormous pressure on him to take care of me, one way or another. If I wanted to come out of this alive, I had to run. And, hell, I wasn't even considering what he might do to Blacker. I swore and tossed the phone on the passenger seat.

I looked at my watch. A little after 9 p.m.

Nine hours to go.

I drove north of the city along the Absecon Bay back to the self-storage center in the marsh. The rain eased up and then stopped, leaving fresh puddles on the concrete. The air wasn't salty anymore. It smelled as fresh and clean as a shower after a workout. The potholes sucked up the water and asked for more. The heat was coming back. Even in the dark the thermostat on the side of the manager's office was in the high eighties. The place was closed for the night, but there was a gate where anybody with an access key could get into their container whenever they wanted. Twenty-four-hour access is essential to the industry. I punched in the code the kid had used to spring the lock.

I emptied the rucksack. The ammunition boxes and the Uzi case and the gun parts and the bundle of twenties and the plain white pills fell out, plus the phone Ribbons never got a chance to use. I took the Uzi out of its case. It was sturdy and the barrel and chamber looked clean for a gun that had been sitting in the heat for a few days. If I needed to, I could fire it with one hand.

I knelt on the floor and snapped bullets into the magazines. There were three mags total, with twenty-five bullets in each. An Uzi fires at least one thousand rounds per minute. Even a short love tap on the trigger could send out a clip-emptying hail of lead. After the muzzle jump and the recoil, accuracy would be an issue. I'd have to keep it down to short bursts. Three clips of ammunition felt like a lot. It wasn't. Three clips meant three trigger taps, or about three seconds of pure fury. Just like roulette, playing the spread is the only way to win.

It took me five minutes to load all the magazines. I tucked the spare clips in my pockets and put one in the butt of my gun. I made sure the safety was on before I hooked the Uzi on my belt loop. My jacket wouldn't cover it if someone was looking, but on passing glance I looked all right. When I left the storage unit, I saw my reflection in the Bentley's windshield. I was looking at a sleepless man with a two-day beard and an expensive new suit with a submachine gun hanging out of it.

I got back in the Bentley and took off again.

I was barely out of the parking lot when a phone started vibrating in my overnight bag. I fished it out with one hand and held the wheel with the other. I recognized the number on the screen. *Rebecca Blacker*. I pressed the green button.

"Tell me you're okay," I said.

"I'm fine," she said. "It's you I'm worried about."

I shot by the place where windmills with blades twenty stories tall spun endlessly all day and all night. My headlights were the only lights except for the distant glow of the casino towers. I was two minutes away from the beach where I'd stashed the money. I could pick it up and be back downtown in less than twenty.

"I just met with the Wolf," I told her.

"You're admitting to that now?"

"Yes," I said. "Are you tracing this call?"

"What?"

"Are you tracing this call? Yes or no."

"I don't know why it matters."

"I'm going back to the casino," I said. "And I need your help."

57

I arrived at the Atlantic Regency twenty minutes later. Somehow it didn't feel right being there. Even if the promised money was waiting for me inside all wrapped up with a bow, this location didn't feel safe. There were still bullet holes from the heist in the glass doors of the side entrance, and a rent-a-cop stationed outside telling people to move along.

I hate returning to a takedown point. I even hate returning to the scene of a crime I didn't commit. It plays into all the worst stereotypes about people in this line of work. Only the most hubristic, prideful thieves would ever go back to gloat. To me that's just embarrassing. A thief is supposed to do the job and get the hell out. Hanging around afterward increases the potential for jail time, nothing more.

I slid the Uzi under the flimsy flap of the blue Kevlar bag. I fitted the bag's strap to my shoulder and practiced pulling the gun out as quickly as I could, at least as far as the dashboard. Assuming the penthouse was a presidential-style skyloft, that would mean five or six bedrooms, a large living room and a dining room or maybe even a kitchen. The money would probably be in a wall safe inside a closet in the master bedroom. I made some quick calculations. There could easily be half a dozen guys up there. Something made me think that even with five of his guys down for the count, the Wolf wouldn't have any problems finding volunteers. He'd run out of guns before he ran out of men to hold them.

I got out of the car. The Regency was lit up like the Fourth of July, even though it was almost ten on a Sunday night. I could hear the music and jackpot alarms going from the street. Atlantic City prime time. I looked at my watch.

Eight hours to go.

I passed through the casino floor toward the hotel main lobby, carrying the bag over my shoulder. There weren't any metal detectors, so I had no problem getting the gun through. It felt strange bringing the money back where it was supposed to go in the first place. The strangeness of the situation excited me, in a way. It was like stealing the payload all over again, just by walking past the blackjack tables. I was starting to get why some men liked to go back to their old targets. It was like being able to see in a room full of blind people. I knew things they couldn't even imagine.

There were three receptionists on duty, with a queue forming in front of them. I slid into line behind a group of tourists in white cabana shirts. When I got to the front, I gave the receptionist the best smile I could muster under the circumstances. "I'm supposed to pick up a room card," I said.

"What room are you in?"

"I'm with the group in the penthouse."

"What's the name on the reservation?"

"Turner," I told her.

I checked for floor security and pit bosses on instinct, then scanned the ceiling for security cameras. There were far too many to count. Every five feet there was a black dome on the ceiling. I must have been on six or seven cameras at once, all told. The receptionist printed me a new card and handed it to me with a smile.

I took the elevator up to the top floor. The top floor had only one room, where a long hallway led to a single set of thick mahogany doors. The penthouse. I swiped my card and walked right in.

The doors opened onto a Roman-style atrium. In the center was a still pool of water with a plaster sculpture of the goddess Juno rising out of it. The ceiling was held up with massive Doric columns, and the walls were covered in frescoes that evoked antiquity. The floors were inlaid black-and-white marble with more mahogany doors on either side. It was the sort of place you'd expect the Wolf to stay. Every detail was extravagant to the point of garishness. The gold leaf and plaster gave it an air of fast money and grotesque overindulgence.

Behind the pool were two men in suits.

They didn't look like the Wolf's other heavies. These men were neatly dressed, clean-cut and well manicured. Their suits were custom-fitted. They both wore plain, gold-rimmed glasses and didn't seem surprised to see me. One stood nearer the statue with a black duffel bag on the floor in front of him. The other stood a few feet away holding a 9mm Beretta at his side and when I'd come through the door he'd raised his gun and taken a bead on my head.

"I'm here to make a trade," I said.

58

KUALA LUMPUR

Liam Harrison wasn't dead.

I merely assumed he was. At the time, I thought this was a pretty reasonable assumption. There aren't a whole lot of bulletproof vests that can withstand a .44 Magnum round at point-blank range. Hell, even if I'd known he was wearing a bulletproof vest, I still would have assumed he was dead. That amount of force carried by that bullet should have broken his ribs and collapsed his lungs. He should've been dead twice over.

He *should* have been.

I can't tell you the number of times I've gone over that moment in my head. Sometimes, when I'm up at night, the scene plays on repeat, over and over again. I feel like there's still a part of me lying on the floor of that armored truck with two nostrils full of coke and a trio of hollow points in my chest. For years now I've been thinking about that moment. Maybe if I'd been paying better attention, I might have saved myself a lot of trouble and pain. If only I'd been more careful, I could have saved Joe Landis's life. I could have saved Jack Delton's.

Over the years I've tried to justify the mistake to myself. I had no idea that Liam Harrison had survived, after all. How was I supposed to know that he'd lived through our encounter and was then able to figure us out? But after a while, I came to see it from Marcus's perspective. Marcus couldn't afford to tolerate failure. On a heist, even the slightest mistake can have consequences beyond the wildest imagination. If he ever saw me again, he'd have to kill me. It was the only way the system worked.

That one simple action—showing my fake passport to a police informant—ruined the Asian Exchange Job. After all my worries, the heist didn't go bad because Marcus set me up. It didn't go bad because we planned something wrong. It didn't go bad because we bit off more than we could chew. No. It went bad because of a bullet-resistant vest, a fake passport and a bag of soy crisps.

I slammed the door to my scatter and locked it.

A guy's not supposed to return to his scatter after a heist except under extreme circumstances. These qualified in spades. After our bloody breakout in the armored truck, everybody in the city would be looking for us. The small room behind the laundry was the only place I knew where I could lie low for a few hours. I knew damn well I couldn't stay there. The police have ways of figuring that shit out. I put the chain on the door and my brain went into high gear. New plan. Right now.

I hadn't left myself much in the scatter. The soap and razor I'd used were still there, of course, but I'd gotten rid of everything else, like my spare clothes and petty belongings. I went to the bedroom, turned on the radio and switched it over to the local news broadcast. I put the police scanner next to the radio and turned it on as well. I wanted to hear both broadcasts at the same time. I needed to know everything the police knew at the moment they learned it.

The rest of the getaway was completely shot. If the police knew about Jack Delton, they must have figured out who came in with him through customs. They'd get warrants for them too. All of our aliases were burned, not just mine. Police would be waiting for us at every point of egress—airports, train stations, harbors, highways. If they knew who we were, they'd be waiting for sure. Going to the airport was a deathtrap now. We wouldn't even make it to the gate before security would take us down. Our only shot coming out of that bank was to break up and take our chances separately.

This would mean I'd never see Angela again, but I didn't have time to think about that. The last time I ever saw her was in the back of that armored truck.

First, I needed to get the hell out of these clothes. Getting rid of the guard uniform wasn't good enough. I couldn't keep anything that had gone into that bank. The costume wasn't the half of it, either. My face was on the security cameras, and in a few hours those images would be on every newscast in the country. I had to find a way to get rid of everything that could tie me to the heist, from the passports to the bulletproof vest. Do you know how hard that is? Ballistic Kevlar is part of a class of synthetic fibers that don't ever burn. Hell, unless you've got an industrial furnace, they don't even *melt*.

Second, I had to change my appearance. There was no way I could get out of the country looking anything remotely like the person who'd robbed that bank. I needed to change into someone else *now*, which would be harder than it sounds. I had already thrown away all my spare clothes and I couldn't very well go out and walk down to the store to buy new ones. The time for that sort of thing had long passed. I had to get some new duds without spending a minute longer out of this apartment than I had to.

Third, I needed my getaway pack. Like I said, I never do a job without a getaway pack. In this case, my closest one was a half-mile away in an alley on the far side of an ikan bakar fish joint in the Pasar Seni marketplace. Inside was ten thousand dollars, twenty thousand ringgit, a 9mm handgun, two prepaid cell phones, two credit cards, a clean driver's license and a Colombian passport with the name Manuel Sardi on it. I brainstormed approach patterns, search strategies, exit paths and patrol routes. Once I picked up that getaway pack, there could be no room for error. I had to stow and go.

I pulled the window open and stripped.

I chucked everything but my undershirt and pants. I tossed the clothing out the window and it fell two stories down into the gutter. I figured this was far more effective than just throwing it in the trash. In this part of town some street-dweller would claim those clothes in a matter of hours. If the police managed to find this place, the incriminating clothes wouldn't be sitting there in the trash can waiting for them. I winced as I unzipped the bullet-resistant vest. Good god that shit stung.

I touched the three spots over my ribs where I'd been shot. Three big black bruises were forming. It was a miracle that none of the bones were broken. I checked to make sure that I wasn't bleeding, then shrugged off the rest of the vest and threw it on the bed. Kevlar may stop a bullet and put out a fire, but unless it's been treated with silica, it won't stop a knife. I pulled out the ceramic trauma plates and threw them out the window, then took a kitchen knife to the Kevlar and carved the vest up into a half dozen little pieces. When I was done the thing looked like somebody'd shredded a backpack. I tossed the big chunks out the window and flushed the little ones down the toilet.

I went to the sink and put my head under the spout. I scrubbed and scrubbed until the makeup and one-day hair dye I'd used for the job ran in thick lines down the drain. Once I was done, I took the same knife to my hair. I didn't have time to do it right. I just bunched it together at the back of my head and cut that part off with a few messy swipes. Once I had the hair down to a certain length, I soaped it up and shaved off whatever remained until I was completely bald. Some people have recognizable hair. A shaved head throws that all off. I looked nothing like the kid who'd robbed that bank.

The news on the radio and police scanner wasn't good. Hsiu hadn't even made it a hundred feet from the truck before they caught her. They hit her with tear gas and she couldn't handle it. She crumpled up into a ball and didn't move until the paramedics came. Alton Hill made it less than a block. He tried to hijack a car outside his scatter and took two bullets from a police officer. Vincent and Mancini managed to beat the dragnet, but the dirty passports did them in. They came up as known associates of Jack Delton when they went through security. They were both arrested before they got to the gate.

There was nothing about Angela.

I pulled the two safe-deposit box keys off the chain around my neck. I looked at them long and hard. Other members of the crew had already been caught. The police would surely notice the keys around their necks or in their pockets eventually and know to look for mine. Getting rid of them meant throwing away almost two million dollars, but I didn't have a choice. That money was already gone. It was gone the moment those elevator doors opened downstairs.

I flushed the keys down the toilet.

I held a lighter to the end of Jack Delton's passport and watched the cotton-polyester visa pages melt, shrivel and turn black. Less than an hour after the heist, Jack Delton was dead. Only the ghostman survived.

I unlocked the door and left without looking back.

I got about two blocks before I found a homeless guy. He was a thin man with pale skin and gaps in his teeth. I didn't have to look close to see the track marks in his arms and jugular. Heroin. He was wearing a dirty tropical shirt with the name of some band on it and a pair of old black sneakers. I tossed him a wad of ringgit in exchange for both. The shoes and shirt didn't fit right, but they'd do for a little while. And they got me to the fish market and my pack.

I took the subway out. I got on the first train going in any direction, then got off two stops later and took a train going in the opposite direction. I ran the way Angela trained me to. I swapped my clothes for a few things from a secondhand shop and changed my appearance with a compact mirror while waiting for the monorail. Manuel Sardi and Jack Delton were entirely different human beings. Manuel didn't speak a word of English and I liked it that way. The identity held up long enough for me to hire a taxi. I gave the driver a whole fistful of ringgit to drive me all the way to Port Dickson so I could get beyond the reach of the local law. From there I got on a bus to the city of Johor Bahru. I went to the port there and bought a boat with cash so I could cross the Johor Strait into Singapore. I scuttled the boat on the other side and went to the airport, where I bought a one-way coach-class ticket on the first flight to Bogotá, Colombia. After that, I did what I do best—I dropped off the grid.

I traveled around the world without ever staying in the same place for more than six months. I became a true ghost, because I knew that if Marcus ever found me, I wouldn't just take the blame for my own mistakes, I'd also take the blame for Angela's. After all, we were the lucky two who'd walked away. Some day we'd all have to pay our debts.

I tried for a few months to get ahold of Angela, but I should have known better. Trying to catch a ghostman is like trying to catch smoke. I'd spend days waiting to see a message from her pop up in one of my anonymous e-mail in-boxes. None ever came.

To be honest, I don't even know if she's still alive.

She was always the smarter one. If she wanted to disappear forever, I knew there was nothing I could do to stop her. Over the next five years, there were times when I'd spend whole days walking through the streets of whatever town I was in, just trying to see her face. I'd see her everywhere, because she could be anyone. It felt like she was watching me. It felt like if only I were smart enough, I could walk outside on any given day and see her waiting there for me with a cigarette and a crooked smile.

Then, five years later and two days ago, Marcus woke me up with an e-mail.

59

ATLANTIC CITY

The suite door closed behind me of its own momentum. I moved cautiously toward the man with the Beretta. I had my hands up to show I didn't want him to shoot me, but then slowly slid the Uzi out from its hiding place and pointed it right back at him. He had the drop on me, but he let me take out the gun anyway. Neither of us wanted to turn this exchange into a firefight.

The Wolf had tried and tried again to get the better of me, and he'd failed every time. If he were smart, he would have told his men to try to take this easy. That seemed to be the case. The guy with the gun didn't look nervous. He had an empty, dispassionate expression that suggested he'd done things like this before. Even the Wolf couldn't weasel his way out of a shooting in a casino penthouse. As soon as either one of us fired a bullet, not one of the three of us would get out of that room alive. The police would respond, fast and furious. So I figured that the Beretta guy didn't intend on firing his weapon unless I did. I kept the Uzi up and steady as I sidestepped around the statue.

"Who are you?" the guy said.

He must have seen the security-camera picture of me going around on the local news, but I looked different now and that must have tripped him up. I'm sure he'd get the picture. There can only be so many men carrying $1.2 million around in a Kevlar sack, and with an Uzi in his face he'd be a quick learner.

"I'm the ghostman." I said. "Where's the Wolf?"

"Mr. Turner didn't wish to be present for this transaction," the man with the duffel said. "He wishes to express the sentiment that if he ever sees your face again, he will most likely put a bullet through your brain."

I nodded and didn't say anything. I kept moving toward the man with the duffel bag. I stopped once I had moved far enough around to place the statue between me and the gunman. He shifted slightly to get me back into his shot frame, but he didn't go very far. I wanted to have some cover, in case of the worst.

I let the federal payload down from my shoulder. It hit the marble with a thud. Once it was down, I gripped the Uzi with both hands and trained it on the guy with the Beretta.

The man with the duffel looked at me, then at the bag at my feet. He said, "Is that what you've promised?"

"I'd show you, but opening up the bag might trigger the ink packs," I said. "The bag's lined with lead to block the GPS."

"I can verify the money," he told me. "We've got a scanner."

He retrieved a large electronic device roughly the shape of a sticker-tape gun from a nearby drawer. The top was a blue touchscreen, and at the end was a laser like the front of a TV remote.

I pushed the money over to him with my foot.

The guy opened the lead-lined bag just enough to get the head of the device past the lead lining and waited for a few moments. The device made a pleasant ringing sound and the man put the device away.

He nodded. "That's it."

"Did you bring what was promised to me?"

"Yes," he said.

"Show it to me."

He stooped down and unzipped the black bag at his feet. He tilted the bag on its side so I could make out the pile of hundred-dollar bills inside. They were the old-style hundreds too. These bills had the large oval image of Benjamin Franklin on the front but no holographic security strip down the center. The straps were held together with rubber bands and paper clips instead of paper, so I knew they weren't fresh from a bank. They'd be perfect for making a getaway, but I needed to be sure they were clean first.

"Take out a strap third from the top," I said.

The man with the duffel gave me a look, then complied. He moved the top stacks aside, took a strap from the center of the bag and held it up for me to see the hundred-dollar bills on the top and bottom. He flipped through the strap so I could see the ink on every bill. This proved that the money pack wasn't packed with blank filler paper. All fifteen ten-grand straps were hundreds.

"Take off the rubber band," I said. "Fan out the bills. Let me take a closer look."

The man with the duffel stripped off the rubber band holding the cash together and fanned out the money between his palms. He made sure I could see the markings on each bill in the pile. All hundreds. I could see the serial numbers printed to the side of the portrait. They had different letter headings, which means they were from different Federal Reserve branches. Nonconsecutive. I could even make out the faint ghost of the watermark to the far right. I nodded. The money was okay.

"Zip it up," I said. "Slide it over to me with your foot."

The man zipped up the money. He picked up the duffel bag and started to carry it over, but I stopped him.

"With your foot," I said.

He stopped and put the bag down. The man with the Beretta moved slowly to the right until he was just at the edge of my peripheral vision. I couldn't pay attention to both of them at once, so I took a step back to get a wider view. I kept the gun pointed at the man with the Beretta, but the other guy was now too close. I thought for a moment that things might get violent, but then the man with the money slid the bag along the marble until it stopped short next to my shoes.

"Another thing," I said. "I've got something that belongs to the Wolf in the trunk of my car. It's the Bentley on the fourth floor of the parking garage. You should check it out when you get a chance."

I very slowly got down on my haunches and picked up the duffel bag with my free hand. The man with the Beretta lowered his gun. I kicked the federal payload over and started backing away carefully toward the door. When I felt the handle against my back, I eased the door open behind me. A second later I was gone. Everything had gone well. It was a clean deal.

Except for the open cell phone line to Rebecca Blacker in my breast pocket.

I took out the phone and ended the call. This line had been connected since she called me after meeting with the Wolf. With the cell phone's GPS sending out a signal every fifteen seconds, she could pinpoint my exact location and, by extension, that of the federal payload. Not only had I just handed her enough evidence to convict the Wolf, but I'd handed her the federal payload and the two guys in the penthouse as well.

And it wouldn't have been possible if she hadn't put out a warrant for my arrest.

I've never been good at law, but after a few bank robberies I learned a few things. You see, when the cops get a good lead on the location of a fugitive, they don't need a search warrant to bust down the doors and look for him. All they need is a good reason to believe the fugitive is really there. They call this sort of thing an *exigent circumstance*, because if they were to wait around to get a search warrant the fugitive could easily escape. When Blacker put out a warrant for me she'd made me a fugitive, and the GPS signal from my cell phone was all the probable cause she needed to go looking for me in the Wolf's penthouse. Once she raided the place, the *plain-view doctrine* would take over. Any evidence she found, even evidence of crimes unrelated to capturing me, she could seize and use as evidence. I just gave her everything she needed to make the charges stick. In twenty minutes, the federal payload would be on a magnetized plate in the evidence locker and the Wolf would be on the run from the police and Feds. Me? I'd be gone forever.

I slung the $150,000 over my shoulder and smiled.

60

I left the Regency by foot and waded out into the crowds on the Board-walk. The wind off the ocean was cool and the boards were slick from the rain. I slipped into the shadows and followed a staircase down onto the sand. There I wiped the Uzi clean, then pulled off the receiver and dropped the parts in a trash can near the surf.

I weaved back through the crowd for a while before cutting through another casino, heading north. After that it was only a few blocks back to the diner where Lakes had parked the red Accord. I climbed in, leaned back in the driver's seat and closed my eyes for a moment. After two days of this shit, the exhaustion was finally catching up. My hands felt like lead. My breath came out in shudders. After a minute or two a pack of police cars barreled down the street in the direction of the Regency. I waited for them to pass before I turned the key and pulled out. I punched in Marcus's number into my cell phone and waited as it rang and rang and rang. It took longer than I expected for someone to pick up.

"Five Star," another Midwestern voice said.

"I need to speak to Marcus."

"You've got the wrong number, man."

"It's the ghost," I said.

It took longer than usual for the front man to bring the phone back. It was still early there, only 8 p.m. I could hear the sound of an industrial dishwasher. When Marcus came on, he didn't say anything. I knew he was there only from his heavy breathing.

"I found the money," I said.

Marcus skipped a beat. "Did you bury it?"

"No," I said.

"What are you going to do?"

"Your package will be delivered to the original intended recipient very soon," I said. "Ribbons is dead and the trail's cold. Once the cash is gone, nobody will be able to connect you to this heist. The Wolf has been taken care of."

"*What?*" Marcus said. "What about the federal payload?"

"That isn't going to be a problem," I said. "The Wolf took the money in an exchange we just made. The FBI should arrest him for possessing it within the hour."

"How the hell did you manage that?"

"You don't need to know."

"Are you sure this won't blow back on me?"

"I am," I said. "Does this make us even?"

"Yeah," Marcus said. "It does."

"Good," I said. "Because right now, I'm going to put this phone down. When I do, I'm going to disappear. You won't look for me and you won't find me. You won't recognize my face and you won't be able to distinguish my voice. You won't know what I do or where I'm from or a single damn thing about me. The moment I put this phone down, you and I are going to be total strangers. It will be like we never met, so even if somehow our paths cross again, on a plane or at a restaurant or across a subway car, you'll look the other way and I'll disappear. Do you understand?"

"Jack—"

"Do you understand?"

Marcus was quiet for a moment, then said, "I understand."

I didn't wait for him to say good-bye. As soon as he said the words, I closed the phone and pried off the battery. I snapped the SIM card in two and threw it all out the window into the street.

I looked at my watch. Quarter to 11 p.m.

I'd done it with seven hours to spare.

This city isn't a good place to make a getaway. It's the geography. Atlantic City sits on a crescent-shaped patch of shoreline that's cut off from the rest of the mainland by miles and miles of uninhabitable salt marshes. While you're standing on the Boardwalk the city may seem like it's the center of the universe, but in reality, compared to most cities, it's actually rather inaccessible. There are only five ways in or out. The first is to head north on a single highway that crosses the Absecon Inlet. Not a good idea. The second is to get on any one of the three freeways heading west across the salt marshes. Any one of the three would be full of state troopers. The third way would be to head through a maze of privately owned roads across the intercoastal waterways to the south. No way. The fourth way was the train station. I wasn't about to try that, either. Even with a new look and identity, I couldn't risk someone picking my face out from a crowd.

So I needed to get out the fifth way.

I needed to leave by boat.

I had bought one for sixty thousand dollars with a black Visa over the phone a few hours ago. If there is one thing I've learned as a criminal, it's that everything is for sale at the right price. Just the cost of the boat wiped out much of the profit I'd taken off the Wolf, but the money was never the point. I live for the rush, not the dollar signs attached to it. Now I could spend the next two weeks drifting anonymously down to Cuba, stopping only for food and gas. From there, I could scuttle the craft and start the whole process of creating an identity again. I'd do what I always do. I'd disappear.

I took an hour or two to get to the marina just to be safe, but nevertheless Blacker was leaning against a pillar across from the boat when I got there. She had an odd look in her eyes and a crooked smile. Blacker stepped back nervously when she saw me and shouted from across the dock. "Over here!"

I waved back.

The boat was sitting in the spot below her. An older thirty-foot Carver that had been built in the eighties, maybe earlier, it was a stubby little thing with an upper deck closed off with mosquito net and a tattered American flag flapping at the back. The hull was dirty off-white and the tinted glass was beginning to show sun marks. It was called *The Palinurus*.

When I got close, Rebecca said, "I got him. The federal payload was found in his suite not ninety minutes ago. If that weren't enough to put him away, we also found one of his guys locked in the trunk of a Bentley in the parking lot. Guy shit his pants twice, and now he's willing to roll on the Wolf's whole operation in exchange for immunity and protection. They must've scared him real bad."

"Why aren't you there?"

"I wanted to see you," she said. "Once before you go, at least."

"Does this make us even?" I said.

Rebecca nodded. She looked out over the ocean.

I threw the black duffel bag off the side of the pier into the back of the yacht. "How did you find out about the boat?" I said.

"Like I said, I'm good at this," she said. "You've got nothing to worry about, though. I'm not going to stop you."

I didn't say anything. I lowered the ladder down to the deck of the boat.

"I have one question," she said. "Tell me one thing before you sail off and I never see you again."

"What is it?"

"You never told me your name, Jack."

I cracked a smile.

"You can call me Ghostman," I said.

Without another word, I climbed down onto my boat and untied the moorings. Blacker watched me for another few minutes before wandering off down the pier. I cast off a few minutes later, just after one in the morning.

My body let out a wave of endorphins that made me weak in the knees. I took my first breath of fresh sea air once I was three miles out. I practically fell into the captain's seat and closed my eyes for just a moment. I'd been on the go for close to two days, but even through the exhaustion I felt the most amazing excitement all over my body. It wasn't because of the bag of money at my feet, either. It was from the pure ecstasy of the job. It reminded me of the exquisite feeling of robbing a bank, or falling in love for the first time. I felt powerful and alive. God, it was beautiful.

Now there was only one thing left to do.

Disappear.

Roger Hobbs is 24 years old and completed the first draft of this novel while still a senior at Reed College. He has worked as a radio host, a rifle range instructor, a note-taker and a security guard. He is a recent graduate of Reed College. He lives in Portland, Oregon.